DRAGON QUEEN

ROD MARSDEN

Night to Dawn Magazine & Books LLC
P. O. Box 643
Abington, PA 19001

www.bloodredshadow.com

Copyright © 2021 by Rod Marsden
Paperback ISBN: 978-1-937769-65-9
Ebook ISBN: 978-1-937769-66-6

Cover Artist SCAR: Steve Carter & Antoinette Rydyr
Editors: Barbara Custer & Keily Blair
Published in the United States of America

In memory of my grandfather who was a Pommy Jackaroo that worked on a Queensland station. He was also a carpenter and toymaker. When war broke out in 1914, he joined the Australian Light Horse and became an ANZAC. Upon his return to Australia, he started a family in New South Wales with my grandmother who was once a London barmaid.

To my friends at the Illawarra Birders – keep on birding!

To SCAR.

To editors Keily Blair and Barbara Custer for fine work.

CHAPTER ONE

Elanora's black scales shone in the early morning light. She smiled at the effect the sun had on her spiked tail and also her legs, arms, and claws. The sun came up over the silvery sea. It was always a welcome sight, the start of a new day on her island. In the distance, waves rose and crashed before they could get to shore. A breeze touched her all too human nose, lips, and ears. It should have been unpleasant, but it wasn't. She found the smell of salt in the air invigorating.

Lizards were bothered by the cold, but despite her lacertilian features, Elanora wasn't a reptile. She was a dragon, and regardless of the plume of white coming from her mouth, she wasn't shivering. In fact, she preferred a cool climate. She looked around for company because it was the loneliness that got to her, not the near frozen air.

She picked up a stick and drew a rectangle in the sand. A small blackish-grey crab came out of the rolling surf, and with its eyes on stalks, looked up at her. "These are the dragons," she told the creature. "They are on the bottom. That's not a good place to be. They're mutants like me, but I'm special because I'm a female, and I'm not supposed to exist."

The crab continued to stare, and so Elanora drew another rectangle, placing it above the first one. "These are the knights. They're not much better off than us dragons. If one of them kills fifty of us, he gets to be a maverick. Only one knight I know of ever did that, and he's on Mars."

With a sideways motion, the crab scuttled off into some nearby bushes. Out of the water, draped in seaweed, came another crab which looked up at Elanora as the first one had done. "Fine," she said. "I'll continue my lecture with you."

She drew a smaller rectangle, placing it above the second one. "Now we have the mavericks. If these fellows behave themselves, they can have long, rich, and fulfilling lives. They can even marry and become fathers. That a knight can't do. If they get up to mischief, then they are downgraded to knight and end up dead. Oh, you ask me if there are mavericks around beside the one on Mars. Yes, there are, and they didn't get to be mavericks by killing anyone. How do they become mavericks then and not knights? Be patient; I'm getting to that."

Elanora drew a fourth rectangle, putting it on top of the third one. "Here we have maidens. They cannot marry knights, but they can marry mavericks. They're female, of course. Oh, I realize you want me to get on with how knights and mavericks come about. Do be patient."

The crab went sideways, shrugged off the seaweed, and scuttled to its mate in the bushes. Elanora drew yet another rectangle which she placed above the one for maidens. A third crab came out of the water and gazed up at her. "To continue," she said. "Now we come to the priestesses. Boys reaching puberty are tested by priestesses. If the boy passes, he automatically becomes a maverick. If he fails, he is a knight. Maiden officers with robots are there to make sure upset boys and parents don't do anything rash."

The crab clicked its claws and Elanora smiled down at it. "No interruptions! Now where were we ... oh, yes! Priestesses are at the heart and soul of this society I am not allowed to be part of. They offer spiritual guidance."

The crab used its claws, once more making a click-clack noise.

"I agree. I'm no theologian. I am just telling you what I know. Now a priestess can rise in influence and power to become a high priestess of a city. One can even go further and become Highest of the High. I believe the High One of Wollongong, who has kept me safe, wants to someday become the Highest of the High."

The crab click-clacked at her a third time with its claws as if making a point.

"What do I do here, you ask? I keep records of vegetation growth and put water samples into test tubes I take back to my cottage to analyse. Don't frown. It's what I am expected to do. Okay, go, join your friends."

Elanora waved her arm in the direction the other crabs had gone, and the third crab left. Soon after this occurrence, the tide bolted in and washed away her handiwork. She tossed aside the stick and sighed deeply. She could hear seagulls squawking a distance away.

On her walk back to where she lived, Elanora wondered what returning to Wollongong for her would be like if that was ever an option. It was where she was born and where she had spent her formative years until it became obvious she was a female and not a male. It was then, according to Wollongong's High One, she had to be moved for her own safety and that of others, first to a secluded shack in the hills then to where she now lived.

At her own expense, Wollongong's High Priestess arranged correspondence to train Elanora in a number of the sciences. It had been one-on-one with a blank computer screen so her teachers had no idea what Elanora looked like.

It was voice and printouts. Elanora had learned, early on at the beginning of her exile, to control her hissing and only did so when she got angry or excited. The hissing, if it was there, could be interpreted as static occurring over the long distance between computers. Not many teachers expected dragons of any kind to be intelligent.

Even if Elanora wanted to, during her years of learning, she could not have made contact electronically with anyone, save her teachers and Wollongong's High One. The computer she was using was set up that way.

From one of her teachers, a maverick into economics, she had discovered that a loaf of bread in Wollongong before the great upheaval of the Third World War was worth twenty dollars. Afterward, thanks to the end of inflation and the creation of new economies throughout the habitable world, the same loaf of bread came to be worth fifteen cents.

"We have kept population numbers stable through knights fighting dragons," the economist had told her in an all too calm voice in answer to how prices in the new economy can be so low. She had imagined him tall in a black suit with red and yellow stripes but had no idea what he looked like or how he dressed. "As you no doubt know, dragons are human mutations created from the last Great War," he had added. "They kill enough knights in battle each year to keep population numbers even and thus the economy stable."

"Isn't there a better way?" Elanora had asked.

"According to the High Ones and the Highest of the High, the answer is no," the economist had replied in a firm voice. "The appropriate numbers of lives are lost, and no damage is done to the environment or to housing or buildings in general."

"What if the appropriate numbers aren't killed?" Elanora had to ask.

"The system from city to city is adjustable," the economist had told her. "When required, more knights are made, and so there are fewer mavericks. When more mavericks and fewer knights are needed, then there are fewer males made into knights and more made into mavericks. As you know, mavericks don't fight."

"Is that all?" Elanora had asked, feeling there had to be more to it than that.

"The High One has told me, since you will be trained in the sciences, to tell you that, when needed, insignificant maidens are sacrificed through giving birth to dragons rather than to more human offspring," the economist had replied in a succinct, matter of fact voice. "It is all a question of balance."

"Why this balance?" Elanora had asked. She had wagged her tail, glad there wasn't any carpet around to get her tail spikes caught in. That had happened long ago when she was young and posing as a boy dragon. It had been ever so embarrassing.

"It is a long-held belief that the last Great War came about because some organization called the United Nations could not come to terms with large population increases," the economist had said. "The population upsurges mostly occurred in what were designated the Third World. In that region, there was great poverty, and many who lived there wanted to go to the more prosperous countries to live. They were the have-nots, made so in part by ruthless businessmen. The have-nots were the Globalists. Their enemies were the Nationalists."

"What were these have-nots like?" Elanora had asked.

"Unlike the haves or the Nationalists, they were highly religious in the wrong way, and that was also a reason why they remained poor," the economist had answered in a superior tone. "The male have-nots did not always allow their women an education even though where women were educated, life improved for all. Yes, I know it is hard to believe there was a time when maidens and priestesses in some parts of the world were not in charge."

There was silence for a moment before this maverick continued with the lesson. Elanora had imagined he was looking over his notes. Then he had said, "Eventually the have-not resentment toward the haves boiled over, and that is how the last Great War started."

"How was order re-established after this Great War?" Elanora had asked curiously.

"In factories, maidens were called upon to design and create robots for war," the economist had revealed. "Thanks to the Great Goddess and the first Highest One, they came to instead build them to restore stability. There was also an organization of knights that aided the first Highest One in doing so, and to this day, this special order of knights remains especially loyal to the Highest One."

"If there are special knights," Elanora had asked, "are there also special mavericks?"

The economist paused for a moment and said, "As far as I know there has only ever been one maverick with exceptional powers. His name is Nathaniel, and he takes his orders directly from the Highest One. He is best avoided if that is at all possible, or so I have been told."

"I do believe in the Great Goddess," Elanora had reasoned, "but how did this now universal belief come about?"

"I am no theologian," the economist had said firmly. Elanora could imagine him shaking his head sadly. "My understanding is that the Great Goddess was always there, in the shadows, especially when the belief in a single male god was prominent."

"How so?"

"I think it would be best if you took this up with either an historian or a priestess," the economist had replied.

Fair enough, Elanora had thought at the time, though a little disappointed.

A week later, Elanora had taken it up with a tutor who was both a priestess and an amateur historian. She had imagined this tutor also being tall like she thought the maverick economist of being, and since she was a priestess, clothed in shining white.

"Before the prominence of the Christian and Muslim god there were, in fact, numerous goddesses representing in their own way the true Great Goddess," the priestess had revealed with some enthusiasm. Elanora had imagined her smiling and opening her hands as if they were spring petals. "My understanding is the ancient Egyptians had, among other goddesses, Bastet, the goddess of cats. The Greeks had Athena, goddess of the city of Athens. Athena had a fondness for owls. The god of the Jews had a feminine side. Diana was the huntress deity of the Romans and also the goddess of the Wiccans."

"But that really was a long time ago," Elanora had interrupted. "What does all of that have to do with our current belief in the Great Goddess?"

The priestess had paused a moment, cleared her throat then added, "In Catholicism, a branch of Christianity, there was praise for our Mother Mary. There was a sect in medieval Europe, banned by the Catholic Church, where the women were called Marthas. They took care of the spiritual life of the community, and their men handled the more mundane, earthly concerns. In the 1970s, there was a woman's movement in America and elsewhere calling for the one god to be regarded as female rather than male."

"But what made the movement after the last Great War so special?" Elanora had asked.

"Men had championed human overpopulation," the priestess had revealed smugly. "Women, after the last Great War, set about doing the opposite. There had to be growth, but it had to be rational based on economic factors rather than a free for all mess like in the past. Our religion looks to preserving life but in a more realistic fashion. No more poverty, rampant disease, or starvation, a near perfect society."

"Yes," agreed Elanora, "a near perfect society."

"One we can be grateful for," the priestess had added in a no-nonsense tone. Elanora had imagined this priestess smiling contentedly.

"But how did the Great Goddess come to be recognized as such throughout the world?" Elanora had asked.

"The first Highest One was most persuasive," the priestess had offered, "plus the populace in general were sick of fighting. Since the major cities were gone, reduced to rubble or worse, the people wanted a new way of life, and the first Highest One promised to give it to them."

"Did the Great Goddess, through the first Highest One, really bring peace and prosperity?" Elanora had asked.

"I believe so," the priestess had said in a firm voice.

But not to the knights and dragons, Elanora had thought but did not feel this was wise to say to the priestess because she felt showing too much sympathy for either knights or dragons dangerous. Maidens, she understood from previous conversations, did not sympathise with either knights or dragons, and to this priestess, as with her other tutors, she had to pretend to be a maiden. The High One of Wollongong had told her that her tutors were informed she had a deformed but human face, and that was the only reason they were not permitted to see her during these sessions.

"On a side note," the priestess had said, possibly with a smug smile, "the term maverick comes from the western part of the USA. It once meant an independent sort of male. I believe the first Highest One envisioned males given that title having a certain swagger, a type of independence to do with being considered superior to those designated knights. I don't believe this swagger has anywhere come to pass."

"Incidentally," the priestess had added after a pause, "maidens were once unmarried women. Now maiden refers to any woman not a priestess. In other words, a woman not wed to the Great Goddess such as a priestess, a High One, or the Highest of the High. Being wed to a mere maverick in our faith doesn't count."

How odd, Elanora had thought but at first didn't say anything. Perhaps, she had also thought, not replying might give away the fact she was a female dragon rather than a true maiden.

"Yes," Elanora had finally said, "we must have our faith."

"You're a good maiden for saying so," the priestess had commented. "It is a pleasure tutoring you."

At the time Elanora hadn't at all felt like a good maiden. She had poked her forked tongue out at the priestess, fully aware the priestess couldn't see her doing so. Despite wanting to, she hadn't hissed.

"The Great Goddess faith may differ from city to city in minor ways, but the Highest One makes sure it remains true everywhere," the priestess had told her with a touch of passion. "There is local custom, and there is blasphemy. The Highest One decides which is which. Remember that if you ever get to travel."

"Just how many people died in this final war you and my other tutors have spoken about?" Elanora had asked during another session with the priestess.

"I haven't got exact numbers," the priestess had replied. "No one has that. But densely populated areas were the hardest hit by the nuclear missiles. Indonesia was virtually wiped out. Thank the Great Goddess there wasn't a nuclear winter! It came close to that, but it didn't happen. New York, Paris, and Sydney are holes in the ground, but recent excavations have given us clues as to those final days leading up to the last Great War."

"I'm glad I wasn't around at the time," Elanora had commented.

"Oh, and besides the missiles, you had food shortages, radioactive winds like you still get in some places even to this day, and plagues in certain minor cities," the priestess had added. "But we've learned from it. No more populations out of control, no more wars."

"Yes," agreed Elanora, "no more wars."

****

Presently, Elanora could only contact, via computer, a select group of University of Wollongong scientists plus the High One. When discussing issues with those scientists, her screen, by order of the High One, remained blank.

She wanted to believe her work on her small island, off the coast of New Zealand, was important in gauging the growth and growing complexity of life on locales newly thrust up from the sea. Fifty years ago, volcanic activity under the sea had created where she was living. Back then, when it cooled down, it was naught but a barren rock. Now there was greenery, birds, and animals. A few small trees tried their luck but without success whereas the ferns, after initial difficulties, did fine. Elanora wondered what, if anything, she could learn from the persistence of those ferns.

"In studying the development of an early ecosystem, we can learn more about how ecosystems work," the High Priestess of Wollongong had told her five years ago before sending her to this desolate place. She knew, however, there was more to it than that.

As the only living female dragon, Elanora understood she was a danger to the society she was born into, and that was not good.

She shouldn't be alive, and it was only through the kindness of the High Priestess of Wollongong that she lived at all. If others found out about her, they would do her harm. "You are best protected being away from humanity," the High Priestess had told her.

Elanora had monthly food and equipment drops that also included books, newspapers, magazines, and letters. She would hear the helicopter before seeing it. Sometimes she wanted to reach out to whoever was doing the drops, but that was not permitted. Her hands were claws, and waving them about would reveal what she was. Her existence meant that people living in Australia and New Zealand thought of her, if they thought of her at all, as a recluse maiden and not the creature she was. Hence, she was expected to hide from the helicopter crew until they were gone then pick up what had been sent to her.

One feature of the island she never mentioned in her reports was a cave that was only accessible during low tide. Once inside, it was possible to first crawl then walk to higher ground within and thus be out of danger if the full tide should return. The entrance was not readily visible, even at low tide, and she suspected that no one could locate it from the air. She thought of it as her safe haven, in case her High Priestess guardian ever decided to get rid of her permanently and she had prior warning of this.

She knew the written and typed materials sent to her were censored. There were bits cut out of newspapers and magazines and blacked out areas in letters. Very little information got to her about knights and dragons.

Elanora was aware of the fighting that went on in May and November between knights and dragons because of that time before her exile. Now it all seemed like a bad dream.

She didn't have much of an image, even in her head, of what a male dragon would look like. How different would he be from her? She knew there were varieties. They no doubt came about through earlier genetic engineering. Some male dragons were black-scaled like herself while others had silvery scales and still others red scales. Would she find any of them attractive? If only she had a photo or a drawing of one to go by instead of vague descriptions and fading memories. In childhood, pretending to be a boy dragon, she did see the males, but being so young she didn't have the biological interest she now had in them.

Occasionally, she looked in the mirror and wondered if the public at large would find her pretty or hideous. She kept in good shape on her two-mile runs around the island and during summer, swam in a rock pool. All things considered, though, she was not quite human. If not the scales, then the spiked tail was the big giveaway.

Taking stock one day in the full body mirror she had in her bedroom, she said to herself, "With my clothes removed, it is obvious I have the downstairs equipment for mating of any female. My smile, though black, is not dissimilar from a more human female, and the same goes for my ears and the contour of my nose. Mind you, I do have scales on my nose that move about when I smile. Maidens don't have that."

She stopped for a moment then went on, "I have high cheekbones if that means anything to anyone and large come-hither hazel eyes. The scales I have for eyebrows are of a lighter hue than the rest of my face and therefore stand out when I raise and lower them. What else? My tongue is red and forked."

Elanora poked out her tongue, then continued: "I have hips like a maiden. My breasts, though they have lovely scales that shimmer if the light is good, are the exact size and shape of any woman my age or so the newspaper and magazine articles would indicate."

She touched her breasts and smiled. "My nipples are free from scales if that would interest anyone. My legs are scaled like much of my person. They are strong and lean from all the exercise I do. Oh, and I have claws for hands, and I have big feet. My spiked tail does get in the way sometimes. It is difficult to get in and out of the short pants designed for dragons, but I do manage. And that should complete this inventory."

After her morning jog, she had lunch in her cottage where she sent off information, via her computer, to the scientific research team situated in Wollongong that, for safety's sake, had no idea she was a dragon. It was enough they appreciated her fine work. Often, she received messages thanking her for her contribution to the study of developing life on earth.

In the afternoon, a pair of magpies knocked with their beaks on her backdoor. She fed them leftovers from the previous night's meal. To her, they were great listeners, better than the crabs, even if they didn't understand a word she said. "Well, my fine friends, you don't mind what I look like, do you? How kind of you to accept food from me. Please call again. When you have young, please bring them here."

She then read over other scientists' reports on ecology and ecosystems sent to her by her Wollongong University contacts. Some included areas of Australia where the radiation was down enough to consider reintroducing humans. She typed up letters she sent, via her computer, to the scientific research team to forward on to other scientists. They too had limited computer access, and this forwarding was generally done via the post office. There, mail coming in and going out, was monitored by lower order priestesses for anything that might be deemed of a subversive nature.

Sometimes, Elanora was miffed that her computer only allowed her access to this team and the High Priestess. She wondered what the Internet was like when it existed, but that was long before she was born. Occasionally, something would turn up in a magazine, newspaper, or letter sent to her, via helicopter dump, that got her thinking about her situation. The Internet, if it came into being once more, would make her life so much better, giving her much wider access to the world, though it might also expose her to the dangers of discovery.

From her scientific contacts in Wollongong, she learned that robots had run amok in Lyon, France, and a priestess, for some reason, had committed suicide. There was an article in a newspaper about Mars and the hope the colony left there, on that planet ages ago, might still exist.

No one wanted to discuss dragons with her. She had always been led to believe robots couldn't kill unless programmed to do so. But why would anyone do such a thing? No one seemed to know, or if they did, they didn't share that information with her.

Before retiring, she ate a simple meal of seaweed and dried fish washed down with lemon juice. Then she did instrument checks on the weather via a control board set up for her to read. It was connected to a measuring device on the roof of her home near the solar panel that provided her with electricity.

Then she went outside to look at the sky. Unless the fog rolled in and it rained the next day, it would be clear with lots of stars. She breathed in the night air, finding it exhilarating, her nostrils flaring and a contented hum from her throat showing no one but herself her appreciation of those dark hours.

Every Sunday, the High Priestess would contact Elanora to see how she was doing. It was also, no doubt, to check up and make sure she was still on the island. "Are you getting plenty of exercise?" the High Priestess would often ask. Then she would want to know if Elanora was bored and, if so, what she might do to help alleviate that boredom. When asked about Wollongong or any other city, the High One would say life is dull there and she wasn't missing much. In fact, life was much better where she was, and so she should continue to appreciate where she had been placed.

Elanora was smart enough to know that her benefactor could not afford to have her disappear and then turn up elsewhere. She might then have to explain how a female dragon could possibly exist, and that would never do.

Elanora wondered what it would be like to be a maiden or a priestess. She had a white scarf she played with when pretending to be first one and then the other. She knew too well that dragons were at the bottom of the social ladder, followed by knights, then mavericks.

She had seen pictures of knights. They were brutish in their armour. Flipping through fashion magazines, she had to admit to herself she thought mavericks looked ridiculous in their brightly coloured suits.

After five years on her island, it was time to move on, but the High Priestess would not hear any argument for such a move.

"I cannot live here any longer," said Elanora one day to the High One. "I am wasted here!"

"You stay at my command," replied the High Priestess.

"And if I refuse to stay?" asked Elanora.

"Death awaits you in Australia," revealed the High Priestess. "If maidens, mavericks, and priestesses see you, they will hunt you down until you are caught, and then terrible things will happen to you. What's more, I will not help you. I may even be called upon by the Highest of High Priestesses to do you harm."

"But I have heard all that from you before."

"And you will hear it from me again and again!"

"But my only crime wassss being born," Elanora snapped in her defence. She spoke with a lisp at times because of the forked tongue all dragons have.

"That is crime enough." The High Priestess's voice was stern.

"But is it truly enough?" asked Elanora.

"Yes, it is," confirmed the High One and broke off the connection.

Like every other dragon, Elanora had clawed her way out of her mother, thus killing her. It was not something she was aware of having done, since she was an infant. Even so, it marked her in ways her appearance alone couldn't. It was because of this, more than anything else, she was among the damned. It was why knights fought dragons.

"You can do better on your island than anywhere else in the world," the High Priestess often told her. This used to satisfy her, but she had become restless, taking longer and longer walks each morning. There had to be a way to escape her cushy prison. Maybe the outside world had changed since she was exiled and it wasn't so bad, and she had a greater destiny elsewhere.

Then one day she thought up a plan. First, she would put aside enough food from every drop over the following three months to last her three weeks without further rations. She could ask for more chocolate bars, cans of peaches, cans of rice-cream, and packets of dried fruit. Then she would take bedding and other material and make a comfortable place for herself within the cave. The idea being that if she could vanish for three weeks, and search parties sent to find her failed to do so, then the assumption would be she had already found a way off the island, drowned while swimming off shore, or had been attacked and eaten by a flying shark or some other predator. Then, when the searching for her had died away, she could leave her hiding place and head off with minimum risk of being caught.

She could dismantle part of her cottage to build a raft. She could sew her bed sheets together to make a sail and cover it in a mixture of salt water, flour, and mud, to stiffen it for added strength, against the high winds once out at sea.

Elanora knew the High Priestess would see this move as a betrayal, but there was nothing she could do about that except to remain where she had been placed. She had already been there too long. Most of all, she wanted to find out more about dragons and why they were the lowest of the low. It had to be more than the way they came into this world.

"I hate disappointing the High Priestess and turning her against me," said Elanora to the magpies who took food from her, "but I must be free. I need to know what it means to be a dragon and if I can make things better for my brethren. I'll leave food for you here and there in various bushes, my treasures, but you will have to go back to fending for yourselves. You have been good company, and I do wish you the best."

CHAPTER TWO

The High Priestess of Wollongong was a tall, lean woman whose white robes were augmented by a silver ring of office on her left hand and a white stone on a silver chain around her neck. In the decades she had been a priestess, she had made two mistakes that could destroy her. One was allowing Dreadnought, the knight turned maverick, to live and fulfill his life's ambition. Thank the Goddess he was now on Mars. The other was showing scientific curiosity and compassion toward a female dragon.

She breathed heavily when she got the letter. It was from the Highest of High Priestesses calling on her to explain how any knight could kill fifty dragons and thus become a maverick. It was a demand for the truth which the High One of Wollongong could not provide without risking her position. Neither the High Priestess nor the Highest of the High believed in miracles. They were supposed to, but despite their religious trappings, they were both practical women.

Something had been off about Dreadnought, the slayer of fifty dragons. Since he had been a Wollongong knight, the Highest of the High wanted to know, in detail, what the trick for his success had been. All the High Priestess could do to save herself from demotion was to write back and state that Dreadnought had been unique for reasons unknown. She could not inform the greatest living priestess that Dreadnought had been born a dragon that shed his scales and tail without condemning herself. When he was a newborn, she had her chance to end his life and hadn't. Now she faced problems with her female dragon, Elanora.

The female dragon she should have eliminated soon after birth had gone missing. She let two days go by without contact then decided she had to send a squad of robots to that island on a kill mission. There was no evidence the dragon in question had left that locale, so she had to still be there or dead and washed out to sea. Now, of all times, the High Priestess could not allow any connection she had with Elanora to expose her to ridicule or worse.

She knew the Highest of the High could do more than demote her if she was found to be a traitor. Messing with the order of life and thus the priestesshood would make her that. The majority of the world's citizens had to think of dragons as male and not male and female, or questions about how dragons came to be would be asked. Dragons had to remain the lowest of the low. For that to happen, they had to be regarded, in this society, as male-only. A female dragon would spoil all of that.

Rumours had it that the Highest One employed well-trained knightly assassins. The High Priestess's fondness for Elanora had put her at risk once too often. If Elanora had stayed in touch on that island, all would have been well. Now,-she had to close all links to past indiscretions for good. The High Priestess sighed, a tear rolling down her cheek at the thought of ending Elanora's life.

The robots were to be flown onto the island by flyer with Malcolm, the dark-haired flyer pilot, who was an expendable maverick. Since any maverick could easily be demoted to knight by a high-ranking priestess, all were deemed disposable by someone in the High One's exalted position. This included the clever ones like Malcolm. The robots were to eliminate him once the death of Elanora had been established. There could be no witnesses to Elanora's demise. When they got back, the robots would be reprogrammed to accept any lie she cared to fill their electronic brains with; thus, they too would be silenced.

Then, when all that was done, the High Priestess could claim the so-called maiden, who had lived in the cottage on the island, had passed away from some unfortunate accident. No one of importance then need ever know she was really a dragon. It was now time to make up for past indiscretions if she was ever to someday make it to Highest of the High status and thus reside in Rome for the rest of her life.

****

Malcolm was nervous about going to some remote dot on the map with six robots, and no technician or maiden officer there in case the robots went haywire. He could not, however, refuse the High Priestess since to do so could mean demotion to knight.

"Are you sure you can't turn this down?" Megan, who was Malcolm's wife, a silvery-blonde haired maiden, asked him the night before the flight. "You don't look well. You're shaking at the very idea of going. If you're sick, the High One can just get someone else."

"It's the robots that spook me," offered Malcolm. "I suppose they do that to everyone. It will be all right. I'll go. As you know, getting the High One annoyed with me would be disastrous for both of us."

"Yes," agreed Megan. "She does have that much power."

The robots had arms, legs, chests, and torsos that mimicked humanity. It was the faces that struck a nerve in the living. Two red eyes and a slot for a mouth made them alien even to the maiden officers who worked with them. Malcolm knew this from conversations he had overheard in various wine bars.

Megan, his wife, wanted to help Malcolm by going along, but he didn't think that was a good idea.

"If it is a harmless flight, then I can go," said Megan. "I'm a maiden. You can't stop me unless you can come up with a good reason why I can't join you."

"I want you safe." Malcolm looked away from Megan.

"The robots are programmed never to harm a maiden," offered Megan. "If I go, there will be less chance of something going wrong with them. So, I'm going!"

"I have a bad feeling about this. I'd rather you stay." Malcolm was still looking away from Megan.

"The robots have given you the jitters, that's all. Any real reason I can't come along?"

"There's none that I can think of." Malcolm looked in her eyes, noticing how her glasses sat snugly on her face. He also saw determination.

"Then it's settled. I'm coming along. Besides, I want to make sure your new robot hand and leg are working properly." Megan added a disarming smile. "I'm no expert at robotic replacement parts, but I have read up on them. I feel that someone, even with only a little knowledge about them, should be with you until I'm sure they are in proper working order."

Malcolm's flyer was standard. It was a circular twin-engine job with flow back wings. It could carry six seated passengers plus a pilot. The robots could go as cargo since they did not require seating during the trip and could lie down without being damaged.

The takeoff from Wollongong airport was smooth. They travelled down the coast, trying to avoid the foul, radioactive winds rising up from Melbourne. Even so,-the winds buffeted the plane, and Malcolm had to use all his skill as a top airman to zigzag out of the trap made long ago by a nuclear explosion.

"Hey!" cried Megan, almost losing her glasses with one of the zags. "Hey!" she cried again when another of those zags occurred. She didn't wear contacts because her eyes were too sensitive for their use. Right then, she thought how much trouble they would be if they did fall out. Searching for them would have been a real nightmare. She was glad when they were far enough away from that swirling hellhole not to be pulled in and ripped apart. They had flown off centre, away from the heart of that forlorn city, but still, they could have lost their lives.

"Someday, Melbourne will be clear of radiation," said Malcolm. He felt the need to say something.

"I can hardly wait." Megan sighed deeply. "I'm so glad the flyer was able to shield us from those deadly rays."

"A crash landing in that mess would have been fatal," said Malcolm calmly.

"I notice there aren't any problems so far with your artificial hand and leg." Megan smiled warmly.

"None that I have noticed," said Malcolm.

As they approached Tasmania, a storm kicked up. The sky blackened, lit up now and then by lightning. Rain spattered against their windscreen. There was the cry of a nearby giant albatross.

A robot got to its feet and said in monotone, "There is a threat."

Megan looked into its red eyes and said, "There's no threat."

"There is danger," insisted the robot, reaching for its weapon.

"There is no danger," said Megan. "Please resume your lying position. All is well. The pilot knows what he is doing."

Thankfully, the robot complied with Megan's instruction, lying down once more with the other robots. She had been calm and matter-of-fact with the robot. Now she exhaled and shivered over what might have happened.

"The last thing we need is a robot taking shots at a huge bird capable of tearing our vessel apart with either beak or claw," reasoned Malcolm. "If bullets from that gun had reached the outside and didn't cause decompression, then a stray one that hit the feathered creature might have gotten it angry enough to attack."

"Thank the Goddess, I decided to come along." Megan smiled a smug smile.

Then the sky began to clear, the albatross turned out to be all noise and quickly lost interest in the flyer.

"The last thing we needed was a shootout in the air." Malcolm shook his head and smiled at the windscreen. Part of him was glad Megan was around, and the other part wished she was home and out of jeopardy.

"Have you wondered why we have these mechanical creations onboard instead of maidens, mavericks, or knights?" Megan offered up a question Malcolm wished he had had the guts to ask the High Priestess.

"Maybe the machines have better eyesight?" Malcolm knew this was lame but said it anyway. He shrugged his shoulders for emphasis.

"I hope that is all it is." Megan suspected it was more than that but couldn't figure out what. Her crossed arms told Malcolm as much.

"We're coming into Hobart now," said Malcolm.

At Hobart airport, they refuelled then waited for the weather, which had turned nasty once more, to clear. Malcolm wasn't about to risk his life and that of Megan flying into rough conditions searching for a locale that would barely register on his flyer's radar.

Megan assured the robots the delay was in everyone's interest. She knew she had to use calming words and non-threatening motions to get her message across to them. Unless programmed otherwise, they wouldn't ever harm a maiden. Even so, she didn't trust them. Something about their inhuman faces made her want to run as far away from them as possible. She had to refrain from wincing when they all nodded their agreement to her.

"We will wait," said the lead robot in monotone.

Megan and Malcolm spent half a day in Hobart. Megan bought bags of apples and strawberries from a market not far from the airport and Malcolm, a newspaper.

It was the first of May, so there were stories about the upcoming bouts between knights and dragons. Some wished Dreadnought would return to the fight. The new champion was Tarsus with fifteen dragon kills to his credit. He would last till the end of May, then die from injuries sustained in an arena in Madrid.

The sun was shining when they left Hobart. There was a chill in the air. Malcolm and Megan knew it was going to get colder as they drew closer to Antarctica. They put jumpers on to combat the cold. After circling Elanora's island a few times to figure out the best place to land, Malcolm brought the flyer down a few hundred yards from the cottage.

"We're here!" cried Malcolm, switching off the aircraft. The robots then got to their feet and marched out of the flyer with Malcolm and Megan bringing up the rear.

A thorough search of the cottage revealed nothing of interest to any of them. Night was coming, and so Megan and Malcolm decided to stay there rather than risk falling down a crevice or finding a large pothole. The robots were also prepared to wait for better light.

The following morning, an hour after sunrise, the robots left Megan and Malcolm sleeping. Special lenses in their eyes revealed the cave and its entrance plus the female dragon. They only had to walk a quarter of a mile west to end their quest.

"We go inside," commanded the lead robot in a flat voice as they approached the cave's mouth. All six of them crawled inside, oblivious of everything apart from eventually standing up and executing their prey. Elanora watched them coming and hoped for something, anything that would stop them. "I pray to the Great Goddess for salvation," she whispered in earnest. Her only reply was a distant sound that grew louder as the robots came closer.

A gurgling was followed by a great rush of water. The tide had come in! Elanora was safe from the flood where she was but not so the robots. They were engulfed and drawn out to sea. One of them tried to claw its way to Elanora, despite the water pressure, but she used her tail to knock it off balance, so it was sucked out with the rest.

Once away from shore, the robots sank to the sandy bottom. Then a creature with great rows of teeth, whose ancestors may have been whales, played with five of them as if they were its favourite chew toys. The sixth, whose sense of direction had been muddled by water, noted what had happened to its fellows. It then started what turned out to be a long, undersea walk of three months back to Hobart. Somewhere along the way, its torso was crushed by a giant octopus. Unfortunately for the octopus, the robot's right arm was free of this embrace. Through its gun use,-the robot was able to get away from the octopus and continue on. Apparently, the gun could fire only once, but that had been enough. Rust wasn't a factor since the gun was made of rustproof material. Water pressure, however, had been the issue preventing the gun from firing multiple times.

What washed up on the shores of Storm Bay was too wrecked to be able to impart why it had come out of the sea or even where its journey had begun. The only thing in the robot's damaged memory circuits was information on what a sea monster could do to five robots that could not get to their holstered guns fast enough. Octopus ink was found inside some of the damaged robot's parts.

Elanora waited for the tide to recede before venturing out of her cave. She looked around, unsure if the robots had really all gone out to sea. Were they meant to take her back alive to the High Priestess or do away with her? She didn't know. With their inhuman red eyes, they looked like they had a deadly purpose. She also reasoned they had not come alone. *There has to be a flyer and, with a flyer, a pilot*, thought Elanora. She knew enough from newspapers and magazines to be aware that robots were not programmed to pilot aircraft. According to what she had read in a newspaper, a helicopter could not take the weight of so many robots. A flyer could. Thus, there had to be a flyer on her island.

She came upon the flyer and found it empty. Over the last two years, thanks to articles in magazines and technical manuals from airdrops, she had pieced together how a flyer worked. So her first instinct was to simply take it to either Australia or New Zealand. Still, she was smart enough to realize she was better off with a pilot at the controls that knew more than she did about flying. There was learning from a book, but there was also firsthand experience.

The smell of fried bacon and eggs came wafting to her from the cottage. *Someone is cooking in my kitchen*, thought Elanora. She circled around the place, looking in all the windows to see who was there. A man, probably a maverick by the fancy clothes he wore, was preparing the food. A maiden wearing glasses was putting cutlery on Elanora's table. Neither the maverick nor the maiden was armed.

Elanora hadn't had a good meal in days, and so, when she did burst in, her first thought was to go for the bacon and eggs. The gasp of horror from the maiden changed her mind. Instead, she encircled the maiden's neck with her tail and pressed her barbs into unwilling flesh.

"Don't!" Malcolm cried in alarm.

"Don't? Is that a command? Forgive me if I refuse to obey you."

"Please let her go!" There was emphasis on the word *please*.

"You will take me back to Wollongong, or I will end her life." Elanora's nostrils flared. Her forked tongue poked out, and she hissed. Megan softly moaned.

"I agree! Now please let her go!" Again, *please* was emphasized.

"First, I will take your food. Put the bacon and eggs on a plate. I'm hungry." Elanora's mouth was watering, her forked tongue wet with saliva.

"Do as she says," pleaded Megan.

Malcolm put all the bacon and eggs he'd cooked onto one plate, and Elanora sat down to eat. In doing so, she released Megan, who was bleeding ever so slightly.

"What did you do to her?" Upon seeing the blood, Malcolm curled his hands into fists.

"It's minor," said Elanora between bites. "There's a first-aid kit in my study. A few sticking plaster bandages should be enough."

Malcolm got the first aid kit and applied the bandages. It was as Elanora said. No lasting harm had been done so far to Megan. Still, Malcolm didn't want Megan further hurt. He knew his fists wouldn't do much good against this creature's scales, but he would do what he could to save Megan, even if it was only to give his wife the chance to run as this creature spent time ending his life.

"I know I could have killed her," said Elanora coolly. "I'm sure I could have snapped her neck. Give me something to drink."

Malcolm sighed, shook his head, and handed Elanora a bottle of orange soft drink straight out of the fridge. Elanora continued eating. She drank as well, feeling her full strength returning.

"Who are you?" asked Malcolm.

"What are you?" asked Megan. Elanora was like no other dragon Megan had ever seen before. The curves were wrong for a male creature and could not be hidden by the shirt and pants it wore.

"My name's Elanora," answered the female dragon between gulps of soft drink. "As for what I am, you can guess."

"You shouldn't exist!" Megan shook her head and sighed deeply. She checked her wounds. The bleeding had stopped.

Megan had been taught from infancy onward that there was no such thing as a female dragon. Yet here was one, and she had injuries to prove it was so!

"And yet here I am, and you are taking me to Wollongong." Elanora smiled at the look of dismay on Megan's face.

"You want to go to Wollongong?" asked Megan in a shaky voice. Why should something that shouldn't exist want to go to a major city? That didn't make sense.

"Yes, I want to go to Wollongong," confirmed Elanora. Her smile did not reassure either Megan or Malcolm. Those claws looked sharp, and her tail was flicking about.

"We'll take you without all the hostility," proposed Malcolm in as restrained a voice as possible. "Besides, we're expecting the robots sent with us to return at any moment."

"They're not coming." Both Malcolm and Megan were open-mouthed shocked by this revelation.

"They're not?" Megan's voice sounded like a squeak toy.

"No." Elanora waved a dismissive claw. "You got more food?" Megan could see that Elanora had put aside a piece of bacon.

"Apples and strawberries in the flyer," said Megan.

"You can show me where in your machine. Let's go." Elanora got up and herded Megan and Malcolm out of what had once been her home.

Malcolm and Megan had to wonder what could have happened to six well-armed mechanical men that terrified most people. Neither was game to ask.

"Those robots...," began Megan in a whisper.

"I know," Malcolm whispered back. He shrugged his shoulders. "For now, let's just stay alive."

Along the way, Elanora threw the piece of bacon she could have eaten into some bushes. The meat was quickly snapped up and shared between two magpies. Despite evidence to the contrary, Megan wondered if Elanora was as fierce as she made herself out to be. *Do monsters have pets?* Megan asked herself.

"Why Wollongong?" asked Megan as they climbed into the flyer. "I take it we were supposed to bring you back anyway, though the use of robots did seem heavy-handed. But no one said we'd be dealing with a female dragon."

"You thought it was some maiden gone astray?" asked Elanora. She shook her head and smiled.

"That's what we were led to believe," said Malcolm.

"Yes. I can imagine that being the case. I've thought about it. The robots are the clue in all of this." Elanora rubbed her claws together. "Would it surprise you to know I was never meant to leave this island alive?"

"I don't know what to say to that," said Malcolm as they flew away from the island.

"We're not killers." Megan wanted to make that clear to Elanora.

"I might be, but not today." Elanora was for keeping her options open.

"So, are there many female dragons?" asked Megan. She didn't think there were but felt she should ask.

"I doubt it, but I believe there are plenty of male ones." Elanora knew she was going mostly by distant memory, hearsay, and the rare newspaper article she was allowed to see on the matter.

"Do you know any?" Megan was curious and needed her curiosity to take her over. She was still afraid but wanted small talk to ease tensions, have her breathe without shivering.

"No. I believe I will be as much a surprise to them as they will be to me." Elanora leaned back in her seat and sighed deeply.

Malcolm, after radioing in to the airport flight tower, put down in Hobart for topping up and to then receive clearance to go on to Wollongong. While that was happening, Elanora had her claws on Megan's throat in the back of the flyer to prevent Malcolm from calling out for help. After takeoff, Megan warned Elanora about the dangers of Melbourne, so she didn't panic when they worked their way past the outer edge of that disaster area. Also, Malcolm noted, Megan had a tendency to talk a lot when she was nervous. With a dragon without a pain collar so close to her, she had to either talk or faint.

"So this major city became a hazard?" asked Elanora. "I think I read about it sometime ago."

"Yes," replied Megan. "It happened a long time ago."

When they did get close to the outer edge of Melbourne, Elanora gasped in horror at what had occurred to what must have been a large metropolis. "And they think I am evil?" said Elanora contemplatively. "I could never have done this!"

They landed safely at Wollongong airport. There Elanora had to rely on Malcolm and Megan not to spread the word about her.

"What are you going to tell the authorities?" asked Elanora.

"An abridged version of the truth," said Malcolm contemplatively. "You've told us the robots went out with the tide from a cave. They were obviously searching for you when the mishap occurred."

"That takes care of the robots," agreed Elanora. "What about me?"

"Once we leave this flyer, we can honestly say we don't know where you are," said Malcolm, "because, by the time they question us, it will be the truth. You will be elsewhere."

"We'll expect you to go from here, and that will be that," added Megan calmly.

"You'd do thisss for me?" asked Elanora hissing emotionally, her forked tongue getting in the way.

"It's for all of us," said Malcolm. "If female dragons are not supposed to exist, and we bring one into a major city, I know there will be priestesses that won't be happy. Who knows what they'd do to us, especially if we weren't supposed to make it here at all with you?"

"There's a coat with a hood in the back." Megan didn't quite know why she was trying to be helpful, except she took her cue from Malcolm. "The hood will hide your face, and the rest of it will go with the clothes you are already wearing. The coat will also hide your tail if you don't move it about too much. You'll be hot in it,-but you'll be safer. Take the apples and strawberries and, for Goddess' sake, be careful."

"Go to Demons, a bar not far from here, to meet dragons," advised Malcolm, "but don't do it right away. Take a couple of days to think about what you are going to do, what you are going to say to those dragons. And good luck!"

Malcolm and Megan left the flyer without looking back. When it grew dark, Elanora made her move. In the meantime, Malcolm reported to the High Priestess that the so-called recluse maiden they were meant to locate could not be found. The fate of the robots sent with him to fetch her, he said, was now uncertain, being somewhere out at sea.

The High Priestess did her best to hide her surprise in seeing Malcolm alive. She accepted his story because it was too fantastic not to be true, and this saved his life.

CHAPTER THREE

The High Priestess of Kiama, a portly woman in her mid-forties, was paying the High Priestess of Wollongong a visit when everything went wrong. Thanks to Malcolm, word had come to Wollongong's High Priestess about the missing fake maiden and the loss of those six robots. A helicopter was dispatched from Hobart to check out Malcolm's story to see how much of it was true. As it turned out, it was possible the robots were now somewhere out at sea, hence Malcolm got to remain among the living. Even so, a female dragon could be on the loose. If she was discovered, it would not bode well for the High Priestess of Wollongong's future.

To impress the High Priestess of Kiama, the One Hundred Knights versus One Hundred Dragons' annual event included the use of pikes, long poles with nasty metalwork on the end. In this instance, there was a spearhead as well as a chopper on each pike. They weighed twenty pounds and were best used when those with them coordinated their efforts, especially in the attack. When this happened, the wielders were like a deadly forest. They were handed out to the collarless dragons as they entered the arena. The knights had swords and shields.

The battle, which lasted the traditional hour and a half, resulted in thirty-nine knights slain to twenty-five dragons butchered. Thanks to the pikes, it was a clear win for the dragons.

Tarsus, the lead knight, managed to slay two dragons, bumping up his overall score to seventeen. When asked by a reporter what his interests were, he said bird watching and origami. Juliet Matong, his maiden, confirmed this and added that he also was keen on rock music. Next, he was off to Madrid to further bump up his score. Madrid would be his downfall.

Some high-ranking priestesses under the High Priestess of Wollongong had publicly questioned why robots were needed to search for one alleged missing researcher and why they had failed to return. This took place while the High One was being interviewed by newspaper and magazine reporters over Kiama's High Priestess' visit to Wollongong.

"Was it a dangerous experiment the maiden was conducting?" asked one priestess coolly. Her eyes narrowed at the High Priestess of Wollongong as she put this to her High One as well as the press.

"Did it have anything to do with radiation?" asked another priestess, just as coldly with narrowing eyes. "Robots would be more immune to deadly rays and hence a reason for sending them."

"Is the public in danger?" asked yet another priestess, her voice icy and her eyes just as narrow.

They were like vultures, willing their mistress, the High One of Wollongong, to slip up and reveal all. Each of them wanted her position and thought they were paving the way to obtain it from the Highest One. She waved away those questions, telling them and the press it was high level state business that did not involve them nor was there any danger to the public. She would deal with those questioners later, after the High One of Kiama had left. After they had been reduced in rank, there were outposts of her city she would send them to where their chances of promotion would be slim at best.

The questions were all an effort to embarrass and thus bring down the High Priestess of Wollongong, but it would not succeed. She would not let that happen. She had been in office too long to be toppled so easily.

"Such expense," muttered one minor priestess as she went about her work mopping floors in Wollongong's major temple. This was a few days later. She was overheard by the High One of Wollongong who thought of taking action against her but decided not to do so.

"We'll have to import more robots from Japan, and where's the money for that coming from?" whispered another minor priestess who was busy wiping down a statue of Mother Mary with a wet cloth so it would shine.

"She knows what she's doing," mumbled the first minor priestess. "Now shush, or we'll both get into trouble."

Such talk from relatively insignificant priestesses was difficult to take while the High Priestess of Kiama was the High One of Wollongong's guest. Being stoic about it and also the gossip of higher ranked priestesses, was all she could do. She was thus a rock weathering a political storm. Her voice remained calm through it all, and her face was as unreadable as she could make it. Internally, she suffered, and this was shown in loss of appetite.

Like Wollongong, the city of Kiama only came to prominence after the destruction of Sydney and Melbourne. Prior to that, it had been a great holiday destination and a place where the well-off lived. Its High Priestess had gained in power in recent years, and the city was now ranked as second only to Wollongong in New South Wales, Australia. Hence, keeping Kiama and its High Priestess friendly had become crucial to the High Priestess of Wollongong's plans. She could not afford to slight her or to openly show weakness. It was fortunate that Kiama still didn't have an arena big enough for an annual event like Wollongong's. Still, the High Priestess of Wollongong needed her city to continue to run smoothly. It had to be an example to all the others.

On the second week in May, a courier brought news from Rome that a special investigator for the Highest of High Priestesses was being sent to Wollongong. It was a middle-aged maverick with a special gift for getting at the truth. His name was Nathaniel, and few maidens and priestesses could successfully lie in front of him.

The High Priestess of Wollongong thought over what she should do in preparation for his visit. She could not have the nurses and doctors who had helped her allow Dreadnought and Elanora to live well past birth murdered without incriminating herself. The best she could do was to send those particular maidens, mavericks, and priestesses as far away as possible for a few months until Nathaniel had gone. The priestesses she could send to Rome to visit sacred sites and then on to Athens and Sparta. The maidens and mavericks and their families could go on a long Mediterranean cruise. These could be seen as gifts to loyal followers and so not at all suspicious. She had her immediate followers arrange these things, saying she was feeling sentimental in her old age. She was, after all, pushing seventy.

As part of her tidying up, she sent Malcolm off to the site of the Mitchell Library excavation in Sydney. The seventh underground floor had been thoroughly explored, but Megan's team still had to sift through six more floors. Jens, Megan's immediate supervisor at the University of Wollongong, thought it was about time Megan got back to her regular job at that site but couldn't fathom why Malcolm would be needed. He knew planes, not artefacts. It didn't make sense. Still the orders had come from the High One, and that's what counted.

"The High Priestess knows best," Jens told Megan matter-of-factly. "Maybe Malcolm has talents for archaeology we don't know about."

Dean Renate, a middle-aged blonde maiden who was in charge of the university, also found this business with Malcolm strange but went along with it because she did not want to openly defy the High One. Malcolm would normally be required to fly in, drop off Megan and her team, and return to Wollongong, then pick them up later, not help with their work.

Malcolm, Megan, Jens, and Dean Renate put the odd instructions down to High Priestess intuition. No one thought it a way of making sure Malcolm would be unavailable to Nathaniel. Why should they? Nathaniel's coming visit or the nature of it was not widely known, except in priestess circles.

Perhaps I, too, had better take my leave, thought the High Priestess. *Since we have had a visit from Kiama's most reverent sister, perhaps it is time I once more visited Kiama. After all, Nathaniel did not ask for my presence, and nor did the Highest of the High, so my presence, during his visit, cannot be required.*

CHAPTER FOUR

Elanora left Wollongong airport after eating the apples and strawberries left for her in the flyer. A robot guard called her to halt near the exit gate. It had her in its sights and had drawn its gun from its holster. It had Elanora cold, so she stopped. If it fired, it would kill her. She suspected dragons that had no business being anywhere near an airport could be executed on the spot. So why was it hesitating, running its scanning eyes up and down her? *Could it be that it doesn't understand what I am?*

She had read somewhere that its red blinking eyes didn't function quite like human eyes. They could see beyond the clothes she was wearing to note that she had breasts and a shape that made her unique and so a puzzle. Why should a robot's programming account for female dragons when most people believe they don't exist?

Unlike the robots that had journeyed to her island to either capture or eradicate her, its scanners couldn't make out what she was. It now holstered its weapon and came closer to her. If she ran, it would take out its gun and shoot. She knew from what she had gleaned from her computer talks with the High One that they were deadly shots, and she wouldn't stand a chance of getting away unless it let her go.

Elanora could imagine that within its artificial brain, it recognized male dragons from humans but had no understanding of female dragons. It knew males from females, and females were never to be harmed unless its programming was changed. Elanora understood this and hoped to use it to save her life. Not fitting in had so far protected her from a bullet. She hoped her female voice might do the rest.

"What are you?" asked the robot in monotone.

"Elanora," she told it in the sweetest, most feminine voice she could manage. "I am a female."

"But what are you?" asked the robot. "I have never come upon your kind before, and your existence is not in my memory bank."

Elanora thought quickly. What would be best to say to a confused machine? "I am a female," she told it. "You should protect me and not hurt me."

"You sound like a female," observed the robot in its dull voice. "You have the general shape of a female, but ... are you a female?"

"I am a maiden with a forked tongue and an embarrassing skin condition," Elanora said, hoping that would work.

"You have a tail," observed the robot as it slipped out from under her coat.

"Yes," agreed Elanora. "I am embarrassed by that as well. May I go now?"

The robot stared some more at Elanora, its brain striving to reach an acceptable conclusion, the no harm to females, including stray maidens, coming to the fore.

"You are what you claim to be," the machine finally told her. "If you had committed a crime, I could detain you without harming you, but I am not aware of any crime. I must return to my post. Please go."

By this stage, Elanora's heart was beating faster than it usually did. *Thank the Goddess I'm such a puzzle*, thought Elanora as she scampered off. If she had been a male, she would now be dead.

It was midnight and, apart from robot patrols, some with maiden officers and others with not, the streets were empty.

Elanora, her nose picking up the smell of salt in the air, headed for the beach and the nearby warehouses. In one of the warehouses, she found a crate to climb into and await the dawn. As she climbed in, she removed a few items, including computer circuit boards she recognized by touch from her own computer back at the island. She threw them away to make room for her person, tail and all. She decided not to take everything out. The packing material was comfortable to lie on.

I can't hide forever, she thought, *but what else can I do?* She remembered her tentative connection with Wollongong University. It was where all her research and those of others accumulated. Even though they had never seen her, only received her scientific information via printout, someone there could help or at least point her in the right direction. She knew she had to avoid priestesses and knights. Maidens and mavericks might be more sympathetic. Despite the scare she had put into them, Malcolm and Megan had turned out to be all right.

Elanora fell asleep in the crate amid the shredded paper and computer parts and awoke to the sound of knights at work, loading goods onto vans and trucks. She knew they were knights because they spoke about doing away with dragons in the arena. Two of them moved her crate to a truck. She thought of getting out and running but decided to stay. Logic suggested the computer parts still with her were headed either to an assembly point in some factory or the university. She couldn't imagine them going anywhere else. Either way, staying put would be better than getting caught escaping from the box or remaining in the warehouse area. She would only be discovered by other knights.

It took twenty minutes for the truck to arrive at its destination and another ten for the knights to unload. Her box was taken from the truck by two strong knights and, by the hum she heard, there was an elevator ride. Then a door was opened, and she, box, and all, were gently laid down somewhere. The door closed, followed by the sound of the knights that had carried her walking away. After she heard the faint sound of the knights driving off with the truck, she peered out to see where she had arrived. The crate was in a storage room. There were mops, buckets, and other yet to be opened boxes around her. *This doesn't tell me much*, thought Elanora. *Beyond this closed door could be anything.*

Elanora got out of the container she was in and cracked the door open a little. She saw tables full of computers, notepads, pens, and strange objects. Some items appeared to be centuries-old according to the reading she'd done back on her island. Possibly they were from old Sydney. A dozen maidens and mavericks were poking around these artefacts, taking notes or typing their reports into a computer. They were young, so Elanora took them to be students.

"I think this used to make toast," said a young red-headed maverick in a colourful suit, studying an object with a grill and a plug.

"This may have been an egg timer," a young maiden with long black hair dressed in blue said. She hovered over something made of glass that contained sand.

"Very good," said a short, spidery, dark-haired maiden in black. "What period do you believe the toaster to be from?"

"It has such a simple design. I'd say early twentieth century." The young maverick smiled.

"What about the egg timer?" the spidery maiden asked.

"Well, Jens, I'd say the same period." The young maiden studied the sand as if it contained a further clue.

"Both are from the twentieth century," said Jens, "but that's all we can be certain of at this stage. These egg timers were mass-produced in great quantities from the 1920s up until at least the 1960s."

"They're from the sixth level of the Mitchell Library," the egg timer maiden said.

"Yes," agreed Jens. "That is where we do expect to find twentieth and twenty-first-century objects. What do they tell us about that period?"

"Someone liked toast and wanted their eggs prepared the way they like them?" The egg timer maiden offered a shy smile.

"Yes," agreed Jens. "But more than that. We know from other sites they were made in their hundreds of thousands, meaning there was once a thriving economy where many citizens could sit down and have a breakfast that was good for them. This had to be before the civil wars and the religious ones that followed. Why do you think these objects were stored?"

"They wanted to remember. They wanted to bask in a time when food was plentiful, and most people could enjoy breakfast." The maverick with the toaster beamed with confidence.

"Very good," said Jens. "Now, you both can do your write-up on these objects for the exhibition we have planned."

Jens walked away, leaving the young maiden and maverick she had been talking to looking elated. They smiled at each other and then got back to work. Next, they had medals from the Second World War to examine. Others were looking at old magazines and aircraft models.

Elanora looked on, contemplating what she should do next. She could open the door and walk out to greet them. *What would happen if I did?* Elanora wondered. *Perhaps these young maidens and mavericks will then go screaming to robot security. I might come across robots not as obliging as the one at the airport. A maiden officer with robots could simply order them to shoot me, and that's what they most probably would do. Some of those young maidens and mavericks might try to stop me from leaving. Thinking it over, it will be best to wait, but for what?* She didn't know.

Then it came to her. *If I have only one of them to deal with, I might have a chance to explain myself and get a positive response,* she reasoned. *If I only get the negative from that one person, then I can handle that one person more quickly than the many.*

****

Three hours later, the students got up and left for the day. Jens returned to go over some of the finds and correct her pupils' work. It was then Elanora opened the door wide and advanced into the room. Jens tried to back away but had her waist encircled by a barbed tail. She wiggled free and grabbed a 21st century kitchen knife.

"Wait!" cried Elanora, waving her claw. "I mean you no harm."

"Who are you? And why should I trust you?" Jens wielded the knife as if she had some idea how to use it against someone.

"Look at me!" cried Elanora, yanking the hood down to reveal her scaled face. "Have you ever seen my like before?"

"You look like a dragon, but..." Yes, the overall features were that of a dragon but were softened around the eyes and mouth.

"No dragon you've ever seen, right?" Elanora pressed the point.

"Yes." Jens's mouth formed an O.

"That's a start. Is there a place where we can sit and have tea or coffee?" Elanora asked.

"My office," Jens said.

"Good. No screaming. Let's go now."

Elanora allowed Jens to show her the way while keeping a close eye on her. They took the elevator to the appropriate floor and got off there. Both were relieved no one was around. Jens had thoughts of being pummelled to death by her captor as she was being rescued. The knife she held didn't seem to her to be much protection against that at all.

Dean Renate's office was nearby, but the dean was out. Jens wondered if that was a good thing or not. The dean handled emergencies well, but Jens didn't want any harm to come to her. It was all Jens could do not to panic.

It was all moving too fast for Jens, who understood the too well danger she was in. The High Priestess had once told her in confidence of Elanora's existence, but she never expected to meet her and certainly not under these circumstances. *Having a hot beverage with a female dragon is too weird, but much better than*

41

being strangled, clawed, or beaten, Jens thought. Thus, she took Elanora to her office, brewed up some coffee, and offered her captor biscuits. She held onto the knife. The knife hand shook. Then it stopped doing so.

"You're taking this calmly," said Elanora.

"What choice do I have?" Jens sounded calmer than she no doubt felt.

"Make trouble, and I may kill you," Elanora told Jens serenely. She wasn't lying, but she didn't know if she could actually do it.

"Have you ever killed before?" After saying it, Jens realized what a stupid question it was. The dragon, female or not, was without a pain collar and thus capable of anything.

"Ha! That I will not tell you, but I do have questions for you." Elanora knew she needed someone's cooperation if she was to get anywhere.

"And you expect me to answer?" Another stupid question, Jens realized, after she had spoken.

"Yesss!" Elanora knew she was hissing loudly but didn't care.

Over coffee and biscuits, Elanora learned about knights and how they had to slay fifty dragons to move up to maverick status. *This was kept from me by the High One when I was on the island. I can't remember, in my childhood, before the island, ever coming across this information*, thought Elanora.

"Fifty dragon kills were once considered impossible by many until Dreadnought succeeded," Jens said with a raised eyebrow. "Now, other knights are hopeful they will be next in getting that score."

"What about dragons?" Elanora asked. "What do they get if they kill fifty knights?"

"Nothing except to live on until the next battle," said Jens. She sighed profoundly, knowing this was something she shouldn't have told Elanora, who was open-mouthed shocked by this.

"I gather I am expected to wear a pain collar," reasoned Elanora, her tail swishing in agitation in and out of her coat. "I remember that much from my time before I was put on that island for my own safety."

"What island?" Jens asked.

"Never mind!" hissed Elanora. "Tell me more about pain collars!"

"Pain collars are worn by male dragons when they are not fighting," said Jens, her voice catching on the word *pain*.

Elanora winced at the injustice of what she had been told. Jens was vague on how all this business between knights and dragons had come about. "It has something to do with the religious wars that devastated great cities such as New York and made it more necessary than ever to control the human population," she told Elanora then shrugged her shoulders.

"I want to know how male dragons will react to a female dragon," said Elanora.

"I have no idea," Jens told her. She also had no suggestions as to what Elanora should do next. Obviously, she couldn't return to the island and pretend nothing had happened, but how she might move forward was not up to Jens to figure out for her.

"What are you going to do?" asked Jens when the discussion seemed to be winding down.

"I must free my people." Elanora clasped her claws together.

"The dragons? That can't be done." Jens sighed. She needed to be careful what she told Elanora, and she understood she wasn't being careful at all.

"Just like a knight slaying fifty dragons can't be done," offered Elanora.

"I have laid my knife on my desk," said Jens in earnest after doing so. "Please leave. I will give you twenty minutes before I call security. You should be able to get away in that time."

Jens tried her best not to show her fear because, in showing it, she might agitate Elanora into action against her. Even so, she exhaled deeply to release the tension she felt. She reasoned that what she had told Elanora she would do was the best move to make. Otherwise, she expected to get clawed to death.

"Thank you for your help," said Elanora before leaving.

"Please don't ever mention it." Jens figured she would get into trouble for aiding this dragon if it became known she hadn't done anything to stop her. But what could she have done to prevent her from leaving without getting herself either maimed or killed? Should she immediately phone security? *No, I can't ring security until the time is up, just in case she finds out and returns,* thought Jens. *I'm tempted, but no. I have given my word. Jens's* hand hovered over her phone for the allotted time,–then she made it known to security that there was a collarless dragon on the loose.

****

Elanora made her way back to the docks and the warehouses. A ship was being loaded. She contemplated spending the night there in the hold of that ship when she overheard talk from a maverick captain that they were not due to sail for a week. Unfortunately, the maverick captain of the vessel spotted her trying to sneak onboard.

"Hey, you!" cried the captain from the command deck, looking down at her. She was about to climb from the main deck down into the hold. "Get off my ship!"

There was not a word from Elanora as she fled, wishing she was better at sneaking about.

Another ship was nearby. She looked for refuge there, among the dozen sacks of grain that had been taken aboard and placed in that ship's hold.

She had been asleep for an hour when she heard a noise. At first, she thought it was a rat scurrying about. It turned out to be knightly thieves! There were three of them. It was then and there she discovered she had a lot to learn about combat. But could she survive the first lesson?

Elanora got to her feet in time to confront them. They were in their late teens and looked fierce.

"Who are you?" asked their leader.

"A stowaway." It was the best answer Elanora could come up with. "Are you members of the crew?"

"Not likely." One of the knights chuckled.

"We're gonna take what we want. Are you gonna stop us?" This was the third knight talking.

"No. Take it all. I don't want trouble." Elanora couldn't see the point of getting into a fight with them, especially over grain that didn't belong to her.

"Very sensible, but then you're the first maiden stowaway we've ever met." This was the second knight.

"A very maidenly attitude, leaving us to our plunder," their leader said. "But you're no maiden, are you? You sound like one, but I see scales, and I glimpsed a tail poking out from your coat. And you are alone, all alone. Look here, boys, we have a dragon to play with!"

Knives came out of belts and glistened in the moonlight that streamed down from the open hatch. They began circling Elanora. One pounced on her tail,–slamming his blade in deep. She screamed and thrashed about, but the blade stuck. Another stabbed her in her right shoulder and the third in her left leg.

Seconds later, metal clanked, and a voice said in monotone, "What is going on here?"

Her assailants fled, leaving the sacks of grain they wanted behind.

A robot came down the stairs into the hold, scanned her, and like a previous robot, could not make out what she was. However, it understood the knife bothering her did not belong where someone had put it.

"I was attacked!" cried Elanora. "I am a maiden. They stole from me and left me here to die!"

"I cannot confirm or deny you are a maiden," said the robot in monotone.

"But I am a maiden!" cried Elanora. "Please help me!"

"What can I do?" asked the robot again in monotone. His mouth was a slot that did not move, yet words came out of it.

"Pull it out!" pleaded Elanora without giving it enough thought. With little effort, the robot yanked the blade from her, and blood began to gush.

"Please sssstop the bleeding," implored Elanora, hissing more than she wished to. The hissing was not a known feature of a human female.

The robot ripped open a bag of grain and poured the contents onto her wounds. It hurt; she winced a great deal. She did not think what the robot had done was hygienic, but the bleeding stopped.

"I will take you to a hospital," said the machine in his lacklustre voice. His arms reached out for her.

"No!" cried Elanora, realizing that if she was taken to hospital, too many priestesses, maidens, and mavericks there would discover she was a female dragon. That discovery would have to get back to the High One. "If you move me, the bleeding will start again, and I will die," reasoned Elanora, hoping this was a good approach. "Please get me a doctor. Say there has been an accident. But bring only one person. Do you understand? Can you do that?"

"Understood," said the robot flatly. "I am on my way."

It clanked back up the stairs that led down into the hold. Half an hour later, a maverick physician in a purple suit with thinning hair was shocked to discover his latest patient was a female dragon and not a maiden.

"Treat her," said the robot, motioning toward Elanora.

"Treat her?" The doctor had his medical kit with him but seemed unsure what to do. He was not expecting this patient. He had treated dragons before but not under these circumstances.

"Yes," said the robot, still motioning toward Elanora. "Maiden hurt."

For some reason, the robot could not fathom what was so apparent to the maverick physician. *Why doesn't the robot see a dragon?* The physician wondered. *Has this machine malfunctioned, or has it somehow been programmed wrong?*

He felt it safer to do what he could for the dragon and then be on his way. There was no point in either getting murdered by a mad robot or a wounded dragon that wasn't wearing a pain collar. He noticed this dragon's anatomy was different from other dragons he had come across but said nothing about it to either robot or dragon. Was the dragon really female? But how can the dragon be female? From childhood, he had been told that female dragons don't exist.

After she had been fixed up, both doctor and robot left her. Despite the painkiller the doctor had given her, Elanora made her way out of the ship and rested under a pier. There she slumbered for a good four hours before awakening to the squabbling sounds of seagulls.

So, there are thieves, thought Elanora upon awakening. It made sense. A percentage of those who are not expected to live for long would band together to steal to make their lives last longer. Possibly, despite the pain collars, dragons were doing the same thing. Perhaps that was her best way into this corrupt society.

CHAPTER FIVE

The Highest One took Nathaniel by the hand and led him out onto her mansion balcony, which overlooked Rome. As per usual, she was dressed in stunning white, and he, a mere maverick, wore a variety of swirling colours. Most priestesses, maidens, and mavericks thought of the Highest One as being as cold and implacable as the white marble she often surrounded herself with. Sometimes, Nathaniel could use his mental power to prove to himself that this was not entirely true. She was not without fire just as the eternal city was not without heat in its summer. She seemed to glide rather than walk. Her little steps plus the long, silk robes that hid her sandaled feet from view gave this impression.

The balcony was small, intimate. Two could stand comfortably there and look out. Unlike much of the rest of the mansion, it was not for show. It did not bewilder underlings with size and expense. Instead, the glory belonged to the view to be had.

From this height and distance, they saw the city as a patchwork of greens and pale greys. Ancient churches and cathedrals, now places where all worshipped the Great Goddess, poked out here and there with their spires and large, oval ceilings. There was a big, uneven area where the Vatican once stood, now a black square on the landscape. It was part of the Highest One's duties to make sure nothing ever grew on that blackened patch. What happened to that place and to the last pope was to remain a lesson to all, including herself and the Highest Ones yet to come. There are enemies you cannot placate, and therefore you must fight them.

"Look over Rome with me," offered the Highest One, letting go of Nathaniel's hand.

"Your Rome," said Nathaniel, choosing to be truthful.

"Our Rome." The Highest One waved her arm over all before her. "With the population controls in place, is it not the most beautiful of cities?"

"Yes," agreed Nathaniel, "and I do not wish to leave it."

"Yet you are a maverick and must obey," reasoned the Highest One. In reading what he could of her mind, he knew she did not want to let him go, yet the urgency to do so was there.

Nathaniel looked into her eyes and rubbed his chin. "You know I do not enjoy travel," he told her.

"But you do find satisfaction in your work," The Highest One waved away his objection with the flutter of her hand. "I rely, perhaps too often, on your judgement. You may be nothing more than a maverick, but I value you and so pay you well for your services."

"As always, I will not let you down." Nathaniel now knew he could not move her to let him stay. His shoulders slumped and he looked down at his feet. He would face the dangers that lay ahead alone.

"Go then," said the Highest One, waving him away and then holding him back for a moment with her hand. She looked intently into his eyes. "With your special powers, I feel that you can always discover jeopardy in time to avoid it, plus there is a certain amount of safety in being my envoy. If you came to any harm, priestesses throughout the world know I would seek out those responsible and have my revenge."

He knew this was most likely the closest she would ever come to expressing any real affection for him.

The flight from Rome to Wollongong took two and a half days. During it, he looked over records dealing with the High Priestess of Wollongong and those under her. Apart from Dreadnought, all seemed to be in order. Dreadnought then would be a place to start after he had landed and stowed his gear away in a hotel room he'd booked in advance.

He would not be able to contact Dreadnought. Mars was an impossible distance away for what was then present-day communication. Still, some people on Earth had known Dreadnought and might have valuable insights into what had made him a champion. Dean Renate was one such person, and so was Jens. Apparently, the High Priestess of Wollongong would not be available during his time in Wollongong. He found this highly suspicious.

The following day, after his journey had ended, he visited Dean Renate in her office at Wollongong University. She had heard about Nathaniel and his visit to Wollongong. Even so, she was surprised to meet him. After all, he was the Highest of the High's chief trouble-shooter. What could he possibly want with her?

"I won't take up much of your time," Nathaniel told her. No visible signs of nervousness,-but he could mentally sense her uneasiness.

"Shall we have coffee?" offered the dean. "I know a place not far from here. Their coffee is excellent. The coffee here isn't as good."

"Very well," said Nathaniel. He smiled. He understood the delaying tactic. The short walk to the cafe would give her a chance to think over any past misdeeds Nathaniel might accuse her of, though she thought there wasn't much for him to discover.

Over coffee at the dean's favourite cafe, he asked his questions.

"Why was Dreadnought, as a knight, so incredibly successful?" Nathaniel inquired while they waited for the coffees to arrive at their table.

"I don't know," replied the dean. Nathaniel knew that this was the truth because of his powers.

"What do you know about Dreadnought?" asked Nathaniel.

"Nothing that everyone else doesn't already know," replied the dean. This was not entirely true. She wasn't sure, but maybe Amelia, the maiden from the past, was why Dreadnought was able to make his final kills. In reading this from her mind, Nathaniel took it to be romantic nonsense, but it was what the dean believed. *This is a dead-end*, thought Nathaniel.

The coffee arrived, and it was indeed good. He spent the rest of his time with the dean putting her mind at ease. She walked away from him, thinking he wasn't such a monster after all.

Next, Nathaniel spoke to Jens in her office. She was just as surprised as the dean had been to meet him.

"I am swamped because of the up-and-coming exhibition," she told him when he mentioned Dreadnought.

"My questions won't take long," assured Nathaniel.

"I really don't have the time," said Jens, her face reddening.

"I am on orders from the Highest One," he told her. "You wouldn't think of defying the Highest One, would you?"

"No." Jens let out air from her lungs as if she were a deflating balloon. "Please sit and ask me what you will."

"Tell me about Dreadnought." Nathaniel sat down and put his hand on his chin.

"Not much to tell." Jens shrugged. "I didn't meet him that often. He made his fifty, and that was it."

"Are you sure?" asked Nathaniel.

"Yes," said Jens.

"Tell me about his intelligence." Nathaniel looked at her. He suspected from her thoughts that there was something hidden that he had to bring to the surface.

"There's nothing to tell. He was an ordinary knight as far as I can recall." Jens kept her voice flat. Nathaniel noticed a crease in her upper left lip that shouldn't be there and didn't last for long. He understood, through his mental powers, that she knew she was being more guarded than she normally would be with her little hand and foot movements replacing her more typical and open gestures.

"Tell me about his leadership abilities." Nathaniel's eyes sparkled.

"Knights don't lead," Jens said, shrugging her shoulders, and hoping that accepted common knowledge would be enough to further deter him from this line of enquiry.

"The Highest of High Priestesses wants the truth." Nathaniel looked sharply at Jens. "It would be best if you cooperated."

"I've told you all I know," Jens lied, the lip crease coming back and then quickly disappearing. "Ask Megan, my assistant, since she spent more time with him."

"Thank you for your time." Nathaniel got up and left.

He sensed that something about Dreadnought's birth didn't add up. He garnered from Jens that Dreadnought was always going to be a knight regardless of his intelligence and leadership abilities. However, she would not say why, and those thoughts were not on her mind's surface. He knew she was hiding something, but it was too soon in the investigation to dig too deep into anyone's subconscious. If he mind-probed to the extent he could do, she would sense his presence, and he was not about to give that game away. Still, he now knew that the secret had something to do with dragons.

The next morning, Nathaniel took a flyer out to old Sydney. It landed near where the Mitchell Library had stood. Malcolm and Megan were busy on underground floor number six, looking for items that might fascinate the general public. They were not interested in his innuendos concerning Dreadnought.

"He and Amelia are on Mars, and we hope they have a wonderful life there together." Megan frowned at Nathaniel. *I don't like the way he's looking at me*, she thought.

"Do you believe sending them to Mars was the right thing to do?" asked Nathaniel.

"It was the only thing to do, and you must know it, too. Not only was it approved by Wollongong's High Priestess, but also by the Highest of High Priestesses."

"But why did the High Priestess of Wollongong take charge of the preparations for launch and not the High Priestess of Houston?" asked Nathaniel.

"You'd have to take that up with them." This was true. He sensed Megan had no idea why.

"Maybe, because Dreadnought came from Wollongong, our High Priestess felt it was more her responsibility to see Dreadnought and Amelia on their way," said Malcolm matter-of-factly. This was something the press at the time indicated and Malcolm found believable.

"We're researchers, or at least I am, and not politicians or theologians." Megan wanted Nathaniel to go away. There was something about his eyes she didn't like.

Nathaniel turned to Malcolm and said, "You're a pilot. What are you doing here?"

"Learning about what Megan does for a living. Don't ask me why, because I don't know. There are more qualified university students that could help her. I'm still getting my pilot's pay for this outing, so it's fine with me."

Nathaniel garnered from both Malcolm and Megan that Amelia, coming from the past in a life pod, was real, and there was some concern about how she would take to present-day society. She caused a stir with local mavericks, knights, and maidens but nothing too serious. It was Dreadnought's fifty kills that were leading to social breakdown. Even now, ripples from that event coursed through over fifty cities, including Rome.

Where do I go from here? Nathaniel wondered in his room that night. He decided a trip to Houston to meet the High Priestess of that city was in order. She must have done some deal with Wollongong's High One to not have been in political and religious control of the spacecraft launch. It had been her big moment, and she gave it to someone else. He had to find out why.

CHAPTER SIX

After the seagulls left, Elanora got a few more hours sleep. Then she was woken by a scuffling sound. She staggered to her feet and looked about so as not to be taken unawares and further injured. She paid for this movement with stabbing pain from her wounds. No one seemed to be around. She groaned, feeling dizzy from blood loss and sore in places she had never hurt before the attack. She knew she was in no shape to take on a determined foe, but Elanora wanted to look as if she could. She was collarless and standing. She understood, from her reading back at the island, that a collarless dragon was supposed to be dangerous even if she didn't feel so at that moment.

"You'd better find somewhere else to rest," a voice came from behind a pier support. "This is knight territory."

"Who are you? How do you know?" Her voice trembled, and her red forked tongue rapidly darted out and in as if it could ward off further injuries. She refrained from hissing.

"We don't come here very often," the voice told her. "It's not healthy."

"We saw you entering that ship," said another voice. "We thought that strange since any dragon with common sense would know better."

"Are you dragons?" Elanora raised her voice slightly. Her tongue stopped darting out and in, and she felt hopeful.

"Tell us who you are first," said one of the voices.

"My name is Elanora, and I'm from an island off the coast of New Zealand." There was no point in not telling the truth.

Pretending to be a local with anyone who, no doubt, knows their way around Wollongong was not going to help her.

"You sound strange, feminine. I have never come across a dragon that sounds the way you do." The voice from behind the pier support hissed this to her.

"I suppose I do, but we all sound this way on that island." Since she had been the only one on that island for ages, she considered this not to be a lie.

A silver-scaled dragon followed by a black-scaled one came out of the shadows. They wore ragged clothes and looked half-starved, their eyes sunken.

"Come!" cried the silvery dragon. "You'll be safer with us."

"We have a shelter nearby," said the black-scaled dragon. "We'll take you there."

"My name is Ronald," the silvery dragon told her. He appeared older than the other one and spoke in a friendlier voice.

"I'm Eric," said the black-scaled dragon.

"We are far too exposed here this time of day," Ronald, the silvery dragon, said. "We must be on our way."

Ronald and Eric's hideout was an old, abandoned house on the fringe of Wollongong's clothing sector. There were warehouse and clothing store bargains to be had by the not so well-off mavericks and maidens. The house was not far from the warehouses but far enough to be considered a different part of the city. The dwelling was old 22nd century with solar panels from that era still on top, and Elanora assumed to be still active. She had read somewhere that they made the panels tough back then, a lot tougher than in the earlier 21st century. There was a special knock on the door for entry, three strikes and a slap. Fellow dragons greeted them as they crossed the threshold. They all gazed intently at Elanora, their tails swishing. None wore pain collars. All except Ronald were around twenty years of age or so, she gathered.

"I'm new here," said Elanora. "Do you fight in the games?"

"Why ssshould we?" asked Eric. He hissed in anger. His mouth was set, and his eyes narrowed.

"You're here to turn us in?" asked a black dragon with a missing digit on his right hand. Elanora shook her head in response.

"No way am I going back to that!" cried Eric. Elanora could see the anger in his flaring nostrils and narrowing eyes.

"We're renegades. We no longer fight for maidens, mavericks, and priestesses." It was Ronald trying to calm everyone down with his soothing voice, and at the same time, explain things to Elanora. "We have a different way of life that suits us best and may suit you, too."

"How is that possible?" asked Elanora.

"Well, it's not easy," said the dragon with the missing digit. "Sometimes, during big matches between knights and dragons, contestants rendered unconscious are mistaken for the dead and the dying. If we are one of them, it is our chance, once we regain our wits, to sneak off and live out our lives as best we can. Oh, there are maiden officers with their robots who make sure the dead really are dead but, when the casualties are high, the bodies strewn everywhere, then a dragon might get lucky and sneak off while other bodies are being examined. But it has to be one of the big matches like the one we have here in Wollongong every May. In no way it could happen with one of the smaller ones, and even with a big one, the dragon doesn't always get away with it."

"We don't have the pain collars because they are never put back on those suspected of being dead or dying," added Eric. "In making our getaway before we are more closely examined, we become collarless."

"We must be careful. A collarless dragon is an easy mark for a robot. It is a wonder you weren't shot by one the way you were moving about last night." So Ronald knew about some of Elanora's movements before finding her under that pier.

"Why didn't you contact me?" asked Elanora. "I mean last night."

"I only saw you from a distance," replied Ronald. "I knew you were a dragon, but I didn't know what you were doing. We try to keep away from the territory claimed by the rebel knights. When you walked into their domain, I didn't know what to do. I couldn't warn you without giving your position away or getting closer. I didn't want to break the treaty we have with those knights, so I waited."

"You waited for what?" Elanora asked, her tail moving slowly in slight agitation.

"I waited for you to come out of the hold in that ship," Ronald told her. "When I saw the robot enter, I thought you were done for and so got on with my foraging. As it turned out, it was a bad night for it."

"You didn't see the knights who attacked me?" asked Elanora.

"No," said Ronald. "It was dark with lots of shadow cast from the few street lights on the wharf area. The full moon was going in and out of cloud. The robot was noticeable from its flashing red eyes. You were moving about like you owned the place, so that made you also noticeable."

"Where were you when I came out of the hold?" asked Elanora.

"I didn't want to run into that robot, so I was elsewhere," said Ronald, shrugging his shoulders. "I came across you later."

"I am fortunate you did," hissed Elanora, moving her tail.

"You can't be out in daylight collarless and expect to live long," said Ronald. "Maiden officers with their robots on patrol will kill you on sight, and there are robots, as you must know, without maiden officers to supervise them. I am surprised you're still alive."

"The knights got me, but I was able to get away from that robot," said Elanora.

"You live a charmed life," replied Ronald, smiling.

"We have some bread and cheese," offered Eric. "Help yourself."

The others introduced themselves, and so did Elanora. Eric thought her name strange, but she told him and the others it was common where she had come from. She was famished but only took a little of the bread and cheese from the table. She sat down in a rickety chair and watched the others devour what was left. There was water to drink, but nothing else. A single ceiling light bulb cut through some of the gloom, but not enough to make Elanora feel comfortable. There was an empty fridge that hummed. She wondered where the power came from for the bulb and the fridge, then remembered seeing the 22nd-century solar panels on the roof as she entered the place. *This house was once state of the art*, thought Elanora, looking about in the semi-darkness, *but that was a long time ago.*

"We plan to raid one of the nearby supermarkets tonight. It's dangerous, but we are out of supplies." Ronald was matter-of-fact about this, but there was fear in his eyes.

"When you are well enough, you will go on raids, too," said Eric. "Ronald will see to your tail and to your other injuries. He can change your bandages. There is some disinfectant left."

After Ronald had changed her bandages, he led Elanora to a corner that had two threadbare blankets. There she rested. She noted there were such blankets elsewhere in piles in other corners but no mattresses or pillows. She missed her cottage with its solid oak bed, plenty of blankets and pillows but would have to, for now, make do with what these dragons were willing to provide. Ronald was visibly relieved not to be going on the raid. He looked less stressed in the shoulders than some of the others.

Despite the clothes she had on to hide her true nature, Ronald, in seeing to her injuries, became aware of, not only her voice being female, but also other feminine traits. A tear rolled down his face after he made his discoveries.

"Why are you crying?" Elanora asked when he pulled away from her.

"You are so beautiful! And I am past my prime. I now know there is more to our dragon existence than I was ever led to believe. I will protect you and the secret of your femininity. Continue to use that bulky coat to cover up what you need to cover. Your curves at any rate can be thus hidden for a time, and so can your breasts. Your voice could also go a shade deeper."

"Am I not safe here?" Elanora needed to know.

"I don't know. We have never had a female in our midst. We were told you were impossible, but here you are. They may love you, they may hate you. Are there more like you?"

"I don't believe so." Elanora shrugged her shoulders and then winced.

"Can there someday be more like you?" Ronald had a faraway look in his eye.

"Possibly." Elanora didn't know.

"Then, we need to strive for that day. You have given me hope for a future I may never see." Ronald smiled weakly. "This grander world you will bring forth."

"How am I supposed to do that?" asked Elanora.

"What we have been told about destroying our more human mothers when we are born may well be a lie, and you could be proof of this," reasoned Ronald. "If it does happen that we do kill our more human mothers when we are born, then perhaps, with a female dragon giving birth instead of a more human female, this need not happen."

"If so, what does that mean to you?" asked Elanora.

"Guilt is a powerful force," answered Ronald, hissing gently. "We are made to feel guilty over the way we are born. Without this guilt, the priestesses will have less power over usss."

"Yesss," said Elanora, also gently hissing. "I can imagine that being the case."

"But you and what you could represent goes against the Great Goddess and what the priestesses have told us," revealed

Ronald. "I don't know how many among my dragons still believe, to some extent, in the Great Goddess, the priestesses, and Heaven when they die. Therein is the danger to you."

"I may not be safe as a female dragon," whispered Elanora, frowning.

"For now, it will be best if we pretend you are a male dragon," Ronald whispered back to her, smiling. "I will keep your secret."

Elanora fell asleep and woke to the sound of dragons returning. The overhead light bulb had been switched off. A couple of candles lit no doubt by Ronald, now provided dim light that cut through some of the gathering darkness of late night. She could smell blood. One dragon had been shot, and she was told two, the one with the missing eye and the fellow with scales gone from his face, were missing. Eric had a sack filled with oranges and cans of vegetable soup. The black dragon with the missing digit had two loaves of bread and a dozen apples in another bag. The rest came back empty-handed.

"We were fortunate to get away," Eric said. "A maiden officer saw us enter our target and sent in a couple of robots to deal with us. We grabbed what we could and ran."

"We can't fight robots when they have guns. We have two dead to prove it." The black dragon with the missing digit said this in anger and regret. The passion was in his rasping voice and the sadness in his eyes.

"The bullet in my leg," said a silvery dragon wincing in pain. "It has to come out."

"I'll see what I can do for you, Don," replied Ronald.

Elanora watched as Ronald tore Don's pant leg with a knife then poured whisky on the wound, making Don scream. He gave Don a drink, then wet the knife with alcohol and used it for fishing out the bullet. Eric helped hold Don down. Once the bullet was out, Ronald applied more whisky. He took a swig and offered the rest of the bottle to Don to drink. A hot iron was applied to the wound, then the bandages were put on.

"It didn't nick the bone," Ronald said after Don came out of a dizzy spell. "You were lucky. Also, the robot was not using a standard firearm. If it had, we would have had to amputate."

"Why wasn't the robot using standard?" asked Elanora.

"Damned if I know," said Eric. "I suppose they issue to the robots what is available on a nightly basis."

"So there is a limitation when it comes to the guns they use?" asked Elanora. "They can't always be outfitted with the more effective types?"

"Yes. I suppose that is true," Eric said, "but the robots still have enough firepower to kill the lot of us, and why so many questions?"

"Should we share our food with this new dragon?" asked Don. "I don't think so, do you, Eric?"

"He needs to eat," said Ronald.

"Don't we all," Eric offered. "He hasn't earned even a crust of bread yet, has he?"

"I've bled for my share," reasoned Don, pointing to his bandaged leg.

"We should at least give him an apple and an orange," said Ronald, his forked tongue active. "He'll earn his keep."

"How do you know?" asked Don, his claws curled up into fists.

"Give Elanora a chance!" cried Ronald, his silvery tail swishing in agitation. "If we're wrong about him, we lose an apple and an orange."

"That's a lot to lose," reasoned Don, touching his wounded leg and flinching.

"We took a chance on you, Don," replied Ronald. "We take a chance on all newcomers."

"Fine," said Eric, his claws open. "Elanora has his chance, but he'd better earn his keep real soon, or he's out."

"And we give him a share of what else we have?" pressed Ronald.

"Yes," said Eric, shaking his head and smiling at Ronald. "We'll do that, too."

A cold meal was made from the cans of soup. Everyone, including Elanora, got a bowl of it to consume with a chunk of bread. There were no spoons.

Poverty, thought Elanora. *This is what it looks like. I have to do something. I must do something. They have suffered enough. No one should have to live the way they do.*

****

Meanwhile, the following day, Jens was rediscovering what it was like to be responsible for educating young children. It had been years since she had taught a class of eight-year-olds, but their teacher had called in sick, and she felt it her duty to take her class.

Wollongong University prided itself on being a place of learning as well as research. Having students as young as eight was unusual. Still, the school where they would normally go for instruction was under repair, so Dean Renate had agreed to allow a few classrooms to be available over the following month.

The classroom where Jens was to teach had practical seats and tables plus a blackboard for the instructor. Textbooks rather than computers were to be used. There was no internet, so the computers with their limited capabilities that would normally have been there had been put away into storage. The room was eggshell white, and so were the desks and chairs. There was air-conditioning, so the windows were permanently closed.

The pupils, in their various coloured clothes, came in on time, sat down, and got out their reading and writing material. They stood out in all this whiteness. Jens, who often preferred to wear a lab coat over her grey blouse and jeans while working, was already there with a welcoming smile on her face.

Jens was not tall, but she was wiry. She knew that some of her more adult students called her the rock spider behind her back. There were a dozen girls and a dozen boys in this class. All were eager to learn, especially the boys because every one of them knew they had to become mavericks or die young as knights. Jens had the notes from the ill instructor's desk to go by plus her own knowledge of the subject.

"Last lesson, you looked at how awful the world was before we were formed into Priestesses, maidens, mavericks, and knights," said Jens. "And, yes, it is true that there was a time when the mutants we call dragons didn't exist. So who can tell me about the first Martha?"

They all put up their hands. Jens allowed a chubby girl with blonde pigtails to answer.

"She stopped the wars and brought everyone together. She did this with the help of the Great Goddess. She is also known as the first of the Highest of High Priestesses."

"Very good!" complimented Jens. "Anything else?"

"She put an end to the false religions," piped up a large boy without permission, one Jens predicted would someday soon be designated a knight. His behaviour was indicative of this. He was already scoring low for good manners.

"Yes, that's right. But hand up next time, please. Turn to your book and the chapter on this subject. I want you to read about how this person who called himself 'pope' turned against his own people and supported the hordes who wished to overpopulate the planet. He was old and stupid rather than evil, but it was still a betrayal. Actually, it was more than one pope who did that, and they are all described in detail in your reading material."

"The people rose up against the pope," said the large boy, again without raising his hand. "I mean the last pope to go against the people. That's why there's a great, big crater where the Vatican used to be."

"We don't know who exactly blew up the Vatican," Jens replied, clasping her hands together. "It may have been those he had given over to the enemy,-or it may have been the enemy. Regardless, the crater remains to remind us of how false beliefs and those who show a lack of care for their own people can meet their just end. In this, the Highest of High Priestesses and our very own High Priestess are in full agreement."

A thin girl with long, black hair raised her hand, and Jens acknowledged the gesture.

"Why were the bad ones so keen on overpopulating the planet?"

"Because they were stupid, like you," answered the large boy.

"That's not entirely true," replied Jens in a calm voice, knowing from previous experience with young children that a raised voice would do nothing more than bring up the volume of noise in the room, which she understood was counterproductive to good teaching. "Poverty leads to all forms of madness. Some of these poor, deluded people thought, by increasing their numbers, they could eat better and have more living space. Of course, this was foolish thinking, and it was opposed by those better educated, hence the civil wars and then the religious wars."

"Breeding to solve all your problems is still stupid," groused the big boy.

Jens's eyes narrowed in the direction of the boy not conducting himself appropriately in class. The rest of the students also looked his way, knowing he was in trouble. He gulped a few times, waiting for Jens to say something to break the sudden tension in the room. There was now the silence of expectation.

"Timmy, I will see you after class," Jens commanded in a soft but stern voice, pointing her bony finger at the reddening boy's face. "Now, all of you get on with your reading."

The chubby girl's hand shot up.

"Yes, Jenny?"

"If dragons are animals, how come there aren't any female dragons?"

"They're not exactly animals or lizards for that matter. If the Great Goddess didn't want there to be female dragons, that's why there aren't any female dragons."

She gave the girl and the rest of the class the textbook answer, even though she now knew it was wrong. *I can't tell a class of eight-year-olds I met a female dragon or someone I think was a female dragon,* she told herself. *It would get around, and Dean Renate would come to believe I've lost my mind.*

CHAPTER SEVEN

Nathaniel had a pleasant flight to Hawaii. It seemed that all the trips he was on were problem-free. Pilots began to think of him as their good luck charm. The truth was he could sense creatures that might harm a flyer and get into their heads and have them go elsewhere. At one time, he had two giant albatrosses attack each other rather than the transport he was in. On another occasion, a whale-sized monster with many rows of teeth ate two flying sharks unwittingly for his benefit.

This sort of mental activity, however, was taxing, and he needed rest afterward. It was also something only he and the Highest of High Priestesses knew about. It was not something he wanted to make common knowledge.

"You have a gift," the Highest of the High had once told him, over coffee when he was young, "but it won't be worth anything, and it might even get you killed if everyone knows about it. What's more, if even my priestess servants are aware of your abilities, and know you have limitations in how you can ferret out damning information about them, they will find ways to exploit any weaknesses you have. They will conspire to be rid of both of us, and they may even succeed."

While in Hawaii, Nathaniel interviewed a journalist who did a write-up on Dreadnought's interest in the statue of King Kamehameha. He found nothing new. It remained a mystery. Maybe Dreadnought simply liked the look of the old king.

The journey from Hawaii to Houston was slow because of winds pushing against the flyer rather than pushing it on. Wind resistance, even with jet engines, remained a factor in flying. This gave Nathaniel extra time to read up on the new space program. The cities of Rome, Shanghai, Hong Kong, Lyon, Liverpool, Wollongong, Houston, and St. Louis had invested heavily in it. The space station that resided halfway between the Earth and the moon was going to be refurbished. New experiments on human ailments were to be carried out in zero gravity. There, few Earth contaminants would be around to interfere with the results.

"It will take years to finish the refurbishing," an astronaut-in-training from Hong Kong revealed in one article, "but it will be worth it."

"In zero gravity, bacteriological proteins can be broken down in relative safety and studied," a scientist from St. Louis reported in another. "That space station will also be a place to gather together the material from abandoned weather satellites for the next venture to Mars."

At Houston, Nathaniel received a grand tour of the facilities for space flight. The head engineer, a rotund maverick in his forties wearing a multi-coloured cap, introduced him to a dozen engineers that bombarded him with a lot of technical information. He also met two of the four astronauts being prepared for the next trip into outer space. He did not have to delve into their thought processes to register their enthusiasm for their upcoming mission.

After talking, even briefly, with these astronauts, Nathaniel almost wished he was going too. If he did, he might be able to contact Dreadnought, who was on Mars, and ask him questions.

The High Priestess of Houston reluctantly allowed him to visit her. She had looked in her mirror that morning before breakfast to confront her fears and calm herself. *I don't know how this Nathaniel maverick, this spy for the Highest One, digs up stuff on priestesses, including High Ones,* she thought, *but I won't be his next victim. I will mind what I say. He will have a short meeting with me and be on his way. I can't refuse him without making the Highest One suspicious, but he will learn nothing from me that will damage my life as a High One.*

She lived in a mansion on the outskirts of the city. It was large, white, and imposing. Marble the colour of fluffy clouds was everywhere. She had the usual statues of Mary and paintings of the Great Goddess. There were models of spacecraft that had made their way into outer space. The pillars holding everything up were of Ancient Greek design brought back for those who had the money because of their elegance.

The high ceilings were meant to create a sense of awe in the visitor. She knew, offhand that such things as the marble, the high ceilings, and even the model rockets would not intimidate Nathaniel. He had spent much time in Rome and so was used to even higher, grander ceilings and more impressive statues and paintings. She knew there were rocket models in the Highest One's private chambers.

The High One of Houston was tall, thin, past middle-age, and dark-skinned with hazel eyes. Her mirror revealed these facts to her. Maybe, in appearance, she had something to offer to throw Nathaniel off with, so she dressed seductively in white silk to meet with him. She arranged for it to take place in a small, intimate room where she had seduced others.

Nathaniel, however, was not to be taken in by this move on her part to disorientate him. "You are a High One?" he asked as he sat down in the white chair offered to him.

"Yes," breathed the High One. She smiled at him, her hand almost but not quite touching his.

"Why were you not the spiritual leader in the launch that sent Dreadnought and Amelia into outer space?" asked Nathaniel.

"I felt, since Dreadnought had been the High One of Wollongong's knight for so many years before becoming a maverick, she should have the honor."

A mind probe by Nathaniel made it clear to him she had been blackmailed by the Wollongong High Priestess and so had given away her place in history.

It was either to be exposed as having had several male and female lovers or letting the High Priestess of Wollongong, from a High Priestess's point of view, handle the launch to Mars.

What the High One of Houston had said to Nathaniel was weak by her standards, yet he seemed to accept it.

"Have you ever been intimate with anyone in a physical way?" asked Nathaniel.

"Never!" cried the High One, indignantly. It was true she was trying to distract him with her appearance but in a look-don't-touch way. She reasoned she could be beautiful and at the same time unattainable. "I am a head priestess," she added, "therefore, I am celibate."

"Of course," Nathaniel mused; he knew her celibacy wasn't genuine, but her power over her own domain was real enough so he had to be careful what he said to her. "That was a silly thing for me to say," he added. "I hope you can forgive me."

"Forgiven and forgotten," said the High One, brushing it aside with her hand. Perhaps the small room and dressing up in silks wasn't such a great idea after all. If he went away thinking she had most probably broken her priestess vows at some stage in her life, then the Highest One could look into the matter, find fault and act against her. Yet Nathaniel did seem to regard her indignation as real, and so she figured that no harm to her had been done.

Nathaniel got the names of past lovers from the High Priestess's mind and later wrote them down. He knew she would most likely be kicked out of the priestess-hood, but no blasphemy charges would be laid against her unless she made a fuss. She might even be allowed to keep her mansion and whatever wealth she had already accumulated for her silence. The public would be told she had retired, and a new High Priestess for Houston would then take office.

How the High Priestess of Wollongong had found out about the High Priestess of Houston's indiscretions was a mystery. The High Priestess of Houston thought it would have to be one of her former lovers, and she was probably right.

Nathaniel left the grand, white mansion with the Houston High Priestess unaware her greatest secrets would soon belong to the High Priestess of Priestesses. However, the High Priestess of Houston had a sense of unease from the mental probing she would later attribute to Nathaniel's visit.

On the trip back to Hawaii, Nathaniel had mentally instructed a flight of seagulls to avoid his flyer.

There in Hawaii, he enjoyed a meal of steak Diane before heading back to Wollongong. He had thought of going to Kiama instead to confront the High Priestess of Wollongong. He decided, however, it was still too early in his investigations to do so. He knew she was frightened but powerful. He might gain all he needed to know from others and thus avoid a meeting with her. He understood that, if the High One of Houston had any idea of what he had gained from her, he would never have left Houston alive. Even with the Highest One's protection, it had still been a risky business.

Near Wollongong airport, Nathaniel ventured into The Great Grape, a known hangout for maverick and maiden flyer pilots. The bartender there, a round-faced maverick in a striped shirt, remembered Amelia as being the strangest damned maiden he ever met. To prove it, he dusted off a half-filled bottle and showed it to Nathaniel.

"That's whisky," said Nathaniel after reading the label.

"She drank it. That says it all. No sane maiden would ever touch the stuff." The bartender shook his head in disbelief. "I know maidens, I know what they drink, it's my business to know and whisky is not your typical maidenly choice."

Nathaniel had a glass of red wine and listened to some jazz.

"Did anyone ever talk about Dreadnought?" asked Nathaniel of the bartender.

"Up until recently, people spoke about him all the time."

"Anyone in particular?" Nathaniel tried reading the top layer of the bartender's mind.

"Everyone. Some were for him, and others were against him, but it was all talk." The bartender shrugged his shoulders, smiled, and added: "I like gossip but don't put much faith in it."

"Would he have ever been accepted here as a maverick?" Nathaniel knew the answer but thought he'd ask anyway.

"That's hard to say. In my opinion, no, but that's just my opinion." The bartender was honest.

Nathaniel came to the entrance to Demons, a dragon watering hole, and looked in. The music that came out was jagged, uneven. Dragons of all shapes, sizes, and colours were getting drunk. This was their place for doing that. So long as they had their pain collars on, they could walk from where they laboured to Demons without maiden officers harassing them and then to their barracks. Nathaniel understood that without those collars they would not have any freedom in any city at all. He also reasoned that dragons would not be welcome in a knight's pub or a maverick's wine bar.

There was talk among the dragons about how knights were more eager than ever to kill them and how maidens continued to enjoy what went on at their expense.

"There's unrest at the waterfront," said a silvery dragon, his smooth tail flicking lightly.

"I heard renegade knights are running loose," claimed a black-scaled fellow.

At the entrance to The Spear and Shield, a knight's pub, Nathaniel heard rock music. He also listened to stories about knights getting up points to become mavericks. Thanks to Dreadnought, fifty was now seen as reachable. If Dreadnought could do it others could too or so some knights thought.

"I hear that the priestesses might bump the number of kills required up to sixty or even a hundred," said a thin-faced knight.

"If they do," a burly knight who had been serving drinks said, "they'll be sorry."

"We need to be able to become mavericks, or what's the point of it all?" This was a young knight cradling his half-empty beer glass.

"You have a long way to go, lad," said the burly knight.

"I know. But I have to know I can get there." The young knight finished his beer.

"Don't we all," agreed the burly knight, handing the young knight another beer.

"I don't know if I could ever get used to sipping wine," confessed the young knight. He took a mouthful of beer and grinned.

"If you ever do become a maverick, you'll sip your wine and like it." The burly knight grinned back at him. "Like me, you'll do anything to stay alive in this crazy world. Plus, you'll have your pick of maidens and not just to play chequers with."

"Yes," agreed the young knight. "There is always that."

"Yes, that particular consideration does make up for sipping wine, doesn't it?" The burly knight hinted.

"Oh, yes," agreed the young knight then took a swig of beer.

Nathaniel had a meal at a maiden and maverick restaurant where locals told him they served the best seafood. Doctors said fish was good for the brain, and he wanted his brain in good working order. That night, he sent off his first report to Rome via computer link. He had his suspicions about the nature of Dreadnought that still needed to be confirmed.

He could inform the Highest of High Priestesses that his investigations were going well. The moral weakness in Houston's High Priestess was discovered by him for the Highest One's consideration. Flaws in the High Priestess of Wollongong would also soon be revealed.

CHAPTER EIGHT

Elanora looked at the dragons with her. Like herself, they sat on rickety chairs in a house made dingy by having only one overhead light. Their clothing was grey and in tatters. She still wore that brownish-grey coat which covered up her femininity but could not hide the fact she was a fellow dragon. She had not been comfortable sleeping in a corner with a threadbare blanket, but that was all they could offer her. She wanted to change that, but first there was the question of food.

The eyes of these dragons had that hollowness associated with a poor diet. She had done enough reading on the island she had come from to know this. *They would think better on a full stomach with good food*, she thought. *Hell, I'd also think better that way myself.*

Eric wanted a raid similar to the one they had the previous night.

"We need to be faster," Eric said, rubbing his claws together. "Right lads, you with me?"

"No," spoke up Elanora. "I don't want to alienate anyone here, but I also don't care to risk my life for little gain."

"Who are you to say what we should do?" Don growled. "You haven't contributed, have you?"

"No, he hasn't," agreed the dragon with a missing digit, both claws curled up into fists. A loud hiss came from him as he spoke.

"He's not yet one of us!" cried Eric.

"Let him speak," said Ronald in a calmer voice than the others, his claws open, his tail moving gently. "There's no harm in that."

"You lossst two dragons," Elanora said in her own defence, hissing with emotion. "Do you want to lose two more?"

"We lose dragons. It is our way. Survival of the group is what counts, and there are seven mouths to feed." Eric glared at Elanora, then sighed deeply. "I don't like losing dragons."

"What if you don't have to lose anyone?" asked Elanora. This surprised Eric and the rest of the group. Scales that were eye-brows were raised, and there was thoughtful hissing. Chairs they were sitting on creaked. There was also the shifting of feet and tails.

"Right!" cried Eric. "So, by some miracle, we're going to suddenly become bulletproof? Do you even know how to fight?"

"I know how to think." Elanora looked away from Eric, wishing she didn't have to be so blunt with him.

"So, what do you think?" asked Ronald.

"I have a simple plan. It will be three of us to act as a dis-traction, and the rest to gather the food."

"I don't get it." Don grimaced, fidgeting about due to his wounded leg bothering him.

"Were you planning on hitting the same supermarket to-night?" asked Elanora.

"No," answered Eric. "That is a dumb question."

"Why not?" asked Elanora.

"Isn't it obvious?" Don slapped his face with his claw. "They'll be expecting us."

"But what if they were not expecting you? What if they had their hands full elsewhere?" Elanora was pushing but knew she had to continue.

"What do you have in mind?" Ronald asked.

"I want to pull this off, and if possible, have someone else blamed. Gather 'round, and I'll tell you how it might be done. If you don't like my ideas, you can always do things the way you were going to." If nothing else, Elanora now had everyone's attention.

"I don't like it," said Eric after Elanora had spoken. "It's too complicated."

"I don't know," grumbled Don. "I realize I was against listening to him in the first place, but we can give it a go. If it doesn't work, we can always go back to doing it your way."

"I agree," said Ronald. "Maybe this is that better way we need."

"It might be at that." Don looked down at his wounded leg and sighed.

"A show of claws then," reasoned Eric, not wanting any divisions among his dragons. "Who is for Elanora's plan?" Claws went up. "Very well, we'll try it, and may the Great Goddess help us if everything goes wrong with it!"

"At worst, more dragons will die, and there will be even less food gathered." The dragon with the missing digit looked down at where his finger used to be.

"At least it's something new to try," said Ronald, his claws open.

Reluctantly, Eric took three dragons to the supermarket and waited outside for the signal to commence looting.

Elanora went with Ronald and Don to a nearby hardware store and broke in. The glass at the entrance was shattered by a rock thrown by Ronald; then Don's claw reached through the space that had thus been made and clicked the front door open.

Upon entering the place, Elanora couldn't help but notice the greyish-blue shelves that were all along the walls. There were also shelves in and around the centre of the room creating a maze of shelving. There was the pungent odour of horse glue that irritated her nose and also the smell of various containers of paints and thinners. Nuts and bolts were neatly stacked as were washers and cans of spray paint. Fire extinguishers were in various spots, close to electrical equipment. What she was most grateful for was the fact it was well lit by lots of overhead lights.

An alarm went off, spurring them into action, her cohorts quick to grab what Elanora told them was needed.

Elanora, Ronald, and Don hid behind shelving as the two robots, with their maiden officer, entered the premises. Then Elanora shook up a fire extinguisher, pressed a button, and let fly the foam directly at the face of a robot, covering the red, blinking eyes with the stuff. Ronald and Don did likewise to the other robot with astonishing results. Blinded by the foam being sprayed at its face, one of the machines closed down. The other, also blinded by the foam, listened for movement and took out its gun. Once the weapon was out, Elanora, Ronald, and Don were still, hoping not to be fired upon. This was not true of the maiden officer. She knocked a fire extinguisher away from one of her robots and tried to wipe the foam from its eyes. This was a bad mistake.

The robot fired and blew apart her head. Elanora and Ronald watched, mesmerized, as chunks of the maiden's brain and skull landed on the floor, and blood spurted from where her head should have been.

Ronald was momentarily reminded of the horrors of the arena in May and so was sickened by what had happened. He moaned to himself. After seeing the worst of it, he lowered his eyes and shook his head to clear it. Elanora, after she had gotten over the shock of witnessing the maiden officer in such a state, also shook her head to clear it so she could continue with the mission. All this happened in a matter of seconds, but the awfulness of it would stay with Elanora, Ronald, and Don a long time.

Then, working out what it had done by its vision beginning to clear, the robot that acted incorrectly deactivated itself. Elanora sprayed its face with more froth from a fourth fire extinguisher she grabbed just to be sure.

"What next?" Ronald asked.

"We leave," said Elanora, "but not empty-handed. First, a few messages."

"Why?" asked Don. "Why not grab what you want us to take and get the hell out of here while we can?"

"If we can confuse the authorities as to who has done what we have done," reasoned Elanora, "all the better. A maiden officer has been killed. We didn't want it to happen, it was an accident, she was just in the wrong place, but the ramifications of her death may be far reaching. If the blame can be put on someone else, the hunt will be on for them and not us."

Elanora grabbed a spray paint can and wrote on the wall in large red letters: KNIGHTS RULE!

"Isn't that a bit obvious?" asked Ronald.

"I hope the authorities are not as smart as you," said Elanora and sprayed another wall with the message: DOWN WITH DRAGONS! She then pocketed more spray paint cans and urged Ronald and Don to do the same. Before they left, she spotted a bow and arrow kit and decided to take that.

****

When they heard the alarm go off at the hardware store, Eric and his team made their move. Not bothered by robots, they collected two large bags of food each.

"We stopped two robots," said Ronald to Eric once they were back in their hideout.

"You destroyed two robotsss?" Eric hissed, finding this hard to believe.

"We stopped them," corrected Elanora. "They'll be up and running again by tomorrow night."

"How?" asked Eric. "How did you stop them?"

"See no evil," said Ronald, covering his face, hiding a grin.

"We blinded them," Elanora told them.

"And we blamed those damned renegade knights for what we did," said Don. "I don't know if that part will work, but it was worth a try."

"I am not sure how wise that was," mused Ronald. "It may make things hot for those renegade knights rather than us dragons, but it could also end the treaty we have with them."

"I wish that maiden officer hadn't been killed." Don sighed.

"I didn't want that maiden officer to get in the way of her robot at the wrong time," said Elanora, eyes downcast. "I was hoping we could have succeeded in doing what we set out to do without anyone, including her, getting hurt, let alone destroyed in such a fashion."

"You weren't to know she'd act foolish," reasoned Ronald, gently hissing.

"No," agreed Elanora. "I wasn't to know, but I still feel bad about what happened to her."

"You may get to feel even worse if our treaty with the renegade knights has concluded," mused Eric.

"It was bound to end sooner or later," reasoned Ronald, claws open.

This time, no one, not even Eric, wanted to begrudge Elanora a share in what had been taken. Elanora understood that Ronald would step in if anyone tried. She also suspected that Don would also come to her aid. He looked at her, grinned, and moved to where she and Ronald were seated.

"We'll do the same thing tomorrow night," said Eric.

Elanora could see a quick end to a short career in crime. Greed, stupidity, and predictability, she knew, could get them all killed.

"That's a sure way to get caught," Elanora warned him, her tail moving in an agitated way. "Besides, we have plenty of food. What we need now are bedding and medical supplies. I need new bandages and antiseptic, and so does Don."

****

The following morning, the newspapers made a fuss over the renegade knights causing a disturbance near the docks. Elanora's graffiti had been photographed and made it to the front pages of all the Wollongong newspapers. Patrols were sent out to specifically catch these knights. There was no suggestion in the media that the offenders might instead be dragons.

Megan and Malcolm both wondered why knights who

should be keeping low profiles would write "KNIGHTS RULE!" on a wall, implicating themselves for no apparent reason. "DOWN WITH DRAGONS" also seemed odd.

"Renegade knights aren't this stupid," said Megan to Malcolm over breakfast in their neat little cottage where the smell of roses wafted in from their front yard garden. This was after reading the morning paper.

"I agree with you," replied Malcolm, who had also read the paper. "There are dragons capable of doing what was done, but no one in the media or higher office wants to believe they can be that intelligent. They prefer dragons to be stupid, which helps make sense of the May and November games."

"Yes," agreed Megan. "We would sympathize more with dragons if we thought them to be as potentially smart as we are, and that would never do. The games might even be called off, and then where would we be?"

"Hence the danger in runaway dragons," offered Malcolm. Megan smiled in agreement.

Meanwhile, elsewhere in Wollongong, in his neatly furnished hotel room which overlooked a charming though small park with its grass, benches and gumtrees, Nathaniel understood the politics of what was going on with the media. It was possible, though not probable, that knights who had been smart enough to dodge robot patrols for months could be so dumb. It was more likely they were being set up. The general public was more comfortable with reports of seemingly clever as well as reckless knights on the loose than, say, intelligent dragons confounding the law. The death of the maiden officer was also a reason to pin what had been done on knights rather than dragons. It was too much for the general public to imagine dragons in any way being responsible for such a death. It was a failing Nathaniel felt someone with brains was exploiting. *Wollongong and its inhabitants just got more interesting*, thought Nathaniel.

After receiving the news, the High Priestess of Wollongong, in her Spartan room that smelled of ink, papers, and books, called up the head of her city's maiden officers. "I want the bad knights mentioned in these reports rounded up and dealt with! I may still be in Kiama, but I keep close tabs on what goes on where you are. Those robots may only have received minor damage, but what happened to that maiden officer is totally unacceptable."

"I will do what I can," offered the head maiden officer, blinking and feeling uncomfortable for the first time in ages in her grey uniform. She was past middle age and had held her position for a decade. She was so glad the High One couldn't see her discomfort.

"If the actions of these renegade knights continue," the High One snarled, thumping her hand down against a coffee table for emphasis, the thump being heard over the phone, "this will speak of a weakness in my administration. Do you know what that means?"

"No," squeaked the head maiden officer, blinking some more and choking up with tears.

"I will have to look for a new head maiden officer!" cried the High One and slammed the phone down.

Neither the High Priestess of Wollongong nor the harassed head maiden officer suggested that rebel dragons might be involved in what had recently gone wrong in Wollongong. *Was Elanora, my missing female dragon, at that waterfront, creating trouble for both of us?* The High One wondered. She dismissed it as highly improbable. *My Elanora is a scientist, not a brigand, and a gentle soul at that.*

****

"Can you get hold of a pain collar?" Elanora asked Eric during lunch at their hideout. He was taken aback by her question, tail twitching, and claw going to the back of his neck.

"No dragon I know wants anything to do with pain collars," he told her.

"So can you lay hands on a pain collar?" asked Elanora.

"I don't know." Eric rubbed his jaw in contemplation; his tail stopped moving. "What do you have in mind?"

"Only dragons with pain collars on are free to walk the streets during the day," replied Elanora. "So, what we need is a pain collar to examine."

"So we can walk around during the day?" Eric shook his head and smiled.

"That's right." Elanora put down her food bowl and picked up the bow she had stolen.

"You do know that will be useless against a robot, don't you?" asked Eric sceptically.

"We'll see," said Elanora. "Anyone care to give me lessons on its use?"

"I will." Don smiled; he was beginning to warm to Elanora's ways. "I used to be good at it until they banned them from the games."

"For all we know, they may have brought them back," said Ronald, amusement in his voice, his tail moving rhythmically.

"Not a chance," said Eric grimly. "They were too effective against knightsss. But at least I got to use them that one time before I decided I had had enough of the whole ssstinking business."

"One bow with arrows won't do much." Don was sure of this, yet had to wonder what Elanora had in mind.

"We'll see." Elanora smiled disarmingly, "Now for that lesson, Don, if you please."

CHAPTER NINE

Gregory threw the newspaper against the nearest bulkhead and watched it fly apart. The shiny blackish-grey surface of the interior of the old ship they were in took it well. He looked at his fellow knights, all but one in their twenties, who grimly shook their heads. He wasn't angry with them. It wasn't their fault the hunt for renegade knights had intensified. He was mad at whoever had done this to them.

Was it in retaliation for that poorly trained dragon those knights in their late teens had boasted about stabbing? He had sent those foolish youngsters away, not wanting to further break the truce with the rebel dragons, even if that stabbed dragon had idiotically wandered into their territory.

A rat scurried by, disturbed by his action. Daylight came in through a hole. *This vessel hadn't been seaworthy in a long time and has been left to rot,* he thought. *What if that had changed? What if they trap us in one of these old tubs? The constabulary with their robots might well search these derelicts in earnest for us and then where do we go?*

"For years, we have kept our heads down," Gregory told his knights. "We steal some goods every now and then to sell on the black market. When it starts to get too hot for us, we live off seagull and yes, even rat, until things cool down. Seagull and rat are not the best food, I grant you, but it has kept us alive along with not making ourselves well known to law enforcement. Now the papers are full of demands for our heads!"

"Five years ago, I was content to be a knight fighting for my life two months out of every year, or so I thought," revealed

Phips. "Then one night, soon after the end of the November games for that year, I was ambushed by two silvery dragons."

"You've told me this before," said Gregory.

"But I haven't told Toff or Craft," offered Phips. He paused for a moment to gather his thoughts then continued: "I was coming out of The Spear and Shield none too sober when it happened. You see, I had killed a good friend of theirs in one of the games. It was all legit on my part, but they wanted revenge. They took me into a dark alley where one held me down while the other carved me up."

"That must have been awful," reasoned Toff, now the youngest of Gregory's warriors.

"It was bad," answered Phips with a sob in his voice. "That dragon peeled my ear like an orange with the knife he had, and I screamed and screamed. I nearly blacked out from the pain."

"What happened after that?" asked Toff.

"A maiden officer with her robots heard me and rescued me," said Phips. "The dragons ran off, but I learned later, when in hospital getting stitched up, that they were caught and executed for harming me out of season, so to speak. Once released from hospital, I was supposed to go back to my barracks, but I ran instead and met up with Gregory. I wanted to get away from this we kill them, they kill us thing we have going with the dragons. Up til now, I thought I had succeeded."

"But what did happen to that maiden and those robots?" asked Toff. "I mean the maiden who was killed and the robots that were damaged. We don't take on robots, and we don't kill maidens. I might steal a purse or a wallet every once in a while, but that's it."

"Those youngsters I dismissed for knifing a dragon for being on our turf, and days later, we're in the shit." Gregory thumped the side of the barrel he was sitting on for emphasis.

"So, you think the dragons did this to us?" asked Phips, a thin knight with a missing left ear.

"It fits," said Gregory. "No knight would do this to us, and no maiden or maverick would care to."

"It doesn't matter," Craft, a knight opening a can of baked beans, spoke up. "We've always been on the run ever since we chose not to be in the games. We are, after all, renegades, but the constabulary have doubled patrols. It's gotten more dangerous. We've already lost five good fighters to the robots, and that was only in the last two days. We need to think fast or die."

"We keep retreating. We'll soon run out of abandoned ships like the one we're in, and then we'll be done." Phips grumbled, touching his face where his absent ear had been.

"One by one, they're blowing up our waterlogged safe places. Then they search through the wreckage for our bodies," informed Aayan, a dark-skinned knight.

"We know where the dragons are," Gregory said between clenched teeth. "We have had a policy of live and let live. They leave us alone, and we leave them alone. That has come to an end. Our territory is no more. If we stay, we might as well surrender to the authorities, and we all know how merciless they are."

"So, when do we attack?" asked Craft. He didn't like attacking anyone but would rather get it over and done with sooner rather than later.

"We eat first," said Gregory. "We have baked beans and some biscuits left, plus sweet tea and pears. That will be the finish of our supplies, but we are not going into battle half-starved."

Craft handed Gregory half a can of baked beans; he'd eaten the other half.

"We'll take them easily." This was said by a husky knight named Alexander. He remembered what it was like in the arena of death, hoping to get out alive. Then not going back to barracks afterwards like he was supposed to but seeking some better way to live. He thought he might have found that better life with Gregory and the others. Now he wondered if he had been wrong.

"We were trained to kill dragons." A short knight named Franko spoke up. Not being tall, he had figured his life expectancy if he had continued fighting in the May and November games would have been brief. Now he wondered if it was going to be brief anyway. The lure of kill fifty dragons and then become a maverick had not appealed to him at all. He felt he had no chance of killing that many dragons.

"Will the dragons have food?" asked Craft.

"Of course! They have to eat, too!" Gregory hoped he was right.

****

Eric, Ronald, and Elanora suspected there might be a backlash to the graffiti and the maiden's death. So, they had two guards posted at the entrance to their safe house, on rotating shifts, at all times. The dragon with the missing digit thought it a waste of time.

Then, on the last day of May, at the entrance to the dragon-occupied house, a spear thrown by the knight named Franko savaged Don. It went straight into his chest. He gasped, shook, and died.

The dragon with the missing digit, which was also on guard duty, was cut down by Gregory's swift sword. This dragon lived long enough to sound the alarm. Then Gregory kicked in the door.

Elanora, who had been calmly sitting at table in the kitchen area, grabbed her bow and arrows. She pulled back and released, pulled back and released. This way, she took out two knightly warriors with two of her shafts. One was Phips, who received an arm injury he would recover from. The other was Alexander, who was slain outright, the arrow penetrating his heart. Eric knocked Franko off his feet with his spiked tail before slicing into him with a battle axe. *No fifty kills for me* was Franko's last ironic thought as he passed away, his mouth frothing blood.

The fighting spilled into the various rooms of the house. It might have gone on if not for Elanora cornering Gregory. She had him in her sights with an arrow poised to deliver death. She called for him to yield.

"What if I do?" cried Gregory. "You will kill me anyway!"

"No, I won't!" shouted Elanora, using her more natural feminine voice. The voice she normally disguised to sound more masculine. "Give up! Tell your knights to surrender and find out! Stop this madness!"

Everyone halted and looked to where the voice calling for an end to hostilities had come from. It sounded too female to be ignored. They had all grown up with either maidens or priestesses in charge, so an authoritative feminine utterance was hard to push aside. This stoppage was Gregory's cue to act.

"I yield! We surrender!"

Tentatively, the knights backed away from the dragons. There had been something in the timber of Elanora's voice, the now more feminine utterance, that compelled them to do so, and it was backed up by Gregory.

"Now we kill the lot of them!" shouted Eric. There was delight in his voice.

"No! We make them our alliesss." Elanora spoke with a passion she didn't know she had.

"You're mad!" hollered Eric. He had hatred in his narrowing eyes.

"Knights and dragons do not work together. We kill each other." Craft was adamant about this, and so were all the other knights except Gregory. He was hopeful.

"Now, you work together. We do this or ssslaughter each other. From what I understand, there are no rewardsss for dragonsss butchering knightsss. And as for you noble knightsss, no one is here to praise your efforts at killing dragonsss. No maidensss to cheer you on or to keep score. Even if there were, is that any way to live?" Elanora let that sink in, then added, "You knights gave up that life, so why pick it up again now? And you dragonsss, I know, never wanted that life in the first place."

"Strange dragons, strange knights, strange times." Ronald leaned toward Elanora. His claws were open and his scaly eyebrows were raised. *She's right in wanting to change attitudes, but how can it be done?* Ronald wondered. *I am surprised by her audacity in trying.*

"But so much blood has been spilled between us over the years," reasoned Craft. "How can this possibly happen?"

"That's what I want to know," said Eric. He had a firm grasp on his sword hilt.

"Fine. Look sharp, dragons. Let's finish this here and now or else use our brainsss." Elanora paused then added, "We are no longer fighting against one another for the pleasure of maidens, mavericks, and priestesses. For most of you knights, those fifty-dragon kills to become mavericks were always impossible. That's why you became renegades in the first place. Don't you see? We all stand a better chance of survival if we all work together."

"It does make sense, but how can we trust them?" Ronald pointed at the knights.

"We have honour," said Gregory with pride, standing tall. "If we give our word we will not betray you, we will not betray you. It is dragons who have no honour."

"You're still alive when you could be dead. There must be honour there, even if it was Elanora's idea." Eric glared at Gregory.

"We'll eat, drink, care for our wounded, and then bury our dead. And we'll think about this some more." Ronald was hoping that, if enough time went by, the putting together of both groups would somehow sort itself out.

"We have no food." Craft looked with an envious eye at what was on the table.

"We will share what we have, and you will help us get more." Elanora hoped no dragon would object to her offer.

"Who will lead?" asked Craft.

"I will not take orders from a knight," grumbled Eric.

"I would find it difficult to take orders from a dragon," said Toff.

"Elanora shall lead." Ronald had thought of a possible way to end the impasse.

"Elanora?" asked Eric. "Why Elanora?"

"She doesn't have much knightly blood on her hands, and this was her idea," Ronald said.

"Her idea?" wondered Eric. "Her as in female? That's impossible! He may sound like a female when he puts the effort into sounding so, but..."

Elanora glared at Ronald, fire in her eyes, her tongue poking out, then a furious hiss and a wild motioning of her barbed tail.

"Sorry, Elanora, I let that slip, but I thought it was time they knew anyway." Ronald noted the anger in Elanora's eyes now dissipating.

"A female?" wondered Gregory. "But that cannot be!"

"I am a female." Elanora removed some of her bulky clothes to prove the truth of that statement. She had breasts like a female despite them being black and scaly. "And I am a dragon."

"And you are our leader." Ronald hoped this declaration would work.

"Just what we need, an impossible leader for an impossible future." Gregory couldn't help but smile.

"We'll see how it goes." Eric shrugged his shoulders. He would have liked to have been in charge, but he couldn't see that happening without a return to bloodshed.

"Do you have plans?" Phips asked hopefully.

"Of course, with the help of all of you, those plans will be less dangerous and more advantageous." Elanora looked around her as she spoke and could see the bloodlust, the desire to kill receding in all of them. Red human faces not so red, and dragon scales were not glistening as much. It was also receding in her.

****

Meanwhile, robots were planting charges on the last of the derelict ships in Wollongong harbour. The maidens and mavericks in charge did not realize such use of explosives were now a waste of time.

The explosions did make good copy at first for the news services. They satisfied the general public that something was being done about the renegade knights. This was before the first of them actually occurred.

Sitting in his Wollongong hotel room, Nathaniel thought that the local Wollongong authorities were being far too heavy-handed with the so-called renegade knights, and in the end, were not likely to get the results they wanted unless they wanted good publicity. Even there, he had his doubts. It was like trying to kill a mosquito with a hammer.

A few bodies would have been good, thought the High Priestess of Wollongong as she watched the explosions on the news in her hotel room in Kiama. *Still, at least one problem has been addressed. I wonder, though, if Elanora is still alive and possibly with dragons, and what part she might have played in the latest disturbance to hit my city.*

Maids, mavericks, and priestesses stood on rooftops watching the display of pyrotechnics. The harbour had not been lit up so much and in so many colours since New Year's Eve. Everyone who had a good vantage point cheered. Then the black, thick smoke and the smell of death made every watcher wonder if the explosions had been such a good idea.

A dozen seagulls circled the area and, instead of landing on the rocks or the sand as they usually did, flew away in disgust. They were lucky to be able to do so.

Jens made some calculations based on the smoke she saw on television and phoned up the harbour authorities. She wanted to know what was in those battered old vessels, the ones the city authorities had so cavalierly destroyed. There was silence on the line for a few minutes, and then the answer came back. "Oh, my Goddess, that's awful!" Jens cried into the phone and hung up. She then got in touch with Dean Renate.

"We have trouble!" moaned Jens to the dean. "Big trouble! Those damned fools in charge of those detonations don't know what they've done, but they'll soon find out. Goddess help us! This is a catastrophe!"

CHAPTER TEN

Nathaniel watched the news as helicopters scoured the Wollongong shoreline. Some belonged to the harbour authorities, others owned by the television networks. The positive reports coming from the harbour turned out to be premature. Several of the hulks the police blew up contained oil drums. The oil spilled into the water and onto the beaches. Terns, seagulls, and pelicans covered in the black muck were not a pleasant sight. Somehow, they had escaped being roasted alive by fires around where the explosions took place. Parks, wildlife officers, and concerned citizens did their best for them. Dead fish floated in the water and piled up on the sand and rocks.

"The clean-up will cost millions," said an announcer from a helicopter. "Was it worth it to deal with a handful of renegade knights?"

The following night, when the fires had died away, body parts from Wollongong hospital were strewn around where the derelicts had been so they could be discovered in the morning. There had to be some proof renegade knights perished even if the evidence had to be manufactured. Robots commanded by well-paid maidens did the dumping.

Gregory heard about the deception from the barman at The Spear and Shield, who got it from a reliable source, or so he said. The word got to The Great Grape,-and the bartender there passed it onto a maverick journalist. The newspapers questioned the nature of the body parts. Some looked too flabby for knights on the run.

Two days earlier, a train heading from Wollongong to Kiama slipped its rails, and three mavericks had been killed. One of the mavericks had an expensive ring with a blue opal at its heart, which mysteriously turned up on the finger of one of the hands found in the waters of the harbour. Beetles feeding on the dead could have allowed this ring to slip off the questionable hand, but that didn't happen. The hand, taken from the morgue and used the way it had been, together with the rest of the maverick's body, was too bloated from being in the water for that to easily occur. This discovery did not sit well with the wife of the maverick that died in the train crash, nor did it go down well with the general public.

The chief aide to Wollongong's High Priestess called for an inquiry. Two maiden officers were dismissed from the force. The robots they worked with would go to new maiden recruits. "We did what we were told to do," offered one of these maidens to the press, but did not elaborate. Her statement was not made known to the public but remembered by those who had heard her utterance. A local newspaper photographer, in a photograph, captured fear in her eyes as if she had said too much. The picture was not published and was destroyed by the publisher who did not want trouble with Wollongong's High One.

The maiden publisher, a dark-haired woman in her mid-twenties who tended to dress in light brown suits, understood that the technology was there to create better forms of communication and to bring back the Internet and the mobile phone. The High Priestess of Wollongong and the other high priestesses also understood this. Not having that technology available to the masses and limiting the use of the computer was all about control. Some high priestesses in certain cities either insisted on the existence of one newspaper or magazine in their province or no newspaper or magazine at all.

Television and radio stations existed only at the sufferance of the high priestesses, and those running such places understood this. In most cities, maiden officers with robots made sure that what was sent out was in agreement with high priestess views and policy. Mavericks who hosted shows were particularly aware of this. None of them wanted to be downgraded to knight for disobedience, or even worse, blasphemy. The wrong words uttered on a talk show could lead to something horrific before death if an example had to be made.

"We can have cars with anti-gravity devices, and we can send maidens and mavericks to Mars," said the publisher to her staff one day in frustration after looking at what the maiden officer with her advised could not be published, "but we can't have the sources of information people used to have, including fancy cameras and talking and listening devices they, those people of the past, held in such high esteem. We have landlines instead of mobiles to make it easier for high priestess spies to listen in on our conversations. Hell, we can't have a free press! It's impossible!"

"And what do you intend to do about this?" asked the maiden officer assigned to this publisher, frowning at her.

The publisher watched the maiden officer's robots, noticing the red gleam in their eyes, looked at their weaponry and said, "I intend to do nothing, nothing at all."

"Good."

The publisher knew that the robots would not kill her because she was a maiden and not a knight or a dragon, but by an order from the maiden officer, she could still be taken into custody. She looked at the metallic arms of one of the walking machines and understood they were strong. One of those robots was more than capable of hauling her off to lockup. She might be fined or have her business taken from her and given to someone else. Either way it was trouble she didn't want.

The search for the rebel knights continued, though at a slower pace. The High Priestess insisted on this. Nothing was to be done that would further upset resident maidens and mavericks. Also, there must not be a violent uprising of knights and dragons in retaliation for acts done to them in this search. "We must crush these renegades," said the High Priestess over the phone to the maiden in charge of the maiden officers, "but not destroy my city in the process."

Jens and Dean Renate were called upon to direct university resources to fix the waterfront. Knights and dragons, many fresh from the games, were required to get the gunk off rocks and pick up debris. Scientists at the university provided knights and dragons with special scrubbing brushes and chemicals. The knights got separate areas of the beach from the dragons to avoid conflict. Robots made sure knights did not wander into dragon spots and vice versa. The work went smoothly, something positive the newspapers could report.

While this was going on, Elanora organized a raid on a bedding warehouse. The lone robot guard was made blind with spray can paint and knocked off its feet by a swinging tail. Shelving was dumped on its head, resulting in its gun skittering across the floor and into Eric's hands. He was tempted to shoot the knight next to him but refrained from doing so. *It's so hard*, thought Eric, his gun hand shaking, but steadied by his other hand. *Still, I have to remind myself that Phips, along with the other knights, is now my ally, not my enemy.*

For years, Eric had been taught to fear and hate knights. He remembered his old instructor at his barracks, before he became a rebel, telling him never trust a knight, and now he was expected to work with them. *I am an outcast*, he thought, *but how much an outcast am I? Doesn't anything I used to know count for anything anymore?*

They loaded beds, mattresses, blankets, and pillows onto a warehouse truck and drove it back to where they were staying. Elanora had insisted on the mattresses. She knew she wanted to sleep on one and reasoned the others would also benefit from better rest if they had such luxury. A good sleep, getting the brain up to full capacity, she told them, could save lives.

Along the way, three of the knights and three of the dragons broke into a liquor store and came away with two dozen bottles of whisky and rum. In this instance, no robot was guarding the premises. Once the renegades unloaded the truck, they dumped the truck a mile away. Aayan, the knight who had driven it, walked back to the hideout.

Elanora knew that tensions still existed between the renegade knights and the rogue dragons. Not long after getting back to the house, Eric took the gun he had acquired out of his pocket and looked down at its barrel. He then stared at the nearest knight, who happened to be Toff, and grimaced. *Why don't I go on a shooting spree, starting with him, and end this damnable alliance before these knights do?* He then looked away from Toff and grudgingly put the gun back in his pocket. He knew Elanora was watching him, and for some reason he was yet fully to discover in himself, he didn't want to disappoint or upset her.

He had been ruled by females all his life. They were in charge of his world from maidens to priestesses, and that was at the heart of why he had mixed emotions about her. He responded too readily to a female voice and hated it. At an early age, he had been taught to obey, and he had had enough of that. *As a dragon, I want to see her dead because she's taken over*, Eric thought, *but as a female I want to protect her like I am supposed to. I know her being female isn't her fault, but her taking over is, and I'm not sure I am ready to be obedient to anyone anymore. I'm not sure at all.*

Elanora hoped the scotch and bourbon would help bring everyone together. After the sleeping quarters had been made up to everyone's satisfaction, they all met in the lounge area to drink to their continuing success.

Bottles were passed around, and the talk turned to how they had all ended up where they were.

Craft took a swig of whisky before passing the bottle to Ronald. Craft then shook his head as if to clear it and said, "I was a skinny youngster back when there was a chance my local priestesses would have me trained as a maverick rather than a knight. But they made me a knight, and so my options became somewhat limited."

"How limited?" Eric asked.

"Could I date and, in the future, marry a maiden? No, that's what mavericks do," said Craft with amusement in his voice. "How about giving me a university education and then a well-paying job? Again no, that's for mavericks, not knights. So, what was left to enjoy? There were three meals a day when in training to be a knight and then in the barracks as a knight. When on the run with Gregory, it was tucker whenever I could get my hands on it."

"I'll vouch for that," Gregory offered with a smile.

"So, you can now understand how food came to mean so much to me," reasoned Craft open-handedly. "It's one of the very few pleasures in life those priestesses couldn't take away from me without killing me outright. So, what's it all really about then, this life of a knight?"

"Most knights don't live long enough to ask that question," Gregory said, also open-handedly. "I wonder what Dreadnought's sex life is like since he became a maverick and married?"

"We all wonder that," Phips mused, fingering where his ear should have been. "When we begin to lose bits and pieces, we come to understand what we are and what will eventually happen to us. I looked for a happier ending, and here I am."

"A quick death is all a dragon can hope for two months out of the year," Eric said grimly, his spiked tail moving briskly. "There are no prizes for us, none at all."

"A quick death, you say? There we couldn't always oblige, but we did our best." As intended by Gregory, both dragons and knights laughed at this.

"I was buried under a pile of corpses." Toff took a mouthful of bourbon and gagged on the taste. "Maybe the pile was uneven or something so I could breathe. I don't know. Some dragon knew I was there, under all that. He was stabbing away, trying to get at me, when a fellow knight shoved the pointy end of a spear into his guts. I was pulled out from under all those bodies, dripping with knight and dragon blood and gore. I survived while others hadn't, but no way could I ever go back to that."

"The pain collars keep us tame most of the time," said Ronald, after drinking from the bottle handed to him by Eric. "Once they're removed, we're no different from you knights. We also have dreams of a more peaceful life. I would rather garden than kill. I used to do chores on a farm. I miss those days."

"Want to know my story?" asked Aayan after taking a bottle off of Eric and downing a nip. "I am thought to be a descendant of those who foolishly tried to overpopulate our world. For a century, my family has tried to make amends for what others did. Even so, most of the males in my line get picked to be knights instead of mavericks. When I realized this was the case and probably the reason for me being selected as a knight, I had to get out. Oh, I know, the priestesses never talk about this sort of thing, except among themselves before selecting. But it is not that hard to work out once you know how you appear to them plus your own family background. Anyway, to hell with being blamed for things I haven't done. I am not responsible for the actions of my ancestors, even if they were guilty. I strongly suspect if I looked different, I'd be a maverick today."

"You can't know that for sure," reasoned Gregory, accepting a bottle off Elanora and finishing it.

"I know enough," said Aayan sourly. "The last maiden I had the company of thought I should be a knight because of what happened in Sydney and Melbourne as if I were responsible for those bombings."

"But you weren't even born when they were bombed." Gregory understood Aayan's angst.

"Also, like I said, my family, going back that far, were not even on the side of those who would overpopulate." Aayan grimaced. "I know this from family records. We just look like we were on their side."

"What about you, Elanora?" asked Gregory.

"What about me?" Elanora asked, blinking.

"Tell us about being a female dragon." Smiling, Ronald passed Elanora a bottle of scotch.

She took a few drams of the whisky before commencing. All eyes were on her, and there was silence.

"I am me. I am a female. I wouldn't know how to be anything else. I have been disguised as a boy dragon and then as a male dragon, but neither can be me. I eat, I sleep. I do a lot of things male dragons do. Who knows? Maybe I think differently, and so we're all alive here today."

She thought for a moment of the trouble she had originally caused the knights with the graffiti she had put on a shop wall. She now regretted having done so but couldn't take it back. *As a pretend boy dragon, I remember being trained with wooden swords and then with real ones,* she thought. *The focus had always been on destroying the knight, any and all knights.*

Looking around, she didn't want any part of her dragon upbringing. Being placed first in her cottage on top of the hill and then on her island away from further contact with dragons as she became more and more a female had changed much in her. The High Priestess of Wollongong had allowed her to develop intellectually, and now she hoped to use that to forge a better life for herself and those around her, including these knights. One dragon in particular concerned her. She wondered if Eric was going to be a future problem.

Soon after they all went to bed, Toff had a nightmare. He was the youngest of the renegade knights and still felt deeply about his experience in the arena. This time, the dream wasn't about being buried under lots of dead bodies like his other nightmares or being caught for stealing since he was a very good pickpocket. He dreamt instead of being hunted down by Elanora, who commanded Ronald to slay him. They hissed as they spoke the way dragons do, and this further unnerved him. They had axes in their hands and the gleam of manic hatred in their eyes. He screamed as they got closer. He could see the shimmer of their weapons. Gregory woke him. He was in a cold sweat, shaking. "It's all right," Gregory said calmly, soothingly. "You're safe."

"Am I safe?" asked Toff.

"We will keep you safe," promised Gregory. "It was only a bad dream."

CHAPTER ELEVEN

The High Priestess of Wollongong had to return to her city on the second day in June to restore order. "They blew up those useless vessels in my harbour," said The High One to herself as she adjusted her white attire in the mirror. "Those idiot maiden officers with their robots caused a spill of contaminated waste oil. It was safe in those drums. It was forgotten in those drums until the leader of my maiden officers blew them up."

She booked passage on the next train heading north to Wollongong from Kiama. It didn't matter now that Nathaniel was still there. *I can't shirk my responsibilities any longer.*

She knew the High Priestess of Kiama was glad to see her go. She didn't say as much, but it was always a case of not having two high priestesses in the same city for too long unless you wanted trouble. No one ever appreciated someone of equal rank continually looking over their shoulder.

Just what has happened to my Wollongong? The High Priestess thought as she got on the train. She had been following the news closely, but that didn't tell her how chasing a few rag-tag knights out of old ship holds could have gone so wrong. There was talk of cover-ups, bribery, and corruption. Undoubtedly, some citizens theorised her absence from Wollongong somehow coincided with the waterfront disaster and that she had planned it before leaving for Kiama.

Reporters at the Wollongong train station asked her about Kiama. They bustled for answers. "Kiama is quaint with its own charms," she told an eager maverick with a microphone, "but I want to make it clear that Wollongong is my home." Badmouthing the High Priestess of Kiama, she knew, was not in her best interest.

On the third day of June, the High Priestess arranged for special prayer meetings throughout Wollongong. In temples everywhere, maidens, mavericks, priestesses, knights, and dragons prayed for the seaside to return to pristine condition.

****

Nathaniel had the visual records of every fight Dreadnought had been in sent to him for study. The replay close-ups were of most interest. On some occasions, the dragon about to be slaughtered by Dreadnought hesitated long enough to give that knight the advantage. This Nathaniel found significant. He noted down these moments. The number of them over the years of combat endured by Dreadnought ruled out coincidence. *This was how fifty dead dragons were possible,* Nathaniel concluded.

It was then he made arrangements for the following morning to meet the High Priestess of Wollongong in the Great Temple. He knew she would have to agree because of his position with the Highest of High Priestesses.

That night Nathaniel ordered coffee to be delivered to his hotel room. However, the knightly waiter who produced it was too nervous for Nathaniel's liking, his eyes furtive. He sensed a trap and skimmed the fellow's mind to find out what was going on. He then had the waiter drink the coffee. The knightly waiter didn't want to, but Nathaniel told him if he didn't, the constabulary would be called in and he'd be in deep trouble with the authorities. And so, the fellow drank the coffee, hoping he'd be out of the room and away from Nathaniel before it took effect. Unfortunately for him, the drug was almost immediate in what it was meant to do, and before the fellow could exit the room, proving he was just a waiter with coffee, he went into a dazed state.

Some kind of preparation to render me incapable of defending myself, thought Nathaniel, *but why?* He wished he had dug deeper into the knight's mind before the drug took hold. He got from the surface of the fellow's mind beforehand that something was wrong with the coffee, then all the ways this fellow could think of to deny this fact. He didn't get who was responsible and how high up in whatever order this abduction might go. He swapped clothes with the waiter, replacing his swirling red and green pyjamas for knightly grey cloth, and hid under the bed to see what would happen next. He was hoping more knights would come to take the disguised waiter away. He could then read their minds and find out in more detail what was going on. The waiter's mind at this point was blank to him.

Twenty minutes later, a robot came in and picked up the disguised waiter and made off with him. Nathaniel crawled out from under the bed and locked the door. *Someone's going to be disappointed*, he reasoned; his mission had taken a dangerous and unexpected turn. What's more, because a robot was used to pick up the knightly waiter, there was no humanoid mind Nathaniel could read and thus profit from. He had never been any good at interpreting the goings on in the head of a walking machine.

A commotion downstairs informed Nathaniel that his would-be captors had discovered they'd been tricked. The waiter, who was in on it, Nathaniel reasoned, would pay for his lack of success. Apparently, someone wanted to take Nathaniel by surprise and to a more secluded locale.

At first, Nathaniel thought they were agents of Wollongong's High Priestess, then realized they were more likely to be connected with Kiama's High Priestess. Wollongong's High Priestess did not want to meet Nathaniel at all and would prefer him dead rather than a captive somewhere. The High Priestess of Kiama, however, would have different ideas. The amount of time Nathaniel had been investigating her rival and what he had gathered might be useful to her.

The coffee would have put Nathaniel in a dream state where it was possible he would be more cooperative in answering questions. The waiter, with his eyes all glassy, looked that way, and Nathaniel should have asked him what was happening before the robot came to take him away.

He suspected that if he had drunk the coffee, he would have eventually found himself back in his bed in his hotel room and could have shrugged the whole business off as something to do with his imagination. The person behind this would have gotten what they wanted from him, whatever that was, and would assume he was none the wiser about it. *A theory worth considering*, thought Nathaniel, wishing he was back in Rome where he felt safe.

The High Priestess of Wollongong received Nathaniel in her office at nine, where he was offered coffee and biscuits. Usually, those who enter the Great Temple in Wollongong are impressed by its size. The ceiling was high. Much of the interior was white marble, including the statues of Mary and the Great Goddess's guiding angels, young girls in gowns and sandals with angel wings sprouting out of their shoulder blades. Nathaniel, however, had come from an even grander temple in Rome. He declined the offer of coffee and biscuits, remembering what had almost happened the night before. Once again, he did not suspect this High One of that wrongdoing. Nothing on the surface of her mind gave him that impression, but he was inclined not to take chances.

Nathaniel asked her about Dreadnought and why he was so special. He got his answer from a mind probe in which he discovered that Dreadnought was born a dragon that shed his scales and lost his tail soon after he was born. That was apparently the reason he had to become a knight rather than a maverick.

The High Priestess would not allow someone who had once been a dragon, even for such a short time, to be appointed a maverick.

Dreadnought might have been able to read the minds of his dragon opponents, but the High One was uncertain in her thoughts about this.

Nathaniel asked the High One if there were any unique dragons around. "What's so special about a dragon?" came her answer. Her mind told him about Elanora.

The interview didn't take long. The High One found she had a mild headache after it and felt she had somehow given too much away, even if her verbal answers had been guarded.

As he turned away, Nathaniel rubbed his chin and frowned, wondering whether he should inform the Highest of High Priestesses about Elanora. She could be a harmless creature, no doubt scraping by if she was indeed alive. Circumstances could change, and she might pose a threat in the future to not only the High Priestess of Wollongong but also to the Highest of High Priestesses. Then again, by studying her, if she was alive and could be located, he could discover insights into his own nature.

Dreadnought wasn't the only male dragon to ever shed his scales and tails at an early age and appear more human, he thought, *and how this female dragon thinks and acts might be the clues I need to further assess my own thoughts and abilities. She is unique, and so am I.*

He smiled at the possibility of finding Elanora as he exited the Great Temple, walking down the ever so white steps and away from the High One.

Nathaniel booked passage on a late afternoon commercial flight out of Wollongong headed for Rome via Hawaii. He had more than enough information needed to satisfy his employer, and it was time he headed home.

Before departing, Nathaniel had lunch at a busy restaurant frequented by maverick shop assistants and then a few drinks at The Great Grape.

It was a short walk to the airport from The Great Grape, but Nathaniel took a cab. Traffic was light, and he arrived with plenty of time to spare for his flight. He was about to board his commercial plane when he sensed good reasons not to do so. Others who were going to board had been given new flights. They had been told the aircraft had developed engine trouble. This he got from their minds.

It was another effort to kidnap him through two flight attendants and two pilots. A mental probe confirmed they were in the employ of the High Priestess of Kiama. Instead of putting himself in their clutches and ending up on a landing strip halfway between Wollongong and Kiama, Nathaniel chartered a flyer to take him to Rome.

He read Malcolm as being an honest, competent pilot more interested in flying than politics or religion. The mechanical hand and leg might have been of concern, but Nathaniel gathered, from the fellow's thoughts, that Malcolm had had those artificial limbs for some time and was used to them. He understood he was lucky to get such a maverick pilot on such short notice. He also felt he needed to be on his way quickly before another attempt was made to kidnap him.

"I've told you where we're going, so can you get us moving and make it snappy," said Nathaniel anxiously to Malcolm. His voice quivered.

"The flyer takes half an hour to refuel," replied Malcolm.

"Does it have to take that long?" asked Nathaniel, wringing his hands. "It's only to Hawaii, and I'm in a hurry. In Hawaii, you can refuel to take us to the next stop after that on the way to Rome."

"Look!" Malcolm informed Nathaniel, "I'm not about to run out of fuel, with nothing but miles of ocean around me for you or, for that matter, anyone else."

Once they were airborne, Nathaniel breathed a sigh of relief. He was going to report how the High Priestess of Kiama had tried to capture him not once but twice. Her agents should have given up after the failure of the first attempt. If they did, he would have left it since he couldn't have confirmed who had made the first go until the second one had taken place. Why they tried a second time, and so blatantly, happened to be beyond his understanding. Just what did she think he knew about the High One of Wollongong?

There was a thunderstorm over Honolulu, making landing tricky. Apart from that, the trip so far went without incident.

As they flew out of Honolulu, Malcolm's flyer was followed a short distance by a flock of seagulls. Nathaniel made mentally sure the birds didn't get anywhere near the engines. He knew that seagulls and engines did not mix well.

Some days later over Rome, they had to circle several times before being permitted to land. Six aircraft were in line to do so before them.

"I hope you don't mind the delay," said Malcolm.

"Do I mind?" wondered Nathaniel, then offered up a broad smile. "I enjoy seeing Rome, my city, spread out before me, even though I have seen this sight, from the air, many a time. Such beautiful architecture! It is the city of cities!"

"The fuel is nowhere near critical, so I am satisfied to wait my turn and drink in the sights," Malcolm said, then smiled back at Nathaniel, who sensed he was being sincere in this.

Once landed, Nathaniel headed straight for the Highest of High Priestesses' home in the hills via rented hovercar, which ran on compressed air rather than wheels.

The Highest of High Priestesses was delighted to see Nathaniel. Over coffee and sweet cakes, he handed her his final report on the Wollongong situation. He dropped the High Priestess of Kiama right in it while, at the same time, keeping Elanora out of it.

"So you think Dreadnought was like you?" asked the Highest of High Priestesses after sipping her coffee. He sensed she did want to know.

"Yes," said Nathaniel. He sampled a sweet cake and added, "Like me, he was born a dragon that didn't keep his scales or tail long after his birth. You let me become a maverick without any fuss or bother..."

"I knew you were smart and that I would be proud of you," said the Highest of High Priestesses. A gentle look inside her mind by Nathaniel proved she had come to believe that. He didn't think it was possible to look at a newborn and work out, then and there, how intelligent that child was going to be.

"You kept an eye on my progress. And it worked out well for both of us." Nathaniel smiled his half-smile.

"But what happened with Dreadnought?" the Highest One wanted to know.

"Out of fear of getting caught keeping alive a dragon that no longer looked like a dragon, the High Priestess of Wollongong insisted Dreadnought be classified a knight," said Nathaniel.

"How tragic that must have been for him," the Highest One cooed. No feelings on the matter could Nathaniel detect emanating from her.

"Just think of what he might have accomplished if he hadn't had to spend those years going from knight to maverick," said Nathaniel. "Just imagine what he might have done with his life."

"He could have outshone you." The Highest One smiled a wicked smile.

"In a way, he was my brother, and I'll never get to know him." Nathaniel sighed.

"Not unless I send you to Mars." There was humour in the Highest One's voice.

"Is that likely?" Nathaniel knew it wasn't but asked anyway.

"No. Now, what should I do about the High Priestess of Wollongong?"

"Leave her where she is. Right now, Wollongong needs stability, and she can provide it. When the time is more advantageous, you can have her dismissed." Nathaniel couldn't see any advantage in replacing the Wollongong High One while the oil spill crisis was ongoing.

"But I should remove the High Priestess of Kiama from her position right away?" The Highest One leaned forward for his answer.

"That's my recommendation. She's getting paranoid, especially toward the High Priestess of Wollongong. The second attempt to make off with me, I now realize, smacks of desperation and muddy thinking. She doesn't have to leave in disgrace. As I have indicated in my notes, she can retire, and you can be financially generous toward her. That would give the people of Kiama a good sense of continuance for whoever replaces her."

"I will keep her in her position a while longer. For now, her paranoia, especially if directed at the High Priestess of Wollongong, can unwittingly be of service to me."

"As you wish, your Highness." This was Nathaniel's reply when agreement was best.

"You will dine with me tonight?" It was as much a command as it was a request.

"If that is what you want, I'll be delighted. I am happy to once more be back in Rome." Nathaniel was truthful.

Why haven't I told her about Elanora? Nathaniel wondered. *Is it the fact that, in a way, I don't yet fully understand, she is my sister?*

The Highest of High Priestess laid on a special feast for Nathaniel, which included all his favourite fish dishes. For the moment, he forgot about Elanora. During the next month, he would be busy in the city he had grown up in. There was no need whatsoever to contemplate what was going on in Wollongong or Kiama since the jobs he was expected to do at those locales were done. He was required, for now, to move onto other work. As far as he was concerned, those places could take care of themselves.

****

In the second week in June, Gregory and his knights raided Wollongong Hospital. They made off with a half-dozen pain collars. Elanora said she only needed one. Gregory thought she would be pleased with the extras, and he was right.

No one at the hospital thought anything was wrong with the knights taking the collars. Drugs that could be addictive or pose a danger to the unwary were locked away where special security clearance was required to obtain them. Since the collars only needed to be worn by dragons, they were considered low priority and not a high-security matter.

The collars were kept in a storage room to be put back on dragons after they had recovered from operations. Also, the collars left over from the games where dragons had died had to be stored somewhere. As for the knights taking them, the hospital staff merely assumed some maiden or maverick had requested them. It would have been inconceivable they were being stolen because a female dragon wanted them.

"I thought the last thing you'd need was one of these gadgets," Gregory told Elanora as he handed them over to her. Eric looked on, wondering what use they could be other than inflicting pain and making dragons more submissive.

"Tell me how a dragon can walk around in broad daylight without getting arrested?" asked Elanora as she tinkered with one of the devices.

"With a pain collar on, everyone knows that! But what good is that?" Gregory shook his head and smiled sadly. "If you wear one, they own your black-scaled skin."

"But what if we can find a way to make the collars harmless?" Elanora smiled back at him.

"I now see what you mean, but can you do it? Can you make them harmless?"

"I can try. By the way, what's the difference between a knight and a maverick?" Elanora was smiling that mysterious way again as if she was teasing something out of Gregory.

"I wouldn't know where to begin to tell you. I have lived as a knight ever since I was designated one." Gregory shrugged.

"Lots of things," Eric said. "Mavericks don't kill us dragons, for a start. That's what knights are supposed to do. Just what are you trying to tell us?"

"Tonight, I want you, Gregory, and Toff to break into a maverick clothing shop," Elanora told Gregory. "I want you to steal enough clothes to outfit three knights and take whatever money is in the cash register."

"There's a clothing store near the university," said Eric.

"What for?" asked Gregory, his face a blank.

"Clothes count." Elanora smiled broadly. "We know you are a knight by the way you dress, even when you are not fighting."

"So what?" Gregory frowned, not getting it.

"I'm a little in the dark, too," Eric admitted. He held out his claw as if he could grasp the answer with it.

"We dress up three of our knights to look like mavericks, and hey! Presto! We have three mavericks!" Elanora smiled a bigger, more triumphant smile.

"Just like that?" Eric looked at Gregory in his knightly rags and couldn't see it.

"Just like that," said Elanora firmly.

Gregory shook his head. "It won't work. We're too rough looking. We have cuts, bruises, and scars. Hell! Some of us, like Phips for instance, have missing parts!"

"I'm whole," said Aayan. Gregory and Eric looked at his dark skin and shook their heads. They knew he was right about being in one piece. But, unless he obviously had Aboriginal blood and features, he would not be viewed as trustworthy by many a local maverick.

Aayan had told them he became a knight rather than a maverick because of his dark skin. He said so during the first drinking bout between these renegade knights and dragons. He still felt the priestesses at his school had made him what he was rather than a maverick because of a war that happened a long time ago, the war that saw the destruction of old Sydney. What was funny was the fact his family was on the right side. They weren't the Globalist enemy.

"There are many dark-skinned mavericks in Egypt and in Lyon, France with my looks," reasoned Aayan after a moment's silence.

"But not many in Wollongong with your appearance," said Craft. "You would stand out too much."

"Thanks mate. I know you're one of my best fighters, but not for this caper. But thanks for volunteering." Gregory didn't want to hurt Aayan's feelings.

"What about me?" Craft asked.

"You've put on some weight of late—mavericks your age like to stay trim, so they don't become knights. Beefing up with muscle is okay, Craft, but the fat you have around your tummy might get you into trouble you can't get out of, and we don't want that. Only mavericks a lot older than you, with a wife and children, can afford to let themselves go." Gregory was warming to Elanora's idea but didn't want to get any of his knights unnecessarily killed.

"We don't need to fool anyone for any great length of time," added Elanora. "I'm sure there are three of your knights, Gregory, who would pass muster as mavericks if not too closely inspected. And money will help."

"I know the three," said Gregory. "There's me, Toff, and Phips. We can put a hat or something on Phips to cover up where his ear should be. All three of us will go along to make sure the clothing fits."

"Good idea. But why have you chosen Phips?" Elanora wondered if Phips was reliable and whether the missing ear could be covered up to anyone's satisfaction.

"Despite the missing ear, he looks all right, plus he's someone I know who can think fast in a tight situation," Gregory told her.

"I would be honoured to be a fake maverick," said Phips, trying to sound noble.

"I take it you have big plans. You want to let us in on them?" Gregory looked to Elanora. He hoped he didn't sound sarcastic.

"I'll let you know when I see three mavericks where I once saw three knights." Elanora hoped the chosen three would take up her challenge.

"You've done well by us so far," said Eric.

"I'm glad you think so. Mobility is our number one ally when it comes to survival. Without it, we're finished. Remember that." Elanora envisioned the fake mavericks and disabled pain collars would have them move more freely in the city. She was trying to get that across to both Gregory and Eric without being too obvious.

"I'm beginning to understand," Gregory told her. He could see some use of maverick clothes.

"Me, too," said Eric. He wasn't sure about the pain collars but knew that mavericks could go anywhere in the city.

While Gregory, with the help of Toff and Phips, invaded the clothing shop, Elanora made progress dismantling a pain collar. She discovered the mechanism that gave electric shocks and put the collar back together again minus that mechanism. Thus, the collar looked whole while missing the part that made it a tamer of dragons. She then did the same to the other collars in her possession.

Fortunately, there wasn't an alarm system in the clothing shop the three knights broke into. Phips picked the front door's lock with two pieces of wire he had taken along for that purpose. He was also able to open the cash register with his wires. Luckily, a maiden officer with robots didn't spot them either entering or leaving.

There was some hilarity when the three knights returned from the clothing shop. They had their regular clothes in sacks and were wearing maverick attire. Elanora could not help but smile at them. She had to stop herself from bursting into laughter.

"Oh, how bright you are, you blind me so, and those silks!" cried Craft, waving a rag about in place of a colourful handkerchief. "They're simply too divine."

"They're no good for digging holes, that's for sure," grumbled Aayan.

"And those pointy shoes are to die for!" cried Craft, more rag-waving.

"Yess." Eric showed some emotion in his hissing. "And I know where you can stick those points!"

"But are they pointy enough?" wondered Craft.

"Oh, they're pointy enough all right," said Eric, his forked tongue poking out.

"I wanna slug someone!" snarled Toff, going red in the face and looking around.

"Relax!" cried Gregory. "They're just funning you!"

"Yess." Eric hissed again. "It's all in fun."

"What do you think, Elanora?" asked Gregory. He felt ridiculous and was close to laughing at himself.

"How much money did you get?" Elanora asked. "The money is also important."

"One hundred twenty-seven dollars and fifty cents," said Phips.

"Good!" Elanora wanted to pat Phips on the shoulder but refrained from doing so since it might be mistaken for an aggressive move.

"What do you think of us?" Phips was eager to know how he looked to Elanora and was a little red in the face over the possible negative response.

"You'll do. Just keep the wool over your ears, Phips, or you'll give the game away." Elanora was feeling more confident about Phips and didn't mind showing it in her voice.

"I will wear hats. All sorts of headgear. Besides, it is the fashion!" Phips strutted around with a particular hand gesture that elicited laughter from both knights and dragons. He stuck his nose up at this and got more mirth in return.

"If everyone can keep a straight face when our mavericks are out in public, this should be okay." Ronald nodded at the potential this dressing up offered and the danger of not taking it seriously enough.

"You really think so?" asked Eric.

"Yes. But our mavericks need to stand right. They have to have more arrogance, more self-esteem." Ronald understood that not making an effort to get mannerisms right could cost lives.

"Out of the way, you filthy knight," snubbed Phips, knocking into Craft to get a drink out of the fridge. Craft laughed and pushed him back.

"You need practice. You need to study how mavericks walk, talk, and interact with each other and their superiors and inferiors." Ronald didn't want to put a dampener on fun, but he wanted to return to the seriousness of dressing up this way.

"Yes. There is a lot to do before our mavericks can go out in public with any hope of fooling anyone, but I can see how this will be, in the end, a success." Elanora beamed with encouragement.

CHAPTER TWELVE

While Wollongong harbor and the coastline were being made safe for traffic, freight came in via plane and train. Liverpool, England, and Wellington, New Zealand were happy to bring in extra food by air at a lower-than-average cost. The train from Wollongong, however, could only go north as far as Hurstville or south as far as Kiama. Both cities had pledged to help Wollongong until its people could get back on their financial feet.

The High Priestess of Hurstville, a friend of the High Priestess of Wollongong, was happy to lend aid. "Tell me what you need, and I will do everything I can for you," the High Priestess of Hurstville told the Wollongong High One over the phone.

Soon after that phone call, there came another. The High Priestess of Kiama understood that she needed to remain on friendly terms with the High One of Wollongong to keep in the Highest of High Priestesses' good graces.

"The Highest One would want me to help out," the High Priestess of Kiama said to Wollongong's High One. She spoke slowly, painfully as if she was forcing herself to do so. "I will be expected to get you past this crisis."

"Yes, I imagine you will do what is expected," replied the High Priestess of Wollongong in a controlled voice. She knew she could not refuse aid, even from one reluctant to give it. "Bringing freight up at cost would be helpful. I believe you are capable of doing that much."

"Yes," agreed the High One of Kiama. "I can do that."

****

Malcolm found work for himself and his flyer, bringing diplomats from various cities to talk over what was being done to address this emergency. Some were nervous about his mechanical hand and leg but soon realized he was still a better than average pilot. "Tell me how you lost your real hand and leg," was usually the first question a diplomat asked. The last question was, "How about working for me and my city permanently? We can pay you well."

The High One of Wollongong and her staff cancelled or put on hold road and building projects. The knights and dragons required to do the backbreaking labour were needed on the waterfront. Instructions had been sent out that every labourer had to help get the clean-up done and as quickly as possible.

When maidens or mavericks expressed reluctance to halt their projects and redirect efforts to the waterfront, priestesses with maiden officers and robots came in, taking charge. Maidens who failed to obey instructions from the High One were heavily fined. Mavericks who did not act quickly enough on behalf of the High One were demoted to knights.

Everyone, from dragon to knight to maiden and maverick, knew the situation would only be temporary. However, it was still bad, considering how important Wollongong had become to the rest of the world. Cities relied on a forward motion to remain viable. There had to be less of that for Wollongong during this emergency.

****

In the meantime, Gregory, Phips, and Toff went out every day to study mavericks. Dressed in their knightly garb of abject greyness, they were not allowed into The Great Grape, but they could hang by the swinging doors and take mental notes of the mavericks within. Some patrons of The Great Grape thought they were beggars and gave them change, which they accepted. Back at the house, they showed Elanora and Eric how much they had earned and learned.

"So, when do we make our big move?" Toff asked Elanora one afternoon near the end of the second week in June. He was anxious to get going with the maverick dress-up caper before he lost his nerve.

"We need to replenish our supplies." Gregory crossed his arms.

"We need more food. We'll run out soon." Craft massaged his belly.

"We should go to another supermarket." Eric smiled broadly and rubbed his claws together.

"And become predictable?" asked Elanora, her tail swishing and her forked tongue poking out. "I wish I could make you all understand how deadly predictability can be."

"So, what do you want us to do now?" asked Gregory openhandedly.

"I need official government standard pen and paper. There's a print shop on the university grounds that does government printing. We need blank sheets with official wording on them and stamps. Can I have two volunteers to break in at midnight tonight?"

"I'll go," said Toff. He bowed his head to hide his nervousness.

"I'll go, too. I once did some heavy carrying in such a place, so I have an idea of what you are looking for." Gregory imagined what Elanora wanted this stuff for had something to do with the maverick outfits.

"Count me in." Aayan's voice was almost robotic, face showing no emotion.

"More delaysss!" Eric hissed, swishing his spiked tail back and forth in agitation. "What good is pen and paper?"

"Yes," said Craft. "I'd like to know as well."

"Add them to maverick costumes, and we might have something," Ronald said, rubbing his chin. He was beginning to see what Elanora had in mind.

"Now you're getting it." Elanora beamed at Ronald, and he couldn't help but grin back at her. She added, "We need to give our mavericks some official approval. I have seen how the requisitions are worded from my time on my island, so we should be able to fool a maverick foreman or two with what I can come up with."

"And if we don't fool them?" asked Toff in a trembling voice, looking nervously at Elanora and then at Gregory.

"We then rely on your charm as a maverick," said Gregory, easing tensions.

Breaking into the print shop was relatively easy. The two robots that made their round of the university went by the print shop once every hour. Gregory, Aayan, and Toff had plenty of time to get in and take what they wanted in the bags they had brought with them. Gregory and Aayan found some sheets with the word "requisition" on them, which they added to their collection. Toff found a stamp and an inkpad he thought might be useful.

They robbed the cash register and scattered sheets around to make it look like a messy robbery. After all, what would anyone want with paper that could only be used for official business?

The following morning, the university staff went for the deception of it being a simple theft, except Jens, who felt there was more to it than that.

"I don't know why," Jens told the maiden officer who was the head of university security, "there was this need for those who broke in to toss paper everywhere. Why not get in, take the money, and get out quick?"

"They were stupid," offered the maiden officer, thumping her office desk with her large fist for emphasis. "Not all robbers are as clever as you."

"Maybe they were hiding their true purpose in breaking in by tossing those sheets about," mused Jens, hand on chin.

"You're overcomplicating things." The maiden officer shook her head. "They were just dumb."

As soon as Gregory, Aayan, and Toff got back to the house, Eric demanded to know what Elanora had in mind.

"The warehouses near the train station are always filling up with goods," said Elanora. "The nearest one to the station will be our target."

"Too open," groused Eric. "Even at night, they'll see us coming at least two hundred feet away from the nearest gate. Then there's the barbed wire to contend with and the robot guards. We'd lose everyone and for nothing."

"Not if three mavericks in broad daylight escorted a crew of dragons to load supplies onto trucks," said Elanora. "The lead maverick could say the items being loaded were for the dragon barracks near the university and also for a university party. One of our mavericks will have the necessary paperwork."

"If we push our luck, we might be able to load two trucks." Phips rubbed his hands.

"We'll have plenty of food." Craft beamed.

"Three trucks," said Elanora. "We'll need one truck per maverick."

"I don't know how to drive." Phips bowed his head.

"Neither do I." Toff grinned. It was in a sheepish way as if he had been caught doing something wrong.

"I'll teach you as best I can." Gregory had to wonder if he could be a teacher.

"What can I do?" asked Craft. He leaned forward, wanting to contribute.

"Sorry, but you and Aayan will have to sit this one out." Gregory wanted them along but had to think of the safety of all. "A pudgy knight might seem too strange, and there aren't many dark-skinned knights around."

"Tomorrow morning, one of our three mavericks will need to hire three trucks," said Elanora. "We have the money, and I will provide the paperwork."

"Why hire?" asked Toff.

"Less suspicious," Elanora told him. "You've told me, through studying mavericks, that the government uses hire trucks all the time since their emergency began. They don't have enough of their own."

"I don't understand why we don't just steal them," said Toff.

"You don't want to be caught in a stolen vehicle at the warehouse." Elanora spoke in a crisp voice, her tail moving slowly across the floor. She looked so intently at Toff she made him shrink away from her. "If the truck is legitimate, and you look honest, we have a better chance. Do you understand?"

"Oh, yes," said Toff, eyes darting toward Gregory and then back to Elanora, "now that you put it that way."

"But do we need three truckloads?" asked Gregory.

"For our needs, we only require one," Elanora replied. "But one is a lot more suspicious than three. You, Gregory, have told me how they operate from conversations you have overheard in The Great Grape. The warehouse maidens and mavericks are used to dealing with large consignments. They will think nothing of three trucks."

"So what happens to the other two truckloads?" asked Phips. "We just dump the stuff somewhere?"

"We'll rent a house on this block to store the stuff," said Elanora.

"I know of one for rent," Craft added.

"Can you do that, Gregory?" Elanora asked. "Can you rent a house? It has to be done before we head off in the trucks."

"I'll do it," replied Gregory. "Craft can show me where this place is. Details of what rental agency to contact should be on the property. What about the stuff? We can't hold onto it forever."

"No, we can't," Elanora conceded. "Do you still have contacts on the black market?"

"Yes, I believe so." Gregory now beamed at the possibilities.

"Good. We can sell it over, say, a couple of months. We'll make money." Elanora smiled.

"What do we need that for?" asked Phips. "Money, I mean."

"You haven't been a maverick very long, have you?" joked Toff.

"Our mavericks will need fake identifications that look real enough to fool anyone. Can the black market provide us with them?" Elanora asked.

"Yes," said Gregory. "For a price, they'd be happy to help. But they're dangerous. No reason why they might not turn on us."

"Money's a good reason to keep us on their side," replied Elanora.

"That's fine," Gregory said, "unless they can figure out how to make even more money by betraying us."

"They are all about making money." Aayan agreed, nodding. "They have no principles. They have no honour."

****

Mid-morning after the break-in, Jens told Dean Renate over the phone what she further thought of the raid on the print shop.

"It has something to do with that print shop being where official documents are printed," said Jens to the dean. "Apparently, items are missing from that print shop indicating something other than the taking of money being the prime motive."

"I'll notify security concerning your thoughts on the matter," offered the dean coolly. "There is no proof that it wasn't a simple matter of breaking, entering, and grabbing the money, so that's how it has been treated. The paper everywhere is inconsequential. The items that have gone missing quite possibly weren't taken by the robbers at all and have simply been mislaid."

"The cafeteria would have been a better target if all they wanted was cash," offered Jens. "There are three cash registers in the cafeteria to the print shop's one."

"I see where you are going with this," the dean said. "However, the cafeteria is in the centre of campus and harder to get into without being spotted. The head of security will tell you they didn't want to come across our robots; therefore, they decided upon the print shop, which is more on the edge of campus. It is the easier target and that's why the head of security thinks they went for it and no other reason. She is determined that is the answer, and unfortunately there is no swaying her toward other possibilities."

****

That afternoon, after work, Jens was invited into the dean's office for a further chat on the print shop break-in.

"You did what you could to offer up a second theory to security. I did forward what you told me to them," the dean informed Jens, offering her a nip of brandy she poured from a bottle into a plastic cup.

"Thanks." Jens accepted the brandy and took a sip. "We never used to have burglaries of any kind."

"I know," The dean swallowed brandy from her plastic cup.

"Times are changing." Jens sighed, thinking for a moment about that female dragon.

"So, what has Megan been up to?" The dean gulped the last of the brandy in her cup.

"She found an old map of Kiama made in 2021," replied Jens. "This was before houses were cleared in the centre of Kiama for the airport to be constructed."

"This sounds familiar," said the dean, with one eyebrow raised.

"Something similar, I know from maps and history books found in our library, happened in Wollongong," replied Jens. "When the population in both places shrank then stabilized, there was less need for so many houses and, because of the necessity to connect with other cities via a modern, close by airport, the houses had to go. Some of the better homes, rather than be demolished, were instead moved elsewhere."

"What reading matter does Megan have for us?" asked the dean.

"There's quite a selection of books on the Mitchell Library's sixth underground floor in Sydney. They're all first editions,"

Jens informed her. "Megan has been slowly going through them with her team."

Jens finished her brandy, and Dean Renate refilled both cups.

"Anything of interest?" asked the dean. She drank more brandy.

"There's *For the Term of His Natural Life* by Marcus Clarke. Then there is Jules Verne's *Twenty Thousand Leagues Under the Sea.*"

"Is there anything significant about either one of them?" The dean watched Jens finish her cup.

"Jules Verne was an early science fiction writer," Jens told her. "The work is in French. I gave you the English title. Since it is the first edition, Megan thought that giving it to the High Priestess of Lyon as a goodwill gesture, via the diplomat we now have staying in Wollongong, would be a good idea."

"I agree." The dean beamed at Jens. "Good thinking on Megan's part." The dean finished her cup, and then took Jens' cup off her. She discarded both.

"I'll pass that along to her," said Jens.

"Please do," replied the dean.

"You know there was a time when alcohol was outlawed in offices such as yours and mine," offered Jens.

"When was that?" asked the dean.

"According to Megan, it was when the Globalists were briefly in charge around here," said Jens, openhandedly. "That was a long time ago, I know, but it was one thing that helped start the rebellion against them. They banned it everywhere they went. What were they thinking?"

"They prohibited a lot of things," replied the dean, shaking her head and smiling sadly. "Paintings and history books had to be hidden away from them for fear they'd end up on some Globalist bonfire."

"Out with the old, in with the new was their most treasured slogan," revealed Jens. "Thank the Great Goddess the underground section of Mitchell Library survived."

"Yes," agreed the dean. "They couldn't have Sydney, so it had to be blown up; but they didn't get the underground section of that library."

"They were religious fanatics believing in a dark and evil god. Thanks be to the Great Goddess they've gone now for good."

"Yes," agreed the dean. "Thank the Great Goddess we now live in more enlightened times."

CHAPTER THIRTEEN

By mid-morning, the lease on the second house and the trucks' rental had been concluded by Gregory dressed as a maverick. The dragons put on their non-functioning pain collars and, when the trucks arrived, climbed into the backs of them. The pretend mavericks got into the driver's seats.

It was half a mile to the warehouse, and they drove through heavy traffic. Gregory and Phips handled their rigs well, but Toff, with all the stops and starts he had to make, got confused between the use of the accelerator and the brake. He slammed into a taxi that was ahead of him. The taxi driver stopped and got out of his hovercar to survey the damage. There was a small dent, but none of the air pockets that substituted for wheels were wrecked.

Toff looked back at Elanora, who was riding in his truck and whispered in a frightened voice, "What do I do?"

She handed him twenty dollars and said, "Get out, confront the fellow, and give him the money. Do not apologize. He is a low-status maverick. His clothes are not as brilliant as yours, and his hat looks old, not new. Gregory has told me of the various statuses of mavericks. I also got this from some of the magazines sent to me on my island. You are dressed in the latest fashion like you have higher status plus you have a truck. Remember that. You work for the government, and he does not. That is also important. Now go!"

Toff got out of the truck and did as Elanora told him to do. The taxi driver accepted the twenty, got back in his taxi, and drove off. Toff followed at a discreet distance until he came to the turnoff for the warehouse. He took it and found the other two trucks waiting for him to arrive.

Gregory had paperwork for three trucks, and the maverick on the gate was questioning why there were only two.

"The third truck will be here," said Gregory. He looked at the guard and imagined how he appeared in return. The guard was wearing a red beret with a goose feather. He was wearing a white beret with two goose feathers. *If anything,* Gregory thought, *I am up by one goose feather. I must be smart to have that extra feather. Either that or these hats and feathers are stupid.*

"I can't let you in until the third truck arrives," reasoned the guard who looked sharply at Gregory and rubbed his chin. "Our robots wouldn't like it."

"Are they in charge now?" asked Gregory, sneering like he thought a superior maverick might sneer at a lower grade maverick. Guards, he knew, were not considered to be top of the line in mavericks.

"Nah!" cried the guard, smiling. "But if you were to open the gate and drive past me without my okay, those robots could get edgy, and we don't want that, now do we?"

"Surely, they wouldn't fire upon a maverick, especially one working for the government, as those papers you are now holding prove," offered Gregory.

"Probably not," said the guard, adjusting the red beret with the single goose feather. "But first, you'd have to get past me to open the gate, and I work out. I would take some flak from my superiors from a dustup with you, but that's better than losing my job."

Despite the fancy clothes he was wearing, the guard looked like he could do all right in a fight. He had bulging muscles under the red and blue striped shirt he was wearing. Gregory thought that he could take him without much effort because of his training as a knight, plus the harsh life he had led as a fugitive. He was sizing the guard up for battle and wondering if the robots would fire upon a knight dressed as a maverick when the third truck finally arrived.

"You're late!" Gregory hollered at Toff. *For twenty uncomfortable minutes, I have been trying to avoid looking at those damned robots on the roof with their rifles at the ready*, he thought in exasperation. *I figure anyone with the right to be here would not be staring at them. But it was so bloody hard not to!*

"A slight accident," said Toff, remembering not to be apologetic though he probably should have been to a fellow maverick who was also working for the government.

"It's not too bad," the maverick guard offered, looking at the damage. "Front fender's bent, but you should be able to get your dragons to do the repairs before you leave."

"We're in a hurry. We don't want to delay loading. Can some of your dragons do it for us instead?" Gregory tried to maintain a steady voice, but he was nervous, and it showed in his hand tremor, which he hoped the guard hadn't noticed.

Gregory had no idea how to unbend a fender. He also didn't know how to get others to do it for him. He didn't even know if the dragons he was with had any experience with fenders, and this was not the time to ask to find out.

"It'll cost you five dollars." The maverick gate guard smirked cunningly.

"That's okay," said Gregory, handing the guard the five dollars. The guard blinked, pocketed the money, then gave him back the papers he'd been inspecting. They had already been freshly stamped by the guard.

"All right, all is in order. Go through to loading bay three to your left. I'll send over some repair dragons." The guard was using his best officious voice. He pressed a button, and the gate opened for the three trucks. When the vehicles were in, the gate closed. The drivers drove the trucks to the designated loading bay. Then the pretend mavericks had the dragons exit the trucks. A short, fat loading supervisor maiden showed the pretend mavericks where the goods were housed.

The dragons in the trucks, including Elanora, were ordered by Gregory, Toff, and Phips to get to work, putting the goods in the trucks. The warehouse dragons commanded to repair the damaged fender did so with some reluctance. The machine that aided in the unbending was tough to handle. One warehouse dragon refused to cooperate and so was shocked by the loading supervisor into complying. This was done via the use of a small device she had in her hand.

Elanora, seeing this happen, responded by hissing loudly, her eyes enlarged. This was the first time she had seen this type of cruelty up front and it affected her more than she expected it would. She lunged forward to slash the loading supervisor with her claws and spiked tail but was grabbed in time by Ronald and Eric.

"Steady on," whispered Ronald, wincing from being hit in the backside by one of Elanora's spikes from her swishing tail. "We would all like to do what you intend to do but, please, steady on."

"Remember the plan," whispered Eric, who was also hit in the backside by one of Elanora's spikes. She then took in a deep breath, hissed one last time, and nodded for Ronald and Eric to let her go, which they did. In releasing her, Eric half expected her to make a self-righteous run at that loading supervisor, but that didn't happen.

"The incident with the loading supervisor and the warehouse dragon is now over," Ronald told Elanora, still whispering, "and best forgotten if we are to be successful in our mission."

"Something's wrong," said the loading supervisor moments later to Gregory. "I'm trying to punish that dragon of yours that rudely hissed at me for disciplining a warehouse dragon, but I'm not getting the results I want. See? I'm pointing my remote control at him, I'm pushing the right button, but that dragon of yours simply won't be shocked. Maybe it's the batteries; maybe I need new batteries."

"Oh, yes, he will," snarled Gregory at Elanora, who got the picture. "It takes a bit of effort to bring that one to heel!"

Gregory pretended to press a remote control, and right on cue, Elanora cried out in pain, making out she had been hurt by him. It was a noteworthy performance.

"Good," said the loading supervisor, impressed by Gregory. "You'll be sure to report this dragon for further disciplinary action? He is, after all, your dragon."

"Oh, I will!" cried Gregory. "Perhaps a hanging is in order or simply a loss of a claw. For now, there is work to be done."

"Yes," agreed the loading supervisor. "There is work."

"Now, get back to work!" Gregory shouted at the dragons, and they all complied.

"You do have a way with them," offered the loading supervisor, smiling.

"They're just like children," said Gregory, touching the feathers on his beret. "A little discipline goes a long way."

"Quite so," agreed the loading supervisor. "Do you have a girlfriend?" She smiled at Gregory in a way that made him uncomfortable. She had been mean. Now she wanted to be romantic? Her eyes, as well as her lips, were involved in this smiling caper. She put a finger to her chin, no doubt thinking this a cute gesture. He started backing away, not wanting involvement with some maiden that could change from violence to thoughts of love in such a short time. However, he did think better of moving away and so stopped and stood his ground and smiled sheepishly back at her as if she was paying him a compliment by her interest in him.

"Yes," Gregory lied. "I have a lovely maiden companion."

"It's a shame all the good mavericks are taken," sighed the loading supervisor before going on to supervise more trucks coming into a different bay.

Elanora found her muscles screaming at her by the time the loading was completed, and they were ready to depart. Ronald and Eric had to help her up onto the truck. The other dragons weren't in such a state. They quickly climbed onboard their designated vehicles without the need for assistance.

At the gate, they were stopped by the guard they had conversed with earlier. Gregory had the gun ready that he had earlier taken from a robot. This was in case they had somehow blown their cover, and he might be able to shoot their way out of trouble. He knew this was wishful thinking since the robots, looking down at them with rifles, would kill him for sure if he was to murder that guard. By his very actions as a killer, he would be regarded as a knight rather than a maverick by robot thought processes, thus freeing them up to shoot him dead. The guard, however, might be taken prisoner by Gregory and thus forced to get them out safely.

"Did the repairs to your vehicle go okay?" the guard asked Toff.

"Fine," said Toff. He shrugged. He had no idea but assumed that the warehouse dragons had done a proper job.

"Do the repairs meet with your approval?" asked the guard of Gregory. "It was, after all, your money. I would have arranged it for three dollars if you had cared to haggle."

"Fine," said Gregory, who was also none the wiser as to the quality of the work.

"Say, why does your mate there have his hat pulled down over his ears all the time?" asked the guard. He was talking about Phips, who was hiding the fact he had a missing ear.

"He has an ear infection," said Gregory. "It's nothing serious, but the doctor wants him to cover his ears. A bit much in warm weather like this, I grant you, but you do understand, don't you?"

"That makes sense," agreed the guard then turned to Toff. "By the way, aren't you awfully young to be driving a truck?"

"I know. My dad is a high government official with a financial tie into this rental firm." Toff hoped this lie wasn't big enough to get him caught.

"That's always the way, isn't it?" The guard looked sour-ly at Toff.

"I'm afraid so." Toff shrugged his shoulders.

"Well, your daddy won't be spanking you for wrecking his truck, thanks to me." The guard found amusement in this and laughed.

"No, he won't thanks to you." Toff gave a nervous half-smile.

"Okay!" cried the guard. "Move 'em out!"

He pressed a button. The gate opened, allowing the trucks to depart into what was thankfully lighter traffic than before.

The trucks were emptied at the houses, and then the drivers took them back to the rental place. After they gave back the keys, they used the rental company's payphone to phone for a cab to pick them up and drop them off on a street a few blocks from their houses. Gregory thought it looked like a better neigh-bourhood for three well to do mavericks to call home. Besides, the fewer links to where they lived, the better. It was something Gregory had worked out for himself.

An hour after the fake mavericks got back to where they did reside, Eric accused the knights who had posed as mavericks of enjoying their roles too much.

"I don't like being humbled by anyone, especially a knight," snarled Eric. The other dragons, except Elanora, nodded in agreement.

"I feel the same way," sighed Ronald, who didn't like be-ing pushed around by those he was beginning to think of as his friends.

"Bloody hell!" cried Phips. "You're dragons! You should be used to it by now!"

"Not from you, we're not!" cried Eric. "We want respect!"

"Respect?" mused Phips.

"Dragons want respect?" wondered Craft.

"Yes," snarled Eric. "We get respect, or we fight!"

"Do not do thissss!" cried Elanora hissing. "We all play our parts. Tell me, Ronald, do you eat well?"

"Since you joined us, yes." It was something Ronald couldn't deny.

"Do you eat well, Phips?" asked Elanora.

"Yes." Phips felt he had no reason to object.

"I don't have any complaints." Craft grinned and patted his stomach. It seemed he was all about the food.

"And you, Eric, do you sleep well nowadays despite sharing your home with knights?" asked Elanora.

"I suppose so." Eric shrugged.

"And, Gregory, do you see a future here for your knights?" asked Elanora. "If not, you are free to leave."

"I see a future." Gregory clasped his hands together to signify unity.

"Me, too," added Aayan, who often had little to say and who also hadn't entered the dispute.

"Then stay. Everyone stay, and let's make that future bright." Elanora opened up her claws and laid them flat on her lap as a gesture of goodwill. She looked at every one of them individually, smiling.

"But what we had to do today...," began Eric.

"You don't think my back hurtsss and my claws throb?" grumbled Elanora. "You don't believe I wanted to rip that gluttonous maiden's throat out and had to be held back from doing so?"

"I believe you wanted to do her harm, and I can't blame you for that." Gregory's voice was cold, but there was understanding in his eyes.

"We need to be clever. We need to play our roles for the greater good of our combine. Can't you see that?" Elanora winced with pain. She turned her claws over, showing where they were throbbing. Her skin was red underneath the scales, as noted in the slight gaps between them.

"I'll put ointment on your claws," offered Ronald, going to a shelf where there were jars of various concoctions. He picked up the appropriate jar, took it to where Elanora sat then tended to her soreness with as much gentleness as he could muster.

"I am proud of you all. Don't make me ashamed by harming one another. We have enemies out there who would gladly do that for you." Elanora was indeed proud of them, beaming at them as both individuals and as a group. They had all come a long way since she first met them.

"That's true," Gregory said. "I can see the logic in maintaining peace."

"We can't fight among ourselves and hope to stay together," reasoned Aayan.

"Let's say no more about it then. Break out some food, and let's eat." Elanora licked her lips, and Craft smiled broadly, rubbing his tummy in anticipation.

"Now you're talking," said Craft, who seemed to be always hungry.

****

The following night, Toff went out dressed as a maverick. He would later claim he had itchy feet and that he wanted to keep certain skills he had acquired from disappearing from lack of use. Also, he later told Gregory that he had never been a pickpocket dressed in such finery and wanted to see if that made any difference in the takings. Theft was something he was good at whereas even the possibility of physical violence continued to irk him.

Toff visited several wine bars and bumped into all sorts of mavericks and maidens. His fingers had that light touch, and he came away with a dozen wallets and four purses. *This is much better than pinching stuff from fellow knights out on the town*, he thought to himself. He took a wallet from a particularly smug-looking maverick. *Dressing like one of them does make a difference like I thought it might.*

Elanora hissed her surprise when he returned with his haul. She thumped her tail on the floor. "You can't just run off and do this!" she cried.

"No, he shouldn't have without our say-so," agreed Gregory, "but look at the loot!"

Toff had collected over two hundred and fifty dollars from wallets and purses plus two bank cards that also came with their own code numbers. Apparently, two of the mavericks he had stolen from had a bad memory for digits and passwords. Therefore, the nearest bank machine had provided Toff with an extra four hundred dollars. Centuries ago, before the wars that ruined cities such as London, New York, and Sydney, this would not have been big money. People considered it so in this time because inflation had long ago been reversed, and the dollar's purchasing power had dramatically increased.

"We now have six hundred and fifty dollars more," said Toff proudly, showing it off. "Minus, of course, the five dollars I paid for drinks. Even so, it's still an impressive six hundred and forty-five dollars."

"What if you were caught?" asked Gregory, poking Toff's chest with his finger. "You would have been shot, and we'd be out one maverick outfit."

"What if you were recognized from the warehouse robbery in one of those wine bars, and some maiden officer had taken you in for questioning?" Phips shrank back at the very thought of that happening to Toff.

"But I wasn't caught, and no one recognized me from the warehouse robbery," said Toff, shrugging his shoulders and smiling at Gregory. He then said in a soft voice, "I thought you'd be pleased."

"We're pleased about the money but more so that you are all right." Gregory cupped his chin in contemplation. "The days of lone missions should now be over. I have admired your sleight-of-hand in the past as I do now, but none of us can just go off on our own anymore. "

"It was fun!" cried Toff, smiling and waving his arms about. "Some of the maidens even got a little friendly, if you know what I mean."

"We'd like to, but we're not young and stupid." Phips' face was reddening in anger. "You could have endangered us all!"

"Six hundred and forty-five dollars says I'm not stupid," replied Toff, sticking his nose up in the air. He then poked his tongue out at Phips, feeling hurt by his friend's seemingly unwarranted hostility.

"It tells me you have been lucky." Elanora had to agree with the others that Toff should no longer take such chances. She frowned as did Gregory.

"You got away with it this time," Gregory told Toff coolly, "but don't do it again, at least not for a while."

"They'll be looking for a young purse and wallet snatcher," put in Aayan, wanting to put Toff straight with his cold logic and even colder stare. "The maiden officers with their robots from now on will be on the lookout for you. Once you're in custody, it may not be too long before they realize you're not a real maverick, and then you'll really be in trouble. Maybe you'll get a flogging and then a public hanging. They could get you to talk about the rest of us. They have ways of doing that, you know."

"You worry too much," grumbled Toff, looking away from Aayan, feeling deflated.

"You don't worry enough. Even so, we have more money, thanks to you. It will come in handy if we have to leave here." Elanora waved her claw in Toff's direction, showing she was pleased about the money.

"Will we have to?" asked Craft. "I like it here."

"We'll see," Elanora said. "I can imagine the dangers of staying in one place too long."

****

Two weeks after Elanora's planned raid on the warehouse nearest the train station, the manager of the warehouse became aware of three truckloads of stock that had gone and had not been adequately accounted for.

Then there were stories told in maverick wine bars and knight pubs about three odd mavericks and also one dragon that seemed feminine rather than masculine. These tales originated from the warehouse dragons and quickly spread.

The guard at the gate on the day the cargo went missing was interviewed by local law enforcement. Too much time had gone by to get a good description from him concerning the mavericks. All he could say was one didn't show his ears, and another seemed to be too young to be a truck driver. The loading supervisor gave a good description of Gregory, but none of the others. She confirmed rumours of a dragon unlike other dragons but couldn't understand how there could possibly be a female type when everyone knew they don't exist.

A member of the constabulary talked to Jens about her theory concerning the raid on the print shop. She could not, however, shed any light on who had committed the crime, but it was now linked to the warehouse robbery. Without the right looking paperwork, the warehouse theft would not have occurred.

The rental company was of little help. They rented out trucks all the time, and the maidens and mavericks there couldn't remember much about the mavericks who rented the three trucks out that day except that they returned them on time. The interviews, done by a tough-looking maiden officer, took place in the rental company's canteen area.

"We don't always get the trucks back on time," said a maverick truck rental clerk in a black suit with a yellow stripe down the middle when he was interviewed by the maiden officer investigating. In fact, he was the last of the rental truck personnel to be interviewed, and her hopes of finding anything useful were already fading.

"Were they anxious?" asked the maiden officer. "Did they say anything strange? By their accents, could they have come from overseas?"

"I honestly can't remember," replied the clerk, shrugging his shoulders. "But I do remember the beret one of them was wearing."

"One of them was identified as having a white beret," said the maiden officer, leaning forward, now she was a tad more hopeful.

"Yes," cooed the clerk. "It had two feathers! I want one just like it!"

"Anything else?" asked the maiden officer, looking away so as not to be tempted to throttle the clerk.

"They may have phoned for a taxi from here," offered the clerk.

"Do you know that for sure?" asked the maiden officer.

"No," said the clerk, "but it is common practice to do so."

****

Jens met Dean Renate to discuss current issues the day after the shortages in stock were discovered at the warehouse and had made the news.

"I tried to tell them someone with brains could use government forms and stationery to their personal advantage," said Jens to Dean Renate. "They wouldn't listen because it had been so long since they'd gone up against a first-class villain."

"How does 'I told you so' feel?" asked the dean. They were having coffee at Jens's favourite coffee shop.

"Irrelevant." Jens shrugged her thin shoulders. "I'm no detective, and there's no money for the university in me being right."

"How is Megan doing?" The dean thought it best to change the subject.

"She's up to the works of Charles Dickens," said Jens.

"Who's that?" The dean was genuinely curious.

"He's a nineteenth-century English novelist and reformer," said Jens.

"That sounds interesting."

Rod Marsden

"I don't know what the government will make out of his writing," said Jens. "According to Megan, his novel *Oliver Twist* wouldn't go down too well with the High Priestess of Wollongong. Neither would his short story 'A Christmas Carol.'"

"Why not?" The dean's curiosity went up a notch, and so did her voice.

"Too much sympathy for people we would nowadays think of as either knights or dragons." Jens sighed deeply.

"But, they didn't have dragons back then." The dean was aware that dragons were mutants and had only come into existence after a nuclear war.

"No, they didn't." Jens held up her hands as if in surrender. "But they did have the lower classes."

"But dragons are subhuman," said the dean matter-of-factly.

"Would it surprise you to know I believe a dragon is responsible for what happened at that warehouse?" Jens smiled. She knew she was being provocative, but she didn't care.

"No! Not possible." The dean shook her head. "Have you told the constabulary about this?"

"And get laughed at and referred to as a loony academic?" Jens waved an open hand. "No, thanks."

"But you actually believe it was a dragon doing the organizing of that raid?" The dean was about to laugh at the idea.

"Oh, yes! But let's keep it to ourselves." Jens put a finger to her lips. "I promise to be as astonished as everyone else if and when I turn out to be right again."

CHAPTER FOURTEEN

It was the first week in July when Gregory and Elanora felt it was time to put the feelers out and see about shifting some of the stolen merchandise.

"Goods are now flowing freely into and out of the harbor but, when it comes to some items, there are still shortages," Gregory told Elanora. "Canned fish and oysters, for example, are still hard to get, or so I have been told by knights at the local pub."

"We should start now, "said Elanora, her tail moving excitedly. "Is there much danger involved?"

"In asking questions, there is some risk." Gregory stroked his chin with his hand. "But nothing I haven't done before and can't handle."

"Who do you plan to contact?" asked Elanora.

"Sam, the bartender at The Spear and Shield," said Gregory openhandedly. "He was my main contact. He's a big fellow knight with a dozen dragon kills to his name. Over ten seasons of being put into the position where it was either his life or that of a dragon, he has stayed alive. He works in the pub because he likes gossip and loves making big money on the side."

"Why big money?" asked Elanora.

"'Before some dragon rips my guts out with a sword in some arena,' he once told me, 'I want to be rich. I smile at the notion of my death hurting the economy.'"

"What else do you know about him?" pressed Elanora.

"Sam knows where just about every illegal deal in the city could be made," Gregory said, smiling. "He is understandably cautious. He figures being lined up against a wall and shot by robots would ruin his chances of ever becoming wealthy."

****

On the walk to The Spear and Shield, Gregory wondered if too much time had gone by since he had talked to Sam. He hoped that this wasn't the case. *Sam might even be dead by now,* thought Gregory as he entered the pub.

As it turned out, Sam was very much alive. Gregory went up to him at the bar and said, "Can we go somewhere to talk business in private? Maybe where we used to talk business?"

"It's been a while," reflected Sam. "You got anything worth bothering with?"

"Let's talk, and you can decide," said Gregory with a warm smile.

"Cover for me," said Sam to another, nearby barkeep, signalling the fellow to do so with his hand. He then went into the backroom with Gregory.

The place, as always, smelled of stale beer and sweat. The empty kegs in two corners were begging to be sent away to the brewery to be refilled. The men sat down at a table that could do with a good wiping down with a wet rag and looked across at each other. Silence stretched for a while. This silence was broken when Sam clasped his hands together and told Gregory, "It has been a while. I thought you and your motley crew of tearaways were dead by now."

"Not yet. I've got five crates of canned meat, vegetables, and tuna. Fifty cans a crate. Are you interested? They're in top condition." Gregory looked into Sam's eyes again, detecting the greed that had always been there.

"Now that's some haul. How did you manage that?"

Gregory figured Sam wasn't expecting an answer, but Sam had to ask anyway. Sam always did so. It was comforting to know that hadn't changed.

"Ask me no secrets," said Gregory in earnest. "Are you interested? Do you have a buyer?"

"I can come up with a buyer," Sam mused, waving a hand to show indifference and sighing. "How does twenty dollars for the lot sound?"

"It's worth a hundred." Gregory smiled, knowing he wasn't going to get that large a sum on stolen merchandise but pushed for it anyway. It was always to be a percentage of what items were worth or no deal. But there was still some room to barter.

"A hundred, you say? Not to my buyer or me." Sam shook his head and crossed his arms. "I'll give you fifty."

"Make it seventy-five." Gregory knew how this game went.

"Done!" Sam cried, slamming an open hand down on the table.

They shook hands, and Gregory arranged for a neutral pickup spot, a vacant lot, not far from the rental property. There, on that spot, money would be exchanged for the crates.

"I have more stuff coming in," Gregory told Sam as a sweetener, a smile returning, "So if you play fair with me with this lot, we'll both do all right in future transactions."

"I always play fair." Sam gave a toothy grin.

"I know you do." Gregory didn't believe it but kept the doubt as much as possible out of his body language. He leaned away from Sam but kept on smiling as if they were mates renewing a friendship.

They met at the agreed place at the agreed time, and Gregory exchanged his cans for cash. Sam had borrowed a brewery truck to pick up the merchandise. Gregory pocketed the money then watched as Sam drove off. He then wandered off toward the university and away from where he lived.

He looked over his shoulder from time to time for knights Sam might have paid to ambush him and get the money back. A couple of rough-looking characters came into view, but they went harmlessly away. The sound of a flyer overhead startled him, and then a car pulled up meters from him. Knights didn't usually drive, but was Sam able to bribe a low-ranking maverick to help steal back the money he now had? A maverick and a maiden got out of the car and walked into a chemist shop. They barely noticed Gregory, who sighed with relief and walked on.

Maybe the notion of more to come has sunk in with Sam, he thought as he continued to walk. *Sam doesn't have a conscience. I know. I nearly lost mine. Sam's was taken away from him years ago in combat with dragons. I have to keep remembering that. I can work with him, like I have in the past, but not trust him.*

When he was absolutely sure he wasn't being followed by one of Sam's associates, Gregory made his way back to where he would share his newly found wealth with his comrades.

"We can do this again next month," Gregory told Elanora upon his return. "As long as Sam and whoever he's dealing with thinks I'm getting it in from somewhere every month, we'll be all right."

"If they suspect just how much we have, they'll want the lot, and they'll want it for nothing." Phips had a good point there. The others nodded their agreement.

"I wouldn't put it past Sam to organize a raid on our rental property if he knew where it was," said Gregory, rubbing the back of his neck. "Even if he paid down and out knights to bash our heads in to get the answers as to where it was, he'd still come out on top. Unless, of course, he and his knights were caught by maiden officers and their robots doing so, but he wouldn't let that happen. He's too smart for that. He knows his way around the city. We don't live in that rental. We live here. So if he knew where it was, he could pick a time when not one of us is at that property and then steal what's there. Then he might also have a go at stealing what's here."

"And it's a good idea to do business with him?" asked Elanora, her forked tongue poking out and a gentle hiss coming from her.

"It is if we want to continue to move what we stole. There are mostly not nice knights involved in black market activities. I can't do anything about that." Gregory sighed deeply and waved a dismissive hand at Elanora.

"I'll go with you next time to the Spear and Shield," said Phips. "I shadowed you on your walk from the vacant lot to make sure you weren't robbed."

"I know. I knew you'd do that." Gregory patted Phips on the shoulder. "I caught sight of you a few times but thought I'd let you have your fun. I'm not that rusty."

"We need a better system of communication when one of us is out on a mission and gets into trouble," said Elanora. "There are two-way devices that could come in handy. I remember reading about them on my island. They're fairly new on the market, but they might save lives if we had a couple of them. I believe they're called walkie-talkies."

"Legend has it before Sydney got blown up, there used to be such things as mobile phones. You're not talking about something like that, are you?" asked Phips. "I once prided myself on knowing something about Australian history. I remember being good at that and hoping my scores there might make up for my atrocious marks in math, but that didn't happen. So I became a knight instead of a maverick, and here I am." He shrugged his shoulders and looked sheepishly at first Gregory and then Elanora.

"They're nothing as remarkable as those fabled mobile phones," replied Elanora. "You talk into the device, and the other person with a similar device, provided you are not too far away, can hear you and reply. The ones I saw can fit into your pocket. The mobile phones I have read about had a lot more going for them than that."

"Where can we get them, these talking devices?" Gregory rubbed his hands together.

"I believe there's an electronics shop near the supermarket we hit. We could do it over tonight." Phips also rubbed his hands together.

"You mean breaking and entering?" asked Elanora, her tail swishing in agitation.

"Yes," Phips shrugged his shoulders. "Why not?"

"That's not smart thinking." Gregory raised his voice, shaking his head at Phips. "A maverick could walk in and buy a couple of sets, no questions asked. We keep menacing the same area, and the authorities will catch us for sure."

"Very good." Elanora praised Gregory, giving him a smile. "Could you buy those devices first thing tomorrow morning? Just ask for what you want, Gregory. I'm sure the shop owner or assistant will be of some help. They will need batteries, so be sure to purchase enough batteries as well."

"I will dress up as a maverick for this," said Gregory. "Knights would have little interest in such expensive and fanciful devices, and too many questions would be asked. We'll also need new maverick duds for winter. We can't continually wear the same clothes without maidens and mavericks getting suspicious. Besides, it will get cold in summer silks. I'll take Phips and Toff with me."

"So it will be a shopping spree tomorrow," Phips grumbled.

"But necessary if we want to continue breathing as mavericks," concluded Gregory.

****

The following morning, Gregory, Phips, and Toff went after the communications devices Elanora wanted them to have plus new clothes.

The middle-aged, red-headed maiden in a red dress who was behind the counter at the electronics store was indeed helpful but also nosey. Therein lay the danger.

"If you tell me exactly what you want them for, I can point you in the right direction," she told Gregory.

"Hunting," Gregory lied, leaning forward and smiling so it wouldn't be too obvious a deception. "We're thinking of going up into the hills, say Mount Keira, and go after wild deer. We might separate and so need to be able to keep in touch with each other in case one of us gets into strife."

"It's just the three of you, then?"

"Yes," said Gregory.

"I know what you need." The maiden came out from behind the counter and walked with them along the aisle of electronic goods on display until she laid hands on what was wanted. "Here! These items should be fine. They come with their own batteries, but you can get more batteries if you want."

"I'll think about it," Gregory replied. He watched as the maiden wrapped up the goods, dropped them into a bag then handed the bag to him. He put the money required in her hands, and they left.

The clothing store they came to smelled of polished mahogany and bristled with untamed suits, ties, hats, and pants. A young fair-haired maiden in yellow beamed at Toff with her lips and her eyes. She waited on him while the more mature owner in blue plus another young maiden, this one in pink, waited on Gregory and Phips.

Toff looked about at how Gregory and Phips were also being handled and took heart. He was marched numerous times in and out of a change room as he tried on lots of clothes.

The colours of everything were too bright, but that was expected when it came to maverick clothes. Dullness in clothing, after all, was a knight and dragon thing. Phips was careful not to show his lack of an ear and selected hats to wear for winter in the change room designated for his use.

Gregory paid and they headed out of the store with their parcels, all of them hoping not to repeat this new-clothes-buying lark too often.

They had spent thirty-five dollars on the lot, electronics and clothes, and felt the money well spent. They thought the clothes looked ridiculous and unfit for hard work but warm and perfectly acceptable for a maverick to be wearing. Phips got three different hats he could pull down over his single ear. Gregory settled for a blue beret with a large white pompon.

"I will not be without headwear," said Phips as they walked back to the house, swinging their parcels. "The fur-lined monstrosity I have for my single ear should be good against the cold."

"If you go into the woods wearing that," quipped Toff, "you could get shot by a deer hunter."

"Yes, I see your point," Phips mused. "We do live in dangerous times."

****

That night at Demons, Ronald and Eric were able to sell ten first-aid kits for fifty dollars to a dragon barkeep with black scales who, no doubt, would sell them on for a tidy profit. They were part of the booty from the warehouse.

"These medical kits have everything you need to take care of wounds that need immediate attention," said Ronald as he pocketed the money.

"Ah, yes," agreed the barkeep, "I know of at least two dragon barracks that want better medical supplies on hand for May and November."

Around the same time, Toff suggested trying The Great Grape disguised as a maverick, but the idea was knocked on the head.

"Sure, we have a case of wine from Kiama that might interest mavericks," Gregory told Toff. "But flogging stolen items in such a place is far too risky."

"But dressed as mavericks, we could do it!" Toff said with enthusiasm.

"Mavericks simply don't deal in hot merchandise!" said Gregory sharply, "and to do so as a maverick would break cover in one of the deadliest places to do so."

"Break cover how?" asked Toff.

"You or any of us, found with illegal wine to sell, could well be taken for knights dressed up as mavericks, and that would not do. Believe me it would not do at all!"

"Mavericks and maidens aren't much trouble," said Toff.

"The constabulary frequent that establishment and gun-carrying robots are never too far away," Gregory told him.

****

In the first week of August, Gregory went to The Spear and Shield to do business again with Sam. He was sitting at the bar, having a beer and waiting for Sam to finish serving a drink to a customer when he felt a heavy hand on his shoulder. He turned and received a face full of knuckles that sent him flying across the room, into a table.

"I know you!" cried his assailant. "I was demoted to knight because of you. I was safe as a maverick. I'm not safe anymore, and neither are you!"

Gregory, stunned by this attack, blacked out for a moment but only a moment. He got up off the floor, wiped the blood from his nose, and advanced on the one-time maverick. It was the guard at the gate he and his fellows had bamboozled into letting them in and out of the warehouse. Apparently, he had lost more than his job. He would undoubtedly be expected to face dragons in the arena in November. Gregory felt sorry for this ex-guard but not enough to be beaten up for his past sins. He realized how much out of training he was when the one-time guard, fuelled by hatred, threw another punch, sending him through an open door into the backroom. Gregory landed on a pile of empty beer kegs but managed to get to his feet to throw a punch at his opponent. The fellow staggered back and then took out a knife.

"I am going to carve you up for what you did to me," crowed the ex-guard.

Gregory rubbed the blood from his cut lip and his nose. He pulled out the gun he'd been carrying. The noise from it going off was loud enough to quieten the drinking crowd a wall away. He pulled the trigger twice. The would-be avenger staggered toward Gregory with the knife in hand and fell dead at Gregory's feet.

Sam came in and saw the gun and the body. Gregory put the gun back in his belt, covered it with his coat, and said, "Clean up for me, Sam."

"Why should I?" growled Sam, his eyes narrowing.

"I'll give you a good deal on the next lot of merchandise due soon," offered Gregory, taking a rag out of his pocket and wiping blood from his face. His left eye was puckering up where he had been struck the second time.

"What if I say no?" asked Sam.

"You wouldn't if you want more of what I can provide you with." Gregory touched his gun. "I don't want to have to shoot my way out of here."

"Okay. But no more deals here, Gregory, between you and me ever again," Sam replied flatly. "You got stuff to sell, you send someone else to me. Have them say, 'I was sent by Gregory,' meaning you. I don't know what this was all about, or how you could have a gun, but Gregory, you're no longer welcome here. Beat it out the backdoor before the robots get here!"

Gregory did as he was told, hoping to make it to safety before getting shot at. Two blocks away from The Spear and Shield, a robot called upon him to halt. He ran instead and was shot. The bullet struck his shoulder. He later learned it was near the bone. If the robot had been closer, he would have either died or needed his arm amputated.

Unless he moved his arm, he didn't feel a thing. When he did, the pain radiated upward, making him wince and grit his teeth. Still, he had to move the arm in getting away or jolt it by doing so. He laid it flat against his side, which helped a little. When he closed his eyes, he saw an image of red blood vessels. He didn't know what that meant, but he didn't think it was good. He tried not to close them but move on to safety.

He didn't fire back at the robot, knowing bullets would be no good against his foe's metal hide. It was once mentioned in an advertising campaign for the constabulary that they were bulletproof.

He kept on running until he was exhausted, stopped to catch a breath, looked at his arm for confirmation that it was still there, and ran some more.

When he felt it was safe to do so, Gregory stopped for a longer moment, got the communicator out of his pocket and, with an effort to stay conscious, switched it on.

"Gregory here!" he cried into the device, not knowing how much longer he would be able to talk. "Help me!"

"Where are you?" asked Phips, concern in his voice.

"I'm at the corner of Palmer Street and Eddie Avenue," moaned Gregory. "Hurry and watch out for robots."

Phips was beside Gregory within minutes and helped him back to the house. There Elanora was open-mouthed startled by Gregory's condition.

"Shouldn't he be taken to a hospital?" asked Elanora.

"No! Not unless you wanted to kill him," said Phips. "Any doctor or nurse will tell you that what he has is a bullet wound, and they hand knights with bullet wounds over to the maiden officers with their robots."

"Quick!" cried Elanora. "We need a mattress and pillow from one of the beds placed in the lounge room. "We have to have a good look at how Gregory's been injured to see what can be done."

Toff went to his room, grabbed the mattress off his bed and the pillow, and brought them to Elanora, who gently laid Gregory down on the mattress, placing the pillow under his head.

"Can you breathe okay?" asked Elanora.

"Yes," said Gregory. "I believe so. My arm is in a mess, though."

"And your poor face!" hissed Elanora as she ripped open his shirt to reveal where the bullet had entered and also exited his body. "We need to stitch up the wound. We can use one of those medical kits. Please, someone, get one for me. I believe they have bandages, pain killers, antibiotic capsules, injection devices, needles, sutures, and other thread."

"I know where we put them," said Toff, running off to another part of the house. "I know we didn't sell all of them."

"What happened?" asked Elanora while waiting for Toff's return.

"I was stupid," moaned Gregory. "I had the gun on me, and I used it. Now they know we've got a gun."

"Who knows?" asked Elanora, new worry in her voice.

"The constabulary knows a knight was shot dead at The Spear and Shield and not by a robot," replied Gregory, blinking and getting dizzy. "The drinkers in The Spear and Shield no doubt have every reason to believe it was done by me. Only Sam knows for sure, and I doubt he'll talk."

"This is bad, real bad." Toff, returning with the kit, shook his head sadly.

"It's done," said Elanora, opening up the kit. She was pleased to find it intact with everything she needed. "We may have to look for someone else we can do business with."

"Sam may still be of use," Gregory replied, his eyes flickering. Elanora gave him a couple of painkiller tablets that took some pain away so that he could sleep plus a sleeping pill.

"You're going to sew him up?" asked Toff in a quiet voice. "Do you know about such things?"

"I'm not a doctor," replied Elanora coolly, keeping concern out of her voice. "How can I be? I'm a dragon. My claws are not suited to this, but your human hands are. I have enough book and computer knowledge to guide you. I have just felt the arm, and the bone seems fine. We must stop the bleeding that may have gone on for too long!"

"I can't do it!" cried Toff. "Get one of the others! How about Phips?"

Phips shook his head vigorously and looked away.

"You're here, now beside me," hissed Elanora, her tongue poking out for emphasis. "Do you want him to die?"

"I can't!" cried Toff, shivering all over.

"You can, and you will," snapped Elanora. "And stop shaking."

Somehow, between Elanora's coaxing and Toff's small but firm hands, the sewing was done. Gregory's bleeding stopped. Toff applied an antiseptic to the wound, bandaged it up, and went outside to throw up. Elanora dabbed some antiseptic on Gregory's lip, nose, and around his swollen eye.

Upon awakening, Gregory had some orange juice given to him by Toff. He then looked at Elanora and asked what she thought should be done about selling more of the goods they had from the robbery. Craft, Ronald, and Aayan were also there.

"We'll give it two weeks for things to cool down," Elanora told him. "Two weeks from now, then Craft will seek out Sam and possibly do business with him."

"Me?" Craft squeaked. He blinked at Elanora and shrugged his shoulders.

"We want a knight who has never dressed up asss a maverick for this particular job," hissed Elanora. "Someone else at The Spear and Shield might recognize our pretend mavericks from that day at the warehouse or possibly from the hiring of those three trucks. Then there's Toff's escapade with the stolen wallets and purses. Someone might recognise him on the street and wonder if he is that thief. We can't take dumb risks right now. We have to be smarter than the authorities."

"Will two weeks be enough?" Craft was shaking, visibly afraid.

"It will have to be," said Elanora. "We can't sit on these goods forever. We either move them or forget about them."

"I agree." Gregory could see the wisdom in Elanora's words. Phips offered him a glass of brandy. He took it and gulped down the contents.

"It makes sense," Ronald concluded after looking at Gregory and then at Elanora.

"We will have to leave here soon." Gregory shrugged his shoulders then grimaced with pain from his injury.

"Yes," agreed Elanora, "but let us depart, if we have to, with enough money to see us right somewhere else."

"But I like it here," moaned Craft, pouting.

"You also like staying alive," said Aayan coolly. "In a few days, I'll look over The Spear and Shield. I'll tell you what I think of the place and our chances of continuing to do business there. I think I'll be better at it than Craft."

CHAPTER FIFTEEN

Eric and Elanora hefted Toff's bloody mattress with Gregory aboard, carrying it to where Gregory usually slept. There, Toff had taken off the mattress already on the bed. Elanora had told him he could have it for his bed as a replacement.

"Thanks," said Toff. "It's a good swap. No way could I have got any sleep on a mattress with anyone's blood on it."

"I understand," replied Elanora, hissing gently. "You did well."

"Thank you." Toff walked away with the cleaner mattress, looking half-dazed, his eyes focusing on the mattress he carried. He moved in a zigzag pattern, occasionally bumping into a wall.

"What do you think he's thinking?" wondered Eric, lightly moving his tail.

"Did I really do what I did? Was I bullied into doing it? I imagine that sort of thing." Elanora stirred her tail in solidarity to Eric's tail movement.

"The way they behave sometimes," remarked Eric. "You'd almost think they were dragons."

Elanora looked over Gregory's wounds and added more antiseptic to them to ward off infection. She covered him with extra blankets to keep him warm and comfortable. The swelling around the stitches was going down. She hoped this was a good sign. Gregory was still asleep, and she expected him to be so for some time.

"Sleep is best for him for now," said Elanora. "It will help. I am glad it was a flesh wound and not a direct hit to the bone. Still, a bone might have been nicked, and if so, a bone fragment will cause complications I may not be able to handle. The best we can do is pray to the Great Goddess that will not be the case."

"Robots don't normally miss vital organs when they shoot," reasoned Eric.

"No, they don't," agreed Elanora. "I take it the robot that did the shooting needs to be serviced, adjustments made to how it functions."

"But why did Gregory run?" asked Eric.

"He had the gun and couldn't dump it somewhere in time to pretend to be innocent," said Elanora, "so he ran. That's what I think was the reason. If he had been searched by a maiden officer and the gun was on him, he would have been executed immediately."

"So, his only chance was to run?" asked Eric.

"Yesss." Elanora hissed. "Now, we do our best to see to his survival."

"It is so strange wanting a knight to live," said Eric, looking down.

"Yess." Elanora nodded. "It is both strange and good."

Elanora and Eric left Gregory to his slumber. Elanora returned an hour later to make sure he was all right. She sat on a chair near him, looking intently at his swollen face and at the other wounds. The swelling on his cheek was going down, which was good. The stitches were the main issue. They looked fine, but it was still too early to tell if they had been done right. She returned every hour after that, sitting for a few minutes to make sure he was still breathing and didn't need further attention.

Seven hours later, Gregory awoke. He looked around and noticed Elanora seated beside his bed.

"I'm still alive," murmured Gregory.

"Yess," hissed Elanora, looking at his face.

Gregory noticed the stitching and asked, "Who patched me up?"

"Toff did so with my help," answered Elanora.

"No," Gregory whispered. He was still weak. He shook his head and then winced with pain from his arm because of the slight movement.

"Yesss," hissed Elanora, her forked tongue poking out.

"How could Toff have done this?" asked Gregory, his eyes wide with amazement.

"My claws were no good for the job," answered Elanora, looking down at the stitches.

"But, Toff?" Gregory shook his head again, winced, and smiled.

"Those stitches are holding. They're good. They will dissolve in two weeks, and you'll have some use of your arm."

"Some use?" wondered Gregory.

"How much? I don't know." Elanora gently poked her forked tongue out. "Maybe as much as ninety-five percent after you have exercised it. For now, it is best to be kind to it while it heals."

"Will I be able to hold a sword or shield with the arm the way it is?" asked Gregory, looking at the stitches.

"In time, I will say yes," said Elanora.

"How do you know?" asked Gregory.

"I once studied human anatomy, but it was from an old textbook," replied Elanora. "You are getting my best guess."

"Where's Toff?" asked Gregory.

"He's around," answered Elanora. "He looks in on you. He's not far away."

"Call him please," said Gregory.

"Toff!" cried Elanora. "Get in here!"

Within minutes, Toff arrived at the door to Gregory's room.

Elanora got up and left, saying to Gregory, "Take it easy. We don't want to have to put in new stitches."

"Come in, all the way in." Gregory motioned with his hand to Toff. "I want to talk to you. I have been told you saved my life."

"It was nothing," murmured Toff as he entered.

"My life is nothing?" Gregory smiled, eyebrows raised. "It means a lot to me."

"Yes," agreed Toff. "Try not to get shot again."

"I'll do my very best," replied Gregory.

"I'll fetch you some broth," said Toff, scurrying away. He came back with a steaming bowl and a spoon. "You must eat to get your strength back."

"I don't think I am up to using a spoon," said Gregory. "I am hungry."

"I will feed you," offered Toff.

"You're a good lad," said Gregory. He reached out to pat Toff on the shoulder but thought better of doing so when his arm protested. He smiled instead and wished he could have done more to show his appreciation.

****

A week after the shooting, Aayan went to The Spear and Shield to find out what the pub's knights made of the incident. He posed as a knight from Lyon, who was the servant of a diplomat visiting Wollongong. He hoped no one would speak to him in French since he didn't know the language and didn't have a translator. Luckily, no one did. Descriptions of the shooter varied since no one who had been there at the time had expected the punch-up and the shooting to occur.

"He was a big fellow," said one knight. "He could take a punch and give one back."

"No," answered a nearby drinker, waving that description away with his hand. "He was a young bloke who had to resort to the gun because he hadn't had enough training to fight like a real knight."

"He was old and well past it," said yet another knight. "Where he got the gun, though, is a mystery. He must have gotten it off either a robot or a maiden officer, and I didn't think that was possible. I hope he doesn't come back and shoot someone else."

"Yeah," agreed Sam. "We want no more gunplay here!"

"We don't want any French crap in here, either," said a red-headed giant. He looked down at Aayan, his fists clenched.

"I have no problem with you."

"I do have a problem with French la-de-da mavericks," snarled the redhead.

"I too have a problem with them," replied Aayan, "but we have to serve who we have to serve. I'm a knight like you. I have limited choices."

"That's the truth," the redhead sighed, unclenching his fists.

"I'll buy you a beer," said Aayan. "We're knights after all, not mavericks."

"Accepted." The giant thumped Aayan on the back. In response, Aayan bought two beers, one for himself and the other for his new friend.

"It's the French mavericks who are bad," said the red-head in good cheer, smiling and then downing the brew given to him. "You can't help being their servant." Aayan did not ask what this knight had against French mavericks. He didn't care.

All the while Aayan was in The Spear and Shield, Sam's eyes were on him. From Gregory's description of the fellow, Aayan knew which barkeep was Sam. He further noticed how Sam was cautious and suspicious of newcomers such as himself asking questions. When Aayan was there, Sam avoided serving drinks to anyone who was new to his pub or was too chatty. Other barkeeps served them, and Sam would listen in on what was said. *Since the murder*, thought Aayan, *Sam probably expects a spy that looks like a fellow knight to turn up. My dark features wouldn't make me a very good agent for the constabulary since I don't look like a fellow knight from around here. No doubt, Sam's also wondering when Gregory's next move will come.*

"The Spear and Shield knights are still nervous," Aayan told Gregory and Elanora when he gave his report. "I could sense some were waiting for something further to happen, but they weren't sure what. The noise level in the place was way down. Maybe they thought Gregory would return and blow someone else away. I guess I can't blame them."

****

Meanwhile, the rumour of a most unusual dragon plus a gun in the possession of an outlaw knight had come to the High Priestess of Wollongong's attention.

"Tell me about it," said the High One to a young priestess who nearly jumped out of her white priestess garments at the High One's voice. She then looked nervously away from her. She had been caught by the High One gossiping with other priestesses who, like herself, had been polishing the wooden seats of the High One's temple. When the High One walked in, the talk stopped and the last priestess to speak was the one the High One addressed on the matter.

"I don't know why a dragon would be different from other dragons," said the priestess, looking down. "They say this one is curvier, but always wears bulky clothes, so it's hard to tell."

"Curvier?" wondered the High One.

"Yes," said the priestess. "All nonsense, if you ask me."

"It is nonsense," agreed the High One. "What of this business about a gun in the hands of a knight?"

"That's real enough," said the priestess. "There was a shooting at The Spear and Shield. I got the details from a servant at the wine bar I frequent. I've been told the shooting might get a mention on local news."

Twenty minutes later, when she was back in her office, the High One called in her top aide for advice. Upon receiving the phone call, the aide left her own office and promptly entered the High One's office.

"Is it true that a renegade knight has a firearm?" asked the High One.

"It's true," said the aide, a tall, imposing woman in priestess white. "We know from eyewitnesses, plus there's the body to consider. We could try hushing this up, but what happened is already circulating. My advice is to let it play itself out."

Dragon Queen

"Just when things were getting back to normal, this had to happen." The High One rubbed her hands together.

"What shall be done?" asked the aide, frowning and shaking her head.

"Despite not having the budget for it, I have arranged for a hundred more robots to be sent to Wollongong from Tokyo." The High One thumped the flat of her hand against her coffee table. "There is growing unrest, and a show of force is needed."

"What kind of show of force?" the aide asked.

"We may have to execute knights who frequent The Spear and Shield," the High One said, smiling thinly. "We must restore order or at least be seen doing something similar."

"Yes," agreed the aide. "Order must be restored."

The High One sent Malcolm to Liverpool, England with a diplomat who was to arrange for a special loan.

****

"Guns should not be in the hands of knights," the Highest One told Nathaniel firmly one night after they had discussed disturbing goings-on in Wollongong from reports sent to her by her spies, the ones stationed there. She was with him on her balcony looking out at Rome when she said this. He observed with her how this ancient city sparkled before them. Even so, that black patch where the Vatican once stood continued to teach every Highest One to ever be cautious when the status quo has been challenged.

"Knights need to know their place," she observed with a frown.

"Yes," agreed Nathaniel.

"Otherwise, our whole society will fall apart," she said.

"You won't need me back there, will you?" asked Nathaniel anxiously.

"I know you prefer your life here in Rome," said the Highest One, "but I may need you more in Wollongong. I'll think about it."

****

The next day, they were in her mansion, standing once more on her favourite balcony overlooking Rome. It was summer, and in the day, the heat cast a haze over the city. The patchwork of greens and browns and white structures reaching to the heavens danced before them. This was even true of the black square where the Vatican once existed as a reminder that ultimate failure to understand the enemy has its price.

Nathaniel hoped to have little more to do with Wollongong for a while, but the Highest of High Priestesses was now insistent he make the journey.

"I need you there," said the Highest One, waving her thin hand. "I pride myself on seeing major trouble in the offering and in dealing swiftly with it. You are to tell me what it is and how best to deal with it."

Nathaniel suspected the difficulties there in Wollongong had something to do with the female dragon on the loose but didn't say anything.

"I will have your thoughts on the matter." The Highest One had used her imperial voice.

"I will return to Wollongong," said Nathaniel, bowing his head. "I will do what I can for you and for the High One of Wollongong."

"Go then," she commanded.

"Yes," said Nathaniel, bowing again and leaving.

She then sighed deeply, looking at the patch of black in the distance. "Now and forever may the Great Goddess help you, my Nathaniel."

****

The flight from Rome to a refuelling stopover then Honolulu gave Nathaniel a chance to catch up on his reading. According to one magazine, the island of May in Scotland continued to be popular among knightly birdwatchers. Also, a Japanese maverick academic had been hired by the High Priestess of Kiama to teach her knights origami and so give them an edge in the November games.

What caught Nathaniel's attention and that of much of the world was Houston's launch of a new rocket that sent astronaut technicians into space to prepare the space station for better future use. Every magazine and newspaper carried something on the successful exit from Earth's atmosphere and the rocket's equally successful joining with the space station.

In Honolulu, Nathaniel witnessed the morning execution of two dragons for theft. They were hanged, for all to see, in the public square. "Good to see justice done," observed one muscular maverick with thinning hair wearing a brightly coloured shirt.

While Nathaniel was there, the authorities discovered that the dragons were innocent. It was a maiden who had been stealing wallets. Ten of those items were found on her. She was fined fifty dollars for being a thief and another twenty dollars for the premature deaths of the dragons that had been executed.

"She should have been fined more than that," a local maiden officer with long, blonde hair streaming out from her cap said to Nathaniel.

"Yes," agreed Nathaniel. He would have liked to have seen the thieving maiden hanged, but he dared not say so publicly. *Maidens are never executed except possibly for crimes that involve espionage*, thought Nathaniel. *The same is true of priestesses.*

Nathaniel was not aware at the time that maidens considered of little value to society that fall pregnant are injected with dragon genes, the needle going to the unborn child. Hence, those maidens die, giving birth to dragons. If he had known this while watching the hangings and then learning the maiden was responsible for the wrongdoings would only be fined, then it might have evened things up more for him. If this maiden thief ever fell pregnant, the powers that be, most probably the High One of Honolulu, would no doubt guarantee she would not survive. If he had known this, it would have been a comfort to him.

Wollongong's High Priestess was furious when she got the message from the Highest One of Nathaniel's return to her city.

"Why has he returned?" cried the High One, thumping her coffee table with her fist.

"I don't know," said her top aide, shrinking back from her.

"What is your advice?" asked the High One.

"He is coming here under instructions from the Highest One," said the top aide, her eyes darting this way and that. "You cannot stop him."

"I know that!" cried the High One.

"You might make use of him," offered the top aide.

"How?" asked the High One.

"He is due to touch down at our airport soon," said the top aide. "Why not request his help in investigating The Spear and Shield shooting?"

"Do you think he will do it?" asked the High One.

"If it is an official request," mused the top aide. "He is, after all, only a maverick and not a maiden or a priestess. He may be protected from harm by the Highest One, but you still have power over him."

"I'll do it!" cried the High One, clapping her hands together. "The new robots from Japan have yet to arrive, so I have changed my mind about killing random knights who happen to drink at that establishment, The Spear and Shield. Go! Get it done. "

"Yes," said the top aide, bowing and leaving the High One's presence.

Nathaniel received the message soon after his plane landed and sent the messenger back; informing the High One he would be glad to be of service.

Nathaniel settled into his hotel room and, that night paid a visit to The Spear and Shield. No one wanted him there. It was a pub for knights and not mavericks, but no law said he couldn't just wander in.

He read the patrons' minds but didn't come up with anything useful he didn't already know from reports the local constabulary had sent him.

Sam was there. Nathaniel sensed waves of hostility coming off that particular barkeep. No doubt, Sam knew about Nathaniel's reputation for getting at the truth. Nathaniel understood, straight off without going too deep into that specific knight's mind, that he had plenty to hide.

"You'd be happier at The Great Grape," said Sam. He smiled a thin smile.

"Why is that?" asked Nathaniel, a grin on his face.

"We don't serve wine here," said Sam, frowning.

"What do you know about the shooting?" asked Nathaniel, rubbing his chin.

"Nothing." However, the question brought to the surface of Sam's mind all he did know, which was gold to Nathaniel.

"Thank you for your cooperation," said Nathaniel and walked out of The Spear and Shield.

"Think nothing of it," replied Sam, rubbing his forehead and wondering why he now had a slight headache.

****

The following morning, Nathaniel visited the vacant lot where the exchange of stolen property was carried out. There was nothing there of much interest. It was mostly weeds and moss with half a dozen bushes. None of this gave any insight as to what had happened there recently. He walked down the street to see if anything came to him.

Outside a modest-looking house, Craft, a chubby knight munching on an apple, saw Nathaniel and dashed inside. This was not that unusual since Nathaniel had a tendency to make all sorts of people nervous. However, he was able to pick the brain of that knight, and he now knew where the items from the warehouse were hidden. The question was what he should do about it. He didn't owe the High Priestess of Wollongong his loyalty, but he had to be, to some extent, faithful to the Highest of High Priestesses. *I wish she hadn't sent me back here*, he thought. From Craft's mind, he also found out more about Elanora, the female dragon, and her location.

****

Two weeks and two days after the shooting, Craft approached Sam in The Spear and Shield to arrange for the delivery of more cans for cash.

"So you're from Gregory?" asked Sam.

"That I am," said Craft.

"How many cans were shifted last time?" asked Sam.

Craft told him and waited for Sam's reaction.

"You'd best come into the backroom with me where we can talk more about this," said Sam.

"Very well."

"How many this time?" asked Sam, sitting across from Craft.

"One hundred and fifty." Craft tried to sound casual, speaking softly.

"I'll give you fifty dollars for the lot." Sam frowned and crossed his arms.

"That's too low. You paid more last time, and there were fewer cans." Craft shook his head. He didn't want to return with such an offer. "Make it seventy-five for your trouble."

"Sixty-five, and you won't do any better." Sam looked at Craft, eyebrows down.

"Done!" Craft cried, not wanting to be there any longer.

They shook hands on the deal and arranged for the same exchange at the same place. Unbeknown to them, Nathaniel had briefly returned to The Spear and Shield. He wasn't there long enough to elicit comments from patrons, so his being there a second time was not mentioned to Sam. It was as if he walked in, changed his mind, and walked straight out. This was not typical of mavericks since they wouldn't normally come in anyway, but it was understandable. Knights liked having a place of their own. Though they couldn't do anything about mavericks turning up, they could make them feel uncomfortable with sneers and black looks.

The exchange of goods for cash went well for Craft. Sam used the same brewery truck to pick up the crates of cans and drove it to the location where it would be unloaded for his profit. Unfortunately, Nathaniel, a tall maiden officer, and four robots were waiting for him.

Sam backed away when he saw the robots, but his front tyres were shot out from under him. He got out of the truck, and Nathaniel tossed him a knife. Sam plucked the weapon out of the air as he had been trained to do for the arena without thinking. He was then shot three times by three of the four robots. According to the robots, it was okay for Nathaniel, a maverick, to have the knife in those circumstances, but not for Sam, a knight.

The maiden officer did not see the exchange. It happened too quickly, and she had been focused at first on the tyres being destroyed by her robots and the sounds that were thus made as well as the smell emanating from that destruction. All she saw when she looked away from the tyres was Sam being blasted for having the knife. It was like he wanted to commit suicide rather than be taken into custody.

The astonished look on Sam's face before he died went unheeded. The expression was put down to the fact that he had been caught and nothing more. No one was going to suspect Nathaniel of any kind of coverup.

The buyer, whose warehouse had been raided by the law, was an old, balding maverick who was demoted to knight by a court judge. His position in life was secure until his dealings with criminals had become known, and he had to be punished. His chances of living past November was slim at best. He had a wife and three children, but that didn't matter. They were now lost to him because of his new status. The knights working for him were fined twenty dollars each. If they had been dragons, they would have been executed.

The High Priestess of Wollongong was pleased. The smuggling ring had been crushed. It was a pity Sam was killed before he could supply any information, but it was still a good result. Twenty percent of what had been stolen from the warehouse near the railway station had been recovered and returned. Where the rest was, apart from the goods already sold on by the balding, demoted maverick would remain a mystery.

Nathaniel typed up a report and sent it to the Highest of High Priestesses via special computer link. She typed back, saying how gratified she was he had solved one problem for Wollongong's High Priestess.

****

The night after Sam died, just past six o'clock, Eric went to Demons with Ronald to flog a case of tuna cans. The bartender, a silvery dragon, and his customers were not interested.

"Get out of here before we call the authorities," said the bartender. "No one's going to do business with you."

Three dragons approached Eric and Ronald.

"I oughta smack you in the head," a large black-scaled fellow told Eric.

"We ought to see if you really do bleed like a dragon," said a silvery fellow with one eye on Ronald.

Another silvery dragon picked up a chair and told Eric, "If you are not gone in five seconds, this will come crashing down on your head."

Eric and Ronald ran out of the bar. The last thing they needed to do was to get into a brawl with their own kind.

Eric told Elanora what had happened. She was not surprised.

"What's left of our haul in that rental house stays put," she told her followers. "After what happened to Sam, the barkeep from The Spear and Shield, no one will buy, and someone may want to turn us in."

"But they were dragons!" cried Eric. "Why should those dragons care about what happened to a dodgy knight?"

"They don't," Elanora spoke plainly, her forked tongue poking out. "They care about what happens to them. Right now, dealing in hot merchandise, or even knowing about it, is far too dangerous for even dragons that face death two months out of every year."

"What now?" Ronald asked.

"We have money," Elanora said, her tail in a slow movement. "We have mobility. If we stay here much longer, we'll be rounded up and eliminated. The sooner we leave, the better."

"What about Gregory?" Ronald asked.

"He will soon be well enough to travel," said Elanora. "His wound remains clear of infection, and he is now on solids."

"Where shall we go?" Ronald asked.

"We'll talk it over with the others and decide," Elanora spoke with open claws.

"Kiama isn't very far away," said Eric.

"Wherever we go, we'll need maps and a plan." Her tail thumped the floor, indicating she was firm on this.

****

Later that night, before eight o'clock, the power grid for central Wollongong went down. Elanora and her followers stayed put in their house, but others used the darkness to rob and murder.

A group of knights broke into The Great Grape and killed as many maidens and mavericks dining under candlelight as they could find. They used battle axes and swords. People screamed and tried to get away. One maverick tried to fight back with a chair, but he was outclassed and was quickly cut down. Fifteen maidens and twenty mavericks thus met their end. The maverick barkeeps managed to escape with a few bruises after giving bottles of burgundy to their assailants. Money was also pocketed by the marauders.

On the way out of The Great Grape, all the offending knights were gunned down by two robots acting on a tall maiden officer's orders who had heard the cries for help from a block away. For many a maiden and maverick, this death toll of their own was staggering and next day would make the papers.

Not long after this incident, at a movie theatre near the railway station, two knights stole that night's takings and slit the maverick manager's throat. They then went to The Spear and

Shield, where they boasted to the patrons about how soft maverick flesh was and how mavericks can't fight worth spit. However, they did not tell anyone there what they had done though the thin-faced barkeep did notice blood on the blade of the murderer's knife he carried in his belt. He also observed how full of money the wallet was of the other bragging knight.

Nathaniel was all set for a short visit with Wollongong's High Priestess, followed by a return to Rome when the blackout occurred. In the dark, he heard a lot of stumbling about and raised voices in his hotel room. He struggled to keep other people's thoughts out of his head. Raw emotion, mostly fear, was everywhere. The general public took the lights going out as yet another sign that their Wollongong was falling apart.

Years ago, Nathaniel trained his mind to exclude the thoughts of others. He had to either do this or go insane. With the help of the Highest One, he had devised a room with a bed and a chair in his mind's eye. The door to this room was bolted shut so no one could get in. However, there was a window he could open to let the thoughts of those he wanted to come in. This room with the locked door and window had given him the control he needed. Now it was as if the window he had created in his head had been smashed by a thrown brick, and other people's thoughts were leaping into his mind room, causing him mental chaos.

There was a young maverick, failing in mathematics, contemplating the beating to death of his priestess university lecturer with a club. *It could be done during this night's confusion*, he was thinking. *No one need ever know it was me!*

Nathaniel suspected the young maverick wouldn't have the nerve to do what was in his mind. Even so, the images presented to him of the young one hitting the priestess repeatedly and of blood gushing everywhere were vivid and quite disturbing. *My biggest fear is to be demoted to knight for failing grades* was the topmost thought for this fellow.

Then the needs of a priestess for the attentions of a maverick came to Nathaniel. The priestess wasn't entitled to lay with a maverick because of her station in life. But her desires were still there and became more pronounced in the darkness. *I must not falter*, thought the priestess. *I must remain what I am, a priestess.*

Meanwhile, the hotel bar's maverick manager downstairs was watering some of the liquor, and at the same time, raising the prices. *This is the perfect time to get away with it*, he was thinking. *There are going to be nervous drinkers around, and so I'll make some extra money.*

There were others, a whole building full of them. Fortunately, after the initial shock of so many thoughts wanting to crowd in, Nathaniel could replace the broken glass in his illusory room. Once more, he only let into his mind the thoughts of others he wanted to let in.

A little after seven the next morning, Wollongong's main generators had been repaired, and the power was back on.

At nine, a maiden officer and two robots from the constabulary called on Nathaniel. It was the maiden officer who knocked on the door and not one of the robots. Nathaniel shook his head to clear it and answered the door, saying, "What can I do for you, Officer?"

"My supervisor feels you may be of help in my investigation," said the officer.

"What are you investigating?" asked Nathaniel to be polite. He had already secured that information from her mind.

"We request your aid, if at all possible, in the apprehension of those responsible for the movie theatre manager's demise," said the maiden. "It took place while the lights were out."

"I'll do whatever I can to help you," offered Nathaniel.

On the way out of the hotel, he met the maverick hotel manager. He said, "Your maverick bar manager is a petty larcenist."

"He's what?" The hotel manager yawned. He hadn't gotten much sleep.

"Your bar manager has recently tampered with the drink bottles at your bar," said Nathaniel. "There's less alcohol content in them."

"Less alcohol?" muttered the hotel manager, scratching his head.

"I would fire him and get rid of those bottles before hotel patrons complain about being cheated, and you find yourself in trouble," revealed Nathaniel. "I know this tampering wasn't your idea, but you better act now. The maiden officer I am with will undoubtedly want to look further into this matter when she has the time. Good day to you."

The hotel manager sighed and waved Nathaniel away. He was too open-mouthed stunned to reply. Moments later, Nathaniel caught sight of him racing into his office to make a phone call, no doubt to hotel staff to get rid of those troublesome bottles.

On the way to the theatre, the maiden officer had to ask, "How did you know what the bar manager was up to?"

"I just knew," replied Nathaniel without a show of any emotion.

"He'll be demoted to knight for sure," said the maiden officer, eyebrows raised.

"He's a thief," replied Nathaniel as if there was ice in his veins, no sign of compassion. Nathaniel was amused to discover that this maiden officer had briefly wondered if he was some kind of sophisticated robot with a pleasant face.

One of the theatre patrons remembered seeing two knights fleeing the scene. "They were knights from the shabby way they were dressed," said the maverick patron wearing a multi-coloured bowtie.

"Anything else?" asked the officer.

"Nothing I can recall," said the maverick, shaking his head.

Nathaniel couldn't get any more out of the maverick being questioned, either verbally or mentally. The ushers' flashlights were trained on the floor to prevent ticket holders from tripping out to the foyer. The flashlights were thus not trained on faces. Climbing and shrinking shadows added to the difficulties, making it impossible to be certain about the villains' height.

On the off chance of picking up a clue from one of the barkeeps, Nathaniel, the maiden officer, and the robots paid a call on The Spear and Shield. It was closed but continuous thumping on the door by the steel fists of a robot got it open. It was unlocked by a tired maverick owner and a knightly barkeep. Nathaniel gathered from their minds that they both lived on the premises. They were open-mouthed startled to see Nathaniel in the company of the local constabulary. The barkeep put down on a table the cudgel he was holding that he had been prepared to use against a robber. The maverick owner said, "What can I do for you, officer?"

"We just have some routine questions," she told him.

"What kind of questions?" the owner asked.

"Do you know anything about the theft that occurred at the theatre last night?" asked Nathaniel. "There was a stabbing. The maverick manager of the theatre was killed."

"No," said the owner, frowning. "I don't know a thing. You know anything, Rex?"

"Not a thing," replied the barkeep, looking away from Nathaniel and the officer. "We don't want trouble, and here we mind our own business."

"Maybe one of your customers said something?" asked Nathaniel.

"No," said Rex, the barkeep. "Nothing."

"I'll say good morning to you then, and thank you for your cooperation." The maiden officer sighed. "I can't see any point in going further with this."

As the maiden officer walked Nathaniel back to his hotel room, he said, "The knight's name is Bruno. He's the one who did the stabbing. His mate's name is Finch. You'll find them at the knight barracks not far from the university. If you hurry, you might catch Bruno still in possession of his bloodstained knife. DNA testing should be able to link the blood with the victim."

"How do you know any of that?" asked the maiden officer.

"Better hurry before Bruno either ditches the knife or cleans it, though I believe it is tough to get rid of all traces of blood," continued Nathaniel. "Oh, and Finch is the one with the stolen money."

"What is this?" asked the maiden officer. "Are you involved in some way?"

"I was asked to give you a hand, and that is what I have done," said Nathaniel, waving her away. "That is my involvement! Now go! Catch them! Isn't that what you want to do?"

"Did you get more out of that talk with the barkeep and the owner of the pub than I did?" the maiden officer speculated. "Can you read body language better than a professional maiden officer? But even if you could, it still doesn't make sense. They didn't mention any names."

"Then let it not make sense." Nathaniel sighed. "I have done what was asked of me to do. I'll do no more. Catch them or don't; it's now up to you."

Nathaniel picked up the question in the maiden officer's head that posed a threat. She wondered if he could read minds. She quickly dismissed it as her foolishness born out of her frustration in not getting better answers from him. Maybe there is something international about this, was the next thought he found in her head. She understood he was the Highest One's maverick, and maybe that, she figured, had something to do with what was going on.

The maiden officer left Nathaniel to go the rest of the way back to his hotel room and took her robots to the mentioned barracks. There she found Bruno about to clean his knife with detergent for the second time. To the open-jawed amazement of the other knights in the barracks, she arrested him and Finch. The other knights were too taken aback to cause the maiden officer any trouble.

Soon after he got back to his room, Nathaniel fell asleep. The city had calmed down enough for slumber to be possible.

Also, he needed recovery time from what he had done for the maiden officer.

Three hours later, the maiden officer visited him, demanding an explanation of how he figured out the theatre killing case. He had nothing to say.

"I'm going to haul you in for further questioning on this matter," she shouted at him.

"You can't do this," said Nathaniel. "There's a phone in this room. Use it to get in touch with your superiors. I have diplomatic immunity. Both the High Priestess of Wollongong and the Highest of High Priestesses will not abide you or your robots rough-handling me. So make the phone call and leave so I can get back to sleep."

She made the phone call.

"It's about Nathaniel," she began. "I want to take him down to the station and ... I can't? Not unless he wants to go? He's what? I'm to say that?"

She slammed the receiver down and glared at Nathaniel.

"Good day," she muttered.

"Good day to you, too," he replied casually.

"Goddess damned immunity," she muttered to herself as she walked out the door with her robots.

****

That night, Nathaniel paid a visit to the High Priestess of Wollongong. It was a courtesy because he didn't expect to discover anything new. She was still concerned about Elanora and what would happen to her if her connection with that female dragon was ever discovered by the Highest of High Priestesses. What was surprising was the fact, gleamed from the High One's mind that twenty members of the Knights of Saint George were going to pay Wollongong a visit. They were elite trouble-shooters who often caused more problems than they prevented or solved. Nathaniel felt he'd better stick around and see what he could do about helping with further damage control.

CHAPTER SIXTEEN

Over tea and scones in her office near her temple, Wollongong's High Priestess asked Nathaniel to divulge what he knew about the Order of Saint George. She exuded a heady fragrance, and he couldn't help noticing the black opal necklace she was wearing amid the whiteness of her skin and garment. The black opal had fire in its heart. He knew he was more ridiculously coloured in his swirling red, blue, and yellow suit and stood out amongst all the whiteness around him.

"Last year, the Order went to Madrid in Spain," said the High Priestess. "There were mass executions of dragons and knights."

"They did put an end to the uprising." Here Nathaniel felt he had to be careful. He sensed tension in this High One's mind. He had to be faithful to the Highest One whom he served but find common ground with this High Priestess.

"What uprising?" the High Priestess persisted. She grimaced and then looked anxiously at Nathaniel. "A handful of dragons ran off and went bush. Local maiden officers with robots hunted them down and eliminated them before representatives of that Order even got there. I have it on the authority of the High Priestess of Madrid that that is what happened. When members of the Order got to Madrid, there was nothing for them to do other than harass the local dragons and knights into action against them. Then eliminate the troublemakers they had created."

"Yes. I have read the reports. Madrid is now peaceful, thanks to the Order of Saint George." Nathaniel combed his hair with his hand. He knew from talks with her that the Highest One had little control over what the Order did in her name. However, she needed her immediate followers, such as himself, to maintain the notion that she did have full control.

"Now, the city of Madrid is as peaceful as a tomb and just as prosperous." The High Priestess sighed then added, "Just who are these Knights of the Order of Saint George anyway? I am naturally familiar with their exploits in the northern hemisphere. They do make the news, and I am told about them by High Ones whose cities have been affected. But this may be the first time ever they will venture below the equator."

"I think I understand what you mean," mused Nathaniel. "It is one thing to read about tornadoes whipping through parts of America. When you expect a tornado to whip through your city, it is something else, especially when one hasn't done so before. The Order is something like that, a righteous tornado."

"That's exactly what I mean," the High One said, leaning forward. "But why has the Highest One sent them here?"

"They move of their own accord but also with the Highest One's blessing," revealed Nathaniel, frowning.

"I know all that!" cried the High One. "But who are they? How did they come to be? They're not like ordinary knights. They are not expected to be in the May and November games."

"They go back many centuries," revealed Nathaniel. He rubbed his hands together while the High One looked on expectantly. He took a sip of tea and then continued. "They have had many names before settling on their current one. They were once based on the island of Malta. After their conversion to the true faith, they came to reside in Constantinople, where they have their main base today."

"Yes. They came to reside in Istanbul after it was renamed Constantinople in honour of the Goddess and her enemies' defeat." Here Nathaniel sensed that the High One wanted to show him she wasn't entirely ignorant and unworldly. "But why did they keep the Red Cross on the white background?"

"It is their symbol. It is centuries old going back to the time of the popes." Nathaniel smiled a knowing smile. He finished a scone and drank more tea.

"But after the last pope turned against the people, sometime in the beginning of the twenty-second century, you'd think the cross, in any form, would have been abandoned."

"Ah, but here, we are talking about Saint George!" cried Nathaniel. "He is the mythical slayer of dragons. The Knights of Saint George support his cause, and therefore they have his cross."

She looked away from him and said, "I just wish those special knights from Constantinople wouldn't do what they do with such vigour."

"The Order of Saint George has a special mandate from the Highest One," said Nathaniel. "It is known in Rome that the very first Highest One gave this mandate to the Order for her own protection. This mandate has been renewed with every Highest One coming into power ever since."

"What kind of mandate?" The High Priestess of Wollongong sipped her tea and looked into Nathaniel's sparkling eyes for the answer.

"The Order of Saint George is fully funded by Rome," said Nathaniel in a cool voice. "They fight at the command of the Highest One, and they also go independently to where they are needed in this world."

"Was going to Madrid their idea?" asked the High Priestess.

"Yes. The Highest One didn't know they were going there until it was too late to recall them if that was what she wanted to do," replied Nathaniel.

"Can she stop them from coming here now?"

Nathaniel understood from a nervous twitch in the corner of the High Priestess's upper lip plus her thoughts that she didn't want what happened to Madrid to happen to Wollongong. Being told about a city where its inhabitants have lived in fear is one thing. Being in charge of a city facing terror on a grand scale was something else.

"The Highest One can stop those special knights from coming here, but she won't." Nathaniel was firm on this, his arms now crossed. He understood the tentative hold the Highest One had on the Order and how she didn't want to push her luck. Even so, he did not care to inform this High One of that.

He knew the Highest One's biggest fear was the Order rebelling against her. For now, it was best to give the impression that the Highest One was all in favour of those knights leaving the northern hemisphere and heading south. "Some maidens and mavericks in Rome and Constantinople believe that the visit here of those Saint George knights is essential to the health of our religious life."

"But it's not!" cried the High Priestess. "What else can you tell me?"

"These knights of Saint George are exempt from the arena or any other combat site during the two months other knights are called upon to do battle," Nathaniel said. He waved his hand, wondering what he would do if he ever came upon one of these special combatants. "Instead, they fight any time of the year, and often enough, against great odds."

"They sound mad." The High Priestess shook her head. Nathaniel, in his mind, agreed with her.

"Be that as it may, some mavericks have chosen to be downgraded to knight so they could join the Order." Nathaniel realized that, too, sounded insane, though, in fact, it was also true.

"And they'll be here tomorrow." The High Priestess sighed. "What do they expect to find here?"

"There have been rumours that your dragons are running amok and need to be brought back into line," advised Nathaniel. "Furthermore, there are those who believe rogue elements among your knights have been in league with these rebellious dragons."

"That's nonsense!" cried the High Priestess, slamming her fist down on her coffee table, rattling the plate containing the last scone. "Besides, I now have an extra hundred robots ordered in from Japan, plus I also have the loan I wanted from Liverpool.

I don't need these knights from Constantinople. I do not require their help."

"You cannot stop them coming here without being in defiance of the Highest of High Priestesses," Nathaniel said in a firm, authoritative voice. *It is best this High One continue to think the Highest One is sanctioning this,* thought Nathaniel. *The Highest of the High has indicated to me, via computer linkup, she is not going to confront the leader of the Order on this issue.*

"Yes," agreed the High Priestess. "I understand it is the Highest One's will that those special knights should come here, but what should I do? I don't want half my dragons and half my knights slaughtered and have nothing much to show for the games in November."

"If all is calm and orderly when they arrive, they may soon leave," Nathaniel told her. He wondered what would register with the Knights of Saint George as calm and orderly.

"And if all is not calm and orderly?" asked the High Priestess, looking deep into Nathaniel's shining eyes. She drank her tea, waiting for him to speak. He said, "If all is not the way they want it to be they'll stay until they are completely satisfied their job here is done."

"In Madrid, maidens and mavericks were accidentally killed by the Knights of Saint George." By saying "accidentally," Nathaniel sensed that the High One was being polite and diplomatic.

"It could happen here, too." Nathaniel understood there was no point in minimizing the harm those knights from Constantinople could do.

****

Meanwhile, Elanora and her knights and dragons had settled on a travel plan. All except Craft, who liked it too much where he was, were anxious to get going.

Gregory was no longer bedridden. He claimed, if need be, he could fight. This was doubtful since he still needed time and the exercises recommended by Elanora and Ronald to get the injured arm moving less stiffly and without pain. Still, the wound was healing well. There was some scarring, but that was expected. If he had to go out as a fake maverick at a future time, he would have to cover up with a long-sleeved shirt.

Elanora and her followers had more than enough money to go to Kiama via rail and find a place to stay for a while. It was hoped that the fake travel passes Elanora had made up would allow them to buy tickets without any trouble.

"We still need a maverick to buy the tickets," said Gregory to Elanora. "Knights don't normally buy tickets, and dragons never do."

"That's true," replied Craft. "Gregory as a maverick will have to buy them."

"I can't do it," said Gregory. "Not so soon after that pub incident and my fleeing from that maiden officer and her robots. My description would have to be circulating, and fancy dress, looking like a maverick, might not fool everyone. If the constabulary recognises me as that knight with the gun, I'd be picked up and shot."

"Yes," agreed Elanora, her forked tongue poking out in sympathy. "Your face is getting to be too well known."

"I'm okay. I'm sure they didn't pay that much attention to me at that warehouse we raided," said Toff.

"Those stolen wallets and purses might still catch up with you," Craft mused.

"Aayan is our best bet," offered Gregory. Aayan nodded in agreement.

"What about me?" Craft asked.

"You won't fit into our maverick clothes." In this, Phips was right.

"We'll have to buy Craft new maverick clothes for the journey," said Gregory, "but for now, we'll go with Aayan."

"What about me?" Phips shrugged his shoulders, looking keenly at Elanora and then Gregory, not wanting to be left out.

"They'll be more cautious than ever, especially at airports and at the railway station. If you're dressed as a maverick and they remove your hat, they'll see the space where your ear was cut off, then arrest you." Elanora hissed gently. She didn't want to be cruel, but she had to be practical.

"We took that chance before," said Phips.

"Yes," agreed Gregory, "but there was a maverick with his hat pulled down over his ears at that warehouse we stole goods from. The guard at the gate noticed and most probably passed on that information before he died in that pub fight."

"So, I'm out." Phips sighed.

"Aayan and Craft are in. They're not perfect, but they'll do. They'll be our mavericks. How much will this cost?" Elanora looked to Gregory for answers.

"You mean new duds for Craft? I'd say around twenty dollars," said Gregory. "The tickets will be another ten dollars. Two mavericks travel first class, as they always do, with sandwiches and coffee provided by the railway authorities. Knights go second class without food or drink provided. The dragons are put in a cattle car with straw supplied for their use."

"That sounds charming." Elanora poked out her forked tongue and hissed in disgust.

"We are, after all, dragons," reasoned Ronald, flicking his silvery tail. "Don't even think about travelling second class, and Goddess forbid, you get the notion in your head to go first class."

"It's less than an hour by train to Kiama. We can put up with a little discomfort for that length of time," Eric said. Elanora was glad Eric had put forward the practicalities of their situation before she could.

"The danger points will be getting on and off the train," said Gregory.

"Agreed," replied Elanora. "Those are when we must be extra cautious."

****

The following morning at nine o'clock, Aayan, dressed as a maverick in a splendid blue suit with white and yellow stripes, went to a maverick clothing shop and bought clothes for Craft.

He had Craft's measurements. He took them from Craft before venturing forth with the hope they were right. Aayan told the sales maiden that he was buying for an uncle's birthday, which satisfied her. She said it would have been better if the uncle could have come in for a fitting but left it at that. As it turned out, the clothes fitted Craft perfectly.

By eleven o'clock, Aayan had bought the tickets and a map of Kiama. The bogus mavericks and knights escorted the dragons, with their fake pain collars on, to the railway station.

The stationmaster, a portly maverick in a blue station master's cap, no doubt with a wife and kids so he could risk being overweight, looked at the forms handed to him by Craft and decided they were authentic. Aayan and Craft glanced meaningfully at Gregory for but a moment as they were taken by the stationmaster to the first-class carriage. They did not like being separated from the others but had to pretend they required the comforts of the better travelling car.

"The seats in first class are padded," the stationmaster said with a grin. "They're more comfortable than what your knightly servants will be sitting on, but they'll still be looked after in second class. I must say we don't get many dark mavericks here."

"As if it is any of your business," snapped Aayan. "I'm from Egypt, seeking trade in Kiama."

"Fair enough," said the stationmaster, bowing his head and opening the door to first class for them. "Kiama is growing. Not as important as Wollongong, but it is getting bigger in terms of trade. I suppose they require a maverick with Egyptian connections."

"Perhaps stationmasters there in Kiama are less insolent," offered Craft, sticking up his button nose in contempt as he joined Aayan in first class. He was right in assuming that the more colourful way he was dressed indicated he was a more important maverick than the stationmaster.

Aayan and Craft seated themselves close to the doors so that, if need be, they could make a swift exit.

Gregory, Phips, and Toff kept their heads down as they boarded second class. Gregory had bought a newspaper to hide behind. Phips, seeing the wisdom in this, bought a magazine, and so did Toff. "It is a case of the less our faces are seen by fellow passengers, the better," Gregory offered to Phips and Toff.

The dragons were shoved into the smelly carriage, where the stationmaster said they belonged, and were locked in for the journey. Elanora hissed, showing she was far from happy with this arrangement, but Ronald and Eric, assured her it would be for the best.

"Even so," sighed Elanora, thumping her tail on the hardwood floorboards, "My fate and that of yours, my fellow dragons are now more firmly than ever in the hands of our knightly allies."

"We must have faith in Aayan and Craft," said Eric. "Believe me, I never thought I'd say that about two knights, but I have said it."

"They will not betray us," added Ronald, his silvery tail moving gently, disturbing some of the straw.

"What smells so bad?" asked Eric.

"Cow dung," replied Ronald. "Cows were transported in this carriage at some time in the recent past."

"How do you know?" asked Eric.

"I've worked with cows," Ronald told him. "We could move the cow dung we find via the straw, so our tails don't get dirty. We have to be careful with the wet bits. If it's all in the upper right corner, maybe the odour won't be so offensive."

"That's a good idea," said Elanora.

Ronald replied by smiling sheepishly at her and getting on with the job.

It didn't take Ronald and Eric long to get the dung as far away from everyone in the carriage as possible.

The train made several stops at smaller stations on the way to Kiama. These were only minor delays as maidens and mavericks from smaller towns either got on or off the train. The stop at Dapto was longer than expected by the dragons, and this worried Elanora. She hissed and shook her head. Then she peered through the slits in the wood and listened in on a nearby conversation.

"We don't see dragons being transported too often nowadays," said a maverick railway supervisor. He was close to the cattle car Elanora was in. She could see his blue cap.

"It still happens. And if the tickets and papers are in order, why should I care?" replied a maiden railway supervisor who also had on a blue cap. "Those dragons are probably headed for a farm somewhere. Someone must have been in the know to get them out of Wollongong in time."

"In time for what?" asked the maverick supervisor.

"The Order of Saint George just got to Wollongong," informed the maiden supervisor. "It just came over the radio. They hate dragons, those Saint George Knights. There's bound to be a massacre somewhere in the city before they leave. Better to have live dragons working on a farm near Kiama than dead ones stinking up the place in Wollongong."

Elanora sighed with relief when the train started up again. Ronald discovered he had been holding his breath, and the same was true of Eric.

At Kiama train station, the maverick stationmaster pulled Aayan and Craft aside.

"Your tickets and papers are in order, but I want to know what you're doing here," said the maverick stationmaster, tilting his blue cap then poking a finger at Craft. "I have the authority of the High One to ask what I want to ask, so out with it."

"You have more authority than the stationmaster at Wollongong?" wondered Aayan.

"Kiama is a smaller city," reasoned the maverick stationmaster. "We are careful who we let in."

Aayan doubted this but chose to keep a straight face as did Craft. There was no point in creating trouble. Craft looked to Gregory, who was waiting nearby with Phips, and Toff on the station platform. Gregory smiled and shrugged his shoulders.

"We want to set up a business here," said Craft, waving his hand about.

"Yes," agreed Aayan. "We've got capital for a farm, and we've heard good things about Kiama."

"Confidentially, we are glad to be out of Wollongong," whispered Craft. "We have dragons we want to make money off of before the games in November."

"Yes, well, it isn't going to be easy," reasoned the maverick stationmaster, taking off his cap and combing his thinning head with his hand. "You will have to purchase a farm."

"We have the money," assured Aayan.

"Do you have a farm in mind?" asked the stationmaster, putting his cap back on.

"No," said Aayan.

"There is a real estate agent close by, "offered the stationmaster. "I could take you there."

"I have a map," said Craft, taking it out of his pocket. "I know where it is."

"Those dragons of yours can stay here until you sort yourself out," offered the stationmaster, a gleam in his eye. "We can sideline the carriage they're in for a couple of days and feed them, but it'll cost you. We can't just have you roaming around with them, now can we? The local constabulary wouldn't like that."

"I suppose they wouldn't." Craft wasn't sure what to say or do next, but the stationmaster did make sense.

"How much?" asked Aayan.

"Forty dollars for three days," said the stationmaster. "Twenty now and twenty when you return to pick them up."

"That's a bit steep," said Aayan, "but we'll take it."

"I thought you would," replied the stationmaster, grinning. He took the twenty dollars off Craft and had the carriage sidelined out of the way. Craft went to the carriage and told the dragons about the decision that had been made.

"I don't want to be in here a moment longer!" snarled Eric.

"We didn't know this was going to happen," said Craft. "I think that stationmaster is already suspicious. We'd better play along with him."

"Fine!" Elanora snapped, swishing her tail in annoyance. "Play along. But please get us out of here as soon as you can."

"It's such a filthy carriage," groaned Ronald.

"I agree," snorted Eric.

"We had to think fast." Craft was apologetic. "I didn't know what else to do. I couldn't ask Gregory for advice because, in his grey outfit, he is obviously a knight, and I am a maverick in this multicoloured nightmare I'm wearing. I take it a maverick can't go asking a knight what he should do."

"I suppose it has to be this way," Elanora mused, her tongue poking out and a gentle hissing coming from her. "Very well, we will stay put!"

After Craft had gone back to Aayan, the knights dressed as knights and the stationmaster, Ronald said, "Now we must have even more faith in our fraudulent mavericks and our knights."

"They won't let us down." Elanora was firm in this, crossing her arms and hoping she was right.

"How do you know?" asked Eric. "They have the money. They could just run out on us."

"I just know," said Elanora. She unfolded her arms and opened her claws. Again, she hoped she was right.

CHAPTER SEVENTEEN

Sir Nicholas strode into The Shield and Spear. There he heard country style music. Two local knights were playing darts. As he passed by them and the drinkers, Sir Nicholas could smell the wooden tables that had been cleaned continuously over the years but still retained the odour of spilt beer.

Sir Nicholas' voice boomed out of the helmet he wore. The music stopped at the beginning of his rumble, ended by the barkeep pressing a button. Everyone wanted to listen to what he had to say. In his white surcoat with the red cross and that great sword in its scabbard not far from his hand, he presented himself well. Even for knights who had fought in the arena, he was a fierce apparition.

"Where is Sam, the bartender?" demanded Sir Nicholas. "I was told by one of your brethren that he is the knight to talk to, so I will converse with him."

"He's dead," said Rex, a twenty-something knight tending the bar.

"Are you trying to be funny with me?" Sir Nicholas drew his sword. The hilt was white bone with a red cross painted on it.

"They cremated him yesterday," said Rex, looking at the blade pressed against his throat. "Honest! I wouldn't lie to you!"

"He was a smuggler," snarled Sir Nicholas, pressing the blade further into Rex's flesh. "Are you a smuggler?"

"No fear, I'm not!" cried Rex, looking at the sword Sir Nicholas had put to his throat.

"Knights who associate with dragons are the scum of the earth!" boomed Sir Nicholas.

"Too true!" agreed Rex, his eyes wide open. Sweat trickled from his forehead, down his neck.

Sir Nicholas took the sword away from Rex's throat and barged his way past knights into the backroom. All seemed to be as it should be. Empty beer barrels plus a table and chairs didn't mean much to him. There was no sign of contraband or knights doing what he would deem to be wrong, such as harbouring criminal dragons, so he made his way back to the bar.

He was about to leave when a knight that had been pushed aside when he had entered the backroom grabbed him by the arm, and shouted, "We don't like being hassled for nothing!"

Thanks to Sir Nicholas, the knight lost his arm and then his head. It was done in just two incredible strokes. It was terrible, and at the same time, mesmerizing in its swiftness. The arm and then the head hit the floor, Sir Nicolas' shinning sword went from white to red in an instant. A knight had to stop himself from shrieking at the sight of eyes and mouth in motion despite the head being severed from the body. Others were disturbed by the headless form thrashing about. These knights expected this type of horror in May and November, but not here and now.

Blood splattered over a dozen seated knights, getting into their drinks, spurring them into action. They put their beer mugs down, grunted, and got to their feet. Swords and knives were drawn, and Sir Nicholas flexed himself for battle. He saw fear and uncertainty in the eyes of those confronting him and so knew he had the edge over them. He had told himself on numerous occasions he had left fear behind. Fighting was a pleasure for him and not a task.

A knight tried to hit him over the head with an empty bottle and was skewered in the neck for his trouble. Two knights barred Sir Nicholas's exit out of the place while two others began to circle him. Sir Nicholas ducked out of the way of a chair thrown his way.

He was now smiling a smile that made no sense to those he was up against. It chilled them. Sir Nicholas knew that only his mouth and his eyes could be seen while he wore his helmet. Did he get a sense of invulnerability being so encased? He didn't know, nor did he care. What he understood was he felt wonderfully charged in both mind and body.

"This is better," enthused Sir Nicholas heartily, "much better!"

A knife broke on Sir Nicholas' plate armour, and the knight responsible was tossed by Sir Nicholas into a fellow knight. Sir Nicholas then laughed a joyous laugh that made those around him cringe.

Sir Nicholas' sword then chopped a knight's head in two and sliced another knight from shoulder to waist. The knight that was cut down the middle screamed momentarily. His moving heart and lungs on display, his face registered astonishment.

Several knights who saw no reason to die at this madman's hands bolted from The Spear and Shield while two more were stabbed through the heart by Sir Nicholas. Blood was everywhere.

Rex watched as knights he'd known for years tottered on their feet, bled out, fell, and died. Sir Nicholas sheathed his sword and said, "Those who defy me also defy the Highest One, and that will never do. I take my leave."

Sir Nicholas strode out of The Spear and Shield. Rex, overjoyed, saw him go.

I'm alive! Rex thought. *I get to live!*

It seemed to him that nothing pleased this Sir Nicholas more than the spilling of blood. It took a while before his brain allowed him to sigh in relief. He was so afraid Sir Nicholas would come back and gut him. It took a bit longer for Rex to find a bandage behind the counter and apply it to his neck.

Later, the maverick manager of The Spear and Shield had a talk with Rex over what had happened while the knights employed to do so by the city put body parts into body bags for transport to the morgue. The manager was glad he hadn't been around when Sir Nicholas made his visit.

"It'll be better when all this mess is cleared away," offered the manager.

"And the High One allows this to happen?" asked Rex, his eyes on a body bag being picked up.

"She has no choice," said the manager. "She can't go against the Highest One."

"So, our maiden officers with their robots can't interfere?" asked Rex.

"They can't get between the Knights of Saint George and the carrying out of their duties to their Order and to the Highest One," said the manager.

"So those knights get to butcher whoever they like?" asked Rex. He downed some beer from a mug, but it didn't help much.

"It could have been worse," reasoned the manager, shrugging his shoulders. "The tables are still in good shape, and so is the dartboard. Not many chairs were destroyed. So we lost some knights. Regrettable, but we still have a working pub. I am so glad I hadn't gone in for carpeting like a carpet firm recommended. Getting the bloodstains out would have been horrendous and terribly expensive."

****

At the same time Sir Nicholas was having fun, Sir Jacque and Sir Ian were at Demons enquiring about the dragon connection to the broken smuggling ring. Like Sir Nicholas, they were well armoured and keen to test their swords. The dragons there, since they were all wearing active pain collars, were determined not to give them an excuse.

"Dealing with dishonourable knights is an offence," Sir Jacque put to the black-scaled dragon tending bar. He leaned close enough to this dragon to activate the dragon's pain collar, making him wince then hiss. Sir Jacque's sword came out, and he rested its tip against the dragon's throat, below the collar.

"We don't do that!" cried the dragon barkeep who didn't appreciate the sword on his more sensitive scales. "We don't deal with dishonourable knights. Please believe me!"

"And how shall we know you are telling the truth?" enquired Sir Jacque.

"Please leave!" cried the barkeep, who felt the sword digging into a particularly sensitive scale, seeking flesh. "They've done nothing wrong, the dragons you see here, and neither have I."

"You have done nothing wrong, and you tell me to leave?" bellowed Sir Jacque incredulously. "A dragon does not tell a true knight what to do!"

Sir Jacque thrust his sword deep into the barkeep's throat. The barkeep bled, gagged, and died.

"Why?" cried a nearby silvery dragon.

"We don't answer to you!" boomed Sir Ian. There was an echo effect because of the helmet he wore. He ran at the talkative dragon, pulled him to his feet, and cut him in two with two swift movements of the sword.

Some of the dragons fled. Those whose way out had been blocked by Sir Ian had to stay. A swung tail knocked Sir Jacque off his feet. The one who did it screamed with pain from the shock of the collar he wore. Sir Jacque stabbed him and another dragon in the crotch before getting up.

Meanwhile, a dragon bashed Sir Ian over the head with a full bottle of bourbon. This activated that dragon's pain collar. The dragon then screamed, running for his life, out of Demons and onto the street. By the time he got back to his barracks, the pain had gone.

Another dragon threw a lit candle. This action activated his pain collar. His cries from his collar were swiftly ended by Sir Jacque's sword coming down on his head. The thrown candle landed on Sir Ian's helmet. Within moments, Sir Ian's helmet, soaked as it was in bourbon, was engulfed in flames. Sir Ian took his helmet off and threw it at a fleeing dragon. The dragon snatched the helmet out of the air and wished he hadn't. He yelped loudly, his eyes watering, his claws burning. Then Sir Jacque joined Sir Ian in slaying this dragon with the blistering claws that still held the helmet. The dragon sliced up landed in two lumps on the floor. The helmet rolled in Sir Ian's direction, and he picked it up. He ripped off the claws still plastered to it and threw them away.

Sir Ian cooled his helmet down with a jug of water from the bar and, while it was still steaming, put it back on.

"The smell of burnt flesh, even dragon flesh, and of course scales, is unpleasant," observed Sir Ian, "but dragons have to be taught their place in this world if, indeed, they do have a place."

Now there were two knights of Saint George plus a pile of dead dragons in Demons. The place's maverick owner was nowhere to be seen and was not likely to surface for a couple of days. He knew he had done nothing wrong other than own Demons, but that might be enough to upset those troublesome knights sponsored by the Highest One into doing him harm, even killing him despite the fact he was a maverick. A maverick should always be more important than any knight, but those of this Order didn't always understand that. He remembered those reports of how mavericks, knights, and dragons were treated by the Knights of Saint George in Spain and felt caution would be best.

****

While The Spear and Shield and Demons were being attacked, the same thing happened to other knight pubs and dragon watering holes throughout the city. Saint George knights such as Sir Douglas, Sir Remy, and Sir Naylor were especially aggressive. Maiden officers, with their robots on patrol, had their walking machines with the blinking red eyes shoot down knights and dragons outside such establishments who appeared to be in too big a hurry to state their business for the constabulary. The maiden officers on patrol had been told not to interfere with the Knights of Saint George.

One rainy night, Dean Renate got soaked going from her office to the cottage where she lived. She didn't think she'd need her umbrella until it started to rain. It hadn't poured in some time. She thought of the farmers and their needs as she trudged inside her home, turned on the lights, and got a towel from her bathroom to dry her hair. *The farmers need the rain, and I want to record a good harvest this year*, she thought. *I'll get out of my wet things, take a hot shower, and everything will be all right.*

Then, just when she was about to have her shower, someone pounded on her door, and a voice commanded, "Open up in the name of the Order of Saint George!"

Oh, dear Goddess! She looked out her window, and it was indeed one of those Constantinople thugs. She recognized the red cross on the white background.

"Yes!" cried the dean. "I'm opening up now. Please don't put a hole in my door!"

Within moments, she was face to face with a dripping knight in full battle gear.

"What can I do for you?" asked the dean.

"I am Sir Ian of the Order," replied the knight proudly. "Together we shall inspect your university."

"Now?" Surprise registered on the dean's face, her mouth forming an O.

"Now!" Sir Ian was insistent, and he had a sword. His hand was on it, lovingly stroking the handle as if it were a cat or a dog. Also, there was blood on his surcoat that hadn't yet washed off completely.

"All right, I'm coming." The dean grabbed her umbrella, even though she was already soaked.

The journey in and around the main university building took two and a half hours. The dean did her best not to anger Sir Ian, who was not looking too happy because of the rain. He moaned, and he clanked.

"This couldn't have waited?" asked the dean as they looked in one of the buildings' basements.

"No," said Sir Ian mechanically. He sneezed, revealing his humanity. She sneezed, too. "Do not be afraid," he told her. "If you are a good maiden, and I believe you are, then you will come to no harm."

"Yes," agreed the dean smiling sheepishly at him. "No harm would be good."

"We protect maidens," said Sir Ian, touching his sword handle.

She was glad when they were out of all the basements and the floors and back in the downpour. Out in the open, she felt safer, even though she didn't expect anyone would come to her rescue if this knight did act up. She simply thought she had a better chance of running from him. The truth was, once that sword was out, and he meant to use it, she was a dead maiden.

She wondered why, despite it being rained upon, his helmet smelled of burnt something. It was discoloured as if it had been in a fire.

It was late, and no one was around except a skeleton crew of maiden officers working security with their robots and a few scientists in their labs. Sir Ian once more sneezed.

"No dragons?" he asked.

"We don't have much use for them this late," the dean told him. "During the day, we mostly have knights doing odd jobs."

"You have an outpost in old Sydney?" asked Sir Ian. "I was told this by airport staff when we landed here in Wollongong."

"We have a research project going on there," replied the dean. "It is hardly a secret."

"When can I see this project?" asked Sir Ian.

"We have Megan, my assistant going out there again to-morrow," said the dean.

"Very well, I will join her in the morning," Sir Ian told the dean.

"You won't find anything of interest there," said the dean.

"My comrades and I must be thorough." He then turned and walked away. Before too long, his receding shape vanished in the continuing deluge.

Dean Renate went back to her cottage for that much needed hot shower, change of clothes, and coffee.

****

The following day, Megan was not pleased with Malcolm's extra passenger but was not game enough to offer any objection to him going with them to Old Sydney.

Megan enjoyed Malcolm taking her out to the Mitchell Library site, working with her, and then taking her back, but Sir Ian made her nervous. Apart from fiddling with her glasses, she also glanced more than she felt was appropriate at the scabbard containing his great sword. An acrid odour came off his helmet. Also, there were patches of blood on his surcoat that hadn't completely disappeared despite the rain the previous night.

She was afraid of saying the wrong thing. She imagined what that surly knight could do with his great sword to Malcolm's flyer, let alone what he might do to Malcolm, who could be too outspoken for his own good. She remembered a priestess who had once told her that he had been too honest with the Highest One in Rome. He was fortunate that the Highest One had found what he said amusing rather than impertinent, requiring some form of punishment.

"Just fly us out there," Megan whispered to Malcolm before takeoff. "The less said, the better."

Despite the tension felt by all except Sir Ian, the flight went without incident. Once they had achieved touchdown near the ruins, Sir Ian turned to Malcolm and said, "You stay with this craft."

"Very well," replied Malcolm blinking in Megan's direction.

"I'll be all right." Megan tried not to sound nervous. She held one hand with the other to stop them from shaking. Then she adjusted her glasses.

Megan took the Knight of Saint George into the underground levels. For two and a half hours, he inspected the corners and containers in which dragons might hide. There were none to be found. He saw something with a tail slither by but discovered, to his annoyance, it was only a small lizard and not a dragon.

On the third level, Sir Ian picked up a copy of the Koran and a copy of the Bible. He weighted both in his hands and then slammed them down on a table. "Rubbish!" he cried. "Not the true faith!"

"Yes," agreed Megan, looking down and then away from him.

Her hands balled up into fists. She hid them behind her back until she managed to calm down. She was appalled at what he had done, and so it took all her willpower not to say or do anything likely to get her hurt or killed. To her, Sir Ian was showing too much contempt for what she considered to be valuable artefacts.

"You look flustered," said Sir Ian. "Is something amiss?"

"No!" Megan shook her head vigorously, wanting it to stay attached to her shoulders. She hadn't considered her face going red with the anger she felt for the mistreatment of those artefacts. "It's nothing, nothing at all."

"There isn't anything of any great interest here," grumbled Sir Ian. He sighed loudly and continued with her down to the seventh level. Then they returned to the surface.

"I don't know why you bother," said Sir Ian. "Everything down there is old; it's had its day."

"It's what I do." Megan took off her glasses, cleaned them on her work apron, and put them back on.

"We leave now," said Sir Ian.

"You want me to leave, too?" asked Megan. "I only just got here. I have things to do. You could go back with Malcolm alone, and he could pick me up later."

"You will do these things some other day," said Sir Ian, glaring at her. He shoved her in the direction of the flyer.

The trip back to Wollongong was quiet. Neither Malcolm nor Megan liked being bullied, but they had that sword to consider. Sir Ian had nothing to say to them.

****

On the same morning, a knight referring to himself as Sir Douglas pushed his way into the University of Wollongong library and found only young maidens and mavericks studying for exams. The maiden librarian didn't tell him to leave, but she did inquire about his reading pleasure. "Something on dragons?" she suggested.

"No books," said Sir Douglas and left.

****

Meanwhile, Sir Naylor and ten other knights explored the taxi stands and bus depots for stray dragons but without any luck. They then went to the official dragon barracks, but no one there had anything to say which was pertinent, even when three of the resident dragons were slain for showing disrespect. Hissing in fear and poking their forked tongues out were all that was required to be disrespectful. No words of defiance. The pain collars kept them from saying anything that might mean trouble for them.

"Dragons lack good manners," reasoned Sir Naylor, cleaning his blade on a dragon tablecloth.

Next, Sir Naylor and his knights went to the nearby knight barracks. They didn't expect to see renegade dragons living with respectable Wollongong knights, but they thought these knights might still know something worth knowing. Here, the knights of Wollongong kept their calm, despite feeling set upon, and so there wasn't any violence.

"You live well," said Sir Naylor after examining the kitchen. "Do you fight well?"

"When we have to," replied a local knight.

Sir Naylor looked in the armoury and said, "You Wollongong knights do have an admirable collection of weapons."

The same day, the High Priestess of Wollongong read with dismay the reports coming in about the activities in her city of the Knights of Saint George. The ranks of her knights and dragons had thinned, and so the November games were looking to be dismal affairs. There was talk, dished up to her by minor priestesses who frequent wine bars, of knights and dragons fleeing Wollongong with their maverick masters for a saner existence in Kiama.

Dean Renate was summoned to the High Priestess of Wollongong's office for advice concerning the disagreeable knights from Constantinople. The High Priestess hoped there was the off chance the university's head could come up with something useful.

Over a glass of first-class sherry handed to her by a High Priestess's aide, the dean thought it over and came up with one possibility.

"Give them something else to do," said Dean Renate.

"But they think they're already on a mission."

"Give them something to do that looks grand and keeps them away from Wollongong," advised the dean.

"Like what?" the High One asked.

"Rumour has it that dragons from here are on the loose in Kiama," said the dean.

"That's hard to believe," reasoned the High One. "Besides, it's not uncommon to transport dragons from Wollongong to Kiama and vice versa. Apart from the paperwork, how are we to know the runaways from those being legitimately transported? How do we know there are any runaways at all?"

"Never mind all of that." The dean waved away the suggestion of sticking to known facts. "Let's say the rumour is true, it is absolutely correct. What is to be done about these Wollongong dragons out to terrorize Kiama?"

"Even if it were true, there's nothing I can do about it," said the High One, annoyance in her voice. "I can't send any of my maiden officers and robots there without upsetting the High Priestess of Kiama and getting the Highest of the High offside. And I will not ask for the High Priestess of Kiama's help in such a matter. You must know that!"

"Oh, indeed, I understand perfectly." The dean spoke in a calming voice. "There is nothing you can do personally to deal with those dragons, whether they are imaginary or not, without unpleasant results."

"Then why bring it up?" The High Priestess was angry, her face reddening.

"You could request the aid of the Knights of Saint George in apprehending these runaway dragons and their maverick masters if they have any." The dean hoped the High One got the message. "You might even hint that they had something to do with the smuggling the knights of Saint George are investigating."

"Ah! Now I understand," said the High Priestess, her anger gone. "Those knights of Saint George are free to go anywhere, and the High Priestess of Kiama cannot deny them passage into her city. Now all I have to do is ask for their aid in this matter. Thank you, Dean Renate. You have been most helpful."

****

After the second day in lock-up in the railway cattle car with bread, cheese, and bottles of water occasionally dumped in by the stationmaster, Ronald and Eric were getting worried. Was it Elanora's imagination, or was there a brown cloud of stink?

"If we're not out of here by the end of today, we're dead," Eric told Elanora. "Those blowflies can't get through our scales, so we're not as bad off as full humans would be in this situation, but the fumes from dragon as well as cow dung are becoming toxic. It's getting hard to breathe."

"They'll be here sssoon," said Ronald, hissing gently.

"Why should they be here at all?" Eric asked, his fists clenched. "They have the money, they have their freedom, and they are knights. Don't forget they were once in the arena and other places killing our sort. Why should they feel any kind of loyalty toward us just because they paled around with us for a while?"

"If past noon and they haven't come, we'll have to break out," said Elanora, looking at her companions, each one at a time, and weighing up what they were telling her. "Some of these boards are rotten, so getting out can be done, but it will make a lot of noise. I noticed from the map that the building housing the local constabulary isn't far from where we are. Once we are out, we will have to move fast or be gunned down by robots commanded by their maiden officers."

"Yes," Eric agreed. "There are risks."

"If we wait another day or so, despite the discomfort, our knightly friends will come through for us," offered Ronald calmly, his claws open.

"I am sorry, Ronald, I know how much you want our knights to do right by us, but we can't wait much longer," reasoned Elanora, her tail moving rhythmically. "The air in here is bad and will get worse. I am not feeling all that well, and if we get too weak, we won't stand a chance when we do escape. Our only advantage on our own is that the maidens and mavericks here don't know our pain collars don't work."

Going by the sun's passage in the sky, as seen through the slits in the wood, it was approaching noon when they heard the lock and chains give way on the doors to their temporary prison.

"Out!" cried the stationmaster. Slowly, they left the carriage, blinking. It took them a while to adjust to direct sunlight on their faces. The stationmaster was with Aayan and Craft, who were still dressed as mavericks.

"They're a lazy lot," confessed Aayan to the stationmaster in good form, "but we'll make good use of them."

"See that you do," said the stationmaster. "Word is out that there are dragons from Wollongong on the run, but these can't be them, now can they?"

"Certainly not!" cried Aayan. Elanora gathered that Aayan was trying to sound as astonished as possible and doing a good job. "Do you see the pain collars?" Aayan added, pointing at the one being worn by Ronald. "You won't find them on fugitive dragons!"

"The very idea!" cried Craft. Elanora understood he was following suit and also sounding convincing.

"Just as I thought," said the stationmaster. "I take it you're all sorted then?"

"We have a truck, and we have knights to make sure our dragons don't act up," replied Aayan, pointing in Gregory's direction.

"I'll have that further twenty promised me," said the stationmaster, holding out his hand. Elanora watched as Craft gave him the money.

"You'd best be on your way," added the stationmaster, pointing toward the exit to his station.

The truck was an old, rusty pickup, and for the sake of propriety, the dragons had to pile into the back. There was enough room in the front for the two fake mavericks and the genuine knights. Those in the front were able to hear those in the back, even over the engine's roar, as the truck moved along the road, away from the train station.

"We're going to a dairy farm in Berry," yelled Gregory to Elanora. "It cost us about three-quarters of the money we had left, but I think it's a good buy."

"Where's Berry?" asked Elanora.

"It's about twenty miles from Kiama," said Gregory. "The farm is a mile from the centre of Berry, so we needed our own transport. Legend has it there used to be a train station at Berry, but that must have been a long time ago."

"We have twenty-three dollars left from our stash," advised Craft.

"Do we have a cow to milk?" asked Elanora.

"Yes," said Gregory. "More than one cow, thank the Goddess! Now, all we need do is figure out how it is done. The equipment came with the house and the cowshed."

"I know how to do it." Ronald's eyes lit up with excitement. "When I was younger, a maverick had me working on a farm."

Back in the twenty-first century, the road was smooth. It had deteriorated with age and lack of care. Elanora was tempted to count the bumps along the way. The farm was off a side road, and the house and cowshed had seen better days but were still serviceable. Both the house and cowshed were on a hill overlooking a valley of good pasture land.

Upon close examination of the herd they now had, Ronald said the cows were in good condition.

Elanora was glad to be breathing fresh air after her time in that horrid carriage, and she knew the other dragons felt the same way. She took Ronald's claw into her own, and for a moment, admired his face and the smoothness of his silvery tail as they looked over the valley they now possessed. Eric looked on, wondering why he, a black-scaled dragon, wasn't getting this kind of attention from Elanora.

"You got us out of that carriage just in time," said Elanora to Aayan.

Gregory showed Elanora the paperwork on the place, and it all seemed to her to be in good order. "The only problem would come," mused Gregory, "if and when the mavericks that signed it and paid out the money were discovered to be knights instead."

"And that would be a problem?" asked Elanora.

"Very much so," replied Gregory. "Knights are not supposed to own property."

The kitchen was large. It was built to cook for two dozen or more knights and mavericks. The bedrooms were roomy, and the beds looked comfortable.

"What now?' Eric asked Elanora.

"We all learn how to milk cows and do whatever else needs to be done around here." Elanora looked toward Ronald, who nodded in agreement. "We have to run this farm as a going concern if we are to stay here for any length of time."

****

Meanwhile, one day ago, Sir Nicholas had conferred with the High Priestess of Wollongong. After having her pray for his cause, he was keen to finish his work in her city before moving on to Kiama. She wanted him to go to Kiama right away with his knights. However, he told her he still had to examine the warehouses, especially the one closest to Wollongong train station.

"I can't be half-hearted about what I do in the name of the Goddess," Sir Nicholas informed her. The High One could see the gleam of the fanatic in his eyes and knew there was no sense arguing with him. At least by siccing him onto Kiama, she was sharing the pain. She wanted to see the High Priestess of Kiama's face when Sir Nicholas and his knights descend upon her city.

That afternoon at the warehouse near the railway station, two Wollongong knights were accused of looking crooked at two Saint George knights.

"You regard us with contempt?" asked Sir Ian.

"What are you doing here?" asked one of the local knights.

"You're not the law," said the other local knight.

"We are the law wherever we go," advised Sir Ian. "You need a lesson." He drew his sword, and so did Sir Nicholas. The local knights, since they didn't have swords on them and knew, by looking into their opponents' eyes, they couldn't avoid a fight without begging, grabbed four by two blocks of wood that were part of a shipment of timber to a building site.

It was no contest. The wood was clumsy to hold, the swords easily handled. The local knights fell, painting the boxes and crates around them red.

"You are fortunate we let you live," advised Sir Nicholas to one groaning victim with missing fingers on his left hand. The other had lost his right hand.

In another area, four dragons were killed outright for hissing at Sir Nicholas and Sir Ian. They were quickly dispatched since the pain collars they wore took much of the fight out of them.

"We lack a worthy foe," remarked Sir Ian, sheathing his sword.

"We are also without what we seek," replied Sir Nicholas. "Perhaps this maiden supervisor I see hiding behind that crate can be of assistance."

"Come out!" cried Sir Ian. "We do not harm maidens."

Once she realized she wasn't going to be gutted by them, the maiden supervisor gave a good description of one of the so-called mavericks involved in the robbery.

"He was a handsome fellow," she added, wanting to be helpful since she wasn't entirely sure she trusted their stated attitude toward maidens.

"Anything else you can recall from that day?" asked Sir Ian.

"One of the mavericks had his hat pulled down over his ears," she replied. "I thought that strange. Also, one of the dragons seemed to resist the pain device I had on me. He screamed after a while, thanks to the handsome maverick and the device he had, but I thought there was something odd about this dragon's shape, despite the bulky clothes he was wearing. Also, his scream was high pitched, which was unusual for a dragon past puberty."

"Something else you know that will be helpful?" prompted Sir Ian, his hand absentmindedly on the hilt of his sword.

"I was told by one of our worker knights," she added, "that the maverick guard recently demoted to knight had died in an altercation with a knight."

"Where did this take place?" asked Sir Ian.

"It happened at The Spear and Shield, "she told him. "I imagine he could have filled in some of the blanks in your investigation."

"Just how did he die?" asked Sir Ian.

"He was shot," she told him. "And it was by a knight." If she could have seen his eyebrows, they would have been raised. His helmet though, did not hide the widening of his eyes upon receiving this news.

Sir Ian thanked the maiden supervisor kindly for her excellent service to his cause. The other warehouses proved to be clear of vice, but this was only discovered after the deaths of four Wollongong knights, ten dragons, and a maverick that happened to get in the way of a sword thrust.

In these warehouses, it was a swirl of swordplay prompted by Wollongong knights bumping into each other to get away and dragons running, hissing in fear.

Usually, the Knights of Saint George would go by flyer to their chosen destination, but this time Sir Nicholas decided they should travel to Kiama by train. The High Priestess of Wollongong bought them their tickets.

At Wollongong train station, the Knights of Saint George boarded the first-class carriage headed for Kiama and enjoyed sandwiches and coffee. As knights, they were supposed to travel second-class, but no one was willing to push that point with them. It was hoped by railway staff that eating and drinking made the Saint George knights less prone to violence.

When the train pulled into Dapto, the Knights of Saint George got off, onto the platform, and then entered the second-class carriage before the train continued on to Kiama. They did this to interview one of the knightly ticket inspectors that travelled this route daily.

The ticket inspector suggested that a knight who had recently journeyed to Kiama looked rather suspicious by how he buried his head in a newspaper.

"Why was that suspicious?" asked Sir Ian. "Knights can buy newspapers."

"Yes, they can," agreed the inspector. "It's just his hand was shaking when he showed me his ticket."

"Did you get a good look at him?" asked Sir Ian.

"No, but there was this knight with a missing ear," recalled the inspector. "I know knights with missing body parts are common enough, but there was something concerning him that made me wonder."

"What was it about the knight with the missing ear that drew your attention?" asked Sir Ian.

"I don't know," said the inspector. "I think I saw him before down by that warehouse that made the news. You know, the one where goods were stolen. But, if it was him, I don't think he was a knight at the time."

"Could he have been a maverick?" asked Sir Ian.

"That's it!" cried the inspector. "He was a maverick with this hat over his ears, so we couldn't see that one ear wasn't there."

"Why didn't you report this?" asked Sir Ian.

"I only caught a glimpse of him at the warehouse," said the inspector. "You can see the warehouse yard and loading docks from the station. And I've only just put it all together if he is the same person."

"Now we're getting somewhere." Sir Ian clasped both gloved hands.

"A knight impersonating a maverick is a criminal offence, punishable by death," said Sir Nicholas, who had been listening in.

"For a knight, a maverick's position must be earned," added Sir Jacque, also listening in.

"And the only knight we know of who managed to do that was Dreadnought," said Sir Ian. "And he is on Mars."

"Yes, he slew fifty dragons," Sir Jacque mused.

"Yes," agreed Sir Ian with awe in his voice. "It was fifty dragons."

****

At Kiama train station, the stationmaster there, despite being a real maverick, was roughed up by Sir Ian while the other knights of Saint George watched.

"We have been told, by the stationmaster at Wollongong, that knights and dragons were travelling here from there," said Sir Ian. "So we know about these knights and dragons and suspect them of being the renegades we are after. So, where are they?"

"I don't know!" cried the stationmaster. Sir Ian walloped him with his gloved fist, sending air out of the fellow's lungs.

"You must know," said Sir Ian, hitting the stationmaster again, this time in the face.

"Stop!" cried the stationmaster. "I will tell you what I do know."

"What do you know?" asked Sir Ian.

"I kept dragons from Wollongong over there in that cattle car," said the stationmaster, pointing in the cattle car's direction.

"Why did you do that?" asked Sir Ian.

"For the money!" cried the stationmaster.

Sir Ian hit him a few more times, blood streaming from the stationmaster's nose. He believed the stationmaster but didn't like the answer.

"Where are they now?" asked Sir Ian.

"I don't know!" cried the stationmaster. "Don't hit me again. They were taken away a few hours ago."

"How were they taken away?" asked Sir Ian.

"It was in a pickup truck," moaned the stationmaster.

"Why a pickup truck?" asked Sir Ian.

"I've told you all I can tell you," groaned the stationmaster, putting a handkerchief to his nose. "I can't tell you any more, believe me. "

"Yes," Sir Ian mused. He was observing the blood tricking down his gloved fist, "I believe I do."

Sir Ian and the other knights of Saint George, those knights who had been content to observe Sir Ian in action, left the station. The stationmaster had by now two black eyes and a broken nose.

CHAPTER EIGHTEEN

In a wine bar frequented by priestesses who worked closely with the High Priestess of Kiama, Nathaniel learned that the troublesome Knights of Saint George were heading his way. He overheard snide remarks to that effect and read the top layers of the speakers' minds for confirmation. Nothing had been made official yet about this occurrence.

It was clever of the High Priestess of Wollongong and a high-ranking member of the university staff to find a way to get those lunatics out of Wollongong, thought Nathaniel after reading the mind of a priestess fresh from Wollongong. He did this over a particularly fine local Riesling served up in a red glass.

I wonder if Elanora and her band have really headed south from Wollongong, he thought. *I suppose it is possible. Yes. They would have to have left soon after those stolen goods were recovered. After that, Wollongong would be too hot for them.*

He sipped his wine, conscious of being admired by two young priestesses who were wishing they were maidens and so free to date him. The colours in this bar were as mild as the jazz being played through the loudspeaker system. The priestesses giving him more information than they intended were all in white. There were mavericks dressed like peacocks like he was and thus standing out as they were meant to do because of their station in life.

I am wealthy by maverick standards, thought Nathaniel, drinking more wine. *Yet, because I am a mere maverick and not a maiden, all I have could so easily be ripped away from me. I must be careful.*

Nathaniel understood that he was only different from other mavericks because of his mental abilities and the Highest One's endorsement. He knew the Highest One could not only take her support away from him at any time but also have him demoted to knight. In that reduced state, he would lose the money he had accumulated as a maverick. Soon after that, he'd have to face death in some arena.

I *can't afford the Highest One to ever suspect I have betrayed her over the existence of Elanora*, mused Nathaniel, finishing his glass and putting it down. *Should I warn the High Priestess of Kiama of the coming of the Knights of Saint George? I can confirm for her that it is more than a rumour. But is this what the Highest of High Priestesses would want me to do? I had better find out.*

Upon returning to his hotel room, Nathaniel contacted the Highest One via computer linkup, asking what he should do. She replied, concerning the High Priestess of Kiama, that he should do nothing.

Hence, the first the High Priestess of Kiama knew about the Knights of Saint George coming into her city was soon after they had arrived.

A maiden was walking by a pub close to Kiama train station when, after a lot of banging and yelling, a local knight bolted out of the place, his grey clothes in disarray, his eyes wide open. Two more local knights followed, bumped into him, collected themselves, and all ran off as fast as they could past the maiden and away from the pub. The maiden noticed one of them had a bleeding shoulder wound. She sprinted off in search of a maiden officer. By the time the maiden officer and her robots arrived on the scene, the Knights of Saint George that had smashed up the knightly drinking hole and cut one of its customers had already gone.

"What was that all about?" asked the maiden officer of the bald, clean-shaven bartender. She looked around at broken tables and chairs.

"Those devils from Constantinople were after information," he told her.

"Did you give it to them?" she asked.

"There wasn't any to give," said the bartender. He shrugged his heavy shoulders, then put an ice pack on his blackening eye.

Further down the road from this pub, the maiden officer came across four more pubs that had been wrecked, other knights beaten up, and three sliced to death. In a nearby dragon watering hole, twelve dragons still wearing their pain collars had been slain.

The maiden officer put in her report. It went up the chain to the High One who asked her priestess servants for verification. She got that after the priestesses interviewed pub owners that had had their staff and customers terrorized or worse by those troublesome knights.

"Where are they now?" asked the High One of Kiama of a subordinate priestess.

"They are staying at a hotel," said the subordinate. "The hotel clerk phoned the constabulary about their signing in for the night. The constabulary then got in contact with me to pass this news on to you."

"Could the High One of Wollongong be responsible for them being here?" asked the High One of Kiama. She looked about at the comforting familiarity of the whiteness of her chamber and put a hand to her throat as if the High One of Wollongong was close by and might strangle her or slit her thick neck.

"I don't know if the Wollongong High One did this," replied the subordinate, "but that is possible."

****

The following day, after breakfast in their rooms at the hotel they were staying at, the Knights of Saint George concluded the dragons they were after had left the railway station's general area.

"We must widen our search," said Sir Nicholas to his fellow knights in the hotel's foyer where there were comfortable seats to sit on and group in a circle.

"Where to now?" asked Sir Ian. He had polished his helmet in the night so that it no longer looked weather-beaten nor smelled of dragon scales and flesh. His surcoat had also been cleaned so that it no longer had traces of blood on it.

"To the harbor," said Sir Nicholas. He touched the hilt of his sword for emphasis. "We must examine the ships coming in and the ones going out to sea."

An hour later, Sir Douglas came onboard a commercial vessel scheduled to make its way to Hobart. The captain, a prim and proper maverick in a white uniform with red stripes and a black beard, waved this knight away, saying, "Leave now. We must be on our way without delay. I don't have time for any foolishness."

To the captain's surprise, Sir Douglas marched up to him and, on the way there, withdrew his sword from its scabbard.

"You don't have time for me to do a thorough search of your ship?" enquired Sir Douglas, brandishing his sword.

"That is correct," said the captain, his nose in the air, no doubt thinking this was but an ordinary knight, and he was, after all, a maverick.

Sir Douglas smashed down with his sword on the electrical board, which powered the ship's propulsion and guidance system. Sparks flew up as the captain's face drooped. "Now, we have plenty of time to thoroughly examine your ship," commented the knight.

"I shall have you arrested!" cried the captain. It was then the second in charge that had come across the Knights of Saint George before and survived, pulled him by the arm aside and explained to him that these Constantinople knights were something special and not to be treated as if they were ordinary knights.

"We shall begin with your hold," advised Sir Douglas, sheathing his blade.

"There's nothing but coal down there," said the captain.

"We shall see now that you won't be leaving the harbour soon," replied Sir Douglas. He sighed in disappointment, finding nothing but coal in the hold and not a single dragon found anywhere onboard.

A navy ship had its maverick captain cut in two by Sir Ian when it was discovered that a gang of dragons had been employed to scrub the deck and load supplies.

"They're cheap labour," moaned a knightly sailor on behalf of his slain captain. "Those dragons don't sail with us. They never have. So, where's the harm? We don't have those renegades you want. So why slay our head officer?"

"It is not good policy to hire dragons," offered Sir Ian, wiping his bloodied sword on the sailor's shirt. "It would do you well to remember that."

Two derelict ships, long abandoned to rust away, were looked into by Sir Ian and Sir Douglas. All they found were a few scrawny rats and some seaweed.

"This is hopeless," said Sir Ian, brushing a rat off his surcoat.

"Not so," replied Sir Douglas, looking about at the gloom around them punctuated here and there by holes made over time by nature. "Have faith. We shall prevail."

Then the knights of Saint George examined the warehouses along the waterfront.

"We shall look here for information about the rusty old pickup truck our quarry was seen climbing into," advised Sir Nicholas before the search commenced. "The dragons we are after might also be here, in one of these warehouses, so keep your eyes open."

Several old, rusty pickups were discovered, but they did not bring the Saint George knights closer to their goal.

A disgruntled maverick trucker objected to having his cargo manhandled and so was slapped about by Sir Jacque.

"We are on a sacred mission!" cried Sir Jacque, punching the trucker in the stomach and then walking away from him.

Complaints about mistreatment were flooding into the High Priestess of Kiama's main Temple in telephone calls and letters sent by messengers. Her subordinates fielded the calls and letters, so she only spoke to important maidens and mavericks being affected by the knights of Saint George and read the more crucial letters.

"Yes," said the High One to the maiden officer in charge of the constabulary. "You can't interfere with what those Constantinople knights are doing unless I get permission from the High-est One. Yes, I have asked her via computer linkup, and she has told me to let those knights do what they are doing. Just do what you can to maintain order."

One letter sent by a maverick warehouse manager called for the knight that had trashed his place of business to pay for damages. The High One sighed deeply and mailed the invoice that came with the letter plus the letter itself and her request to pay to Constantinople where it might be acted upon. She replied to the manager that she had done so but did not know if and when the leader of the Order of Saint George was likely to act.

In desperation, the High One, feeling overwhelmed, called Nathaniel to her office in the hope he might have the answers to her mounting problems.

All that Nathaniel, the ambassador from the Highest of High Priestesses, could advise her to do was sit tight until it all blew over.

"I would love to send in my maiden officers with their robots to wipe out these crazy knights, but that would be going against the Highest One," she told Nathaniel. "That's something I would never do."

"That is something you cannot do and keep your posi-tion," he told her over sweet cakes and coffee in her office.

It was over drinks at a local knight's pub they hadn't to-tally wrecked, that Sir Ian came up with the idea of searching for information about the truck they were after in local used car and truck lots.

"If they didn't steal or borrow a truck from one of the ware-houses, then they bought one or rented one," reasoned Sir Ian.

"There are three used car and truck lots near the train sta-tion," said Sir Nicholas. "I remember walking by them on the way to those pubs. If we split up, we can cover them in no time. Also, we can have knights searching other locales for clues to the whereabouts of those dragons."

Two of the used car and truck lots hadn't sold a pickup in months. The third had sold one the other day and had the paperwork to prove it. Two mavericks accompanied by knights had bought it. The maiden owner of the lot thought they might have come from Wollongong even though the paperwork said Hobart.

"They could still have flown in by flyer from Hobart to do business," suggested the owner. "We get the occasional maiden or maverick from Hobart buying up local property. There's no law against it."

"So why do you think they're from Wollongong?" asked Sir Ian.

"If they did fly in from Hobart, why didn't they buy a brand-new pickup or one in better condition rather than an old rust bucket?" asked the owner. "Anyone who travels by air or sea from Hobart should have plenty of cash."

"That makes sense," said Sir Ian.

"And if they just want to see the property they've bought before handing it over to some local manager to handle for them, why not rent a hovercar instead? It would be cheaper." The owner was warming up to the idea that those mavericks were not from Hobart at all.

"Another good point," said Sir Ian.

"Which way did they go after they left here?" asked Sir Nicholas.

"Down the street to the left and then around the corner to the right," replied the owner. "After that, I wouldn't know. They could have been heading toward the train station."

"What else do you remember?" asked Sir Ian.

"One of the mavericks was dark-skinned, and the other was chubby," said the owner. "We don't get many dark-skinned mavericks around here. The plump one was a bit young to be so fat. Mavericks usually stay in good shape until they marry."

"What now?" Sir Jacque asked Sir Nicholas.

"We hire trucks and get back on their trail," said Sir Nicholas with rising energy in his voice. "We're getting close. I can feel it. What would they want with that pickup?"

The owner shrugged and said nothing. She didn't know. Apart from transporting dragons somewhere, Sir Nicholas and the others could only guess.

"From Kiama train station, they were no doubt headed for one of the smaller towns," said Sir Ian, "Possibly Gerringong or Berry."

"Why those smaller towns?" asked Sir Nicholas.

"A good place to hide," said Sir Ian.

"First, we search Gerringong and then Berry. The hunt continues." Sir Nicholas was pleased, and so there was a rare smile on his face.

"I'll send a runner to gather up our fellow knights," said Sir Ian and did so.

****

Not far away, Sir Naylor and Sir Remy, with other knights of Saint George, came across Kiama knights digging a ditch for the local council. Sir Naylor asked them if they had seen any stray dragons. The Kiama knights answered in the negative. Then one knight asked Sir Naylor what business was it of his since this was Kiama and not Constantinople. For his insolence, he was introduced to Sir Naylor's sword, which sliced him from shoulder to waist.

"Are there any further objections to us being here?" Sir Naylor enquired.

"No trouble," said one of the local knights, laying down his shovel. "Pickaxes and shovels aren't much good against swords carried by well-trained warriors. I think you know that."

"You are being sensible," reasoned Sir Remy, "though I was hoping you had more of a fighting spirit like your dead comrade."

CHAPTER NINETEEN

On the sixth underground level of the Mitchell Library in Sydney, Megan found the first edition of Charles Dickens' *A Tale of Two Cities* right next to Aldous Huxley's *Brave New World*. There was also a first edition of 21st century New Zealand author Lyn McConchie's *Farming Daze* and *Coals and Ash*.

Furthermore, there were abstract paintings from the 1930s and 1940s. A couple of these paintings depicted horror scenes of what the Japanese might do if they invaded Australia. One had a maiden menaced by a grinning Japanese soldier brandishing a knife. Of course, there hadn't been an invasion, but the fear of one had undoubtedly been there during the Second World War. Fear had made the Japanese of that era seem less than human.

War! Megan thought in disgust. *Thank the Goddess, we don't have that anymore.* Then she remembered Amelia, Dreadnought's wife, and how she felt that the two months a year of death in the arena and elsewhere for knights and dragons being no better than any war except in its horrid continuance. *Have we really contained evil, bottled it up*, wondered Megan, *or merely spread it out like butter on bread?*

After more rummaging around with Malcolm's help, Megan found a metal box containing a computer disc the size of a button. By the look of it, she knew it was from the middle of the twenty-second century. A computer disc reader device was beside the box. The box's content and the reader would need careful analysis back at the university by a maiden computer expert Megan knew before it gave up its secrets.

It took a week for the computer expert to get the reader to play the disc.

To appreciate the material, Megan sat in a university room with a white wall to project the reader's results onto while she listened and watched. The disc had a number of files, some of better quality than others. She had on her head the translator that would help with archaic English. She began with file one.

There was a film showing black planes with the Globalist flag on them flying over Berlin. There was also a grand parade followed by speakers on a raised platform calling upon all in the crowd of onlookers to praise the Globalist movement. Megan noted smiles among those in the group dressed in black and frowns expressing displeasure by those wearing more colourful clothing.

This is how it started, thought Megan. *This was when the civil wars that ravaged Europe in the late twenty-first century began.*

The film concluded with the Globalist motto, in blazing red letters across a white screen: *Erase the past for a better tomorrow. European history ends now. It never happened. There is only and forever Globalism.*

The Globalists would never get their united world under one black-gloved fist, thought Megan. *Though diminished, the world would eventually be united, but under more benevolent rulers, in the name of the Great Goddess.*

File two dealt with the middle twenty-first-century uprising in London and the twenty-second-century troubles. The film shown ran from the major issues raised by both sides to the attempts at peaceful resolutions to the fighting. Megan noted that, by the mid-twenty-first century, promises made by the British parliament to the general population of Britain had been broken too many times for further assurances to be believed. The authorities could not protect the children, and this angered the Nationalists who raised their fists against the Globalists. There were threats and counter threats. The results of all of this were street brawls, as shown to Megan. Here, the emerging Globalists had knives and batons, and the developing Nationalists had cricket bats and cricket balls.

Megan watched as pubs were blown up, and in retaliation, pig's blood was splattered all over the walls of certain places of worship. There was a king who might have brokered peace between the warring factions, but he proved to be unworthy of the task. Megan saw his limp message to the people to unite and to behave. She sighed in disgust. From her earlier readings of this period, she knew that he would go down in infamy for his failures as a monarch.

File three nearly brought Megan to tears. In a documentary, a team of Globalists blew up Big Ben, the grandest of London clocks, in the name of "Out with the old and in with the new." She had no answer for why it moved her so except she was used to witnessing death, but not the simple-minded destruction of something centuries old that need not be destroyed.

On file four, there was a movie about Twenty-second Century Nationalist/Traditionalist hero Wilder Smith. Born in a ghetto in London, he had gathered together a group of followers that became an army. They called themselves The Royal Blues. The deep blue of the sea was their chosen colour, together with the type of sailing vessel that had taken on the Spanish armada, many centuries ago, and had won. *Wilder was one of my childhood heroes,* thought Megan.

One thing Wilder was famous for was using stun grenades against enemy Globalists then burying them alive. He was once quoted as saying, before burying a group of them, "You want our soil? You don't deserve it, but we will give you a portion of it. We are that generous."

Megan was mouth-dropping surprised at seeing a small, weedy man with a big grin announcing on camera that he is Wilder Smith.

The history books Megan had read as a child had him as being much taller and more powerful looking. She concluded that how he looked fitted into the times in which he lived much better. Born in a bad part of overcrowded London, he would have grown up malnourished and therefore small and weedy.

Megan enjoyed seeing The Royal Blues with their flag on display and pints of lager in their hands. She wished she could raise a glass to them.

The film came to its conclusion with a set of artist drawings, depicting what happened to her hero and a large body of his people. Wilder Smith died in a famous charge against a Globalist army that resulted in neither side being able to claim victory. According to the film, The Royal Blues cause persisted and, for decades to come, remained a problem for the Globalists.

Megan knew that London was eventually destroyed. However, the memory of the Globalists and their enemies lived on in these discs and in the history books.

History isn't as simple as working out who the good guys were and who the bad guys were, Megan reminded herself. *It's never like that.* Even so, in her mind, she did take sides.

Megan understood that many of the Globalists were fighting for space, though they were, at the same time, using up what they had at an alarming rate. Therefore, it went against Megan's Goddess faith to ever think of them as the good guys since she knew that overpopulation was at the heart of everything that went wrong. Unfortunately, those against Globalisation were slow to act, which made the civil wars inevitable.

On file five, there was a documentary on Australian inventor Thomas Cooper. He invented both the stun gun and the stun grenade in the belief that his inventions would be used to pacify hostiles and prevent bloodshed. He was later dismayed to discover how Globalists in France, Germany, and Belgium were using them. They were also being exported from the USA, where they were manufactured, to mainland China, India, and Mexico, where they were used in whatever manner the governments in those countries chose to use them.

According to the documentary, Thomas Cooper did not live long enough to see how Wilder Smith and his Royal Blues were using stun grenades. It is uncertain, according to the documentary maker, whether or not he would have approved.

"You can't ignore the past," said Thomas Cooper in an interview in Sydney's old town hall building. "It will bite you in the bum if you do. Most people won't stand for anyone taking who they are away from them. Hell, I want to be me, don't you?"

Megan smiled at this. She would have liked to have met Wilder Smith and Thomas Cooper, though she had no idea what she would have said to them.

File six showed men in black outfits and masks using flamethrowers on poorly constructed housing in a slum district in Indonesia. Men, women, and children in tatters fled their rat-infested homes, fighting one another to get away. The cameraman then moved his camera up, away from the turmoil created by the fires to the towers of glass and steel where the elite lived, overlooking everything.

An unseen commentator stated in English that the people in the towers had organised the slum's burning because they had grown sick of looking down and seeing such squalor. He also noted that those in the buildings, those with the flame throwers, and those fleeing for their lives were all Indonesians but of different classes. The ones with the flame throwers did what they did because they didn't want to be downgraded and lose what they had. *Are we really better than these tower people?* Megan wondered. The film ended with the man with the camera running from armed security guards.

This was in the late twenty-first century, thought Megan. *This was a time when, in Indonesia, the rich were exceedingly rich and the poor very poor. We don't have poverty like that anymore, thank the Great Goddess and, of course, the Highest of the High.*

Moving on to file seven, there was film footage of the United Nations building in New York blowing up. Moments later, a crowd in the street cheered. "No more Globalism!" a young man wearing a USA flag on his jacket shouted. Later, Megan knew, the whole of New York would be destroyed.

Megan viewed file number four a second time because of Wilder Smith, then took the disc out of the reader and put it back in its box. Next, she spent two hours typing up a report in her office on what was on the disc, a report she'd hand to Jens the following day.

****

A few days later, Malcolm took a priestess diplomat to Rome. She was sent to advise the Highest of High Priestesses that all was now well in Wollongong and that the city wasn't falling into ruin. To some extent, this had already been done by earlier reports. Even so, the High One of Wollongong felt the diplomat necessary. It was a more personal touch. She did not want to be replaced as High One through some misunderstanding. She had faith in the diplomat to see that this did not happen.

Wollongong harbour was once more teeming with vessels, and trade was going back to the way it had been months ago. However, it would be a while before the fish came back.

It was a long journey to Rome for Malcolm and Priestess Elba, the diplomat. "I want to go via Egypt so I can visit old friends there," she told Malcolm. He didn't see a problem with this. It would make the journey longer, but if he wasn't paying personally for the extra refuelling stops, then that was fine with him. She was a skinny, dark-skinned priestess whose pencil-thin nose poked out of her white priestess hood.

She had light blue eyes, which was surprising. "If you don't mind my asking," Malcolm said, not long into the trip, "why are your eyes blue?"

"I have some French blood from long ago in my family line," she told him, smiling and shrugging her shoulders.

Malcolm wasn't the history buff his wife, Megan, was. Still, he knew enough to say that Egypt's cities, including Cairo, came close to annihilation during the religious wars of the twenty-second century. Some had been knocked about but never nuked. Cairo had been spared by both sides. This meant that Cairo had, for centuries, bustled with economic activity and that

220

it still contained some of the more intriguing mysteries from the long-dead past, including the origins of the belief in the one true Goddess.

The trip to Cairo from Colombo was not without incident. Deadly radioactive winds over Somalia and Saudi Arabia threatened to bring their flyer down, but Malcolm made sure not to alarm Elba to their peril. If they were forced to land in that desolate and destructive wasteland, covering what were once two countries, they would not have lived for long. There was a safe air corridor in all this mess. It was a case of finding it, which he did. Later on, Elba said to Malcolm of their trip through this gap, "I am grateful your craft has some protection against radiation or, coming into Cairo, we would have glowed in the dark."

They touched down at Cairo airport and made their way on foot to the centre of the city. Small stalls everywhere were selling everything from oranges to delicate carvings of the Mother Goddess with the head of a cow. The smell of various different kinds of spice, including cinnamon, was heavy in the air.

"I grew up here," said Priestess Elba to Malcolm as they walked. "When I was ordained a priestess, I wanted to travel and see other lands. My skills at negotiation have allowed me to do that, but every once in a while, it's always nice to come home."

A maverick vendor tried to sell Malcolm a bag full of black peppers and then a jar of fresh olives. The fellow was so insistent that Malcolm half wished the translator he wore had been switched off. The colourful outfit the vendor wore to prove he was a maverick had faded. Two young girls ran past them, and an old maverick in clothes that hadn't faded hobbled along on a stick, no doubt heading for one of the many cafes in the area. It was all so much white noise and exotic smells to Malcolm until he heard a whip crack. It was so sharp it cut through the other sounds around him.

Malcolm looked on as a dozen red dragons with pain collars on were marched past him by four knights and a young maverick in a colourful robe to an office building in need of repair.

There was a second crack of the whip delivered by one of the young mavericks, which made Malcolm shiver.

"Why so jumpy?" asked Priestess Elba.

"We don't use the whip in Wollongong," said Malcolm.

"The whip is only there to get their attention," assured Priestess Elba. "They're dragons from Greece. They're hard workers, but they can be a little difficult to handle. You can't use their pain collars all the time to get them moving, or you'd end up with dead dragons."

Malcolm watched the dragons as they were urged by the young maverick cracking the whip to move broken stone onto a truck. The dragons weren't being hit by the whip, but they looked resentful of its use. One hissed at the whip carrier but still got on with what he was supposed to do.

"Are they paid?" asked Malcolm.

"Of course!" cried Priestess Elba. "And they have lodging as well."

"But the whip...," began Malcolm.

"It's just noise, nothing more."

This is slavery, thought Malcolm, *but is the way we treat dragons in Wollongong much better?*

Priestess Elba introduced Malcolm to the High Priestess of Cairo and other dignitaries, but despite their friendliness, he couldn't get his mind off the whip and the dragons. His eyes darted this way and that. He didn't say anything to Priestess Elba, but he was glad to leave Cairo for Rome.

Rome was everything Malcolm remembered it being from his last trip there. He had to wonder about the Colosseum and how it was being used in the May and November games. *You're getting soft*, Malcolm told himself as he escorted Priestess Elba to the residence of the Highest of the High, *and you better keep your mouth shut about things that do not concern you like what happens to knights and dragons in the games.*

Over tea and biscuits, Priestess Elba, with Malcolm present, told the Highest of the High everything the High Priestess of Wollongong wanted her to say then added, "The Knights of Saint George are active in Australia."

"Yes. I have a report from my diplomat Nathaniel about that. It seems they have moved on from Wollongong to Kiama." The Highest One shrugged her shoulders.

"That's true. You could recall them from Kiama." Priestess Elba put this forward in the slim hope the Highest One might act. She was thinking of property damage.

"And spoil their fun?" The Highest One smiled. "No. Wollongong needed shaking up, and the same can be said for Kiama."

"Highest one," interjected Malcolm, who had been silent until now, "what about the loss of life?"

"They were mostly lives that would have been lost in November. That's hardly a serious matter." The Highest One wondered why Malcolm was bothering her with trivialities.

"That's true, Highest One," agreed Priestess Elba.

"I stand corrected, Highest One," said Malcolm because he knew that is what he had to say to keep his position. Megan would not like it if the Highest of the High, on a whim, downgraded him from maverick to knight. It would be the ultimate disgrace, and he knew, come November, he wouldn't last ten minutes as a knight in the arena. He might be physically fit enough, but he understood he hadn't had the training required for survival there.

"I tire." This was the Highest One's way of saying the audience was over. "Go now. We'll talk more tomorrow and without your flyer escort. You, Malcolm, are to return to Wollongong with my thanks to your High Priestess. Elba shall stay here a while."

The following day, the Highest One wanted Elba to tell her, in confidence, all the dirt she had on the High Priestess of Cairo and the High Priestess of Wollongong.

"Which is in better control of her subjects?" asked the Highest of the High.

"The High Priestess of Cairo is more the traditionalist," said Priestess Elba guardedly.

"That doesn't answer my question," observed the Highest of the High.

"It does in a way. The High Priestess of Cairo is ridged and entirely too conventional in her approach. The High Priestess of Wollongong is less traditional and is thus more flexible. The High Priestess of Cairo is all about keeping order and good discipline. The High Priestess of Wollongong is all about the prosperity of her city above all else."

"So, you favour the High Priestess of Wollongong?" There was surprise in the Highest One's voice.

"Wait a month, and we'll know how truly good the High Priestess of Wollongong is in her position," advised Priestess Elba. "Don't forget Cairo is much older than Wollongong, so you would expect Cairo's ruler to acknowledge those deep roots. On the other hand, Wollongong only came to prominence with the fall of the city of Sydney."

"What do you think should be done with your recent pilot, Malcolm?" The Highest One leaned forward, interested in Priestess Elba's answer.

"He is of little consequence when it comes to matters of religion or politics." Priestess Elba waved a dismissive hand. "I'd let him be and forget his momentary indiscretion. Despite his artificial hand and leg, he is useful in his present station in life. To demote him to knight would be a waste of resources."

"That is also my conclusion," said the Highest of the High.

****

Soon after Malcolm left for Wollongong, there was a dragon rebellion in Cairo. They smashed their pain collars with rocks. This resulted in some, though not all, being electrocuted by the feedback. Then they trashed their living quarters and went on a rampage throughout the city.

They found the maverick that had cracked the whip earlier on and took it off him. "Dance!" cried one of the dragons, and so the maverick was forced to do so at the whip's sound. After a while, a dragon, tiring of hearing this maverick whimper as he moved about, snapped his neck with his claws.

Robots were sent to deal with the dragons. A dozen of the dragons were shot dead; the rest surrendered. Those that gave themselves up were hanged, for all to see, in the city square.

A day later, in his cottage, Malcolm read about the goings-on where he had recently been in a newspaper account and was dismayed. *Could this happen in Wollongong?* He wondered. He didn't want to be around if it did. He was having breakfast with Megan. He showed her the article about the Cairo dragons running amok and said, "What do you think?"

"Stay out of Cairo if you can," she answered. "They don't know how to treat dragons."

"But are we any better?" he asked.

"We don't have dragons rioting in Wollongong, so I suppose the answer is yes," replied Megan.

The article mentioned the Cairo authorities obtaining more dragons from Greece, so their rebuilding projects could continue. There was also a note about a Wollongong maverick salesman willing to sell the Cairo maidens and mavericks superior pain collars for their dragons at a reasonable price. They were pain collars guaranteed not to break if set upon by rock-wielding dragons.

Two weeks later, Priestess Elba returned to Wollongong. She met up with Malcolm in The Great Grape. At the time, he was having a quiet drink with Megan.

"I smoothed things over with the Highest of the High for you," said Priestess Elba to Malcolm after he introduced the priestess to Megan. "You're too gentle for politics, but you are a better pilot than the one I had hired to get me back here."

"What do you mean too gentle?" asked Megan, adjusting her glasses to better glare at the priestess.

"It seems your husband is bothered when a few knights and dragons, here and there, are executed," observed the priestess. "He also doesn't like it when mavericks use the whip to get more work out of dragons."

"I suppose I am soft," said Malcolm, not wanting to get into an argument with someone who had recently spent time with the Highest of the High and could have him reduced to a knight.

Both Malcolm and Megan sighed in relief when Priestess Elba left. Some of the other patrons did the same. No doubt, they were also glad to see her go, but no one said anything. Now, there was more chatter and fewer maidens and mavericks looking into their drinks as if answers to world problems could be found there in the Riesling or Claret.

"There's something cold and calculating about her," said Megan after sipping some of her Riesling.

"You mean Priestess Elba?" asked Malcolm.

"Yes," said Megan. "Her coldness and calculations will either see her dead someday or in a position of great power."

"I suspect it will be great power."

"You can tell me what you said to the Highest One when we get home." Megan's eyes narrowed. "You can't be in too much trouble if the Highest One allowed you to leave Rome, but I'll need to know." She grasped his hand tightly and added, "I don't want to lose you."

"Good to know," replied Malcolm, smiling at her and then gulping down some wine. Megan gripped his hand for longer than it felt comfortable.

CHAPTER TWENTY

The farm was both a blessing and a curse. The homestead and milking shed were on a hill that looked down on, according to Ronald, good pasture land. There was a stream in the little valley that Ronald also found agreeable. The farm was far enough away from the seaside for Elanora and her rebels to smell the grass and eucalyptus leaves rather than sea salt. At night, if the wind blew the wrong way, they could smell cow dung.

Ronald suspected that those who were with him for days in that cramped cattle car would have had enough of the odour of cow manure. Of course, that was not to be since cows tended to produce a lot of it, and it was not possible to have a dairy farm in the Berry area or anywhere else for that matter without those particular beasts providing plenty of dung.

"Do we have to have cows?" moaned Eric, after looking at the ones that came with the property.

"Do you drink milk?" asked Ronald.

"Only when I have to," replied Eric.

"Then we have to have cows," said Ronald, "for when you have to do so." He hissed in amusement and poked out his forked tongue at Eric. Rather than react, Eric walked away.

Elanora's knights and dragons found work on the farm both testing and promising. Ronald tried to remember how everything was done. The years he had spent dodging the law in the big city of Wollongong didn't help. He had to think back to his youth.

The first morning there, Ronald sat on a stool in front of a cow in the milking shed with fellow dragons and knights looking on. Elanora was seated next to him. She wanted to find out all she could about this milking business. There was a metal bucket positioned just right, Ronald hoped, to catch the milk.

"We'll call this cow Bessie," said Ronald to those looking on. "I'll see if I can get any milk from her."

It took a while, but Ronald, with gentle pulls from his claws, got a few squirts from Bessie's udder that unfortunately landed in Elanora's face rather than in the bucket. Elanora hissed in irritation, wiped her face on her coat sleeve, then smiled and said, "Now, Ronald, please get the aim right."

Ronald persisted and so was able to do so. "When we can arrange for electricity, we will be using the milking machines," he told Elanora, "but they can break down, and so we'll all need to know how to milk by hand. The cows need to be milked, one way or another, of a morning and a couple more times a day. The morning milking needs to be on schedule, too. Otherwise, they can get sick and die from mastitis. They have dry periods, but we won't worry about that for now."

"What time in the morning is best?" asked Elanora.

"It's five o'clock," said Ronald, "if my memory serves me. We were late this morning, hence the noise from the cows that woke us up. Now I'll show you how to operate the milking machine. I can't get it started, but I can still show you a thing or two. Then back to milking by claw or hand. All the cows we have need to be milked, not just Bessie."

"What else needs doing?" asked Elanora.

"Fences have to be mended, and we have to get rid of the Scottish thistle encroaching on our land. We will have to spray. I notice we do have cans with spray nozzles in this shed for such a purpose. Not sure if the cans should be kept so close to where we milk."

"Anything else?" asked Elanora.

"Lemon and orange trees are in the back of this cowshed. They need attending to if we want fresh lemons and oranges," said Ronald, his claws open. "The eucalyptus trees are not too close to the house. They will give us shade in summer. Oh, by the way, cows don't live on grass alone if you want good milk from them. They need grain and mineral supplements as well. Salt licks are a treat for them. We should be able to make our own butter and cheese. That is worth looking into. Yes, there is a lot to be done."

Both dragons and knights were put on fence-mending duty by Elanora.

None of them, including Ronald, could escape exhaustion from the kind of labour they were not used to doing. Toff grumbled, and so did Craft.

"We can get ointment for blisters," Elanora said to both Toff and Craft. "From what I have read, though, your hands will eventually harden, and you will be free from them."

"I remember getting blisters once from overtraining with a sword and also the first time I had to dig ditches," Aayan told her.

"This farm, it will all be worth it," said Ronald in a cheerful voice to all the others at suppertime as they gathered around the kitchen table on sturdy but ancient chairs. "What we put into this property, we will get back tenfold."

Everyone looked at the bread and cheese on offer to be washed down with water. The bread and cheese were what Craft, disguised as a maverick, had bought at a grocery store in Berry. All at the table were too tired to have much of an appetite. They nibbled on the bread and cheese. Most of it remained on their plates to be eaten in the morning before they renewed work.

Aayan and Craft took turns as lookout mavericks. If there were visitors, at least one maverick had to be seen in charge. Otherwise, suspicions would mount, and everything would fall apart.

"No one in any town could believe that any farm could be run by knights and dragons alone," Gregory told Craft and Elanora.

"We're not supposed to be all that bright," reasoned Craft in his tattered greyish knight clothes. He pointed in a dramatic gesture to his maverick clothes that were drying on a line, after a wash, back of the house, and added, "but put me in a fancy suit and see me change!"

"Yes," agreed Gregory, "intelligence up twenty points at least."

"Remember," cautioned Elanora. "A maverick presence at all times is a measure to keep the farm and to save our lives. Please treat it as such. Aayan is now on duty. Tomorrow you, Craft, will be."

****

One week after they were at the farm, Aayan and Craft purchased dragon short pants and T-shirts for the dragons from a Berry store. When not seen by strangers, Elanora was happy to walk around in short pants made for dragons as well as a T-shirt. If seen thus by someone not in her group, it would be too obvious she was both a female and a dragon, and she understood that could be fatal, not only to herself but also to her companions. She hated wearing a bulky coat, especially in summer, but it was the only way she could think of to disguise who she was from those who might, through her, do them harm.

New clothes were also bought for the knights to wear as knights and new hats and shirts purchased for the pretend mavericks.

****

Two weeks after Elanora and her gang had settled into their farm, a nearby maiden farmer sold a dozen bales of hay to Craft for five dollars to keep the cattle in feed until the farm could once more produce hay of its own. She also provided salt licks for free in the way of a friendly gesture.

"It's a good farm you have. It just needs a bit of effort put into it," said the maiden, smiling up at Craft. She was small, plump, and in her twenties, but since she was a maiden, the plumpness didn't matter. She could not be made to fight dragons, though that could happen to Craft if locals wanted to turn a made-up maverick back into a real knight. *I must lose weight*, thought Craft as she walked away. *She's all right the way she is, but I'm not. I wish I didn't love food so much!*

Another maiden farmer sold a blue heeler to Aayan for two dollars. She was a tall woman with green eyes and long red hair waving about in the breeze. She was, at first, taken aback by his features enough to blink twice at him. Dark skin was unusual in a local maverick, but word had gotten around that he and his companion maverick were from Hobart. Perhaps it was less unusual in that part of Australia. Of course, he and his companion and the rest calling the farm home were not really from Hobart but Wollongong.

"You'll need a dog," she told him. "And blue heelers are the best."

She had with her a bluish animal that jumped about on a leash.

Before coming to this farm, Aayan had only eaten the occasional stray dog that wandered into the rusting hulls of abandoned ships. He got the impression, though, that this particular creature was not for eating. Since he couldn't ask Ronald if it was true that this blue heeler was necessary without giving away that he was new to farming and a dragon knows more than he does, he nodded in agreement.

"I'll name him Hector," said Aayan, taking the animal's leash off of the maiden. The dog looked up at Aayan with its big brown eyes and wagged its tail.

"He's still young," said the maiden. "He has a lot to learn, but he already has the instinct to round up cattle. I can also sell you three great sacks of apples for a dollar. Are you interested?"

"Yes," replied Aayan. "Three sacks for a dollar would be fine."

Once more, he wished he could have talked over this purchase with Ronald, but he was supposed to know more than a mere dragon. He handed over the two dollars for the dog and the one dollar for the apples.

"I'll be on my way," said the maiden. "I'll see that a knight servant delivers the apples to you in the morning." She shook his hand, and then, surprisingly, for Aayan, she kissed him on the cheek before leaving. "We're friendly here to new mavericks in our district," she added as she walked away. He touched his cheek where she kissed him and smiled broadly. "Oh, my!" he cried softly to himself. Maidens are not supposed to kiss knights, but then again, he was dressed as a maverick.

Aayan took the dog into the house. There, Ronald was delighted to see the animal. "A blue heeler!" Ronald petted the dog softly with his claws. "Now, we have a real farm!"

Aayan mentioned the apples, and Ronald told him he could probably have bargained her down to fifty cents for the lot, but a dollar for large sacks of apples was still a bargain.

Hector, the blue heeler, turned out to be a useful and friendly cattle dog that didn't discriminate between knights and dragons. He'd go up to anyone for a pat and was happy to gulp down leftover cheese and bread. The apples were good for eating.

At the nearest grocery store, Craft traded milk from their cows for flour and cans of Irish stew, dry dog food for Hector, plus two old swords. The proprietor, a plump maiden in her forties, was glad to meet Craft and do business with him.

"We need new blood around here," she told Craft. "You're most welcome as long as you intend to stay."

"That is our intention."

"Good. You'll need the electricity put on. Would you like me to see to it? I could have some locals at your place tomorrow if you like."

Craft thought about this a moment. He didn't like doing it without either Elanora's approval or Gregory's nod, but it did sound like the right thing to do. Yes, it did make sense. "All right," he finally said. "If you can do that for me, I'd be grateful."

Neither Elanora nor Gregory saw a problem in what Craft had done. The electricity was put on in the house and the shed by competent maverick technicians.

Craft bought a television screen at the local electronics store to keep up with what was going on globally.

"We don't get much local news," said the maverick store owner with the greying hair who sold Craft the screen, "but it's good to keep up with what those folks in Wollongong and Kiama are up to. By the way, you'll need a telephone. Would you like me to arrange that?"

"Yes. That would be good." Craft reasoned that not having a phone would have seemed too strange for the locals.

A telephone line was reinstalled, together with a new phone from the maiden who did the reinstalling.

"The phone line had simply been disconnected when the last owner left," the maiden told Craft. "If you're hard up for cash, we can put what I've done on credit for a month. You should be on your feet by then."

"That would be good of you," said Craft.

"I know how it is to move into a new place," offered the maiden. "In time, you'll discover us locals aren't so bad."

Meanwhile, Elanora was helping Eric dig a new well for fresh drinking water. "Hauling buckets up from the stream in the valley below the house each day," Ronald advised Elanora, "won't look right to the locals if we continue doing it."

Milking time did not agree with Phips and Toff who preferred late nights rather than early mornings.

"These early starts are killing me," moaned Phips to Toff.

"It's still better than a sword in the guts," offered Toff.

"Only a fraction better," groaned Phips. "My fingers feel half-frozen, and I'm supposed to play with cow udders?"

"Playing with them will warm up your fingers," reasoned Toff. "That's how I'm warming mine up. Mind you, I'd kill right now for something hot to drink."

Those mornings were also a struggle for Ronald and Eric.

"I have forgotten about mornings and lack of sleep from getting up too early," yawned Ronald as he looked at getting Bessie milked. "I suppose in my youth before they sent me to Wollongong, I was always getting up early, so I was more used to it and also more acquainted with the cows I was to milk."

"This is a strange way to live," observed Eric. "The cows don't seem to mind who does the milking as long as they have the right touch. Claw or hand just so long as it's firm, but not too firm. I think I'm getting the hang of it."

A short distance away in the shed, Elanora walked briskly up to Gregory, who was making a cow unhappy with his attempts at milking her. The sounds the cow was making, not mooing gently but straining its lungs in loud bleats, would have been evidence enough. The futile attempts by the cow to kick Gregory made Elanora act quickly. Sooner or later, no matter how much dodging Gregory did, the cow would move forward fast enough in the right direction to land a blow with its leg. There was also the possibility the cow might step on Gregory's foot and do damage that way. Elanora didn't want either a hurt cow or an injured knight. She got Gregory off the milking stool and took over. She wasn't the best at milking, but at least the cow being treated by her didn't mind her being there. The kicking stopped.

"I suppose milking's not my line of work," said Gregory.

"I have always enjoyed the crisp, cool air found at the beginning of the day," Elanora offered. "Maybe that's why I am better at this than you are."

Aayan and Craft also turned out to be no good at milking.

"I'm tempted to dress as a maverick and go into Berry to nick stuff to keep my hand in," Toff told Gregory and Elanora that night during supper.

Gregory and Elanora were against the idea and for good reasons.

"Where have you come from?" asked Gregory of Toff.

"What do you mean?" asked Toff, startled by the question.

"Quick!" Answer the question!" demanded Gregory.

"What question?" asked Toff, shaking his head.

"If you come into town, you must have come from somewhere," advised Gregory, his voice rising and speeding up.

"If you meet up with a maiden officer with robots here, and you can't answer the simple question of where have you come from, then you're done. They'll have you in custody. Mavericks that are strangers here don't materialize out of nowhere. They have a place to have come from and a purpose in being here. This isn't the city. This is a smaller community."

"What about Aayan and Craft?" asked Toff, in a small voice sounding hurt.

"They have a cover story, and they backed it up with the purchasing of the farm," said Gregory, calming down, his voice softening. "It's as solid as we could make it."

"I could go with him," suggested Craft.

"And you'd be taking the pickup into town?" asked Gregory.

"I suppose so," said Craft.

"And if they link the pickup and you to the theft of a few wallets and purses, what then?" asked Gregory. "And what would Toff be to you? Maybe he's your cousin or something?"

"My cousin? I suppose so," said Craft. "But there needn't be a link between me, the pickup, and any theft."

"Why not?" asked Gregory. "How many thefts and how many thieves do you think would be in a town like Berry?"

"We need the goodwill of the maidens and mavericks of this area. We do not want them suspicious of us or why we are here. And we already have plenty of stuff." Elanora glared at Toff to get her meaning across to him.

"Okay!" cried Toff, throwing his arms up into the air in surrender. "You win! I won't do it! I won't take the pickup and go out as a maverick. It's just, despite the hard work around here, I get bored sometimes."

"I understand," said Gregory. "This is a different kind of life, isn't it?"

"Yes. Don't worry. I'll keep my bad habits to myself. I'll get used to it." Toff looked crestfallen. His eyes were downcast, and his face drooped.

"We'll all get used to it," offered Gregory, patting Toff on the shoulder.

****

The local priestess visited the farm. Her name was Anna, and she was originally from Athens. She was thin with her white garment loose fitting. After looking around, she said to Craft, "I love what you have already done to the place, but if you need help with anything, all you have to do is get in touch with me, and I'll roust the community to lend a hand."

Craft further noticed that this priestess was old with hollow cheeks. Her eyes, though, were sharp hazel as if they were the part of her that wouldn't age. She had a threadlike smile that could calm a rampaging bull, as legend had it among the Berry folks.

"I hope to see you, your partner, your knights, and dragons at Mass this coming Sunday," she told Craft. "My little temple is not far from the grocery store. It's made of stone and wood with comfortable seating. You can't miss it. I know I should have seen you sooner about this."

"We'll think about it," said Craft.

"Think about it!" cried Anna, sounding hurt. "It is your spiritual life I'm talking about. You also must see that your dragons and knights have what they need from me. You must go to temple unless, of course, you have a good reason not to do so. Are you ill? Is anyone on your farm sick? If so, we do have a marvellous doctor."

"All right!" howled Craft, going red in the face. "We'll be there! We'll go to temple."

"Good," replied Anna. She gave one of her thin smiles and left.

Craft told Elanora about this going to Mass business. At first, she wasn't sure if mixing with the locals in such a way was a good idea. But Gregory, when asked by Elanora in Craft's presence, reasoned that if they were to stay for any length of time, they must not appear to be too mysterious and foreign to the families that had worked the land for generations.

"If we don't have this sort of contact with these temple go-ers," warned Gregory, "they'll know something's wrong with our setup, and the constabulary at Berry will investigate us."

"Well then, we will have to be sure to behave the way we're supposed to behave," reasoned Craft, putting hand to chin.

"Yess!" Elanora hissed with emotion. "We will have to act proper, or at least the rest of you will. I won't go. I can hide away in our house. The coat is too absurd to wear right now. But the rest of you must go."

Sunday Mass involved prayers and a couple of sing-alongs enjoyed by all the parishioners, including the knight and dragon labourers. It began at nine in the morning and went on until eleven.

Eric looked at the dragons from the other farms. Many of them were leaning forward when the priestess spoke, indicating they took their religion seriously. He understood from the preach-ing it promised a better life for them after death. They were bet-ter dressed than Wollongong dragons. They didn't have holes in their short pants or their shirts. He concluded they were still at the bottom of the social ladder, but life could be worse for them.

"This community is solid, dependable, and friendly," said Craft to Aayan, "It may be years before we would need to move on."

"I hope you're right," replied Aayan.

****

The third week at the farm Susan, a young freckle-faced maiden from a nearby property, came to warn Craft, who was dressed as a maverick at the time, that well-armed and crazed knights claiming to be from Constantinople were causing trou-ble in Gerringong.

"I don't know what it's about," Susan told Craft, "but twen-ty Gerringong dragons and a couple of Gerringong knights have been murdered. And no, the games haven't started early. From what I can gather, they are not justifiable killings."

"So they just turned up in Gerringong?" asked Craft, astonished.

"They ran amok in Wollongong and then Kiama," added Susan. "It was on the news. If they come here to Berry, I suggest you hide your dragons. I will hide mine."

"What are they after?"

"They want fugitives from Wollongong," said Susan, shrugging her shoulders. "I know that shouldn't concern you because you're all from Hobart, but even so, it's best to be cautious. You don't want to lose your field hands over some misunderstanding."

"We don't want any trouble."

"The same was said about the maidens and mavericks of Gerringong. Look! We need you here. We need all the farms in our district up and running to meet our milk quotas. There are twenty of these insane knights. So, for the Goddess's sake, be careful."

Craft passed on the information to Elanora, Gregory, Eric, and Ronald.

"I thought we'd be sssafe here," said Ronald, hissing. "I like this farm."

"I knew it would only be temporary, but I thought we'd at least get a good six months out of the place before being forced to move on," said Gregory.

"I had plans for improving the milking schedule, "said Ronald. Elanora patted him on the shoulder.

"I hope I didn't help dig that well for nothing. We did hit water," Eric told Ronald. "I have put quite a bit of myself into this farm."

"There are plenty of these knights, and they like to kill," said Gregory to Eric in an apologetic voice. "We haven't trained for ages. We're not in good shape. We don't stand a chance. We must get out now."

"If we run, they will find us and end our existence," observed Elanora, who had been quiet up till now. "I am sick of running. We may expect help from other farmers and their farm-hands if we hold our ground."

"What kind of help?" Ronald asked. "I want to stay."

"At the very least, they will keep out of our way. If they are also besieged, we may be able to get them to resist and buy us time." Elanora rubbed her claws together in contemplation.

"Why wouldn't they just hand us in?" asked Gregory.

"They don't know who we are. To them, we are farmers and farmhands from Hobart, right?" Elanora smiled, hoping this was still the case.

"Those farmers won't hold them up for long," said Gregory. "Those Saint George knights are said to be mean and good at what they do."

"Those farmers may hold them up long enough," said Elanora, smiling. "Do you still have that gun?"

"Yes, but we only have three bullets in it, and there are twenty of them." Gregory shrugged his shoulders, knowing the gun would never do as the only solution.

"Anything to reduce the odds has to be a good thing," said Elanora. "They're not in Berry just yet. We have preparations to make."

"Like what?" Gregory asked.

"We need at least a dozen flashlights. The more powerful they are, the better. We also need more holes dug." Elanora's mind raced with ideas as she scribbled them down with a pen on a pad she took out of a drawer.

"How many?" Gregory asked.

"At least a dozen," said Elanora.

"We also need our mavericks to become even friendlier with the locals. Can you do that, Craft? Is that all right with you, Aayan?" Elanora knew for any plan to work, the locals, at some stage, would have to be involved.

"For a couple of dollars, we can have drinks at The Flowing Red wine bar in Berry," suggested Craft.

"We haven't visited the local butchers," said Aayan. "That's another meeting place that might come in handy. It may be too soon to visit the maiden who warned us."

"Yes," agreed Craft. "She's young, and her parents no doubt own her farm. She was kind in telling us about those horrid Saint George knights, but her parents might not be as friendly to relative strangers."

"Yes. We must avoid antagonizing the locals at all costs, but I could have a word with Berry's priestess," said Aayan, smiling broadly. "That shouldn't do any harm, and it might do some good. In times of strife, we must look to the temple for spiritual aid."

"Flashlights and holes," muttered Gregory, frowning. "I don't get it."

"You will," answered Elanora. "We also need bows and arrows. And we could do with as much practice time with the bow as we can get."

"Arrows won't get through their armour," advised Gregory. "From my time in the arena, I should know something about armour."

"Yes," agreed Elanora, "but if we manage things right, they will be useful."

"How?" asked Gregory.

"I once read an article about the ancient battle of Agincourt," said Elanora. "The article was written by a maiden called Megan. Anyway, if we can manage to do what the English archers there did at that battle, we may stand a chance."

"What did they do?" asked Gregory.

"They slowed down the enemy, or at least they did with the help of the terrain," said Elanora, contemplatively. "Now, if we can slow down our enemy, by use of arrows plus picking the right terrain, we could have a chance."

"So running is definitely out then?" asked Craft.

"Even in the pickup, we'll only get to the next town along the coast before we got pulled over by a maiden officer in an official vehicle with two robots to make sure we don't run any further," reasoned Elanora. "We don't have any papers, fake or otherwise, stating we have business in the next town. That's highly suspicious! We won't be able to afford to buy property, and they don't know us there. If we try to hide, the locals will find us and turn us into the authorities. We could try doubling back to Kiama and then to Wollongong, but I can't see that being a good idea."

"And what you have in mind is better than running?" asked Craft. "Not that I am keen on running."

"I hope so, "said Elanora, "I would like to promise success, but that wouldn't be realistic. At least here, we do have a property and a believable story for the folks of Berry. We don't have to steal from them to stay alive like we might have to if we went elsewhere, and that can be a big advantage."

"We do have enough fuel in the pickup to get us to the next town, but virtually all our funds are tied up in the farm," observed Gregory, hands open and no doubt warming to the idea of staying. "If we run, there's a good possibility the Berry constabulary will go after us because we'll look guilty of something. It's best not to risk that."

"Right now, we're on friendly terms with those Berry officers," said Craft.

"You've spoken to them?" asked Elanora.

"A maiden officer spoke to me," said Craft. "It was when I was trading milk for supplies. I was nervous but I kept it together. She wants us to stay, and it would look highly suspicious if we suddenly left."

"We can buy more food. We can build up a supply of canned beef and beans for when there's a siege," said Eric.

"More food would be good," Craft reasoned.

"We need more buckets," added Elanora, writing that down. "They must be made of steel and not plastic."

"We'll get them, too," said Aayan. "I believe our credit is still good in Berry."

"I suppose we should have more food now that I think about it, "Elanora revealed with a smile. She was glad at the input and wanted to show it. "We also need bottles of whisky and three ten-gallon drums of gasoline."

"How many bottles of whisky?" Gregory asked, frowning. "This is stretching our credit! And I don't believe this is an appropriate time to get drunk."

"Ten bottles should suffice," said Elanora, writing them down.

"What's the whisky for?" asked Gregory.

"It is for drinking," said Elanora. "When all ten bottles are empty, we'll fill them up with gasoline."

"I'm not drinking gasoline!" protested Craft.

"I doubt that's what Elanora has in mind," said Gregory shrugging his shoulders. "At least I hope that isn't what she is thinking."

"Hector will let us know when someone is coming. He's a good boy!" Aayan patted the dog, and the animal wagged his tail in response.

As agreed upon, Craft and Aayan did go to The Flowing Red, a wine bar in Berry, to hang out with the locals and try to garner useful information and form acquaintances. It had red carpeting and redwood furnishings. Jazz music played from a recording. Apart from the music, it got quiet. Conversations ended when Craft and Aayan entered until they ordered wine and sat down on the stools provided. Then conversations started up again.

"Are you the new mavericks from Hobart?" asked the barkeep, a brawny maverick with a flowing red moustache.

"That's us," said Craft.

"I was wondering when you'd be paying my establishment a visit," said the barkeep smiling through his moustache. "We're always glad to have new regulars."

"We're still settling in," said Aayan.

"Yes," agreed the barkeep, "it does take a while."

"So you're still with us," said a twenty-something maiden who was the real estate agent that sold them the farm.

"Good to see you again," said Craft, smiling.

"I travel down to Berry every once in a while, to see how the folks here are doing," the real estate agent told them.

"We needed a friendly face," said Aayan.

"We can be friendly." This came from a blonde maiden farmer in her twenties dressed in black.

"I'm glad to hear it." Aayan smiled.

"We don't need the kind of trouble they're having in Gerringong," said a heavily built maverick farmer dressed in leather dyed red.

"Does anyone know what all the fuss is about?" asked Aayan.

"I haven't a clue," said the maiden farmer.

"They're looking for dragons that don't exist," said the maverick farmer. "At least, they don't exist in Gerringong, and they don't exist here."

"Those Saint George knights will kill any dragon they come across on the off chance it's one of the ones they're hunting for," the maiden farmer told them. She turned to Aayan, frowning at her revelation. "Enough of us have dragons working on our properties for it to be a worry."

"It's a crazy business," said Craft. "What do you think we should do if those Saint George knights show up here?"

"There's nothing we can do," the maiden farmer replied. "They're professional murderers."

"Maybe some of your knights and dragons can fight," said Craft.

"They wouldn't be a match for those Saint George knights." The maiden farmer was definite about this; he could see it in her eyes. "Those killers from Constantinople love their trade in blood and guts too much."

****

The following day, Aayan and Craft visited the butcher who regaled them with all kinds of gossip but had little to say about the Knights of Saint George and the town's pending doom. He was a jovial, balding maverick in his mid-forties with a maiden and two children. He couldn't see why anyone, including the Knights of Saint George, would want to bother either him or his family. His wife loved him and was going to keep him, so he couldn't imagine too much trouble coming his way, or so he told Aayan.

Berry's priestess thought a prayer to the Goddess and a letter to the High Priestess of Kiama might help alleviate the spreading fear. Despite what Priestess Anna had heard about Gerringong, she wasn't yet ready to believe anything bad would or could happen to her town. They had met her outside the chemist shop, and she wanted, most of all, to assure them they had not made a mistake in choosing the outskirts of Berry for their home.

"Life is good here. I can't see it changing much at all," Priestess Anna told them.

CHAPTER TWENTY-ONE

Sir Nicholas cleaned his blade with a rag. He looked at his knights and smiled. Two farmhouses were burning in the distance. They were the last of a row of farmhouses to be visited by him and his warriors. Those who had engaged Gerringong knights to work on their farms only fared a little better than those who had employed dragons. Dragons were cheaper to hire, but not when the Knights of Saint George were on the move. Having a couple of dragons around could cost you your very existence. Even without the dragons, your life could be in danger if you say the wrong thing, whatever that might be.

"They're not here," said Sir Jacque, breathing in the smoke from a recent blaze he had created. He found the smell sharp and exhilarating.

"We press on." Sir Nicholas was firm in this. It could be seen in his eyes.

"Very good," said Sir Douglas, adjusting his helmet.

There was blood, gore, and the severed head of a silvery dragon on the green near Gerringong's tavern. Sir Nicholas kicked the head into the street. A stray dog followed it as it bounced and rolled.

"Over there!" cried Sir Douglas, pointing. "Aren't they local maiden officers?"

"Yes," agreed Sir Nicholas, "they have their robots with them, but they won't bother us on our sacred mission. They are not authorized to do so. The High Priestess of Kiama has made it clear in broadcasts. They have orders from her not to interfere. "

"Of the dozen farms at Gerringong we've raided in search of those renegades," said Sir Jacque, "five are still serviceable with staff physically capable of work. I suppose that's a good thing."

"If they want fresh milk in Kiama," said Sir Douglas, "those city folks are going to have to rely on Berry for a while."

"After we get through with Berry," reasoned Sir Jacque, still breathing in smoke, "Kiama city folks will have to forget about fresh milk for the foreseeable future if, of course, we don't get more cooperation from these locals."

"Yes," agreed Sir Nicholas. "These farmers and their pet dragons must know where the renegades are."

Meanwhile, cows from Gerringong were making their way from the wrecked Gerringong farms to Berry, smoke and flames urging them on. They were being rounded up by the Berry locals and kept in a cooperative shed to be milked daily until they could be safely returned to Gerringong.

It was now the sixth week since Elanora and her knights and dragons moved into their farm. Four extra holes, deep enough to be wells, had been dug, but Elanora knew that wouldn't be enough, so she had six more shallow holes added to the score. They had food, flashlights, and bottles filled with gasoline with cloth wicks inside but with part of the wick sticking out. There were five bows and forty arrows. Everyone under Elanora had been trained in the use of the bow and arrow. They also had buckets filled with gasoline, a handful of kerosene lamps that could quickly be lit, and extra bales of hay.

"What more can be done?" asked Eric as he patted Hector, the blue heeler.

"Nothing," said Elanora. "We wait."

Aayan was in Berry with Gregory buying dog food for Hector and salt licks for the cows when the Knights of Saint George, in three trucks, drove up to the centre of town. This was just after ten in the morning. They got out of their vehicles and were about to cross the road to the Lions pub, a knight's hangout, when two maiden officers and four robots came out of the nearby constabulary building.

"Please state your business in coming to Berry," said one of the maidens. She was a lean woman with a sharp eye. Beside her, two robots with blinking red eyes studied the Knights of Saint George.

"We are after the renegade dragons," replied Sir Nicholas. "We believe they are being aided by dishonourable knights and mavericks."

"You won't find them here," said the other maiden who was shorter but just as slim. The robots beside her were also blinking.

"We will look and see," replied Sir Nicholas, a hand on the hilt of his sword. "You have your duties, and we have ours."

"We protect the people of Berry," said the first maiden officer.

"And we have our sacred duties," replied Sir Nicholas, bowing at the maiden officers. They nodded in return but did not smile.

Sir Nicholas, Sir Jacque, Sir Naylor, and the others, after listening to the maiden officers, shrugged their shoulders and were about to move off to the Lions pub when a shot was fired. The bullet came from the direction of one of the robots, but Gregory was responsible. He was hiding behind a dumpster near a robot. Gregory fired again. Sir Nicholas and Sir Jacque crumpled to the ground. Both hit in the chest. It was so sudden and so startling that this should happen, the maiden officers having no jurisdiction to order their robots to act in this manner and there being no obvious other culprit in sight.

Gregory, unseen in the confusion he'd created, scampered away with Aayan, got in the pickup, and drove off. This left a mess for the maiden officers who had no intention of attacking the knights but who would now have to defend themselves with their robots.

Angered by his leader's death and unfamiliar with how best to fight against robots, Sir Naylor charged, sword in hand, and was cut down by two bullets before coming close to doing the walking machines any harm. Three other knights, following Sir Naylor's example, also rushed at the robots. One managed to damage a mechanical hand with his blade. Unfortunately for him, it wasn't the hand holding the firearm.

A maiden officer, the one who had first spoken to the knights, was cut down by a knight before a robot could save her. When it did act, the result was the demise of three knightly warriors. However, two of Sir Jacque's knights got into their trucks and ran down the four robots. Bullets from the walking machines, before they were crushed, killed one of the drivers. The remaining maiden officer fled. The unpleasant grinding sound of her robots crumpling under those wheels would remain with her for a very long time.

Aayan and Gregory got back to the farm as fast as they could. Word was already spreading among the Berry locals about a maiden officer's death and the robots' destruction.

"Goddess damn those Knights of Saint George!" cried the local barkeep of the wine bar, curling his red moustache with his fingers then raising a fist. No one was quite sure how old he was, but according to his moustache, he was most likely in his late thirties.

"Now, what can be done?" asked a farmer maiden. She pointed to having her glass refilled.

"I don't know," said the barkeep, shaking his head. He sighed deeply and then refilled the glass. "We've lost what protection we might have had. I don't know what's to become of us. I really don't know at all."

"We know what happened in Gerringong," said the maiden, taking a sip of her drink. "And I know we won't get any help from Kiama unless the High Priestess decides to give it to us. We'll have to arm ourselves as best we can."

"That's dangerous talk," advised the barkeep.

"These are dangerous times," replied the maiden, who downed her drink and motioned for another refill.

****

When Gregory got back to Elanora's farmhouse, he informed her of recent events.

"I saw an opportunity, and so I used the gun," he told her. "I know I was taking a big chance going into town with the gun, but everything has worked out to our advantage. I only have one bullet left. That's a worry, but we now have less of these Knights of Saint George to contend with."

"Hopefully, you'll be able to make excellent use of that one bullet," reasoned Elanora.

The phone rang, and Craft answered it. On the other end was a nearby maverick farmer.

"What can I do?" asked the maverick. "Those Saint George knights will be here soon. I haven't done anything wrong, and neither have my field hands, but I'm scared."

"Do you have dragons in your employ?" asked Craft after being prompted by Elanora to ask.

"Yes," replied the maverick.

"Arm them with clubs, pitchforks, staves, and whatever else they can lay their hands on," said Craft. "If you have keys and can get their pain collars off them so they can really fight, all the better."

"But that's illegal!" cried the maverick. "If I take off those collars, I'm as bad as the renegades they're after. Besides, only the local hospital staff would know how to remove those pain collars. I thought you'd know that."

"Just thinking about possibilities," smoothed Craft, realizing his knowledge of being a maverick wasn't as extensive as he would have liked. "Do you have knights in your employ?"

"Yes," said the maverick, "but I only have a few."

"Good," replied Craft. "You'll have no trouble arming them, and I wish you good luck."

"Have my knights go up against the Knights of Saint George? They'd be slaughtered and damned for all time if they did. I can't ask that of them," said the maverick. "Those knights have the blessing of the Highest of the High to act the way they're acting. My knights only have my orders. Besides, we've done no wrong so far. Surely, those Knights of Saint George will know that and do us no harm. If we start now, if we act illegally, where will it end?"

"Yes," agreed Craft, sighing deeply, "Where will it end?"

Craft hung up the phone.

Elanora's farm was the eighth one heading south from town. Two of the farms the Knights of Saint George were likely to visit first would show no resistance to them and would likely be all right. They had never had dragons as workers. The others would have to fight. Elanora wanted the mad knights to arrive at her farm either late in the afternoon or at night.

After one in the afternoon, Hector's barking announced the arrival of the first lot of survivors from one of the other farms. First, the cattle arrived. A stray maiden turned up. Finally, three Berry knights appeared.

"We've been burnt out and chased out!" The stray maiden coughed as she approached Craft. Her name was Cybil, and she was a frail woman in her thirties with long, silky yellow hair. She was puffed out from running.

"How did it happen?" asked Craft, concern in his voice.

"Our knights and dragons couldn't cope," Cybil told him, her voice now steady. "Our knights tried reason because they were reluctant to do battle with them, but there was just no reasoning with them."

"You're safe now," said Craft, showing her and the knights where to step as they made their way up the hill to the house. It wouldn't do for any of them to fall down a hole. Elanora and Eric put the cattle, with their own, in the barn.

An hour later, more refugees arrived. There was one maverick in his forties footsore because his pointy shoes were for admiring and not walking. Two knights, in their twenties, that had sustained minor injuries hobbled along. The surviving maiden officer from Berry, the one who couldn't understand why one of her robots would shoot a Knight of Saint George when she had given it no such instructions, also turned up.

The refugees looked to Craft in his maverick finery, who told them, "You can stay here, but you have to make yourselves useful if any of us have any chance at survival. This farm will be defended."

By four o'clock, Elanora and Gregory could smell smoke. It was visible in the distance as rising black clouds. A half an hour later, Priestess Anna arrived with six boys and six girls from the town plus two maidens, including Susan, the young freckle-faced maiden from a nearby property who had warned them of the approaching menace of the Knights of Saint George. She was upset over the death of her parents. There were also two Berry dragons. There were more cattle that, for their protection, had to be squeezed into the barn. This meant taking out the milking devices and stools and hiding them in the brush. Hector, for his own safety, had to be put in with them.

Aayan, looking like a maverick and knowing Elanora's overall game plan, helped Gregory by putting the newcomers to work. Some added more brush to hide the holes that had been dug. Others sharpened knives and axes. The kerosene lamps were lit and kept where they could easily be grabbed and used. Cloth soaked in gasoline was wrapped around the heads of arrows while fires were lit and maintained outside the house.

"More firewood!" cried Aayan at one stage. "Also, we need buckets filled with water from the well placed against the house and barn."

"Anything else?" asked Priestess Anna, sweating profusely from labour she wasn't used to.

"Yes," replied Aayan. "The buckets containing gasoline are to be kept well away from the house and barn but still handy. Near that tree will do for now."

The Berry dragons had cuts and bruises, but nothing serious. They still carried the pitchforks that had so far kept them alive.

They were nervous about being with knights in a combat zone, their eyes darting this way and that as a knight walked past them.

"It's weird to be fighting alongside knights rather than against them," said one Berry dragon, shaking his head, swishing his barbed tail and gripping his pitchfork. "These pain collars we still wear hurt when we do fight. They are removed when we go into an arena in May or November. But this isn't May or November, and we have to do battle with the damned things on."

"I'll get them off you," said Elanora to the Berry dragons.

"It will be all right fighting alongside the knights here," assured Ronald, his forked tongue poking out. "They, and the maidens and mavericks, know the real enemy are the Knights of Saint George."

There were also Berry knights who did not want to fight alongside dragons but could see no alternative.

"Once their pain collars are removed," asked a Berry knight, "what makes you think they won't attack us and then run off?"

"We all have a better chance of living through this," hissed Ronald, "if we work together. See? I am collarless, and I am not attacking you."

Meanwhile, the maverick with the pointy footwear became a gibbering wreck, and so was of no immediate use to anyone. He sat down under a tree and muttered, "Why? Oh! Why?" It was as if he expected the Great Goddess to drop the answer into his lap.

Cybil, one of the maidens, was in shock, her eyes widened by what she had recently witnessed. "They burnt it," she moaned softly, her voice rising as she continued to speak. "My farm! They burnt it all. Gone! All gone!"

Elanora noted that those who had only ever viewed violence from a comfortable distance, such as in the stands, looking down at knights and dragons doing battle, were now being confronted with the reality of it.

The maiden officer, who was used to having two robots do her fighting for her, gaped open-mouthed at Craft when he handed her a shovel. "What is it for?"

"You can hit Saint George Knights with it," Craft told her.

She blinked, nodded her head, and smiled sheepishly. "Why didn't that occur to me?"

Susan, who had been listening in, said, "I want one, too!" Craft gave her a shovel and handed Cybil one as well.

Just as the sun set, the three trucks containing the Knights of Saint George arrived. They parked in the valley, got out, and began what should have been a short, easy walk to the house. There was a cry, and the clank of armour as one of them fell into a hole followed by another and then another.

Once past the holes, the knights drew their swords to do in whoever came within reach. On Aayan's signal, they had lights in their eyes from the twelve children's flashlights. Blinded for at least two minutes, they stood like statues. Gregory and Elanora loosed flaming arrows. Most could not get past the armour, but one managed to go through an eye slit, into an eye, and then into a knight's brain. Another stuck in a knight's throat, choking him to death as he tried to pull it out.

Three bales of hay that had been soaked in gasoline were set alight by the two Berry dragons and rolled down the hill. The bales collided with three of the advancing knights, bowling them over. They struggled to get the hay off and to put the flames out on their armour. Coughing ensued. They either roasted alive from the heat and died that way or were overcome by the toxicity of the burning hay.

After this incident, it took the remaining Knights of Saint George a good twenty minutes to regroup and resume their journey up the hill.

The ten bottles filled with gasoline were thrown, smacking into shields and flaming but otherwise doing no harm to the Constantinople knights other than spooking them.

A Saint George knight that got further than the others received a bucket full of gasoline splashed in his face via the eye and mouth slits in his helmet. This was Toff's doing. It was followed by a kerosene lamp smashed by Phips over the unhappy knight's head. The flames and the pain sent the knight crazy. He blindly slashed away with his sword, mindful of where his enemy was even if he could no longer see, even if his nose and lips were agonizingly melting away with his eyes, and his brain was barely functioning in a haze of red. All he knew was to move and slash, move and slash. His sword in movement was all that was left, that and his training with it.

In his madness, the Saint George knight took out Phips' stomach. Both good, loyal Phips of the missing ear and the Saint George knight fell to the ground, screaming. Neither could be saved. Both, in their agony, as they lay dying, prayed for a better life in the hereafter. Gregory stabbed both to death with a pitchfork. It was the merciful thing to do.

Toff saw it all and was so shocked he couldn't move. He remembered the time he had been in an arena facing death. He recalled those corpses piled on top of him, and it being hard to breathe. The horrid stench of blood, urine, and body parts crept down his lungs. He had played dead. He'd gotten out. Now here he was, having seen a good friend of his butchered, and for no good reason. The horror had returned!

Gregory slapped Toff in the face to bring him back to his senses and said, "Please stay alive, Toff, we need you. We'll mourn for Phips later."

The remaining knights, wanting to enter the house by force, were greeted with thrown bottles filled with gasoline. The wicks had been lit, so the bottles, when they hit, spilled burning liquid onto armour. The Saint George knights retreated while three others remained trapped in the holes. A flight of flaming arrows followed those in retreat down to the valley.

There were laughter and threats aimed at the Saint George killers from knights, dragons, and maidens who had been sure they would die that day. Elanora found it was good to hear those sounds, though she wanted guards posted in case the enemy tried something in the dark. She also called for the fires to be maintained and a watch kept on the barn. By now, everyone on her side realized that Elanora was organizing and giving the orders rather than either Aayan or Craft. They were merely passing along the information. It was also becoming obvious she was no ordinary dragon.

"They're not through with usss yet," Elanora advised Gregory, Eric, Aayan, and Craft.

"Yes," agreed Gregory, grimacing and shaking his head. "Reputations are at stake, and too much of their blood has been spilled. They have to attack again."

Elanora marvelled at how light the casualties so far had been though she regretted the loss of Phips of the missing ear. Making sure everyone was fed now became the number one priority.

There wasn't anything stronger than coffee, but there were plenty of beans and canned meat.

Ronald got together some flour, salt and water and made a dozen dampers, Australian style bush bread on the kitchen table. He got the children, who were frightened at first because of his silvery scales, to help.

"Please lend a hand," he said to a scruffy looking boy who was watching him make a damper. "We have people to feed."

"But you're a dragon!" cried the boy.

"I won't eat you," said Ronald, "but it would be good if you and your friends could be my helpers. Lots of people here are hungry."

"I suppose I could try," mused the boy, scratching his head. "I'm not supposed to help dragons."

"I won't make you," replied Ronald, "but if you could put aside what you've been told about my kind, we'll all get along much better. See? It's flour and water. Easy! Would you like to have a go? You can work up one end of the table, and I'll work up this end. Is that okay with you?"

"Okay," said the boy in a timid voice. Once he made his first damper, the other children joined in. They stayed up the furthest end of the table from Ronald at first but slowly inched further and further down until they were close to him.

Once enough dampers were made, Ronald and the children warmed them over an open fire until they were ready to eat.

The smell from the cooking dampers so intrigued the children they forgot all about once being scared of their silvery companion.

Maidens, who usually expected a better meal, appreciated Ronald's fresh bush bread with what else was on offer.

"A simple repast," said Cybil, taking a chunk of bread, sniffing it and putting it to her lips, "but oh so good."

"I bless this food and all who partook in its preparation," offered Priestess Anna.

Elanora was happy with Ronald's contribution; she could see how valuable it was and beamed at him. He smiled back at her, wrapping his silvery tail around his legs. She noticed he was still a little shy around her. She envied his tail, thinking hers was too spiky and so rather ugly.

"You and your little helpmates are champions!" declared Craft as he tasted a damper.

"Why thank you," said Ronald. "They are good kids."

"Always thinking of your stomach." Gregory crossed his arms and smiled.

"My stomach? I look after it, and it looks after me." Craft grinned. "Right now, we're delighted."

"I will arrange for a prayer meeting for the children to settle them down for the night," said Priestess Anna. "All who want to attend are free to do so."

Gregory, Craft, Aayan, and Toff attended, and so did the maidens and the one authentic maverick. All the dragons, including Elanora, declined.

"Prayer isn't for me," said Elanora apologetically to Priestess Anna. "Perhaps I can believe in the Great Goddess and the land after death, but not as it has been preached to me in the past."

"Perhaps I can help you find your way back to the Great Goddess," offered Priestess Anna.

"Anything's possible," said Elanora, shrugging her shoulders, "But for now, the answer is no."

"We need all the help we can get," said Gregory as he joined the others in prayer.

****

At dawn, a Saint George knight arrived to set fire to the barn. He had figured out where the holes were located. He had a torch he was going to light.

Unfortunately for him, Hector barked. The cows mooed, making a fuss, and thanks to Eric, the Saint George knight found the business end of a pitchfork stuck in his chest. Despite the armour, Eric was able to push it in deep enough to make the intruder cough blood. Elanora bowled the intruder over with the swing of her spiked tail, and he was sent back down the hill with the pitchfork still stuck in him. An hour later, he died.

By five in the morning, the knights still in holes were rescued by three of their comrades. Over coffee, Sir Ian planned the next phase of the operation against the farm.

"We shall split our force in two," said Sir Ian, his eyes narrowing. "We will attack from two different sides of the hill. They will pay for what they have done to us. I will need two of you to drive into Berry and pick up three pikes and three spare guns from the armoury inside the constabulary building."

"But we're not allowed to use guns," pointed out a knight. Sir Ian snarled at him and struck him in the chest with a mailed fist.

"We use guns now," grunted Sir Ian. "We will apologise to the Great Goddess and whoever else we need to say sorry to later. At the sound of gunfire, some of those in the farmhouse will surrender."

"We will take prisoners, then?" asked a knight.

"No prisoners," said Sir Ian flatly, crossing his arms and frowning. "We are not even going to spare the children."

At seven, the Knights of Saint George started their march up the hill. Flaming arrows flew, but they were not the distraction they had previously been. The bottles that had once contained whisky and then gasoline had all been smashed from the earlier battle, and so Molotov cocktails were out. It now wasn't dark enough for the flashlights to be useful.

The children were given apples to throw at the enemy. One knight lost his balance because an apple hit him on the helmet. He then found an axe slicing into his throat. This particular knight had a gun. Craft grabbed it off him. Another of the Saint George knights had his pike struck from his hand via a well-aimed apple. Then his pike was used by Eric to cleave into both his helmet and skull.

Craft put two bullets in a Saint George knight that had a pike then got shot to death by a Saint George knight with a gun. Surprise registered on Craft's pudgy face as he fell. He no doubt wondered for, but an instant before death, if there will be plenty to eat in the afterlife the priestesses had promised to him before he had turned into a renegade.

The knight that killed Craft advanced on Toff. He was about to be shot when Gregory used the remaining bullet in his gun to save Toff's life by blowing the aggressor knight away. Both the Knight of Saint George and Toff fell to the ground. The Saint George knight bled out, and Toff assumed the foetal position. Toff was physically unhurt, but his mind had gone back to him being trapped under all those bodies.

Gregory shook Toff and slapped his face but couldn't get him out of it. All he could do was throw away his empty gun and pick up the gun left by the dead Saint George knight. It still had bullets. Gregory couldn't comprehend what was happening to Toff but knew it wasn't good. He also realized the fight wasn't over, and he had to get back to it.

Meanwhile, the genuine maverick, who had been panicky and useless yesterday, was now a firebrand. He had turned a corner in his mind. Gregory had seen this before when the bullied had had enough and had become suicidal for revenge. With nothing but a stave, the maverick took on a Saint George knight with a sword. He gleefully knocked the astonished knight around with what amounted to a wooden pole, doing no damage to the knight whatsoever. The knight laughed heartily at this pathetic assault; then, his sword did its work, and the maverick's colourful outfit was sliced up. Finally, the owner's arms, legs, and chest went their separate ways.

Gregory shot the victorious Saint George knight and then had his gun shot from his hand. He was about to die when Elanora tripped up the offending Saint George knight with her tail and brought her axe down. It went through helmet and bone. She dropped her axe and grabbed the dead knight's gun.

Elanora looked about. Only six Knights of Saint George were standing, and all they had were swords. One advanced on a five-year-old maiden. Elanora fired and saw both Saint George knight and sword tumble down the hill. She fired again, stopping a Saint George knight from carving up the Berry priestess.

The five Berry knights, armed with swords, proved to be no match in close combat for two of the Saint George knights. The Berry knights were swiftly cut to pieces.

Elanora shot one of these Saint George knights. Gregory bested the other, his sword carving through the attacking knight's neck. With satisfaction, he watched the head leave the body and tumble down the hill, followed by the rest of the knight, spraying blood everywhere.

A Saint George knight advanced on Priestess Anna and was stopped by the maiden officer, Cybil, and Susan. All three used their shovels to disorientate him while Eric swept him off his feet with his tail, and then delivered a fatal blow to the knight's head with an axe.

Sir Ian, the last standing Saint George knight, advanced on Eric. Two bullets later, delivered by Elanora, and Sir Ian was lying on the ground in his own blood, dying.

Elanora was about to put a third bullet in Sir Ian when Eric hissed. "Stop! It'sss over! There's no point in killing the dead."

"Yes! Save the last bullet!" Elanora felt the bloodlust in her and hated herself for it.

Gregory picked up Toff and took him inside the house. He tucked him in bed then sought Elanora for her advice.

"What can be done for Toff?" Gregory asked Elanora. "I can't see any bleeding or bruising. I don't know what's wrong."

"His mind needs time to heal." It was all Elanora could think of to say.

"I don't understand," said Gregory. "He's been in danger before. We're always in danger."

"Not like this! There's a big difference between being a thief and a scoundrel and being a front-line warrior."

"He is a good thief, but he had been in the arena," reasoned Gregory, crossing his arms. "He's been in this sort of battle before."

"He wasss in the arena once, or that's what I have been told." Elanora hissed. "I imagine it is not easy being in such a terrible place."

"He was there one time only," said Gregory in a contemplative voice, running his hand through his hair. "He ran from it. He never wanted to go back. I believe he was meant to be either a good thief or a maverick. He never should have seen his friend go the way he did. Phips and Toff had been good mates."

"And how do you feel?" asked Elanora.

"I'm all right." Gregory blinked twice, taken aback by the question. "I have to be all right. I saw more combat than Toff, and I'm older. I ran, too, when I knew the whole thing stank. I could never score fifty dragon kills like Dreadnought. I was trained to take the loss of comrades, so I'm fine."

"We have to dispose of the bodies strewn about and quickly," said Elanora. "The less the outside world knows about what has happened to the Knights of Saint George, the better."

"You can't keep what happened here a secret for very long," advised Gregory, looking down.

"Of course, I don't expect it to remain a secret forever, just long enough for us to find a way out of the mess we're in," offered Elanora. "I notice the holes came in handy. They will do so again with the burials."

"Yes," agreed Gregory. "We'd best get to them right away."

Just then the ex-maiden officer approached Elanora, looking worried.

"Is Toff badly hurt?" she asked. "I saw him taken away. I know a little first aid from my training as a maiden officer."

"He'll be fine," said Elanora.

"He'll recover?" asked the ex-maiden officer, still looking worried.

"It's in his mind," offered Elanora. "Why the interest?"

"I don't know," said the ex-maiden officer. "There's something about him that reminds me of me when I was first made a maiden officer. Besides, I can talk up a storm when I want to, and that might be good for him."

"Yes," agreed Elanora. "No doubt when he is feeling better."

Later Elanora saw the ex-maiden officer sneak into the room where Toff was kept. She didn't say anything to anyone about this, figuring, so long as her interest in Toff didn't interfere with this ex-maiden officer's ability to help out, it was none of her business. What's more, having someone other than Gregory talk to Toff might bring him around quicker.

****

After all the dead had been laid to rest, Gregory, Eric, and Aayan took one of the Knights of Saint George trucks into town. They loaded it with as many supplies as it could handle. They had money from the maidens and mavericks that had sought shelter on their farm plus cash from the Saint George corpses.

They emptied out two grocery stores and the butchers. They took medicines and bandages from the shelves of the local chemist shop and picked up bottles of scotch, bourbon, wine, and beer from the various drinking establishments. No one opposed them. Shop owners and their assistants who were still around meekly accepted what money was given to them and were grateful for that. What few people were left alive in town didn't want any more trouble. When Gregory, Eric, and Aayan got back, everyone was pleased with their haul.

"We can stay here for quite a while," said Eric to Gregory after examining the booty.

"We won't starve," replied Gregory.

"We're in a trap! Sure, we won't starve, but they will come for us. We have killed fifteen **Knights** of Saint George. That is something their **Order** will not tolerate." Elanora felt she needed to bring them all back to reality.

"What can we do?" asked Eric.

"I hope we have enough time now to come up with a solution that doesn't get everyone killed," said Susan.

"I hope so, too," replied Priestess Anna. "May the Great Goddess protect us."

All who had survived the siege wanted some assurance they had a future somewhere. It was true that neither the High Priestess of Priestesses nor the Order of Saint George was likely to be pleased with them. The fact that the killings by the Knights of Saint George would now not extend to the next town past Berry was going to be noticed. All looked to Elanora for answers.

"Those who feel they can sneak back to Berry and resume their lives there should do so. We have no intention of stopping you." Elanora felt this was something she had to say. She needed nothing but loyal followers.

"I can't go back to my former life," the now ex-maiden officer told everyone. "No way could I account for the deaths of those Knights of Saint George at the hands of those robots. My name's Celine, by the way. No point calling me the maiden officer anymore, as you have done so far, since I can no longer be a maiden officer. I must face facts. I cannot go back to my former life."

"I don't believe going back is an option for any of us, including the children," said Cybil, and there was the murmuring of general agreement. Cybil looked toward Aayan who took her hand and kissed it.

"We're weaker if we split up," reasoned Aayan. "We should not make it easy for them to pick us off."

"I agree with Aayan," said Eric.

"I do too." Gregory didn't believe any of those returning to their farms would be any safer than if they remained where they were. Susan looked to Gregory for assurance and pecked him on the cheek. He was taken aback by this gesture.

Elanora smiled at Ronald and took his claw in her claw. He smiled back and they kissed one another on the lips. It was something that was a long time in coming both knew, but it felt right. What's more, none of the others raised an objection, including Eric who frowned, less than happy about this happenstance. Secretly, Eric wanted Elanora for himself, but now he realized that was not to be.

Then the phone in the living room rang, startling everyone to attention. Aayan picked up the receiver, and the voice on the other end asked to speak to Elanora.

CHAPTER TWENTY-TWO

Malcolm and Megan were open-mouthed surprised by Nathaniel. At seven o'clock at night, the Highest of High Priest-esses' right-hand maverick was at their front door, paying them a home visit. "Please come in," was all Malcolm could think to say to the maverick of mavericks. This visit was most unusual since Nathaniel rarely left his hotel room except on official business or so wine bar gossip went. *How could this be official business?* Malcolm wondered.

"I need your help and your discretion," Nathaniel told Malcolm as he settled into a plush sofa in Malcolm and Megan's living room.

"What can I do for you?" asked Malcolm as he prepared to brew coffee in his kitchen. A half wall separated the kitchen from the lounge area, so he could see what was happening in the lounge room, and those in the lounge room could see him. He always thought of this structural arrangement of the cottage he shared with Megan to be friendly to both those who lived in it and guests. He put coffee powder and sugar into three cups and set the kettle to boil.

"Yes," echoed Megan, who was sitting on her favourite armchair yawning after she spoke. Malcolm understood she was tired from her work at the Mitchell Library site. She was looking sharply at Nathaniel, not keen on this intrusion into their domesticity by a strange maverick. Malcolm looked intensely at her and sighed, hoping she got his signal and wouldn't say something that might later upset the Highest of the High when she heard about it. Megan, possibly realizing the danger they were in thanks to Malcolm, calmly added, "What can my husband do for you?"

"It shouldn't be hazardous," said Nathaniel, dismissively waving his hand. "I'll just need him as a pilot for a week, maybe two."

"To do what?" asked Malcolm, coming out of the kitchen and taking a seat close to Nathaniel.

"To fly me around," said Nathaniel.

"Where?" asked Malcolm. "I'll need to know our destination for gauging fuel consumption."

"South of here," said Nathaniel. "First, Kiama and then wherever I say we should go."

"Kiama is only half an hour away by flyer." Malcolm wondered what could possibly be there that would interest someone with this maverick's power. Why hire a pilot for a week, maybe two for such a short hop?

"I know where Kiama is located," said Nathaniel. "You'll be expected to wait for me when we get there, and then I will tell you where we go next."

"I don't understand," said Megan, adjusting her glasses. "What do you expect to find at Kiama?" she added.

"If this is an official investigation of some sort, will there be a maiden officer and robots onboard my flyer?" asked Malcolm, frowning. He did not want robots in his flyer.

"It's not official, and I am not sure what I will find," said Nathaniel. Megan removed her glasses, cleaning them with a tissue she got from a nearby box on her coffee table, and putting them back on. Malcolm didn't need to read her mind to understand that Nathaniel's last statement did not sit well with her. Her glasses' cleaning was a sign of her nervousness. He gulped a few times, showing Megan he also had concerns about what Nathaniel had just told them.

The kettle whistled. It broke the tension that had gathered in the lounge room. Malcolm went into the kitchen and, minutes later, returned with three steaming cups of coffee on a tray and placed them on the coffee table. They each took a cup, and Malcolm seated himself on a lounge chair facing Nathaniel.

"What is it then?" asked Megan. "Why not official? And why don't you know what you will find?"

"I will be sightseeing," said Nathaniel.

"A risky part of the south coast for that," Malcolm replied. He had heard about the recent problems there with rampaging Knights of Saint George slaughtering knights and dragons and wanted nothing to do with that lunacy.

Nathaniel took a sip of coffee and said, "The Knights of Saint George have moved on from Kiama. If anyone asks why I am in Kiama, I can always say I'm looking to buy land cheap. It should be at a reduced price because of recent trouble. I'm a bastard. I want to cash in on someone else's misfortunes."

"That makes sense, but that's not the real reason," said Megan. Both she and Malcolm could sense there was more to it than that.

"No," agreed Nathaniel, "It isn't the real reason, though I may buy land."

"So I fly you to Kiama then wait for you to work out where to go next?" asked Malcolm. He took a couple of gulps of his coffee. He needed a pick-me-up.

"That's right," said Nathaniel. "And it is a paying job. That should be understood. After all, a sightseer pays his pilot."

"Anything else I should know?" asked Malcolm. He finished his coffee and watched as Megan took a sip of her own.

"I want Megan to go along as well," said Nathaniel.

"Why me?" asked Megan. Her eyes widened in surprise at this.

"Three intelligent people are better than two." Nathaniel finished his coffee and watched together with Malcolm as Megan took another sip of her own.

"What about my university work?" Megan asked. By the barely subdued anger in her bespectacled eyes, Malcolm suspected she wanted to know why she should be involved and why she should be required to neglect her paid work and go off gallivanting into Goddess knows what with her husband and this Nathaniel person. Malcolm knew how precious what she did for the university was to her and how reluctant she was to break with routine.

"Your university work? Go on sick leave or take some holiday time," said Nathaniel. "This is important."

"You don't want anyone asking me questions as to where Malcolm has gone and why," reasoned Megan. Malcolm noted that his clever wife could figure out that much. "They'll find out sooner or later," added Megan, "but you want it to be as late as possible. That's why you want me along."

"I said you were intelligent." Nathaniel smiled a cold smile at her.

"And the High Priestess of Kiama will think it's sightseeing?" Megan asked. By the edge in her voice, Malcolm understood she wanted to know more about what they might be getting themselves into if they went on this adventure with Nathaniel.

"Oh, when she does find out about it, she'll suspect it must be more than that, but she'll think it has something to do with the Highest of the High." There was humour in Nathaniel's voice. "At worst, she will contact Rome and find out it has nothing to do with the Highest of the High, but she'll continue to suspect it has everything to do with the Highest One."

"I think I will pass on this job. We don't need the money that badly." Malcolm frowned, looking down. He didn't like going anywhere near those Knights of Saint George, especially if he had Megan with him. If it means a displeased Nathaniel would recommend to the Highest One he be reduced to knight, then so be it. Above all else, he wanted his wife to be safe.

"What if I were to double your fee?" asked Nathaniel.

"No deal," replied Malcolm firmly.

"What if I was to tell you that you will most likely be saving lives?" Nathaniel pressed, leaning forward. This got Malcolm's full attention. He also leaned forward.

"Maverick lives?" asked Malcolm.

"There is that possibility," replied Nathaniel.

"How about knight or dragon lives?" asked Malcolm.

"That would be a stronger possibility," replied Nathaniel.

"I think we should do it," said Megan. Malcolm suspected she was all for saving lives, especially his life. He was confident the last thing she wanted was for him to be demoted to knight. "If we can save anyone and not risk our own skins, we should do it," offered Megan. "We won't be in danger, will we?"

"I will keep you out of danger," said Nathaniel, clasping his hands together. Malcolm both felt and hoped this great maverick meant it.

"All right. Double the usual fee, and we're in. When do we start?" Malcolm hoped he was doing the right thing. He could see that Megan wanted him safe, but he also needed her to be safe as well. In the end, he didn't care to go against Nathaniel and end up in some arena with a sword in his hand.

"I'll meet you tomorrow morning at nine o'clock at Wollongong airport," said Nathaniel. "I'll expect your flyer to be fuelled and ready to go."

"Fine," replied Malcolm.

"We'll see you there then," said Megan. She finished her coffee, and both she and Malcolm watched Nathaniel get up to leave.

Malcolm could see by the pensive look on her face that Megan wondered what she and Malcolm had just bought themselves into and whether or not they would be called upon to go up against some powerful priestesses. However, Nathaniel was a power in his own right.

Nathaniel left, leaving Malcolm and Megan feeling stunned in his wake. They looked at each other and shook their heads in disbelief. Even in conversation, Nathaniel was a force to be reckoned with.

"Do you know what we have just agreed to?" asked Malcolm.

"Only some of it," replied Megan. "I'm sure we will find out more tomorrow."

****

Morning came, and Nathaniel was on time. The lift-off from Wollongong airport was smooth and the flight, as predicted, only lasted half an hour.

Kiama's airport was only a quarter of a mile from the railway station. Nathaniel left Malcolm and Megan with the flyer and walked the distance. Nathaniel understood before leaving the flyer that both Malcolm and Megan were glad not to be accompanying him.

Nathaniel found much confusion in the minds of the maidens, mavericks, and knights he came upon. Fright did that to all sorts of people. All these passersby wanted were to get away in case the Knights of Saint George returned. Some looked upon Nathaniel momentarily with suspicion, eyes narrowed but also glazed with terror, mouths open.

None could say where the renegade dragons the Saint George Knights were hunting could have gone if they existed at all. However, the train stationmaster recalled being in charge of some strange dragons for a short time.

"I don't know what I can tell you," said the stationmaster to Nathaniel, looking every which way but directly at him with his blackened eyes. "I kept those dragons here for a while as a favour to maverick gentlemen."

"They paid you," said Nathaniel, a sinister smile at the edges of his lips and a menacing glint in his eye.

"I never said that!" cried the stationmaster, trying to sound aghast at such an accusation.

"Never mind," said Nathaniel crisply. "I know it to be true."

"But who told you!" cried the stationmaster, wiping sweat from his forehead with a blue handkerchief, being careful not to touch his damaged nose and bruised eyes.

"Never mind!" snapped Nathaniel. "Tell me about the mavericks who took the dragons away and be quick about it."

"They were just mavericks, one was dark-skinned, that's all I remember! Am I in more trouble? Another beating? Have I lost my job?"

"I am done with you," said Nathaniel in an even voice and walked away. When prompted to think about the not-so-typical mavericks, the stationmaster's thoughts revealed the pick-up truck the dragons had been taken away in and the direction it was headed. The stationmaster's bandaged nose and black eyes showed Nathaniel how manic the Knights of Saint George could be in their questioning of even mavericks.

Nathaniel was about to return to Malcolm and Megan when he caught some valuable information off the passing thoughts of a maverick real estate agent. Unlike the Knights of Saint George, he would not have to venture into Gerringong, searching for his quarry. Instead, he would go straight to Berry. He got back to Malcolm and Megan and told them where they were off to next.

On the way to Berry in the flyer, Malcolm, Megan, and Nathaniel couldn't help noticing burnt out and wrecked farms and lots of smoke.

"What happened here?" asked Megan, pointing at a badly damaged farm as they flew by it.

"The Knights of Saint George happened," replied Nathaniel.

"So they're heading south, and we're heading south?" enquired Malcolm. "Is that a good idea?"

"We'll find out when we get there," replied Nathaniel. "I'm not predicting we'll run into any trouble."

"Well, I am!" cried Malcolm, his eyes on the controls and in the direction they are heading, but his face noticeably reddening.

"Remember, lives are at stake," said Nathaniel.

"Our lives are at stake," retorted Malcolm. "I don't mind a humanitarian mission as long as it doesn't involve us getting stabbed to death."

"It won't come to that. We can always fly away." Having said it, Nathaniel wondered if that was true. Once on the ground, the plane would be vulnerable to attack from the Knights of Saint George or any other foe. Malcolm might not be able to get them airborne in time to stave off harm.

"Okay," said Malcolm with a deep sigh. "I'll touch down where I can at Berry, but at the first sign of danger to myself, Megan, or the flyer, I'm gone."

"If we see something bad happening before we land," added Megan, "Malcolm can always radio the authorities for help."

"Fair enough," replied Nathaniel, who had no intention of getting into any sort of battle. He had been trained to think, not to fight. From what he had gathered so far, any fighting would be over, by the time he got to where he was going. The tricky part would be in assuring the victors, whoever they might be, that he is on their side. He suspected the ultimate winners would be the Knights of Saint George, but he felt he had to be there to make sure. He wanted the victors to be Elanora and her followers, but he couldn't see how that would be possible.

After a ten-minute flight, they touched down in the centre of Berry at a park that now had patches of blood soaking into the grass.

In ancient times, there had been a railway station at Berry. It used to get awards for excellence because the stationmaster, in its heyday, had a green thumb and prided himself on how he attended the plants that grew on his station.

Decades ago, what had remained of the station structure had been converted into the local constabulary's headquarters building. The maiden officers and robots that made up this constabulary were mysteriously absent. At least one maiden officer plus robots should have greeted them since where they landed was only a short distance away.

The state of the entrance to constabulary headquarters was a clue to what had occurred. The doors had been forced open, and there were signs of looting. The fridge was empty, and the blankets were taken from the linen closet. The computer used to communicate with Kiama headquarters had been smashed. The storage area where spare guns and ammunition for the robots were stored had been emptied.

The food and blankets could have been taken by anyone, but smashing the computer and stealing the guns could only have been done by the Knights of Saint George. Only they would dare do such a thing, thought Nathaniel. Then, in a darkened room that served as a bedchamber, he came across five dead Knights of that Order.

There was also the body of a maiden officer. Her smart greyish-black uniform, despite the bloodstain, revealed her to be such. She was a lean woman with wide-open eyes as if surprised at being killed. He closed her eyes for her.

He suspected the action had occurred outside. The bodies were taken into the building either by locals or surviving Knights of Saint George.

Nathaniel left the building frowning, feeling bewildered. Knights didn't usually attack maiden officers, and he knew that maiden officers with their robots had been advised not to interfere with the activities of the Knights of Saint George. So what did happen here? All he could fathom from the dead was that it shouldn't have occurred.

He then received information from the mind of a curious child who had been observing him from a short distance near the chemist shop. The child painted the picture in his head of an epic battle in which the Knights of Saint George had won. Nathaniel went back inside to search for more information.

Malcolm and Megan, Nathaniel noting their curiosity getting the better of them, left the flyer and joined him.

Nathaniel hovered over the body of the dead maiden, further wondering who, besides a Knight of Saint George, would have the nerve to kill her.

"Over there, in that corner!" cried Malcolm. "What's that?"

"I don't know," said Nathaniel. "Let's take a look."

"They're robots!" cried Megan. "They've been dismantled."

Malcolm picked up the head of a robot, saw the empty eyes, and said, "I have never seen robots in such poor condition." He put the head back where he found it.

"No ordinary knights could have done this," added Malcolm upon reflection, looking at his mechanical hand.

"This needs to be reported," reasoned Megan, shivering with fear.

"We'll have a look around first," said Nathaniel as he walked out of the building. The others followed.

"I don't like this," said Malcolm, his eyes going this way and that. "It's too quiet."

Not even a dog was barking, or a bird giving song to the day. In the nearest wine bar, Nathaniel found a frightened barkeep. He was loading bottles into boxes, getting ready to flee. *He won't leave his stock behind*, thought Nathaniel. *I sense he's put too much into this place to abandon it all to looters and crazy foreign knights.*

"Look! We don't want any more bloodshed," admitted the barkeep upon seeing them enter, his red moustache twitching. "We didn't ask for those Knights of Saint George to come here, and we don't want them back. We don't know a damn thing about runaway dragons, and we don't want to know anything!"

"We'll have three glasses of your best white," said Nathaniel, plunking down a handful of coins on the counter. "We're not going to ask you anything about dragons, so relax."

The barkeep sighed as he got a bottle out of a box and poured the wine into three glasses. "You picked a funny time to visit."

"I suppose we did," agreed Nathaniel, then took the glass offered to him and downed the contents. His companions did the same. Nathaniel noted that Malcolm wouldn't usually have indulged since he knew he would soon be flying again but felt one drink wouldn't hurt. It might even be good for his nerves, but it would only be one drink.

Apart from an old knight with a broom who had nowhere to go unless he joined the barkeep when he left in his truck, the place was empty. From both the knight and the maverick bar-keep, Nathaniel got all the information he needed. The real estate agent at Kiama, whose mind he had probed, had been vague. Both the janitor and the barkeep had been much more precise in their heads as to where Nathaniel should venture next.

There was another piece of luck. On the way out of the wine bar, Nathaniel came across a maverick telephone techni-cian. He explored the fellow's mind for a recent reconnection and got a phone number. It had been the first reconnection in the area the technician had made in months. Usually, he got such work in Kiama, not Berry, even though he lived in Berry. Hope-fully, it would be the number of the person Nathaniel wished most of all to contact before eventually meeting her. He so want-ed to avoid messy misunderstandings.

CHAPTER TWENTY-THREE

Megan startled Jens with her phone call into almost but not entirely dropping a half-eaten toasted bread slice covered in butter and Vegemite onto the floor in her lounge room. She had been looking dreamily out her kitchen window at a noisy miner chirping on a tree in the University Park. The bird was being knocked about by a cold August wind but still making noise. It was a small grey fellow with yellow around the eyes and on some of its wings. It was a typical sight in Wollongong, and its greyness suited her lacklustre mood.

She immediately resented the sound of the telephone before picking up the receiver. *Too damned early* were her thoughts. This was seven o'clock in the morning in her cottage. It had interrupted her breakfast routine.

"Hello!" called Jens.

"Megan here."

"What can I do for you," yawned Jens. "And why couldn't it have waited until I was in my office?"

"I need to go on leave starting immediately," Megan told Jens.

"Immediately?" wondered Jens, wiping sleep from her eyes.

"Yes," murmured Megan. "It will have to be right away."

"Right away?"

"I have to help my husband on a project that can't wait," replied Megan.

"What project?" Jens asked, tension in her voice.

"I can't be more specific," said Megan.

Jens sighed deeply. "This is not like you. How long will you need to be away?"

"Two weeks."

"If you and your husband are in trouble, maybe I can help," offered Jens, concern in her voice. "I have some influence in high places."

"That won't be necessary," said Megan. "Can I have leave starting immediately? I want to keep my job if that is possible, but I need this time off for my husband. I have been so happy working for you and the university, and there's so much left for me to do at the Mitchell Library site."

The line went silent for a moment. Jens had to think about what best to say next. She had eaten half a slice of toasted bread with vegemite and butter on it and had half a cup so far of her morning coffee. She usually had breakfast in peace at her coffee table in her lounge room before showering, dressing, and leaving her dwelling to get on with her day. The possible loss of Megan, her number one maiden worker, registered sharply with her. It was a prickly feeling she didn't like. She found herself twisting the cord of her phone as if that would make any sense of what was going on with her subordinate.

"No," agreed Jens after the pause. "We can't have you going away for good just because you need to be absent for two weeks. We value what you do too much for that. Two weeks' disruption we can live with. It would take months to train someone to replace you. Some of our students have promise, but they are not you. Then again, you have accrued plenty of leave time, so I can give you permission to take some of it now, but I stress it can only be two weeks."

"Two weeks should be fine," said Megan. "If I am not back by then, I may not be coming back at all."

"Please do come back!" cried Jens forgetting her position for a moment, not having that calm, passionless voice with a subordinate she normally had. Then the phone went dead. The call had ended.

Jens finished breakfast, showered, dressed in a black outfit with white zig-zags, and made her way to the university building where she did the bulk of her work. Along the way, she thought, *I hope you know what you are doing, Megan. I truly do.*

At ten o'clock, in Jens's office, she got another phone call, this one from Dean Renate.

"Nathaniel has gone south to Kiama in a flyer piloted by Malcolm," the dean told her. "He stayed only a short time at Kiama and then headed further south."

"What has this got to do with me?" asked Jens.

"Do you know what Nathaniel is up to?" asked the dean.

"No idea," said Jens.

"I thought you might know since Megan went along."

"I got a phone call this morning from Megan saying she needs a two-week break from work," said Jens, "so it's something that's just come up."

"The High Priestess of Wollongong is asking." Dean Renate emphasized the words "High" and "Priestess." "She wants to know if Nathaniel is doing something for the High Priestess of Kiama. I would say Nathaniel has been in Wollongong too long for our High One's liking. Our High One is glad he is elsewhere, but Kiama is too close for her comfort, and she wants to keep tabs on him."

"I'm sorry," said Jens," but I can't help. I've told you all I know." *Whatever you're involved in, Megan, I hope you really do understand what you are doing.*

At eleven o'clock, Jens took a flyer to old Sydney to look over the Mitchell library's fifth underground level. Megan was supposed to start on this level that day. Jens could have left the whole thing for two weeks and continue on other projects, but she was curious about the site.

Megan had made some remarkable discoveries on the lower levels, and the fifth one promised to be just as important. Her assistant Megan was better at finding archaeological gems, but sometimes Jens felt like getting back into actual fieldwork. *I have been behind a desk giving orders too long*, she thought. *It's about time I got my hands dirty again.*

While en route, Jens and the pilot heard over the radio an operator at the airport tower in Wollongong warn them of a dust storm coming their way. Then there was the scream of the storm as it got nearer to them. They couldn't see it at first, but the sky quickly darkened to a muddy hue.

"We're too close to old Sydney to turn back to Wollongong," advised the pilot. "We're already getting hit by dust and debris, and it'll get worse. Our radio is cutting out. I can't contact Wollongong airport to tell them we're in strife. There's too much static."

"What do you recommend?" asked Jens.

"We land at old Sydney as planned and take shelter underground at the Mitchell Library site, "the pilot told her. "We can wait out the storm there. Believe me, it's better than trying to make our way back to Wollongong. We're too vulnerable in the air. We need to land as soon as we can."

"Fine," said Jens. "Fly us to where we planned to go, and we will take shelter there."

"When we land, the flyer will be buried under a lot of material. Some of it may be radioactive from the bad days before we came to believe in the Great Goddess," advised the pilot. "The flyer has some interior protection against radioactivity, but it is better if we take as few chances with exposure to high radiation as possible. Once we're down, it becomes a choice to wait it out in the flyer or go underground. I favour going underground and to your seventh level."

"We will do as you say," replied Jens coldly. "Do these storms happen often?"

"No," said the pilot. "I'm landing now. When we get out, you run for the library. I'll make sure the flyer is sealed up tight, then join you. Cover up as much as possible on your run. I'll do the same."

Both Jens and the pilot were whipped about as they made their way to the library. The ladder down to level one was now more treacherous than it had been because of the wind and the dirt flying about, but they both descended without slipping on the rungs and falling. On the way down, Jens felt closer to being the human rock spider some of her students claimed she was. Once on the first level, stairs were going down to the second. There was also an elevator, a cage contraption, but it was so ancient it was not considered trustworthy.

On the second level, as they descended the stairs, Jens came across a cabinet that contained a stun grenade from the early twenty-second century. She left it where it was since she didn't know how to handle it and didn't want it accidentally going off in her hands.

On the third level, going down via the winding stairs, there was an old-fashioned Geiger counter from the 1960s Jens figured would later come in handy and might even be suitable for an up-and-coming exhibition. She put it in the sack she carried for gathering up finds.

When they did reach the seventh level, the howl of the wind could still be heard.

"We're going to be here for a while," said the pilot, "and we have no way of communicating with the outside world."

"At least we have plenty of reading material." Jens pointed at shelves of books.

****

By three o'clock in the afternoon, Dean Renate tried to contact Jens but without success. *Now Jens is missing*, thought the dean, *what the devil is going on?* She frowned, rubbed her chin contemplatively, and got in contact, via phone, with the airport. No, they hadn't heard from Jens or the pilot assigned to her either. She was then told of a dust storm that had interfered with communication.

"Great Goddess, help them if they got caught in the middle of that!" cried the airport controller. "We'll let you know as soon as we hear anything. The storm should clear in four or five hours, and communications in the area where they were scheduled to go should be restored."

Just as the dean was settling back into paperwork with a much-needed mug of coffee steaming away at her shoulder, the phone rang. A priestess named Elba wanted to know what was going on with Nathaniel, Malcolm, and Megan. "I smell a conspiracy!" the priestess cried.

The dean took a sip of her coffee, basking in the smell of the beans ground to perfection with hot water added and a touch of milk. She then said, "No conspiracy here that I know of. Your olfactory nerve must be out of whack."

"My what?"

"Never mind."

"Where is maiden Megan?" demanded the priestess.

"She is on vacation," replied the dean.

"And where has she taken her vacation?" snapped the priestess.

"I have no idea," said the dean. "You would have to take that up with Jens, her supervisor."

"And where is Jens?" demanded the priestess.

"I don't know," answered the dean. "She meant to visit old Sydney. Maybe she's there and maybe not. No communication with that area is possible for the present." The dean shrugged her shoulders, despite knowing this priestess couldn't possibly see her doing it. She drank more of her coffee.

"How convenient! I am not impressed, and I am far from satisfied," snarled the priestess. "I will take this up with the High Priestess of Wollongong."

"Please do," said the dean and hung up.

Priestess Elba did visit the High Priestess of Wollongong with her thoughts on a supposedly current plot unfolding. The High One was busy watering the flowers in the flower pots in her study. The High One sighed deeply, uncertain what she should do about it if it were true.

"And what do you think I should do?" asked the High One as she gave a white rose a drink.

"You must act!" cried the priestess, waving her arms about, making her white robes swish comically this way and that.

"How?"

"Send agents to capture them," said the priestess, "and have them brought back here. Malcolm, the pilot, you can let go and possibly Megan, but Nathaniel is definitely up to something."

"And what if Nathaniel, this Megan, and pilot have done no wrong or are in the service of the Highest One?" asked the High Priestess of Wollongong. "Bring me facts, and I may act. Otherwise, please go away."

The High Priestess, no doubt feeling troubled by what Priestess Elba had told her, rang the dean who by now had had enough of phone calls for the day. She perked up when she heard the High One's voice on the other end, talking about conspiracies. Dean Renate told her it was doubtful any of her staff would be involved in anything so underhanded. "A sinister plot is out of the question," she told the High One. "I can assure you such a thing is pure nonsense. I know my people."

"Yes," agreed the High One. "I suppose you do." The dean made sure the High Priestess hung up first. She didn't want to risk seeming impolite by putting her receiver down before the High One could act.

The dean took out a bottle of mead from behind a house plant, uncorked it, and poured herself a glass. She examined the colour of it in the glass before tasting it. Yes, it did look like liquid honey with a kick, gold from the sun. She downed a glass and took another. She would have preferred to have punched that Priestess Elba, whoever she was and whatever she looked like, right in the nose for Megan and Jens' sake but knew she would never get away with it. *I don't want anything to happen to either Jens or Megan over politics in high places*, she thought as she recorked the bottle and put it back into hiding.

****

Five o'clock came around. The wind had died, and Jens and her pilot decided it was time to leave the seventh level for the flyer.

The flyer was covered in dust and debris. Jens used the Geiger counter she had to see if there was any radiation danger. The count was low. It took them an hour of digging to get inside and for the pilot to access the radio.

Once inside, the pilot showed Jens how to contact Dean Renate with the news of what had happened to her. Thankfully, takeoff in the flyer was possible, and they made it back to Wollongong airport without any further trouble.

****

A few hours earlier, Nathaniel made contact with Wollongong airport and requested three extra flyers to meet him south of Berry. "I am planning a trip with friends to a place I have just purchased near Tasmania. Fuel consumption for them shouldn't be a problem," Nathaniel said to the maiden airport supervisor. "Also, where they are landing will be safe from violence, so tell the pilots I not only pay well, but there will be no danger to them, none at all."

Minutes after this transmission, the maiden airport supervisor contacted the High Priestess of Wollongong to let her know that Nathaniel was well and that he had further travel plans. "What further plans?" the High One asked.

"Nothing likely to concern you or me," concluded the airport supervisor. "He's heading toward Tasmania. He has bought property near there, or so he says."

"He's been out property buying?" asked the High One.

"That seems to be the case," agreed the airport supervisor.

****

Priestess Elba was brought before the High Priestess of Wollongong, who was in her garden and in a frightful mood.

"So you wish to destroy me!" cried the High One, shaking her fist at a now quaking Priestess Elba.

"No!" yelled the priestess, face down. "I mean no offence. How have I offended?"

"Your words!" cried the High One.

"My words?" wondered Priestess Elba, her eyes wide with horror.

"You could have ended my career with your urgings this day," said the High One, both frowning and seething with fury.

"I am but a servant," offered Priestess Elba, a sob in her voice.

"I could have made grave errors this day because of you," said the High One, her nostrils flaring.

"My apologies." Priestess Elba sighed, and the sigh caught in her throat. She knew she was in disgrace, and it would be a while before she could win back the High Priestess of Wollongong's favour.

"I could have made the sort of decisions this day that could have cost me my position," continued the High Priestess. "Now go! Do not return until I have summoned you."

****

Around this time, Kiama's High Priestess sent maverick agents into Gerringong and Berry, but they found nothing she could use. She wanted to pin the disasters that happened in Kiama and those outlying towns on the High Priestess of Wollongong. Still, she couldn't find the evidence to take to the Highest of the High. *You get away with it this time, Wollongong,* thought the Kiama High One, *but one slip, and I will have you and your position.*

****

One day later, at one in the afternoon, Priestess Elba was walking toward her favourite wine bar when she went into shock. She gasped out loudly, blood exiting her mouth and nose. It wasn't until the blade that had been thrust into her back had been removed that she felt pain. It wasn't a knife. That would be established at the morgue. It was too thin for that. It was more like a knitting needle, only exceedingly sharper and undoubtedly wielded by an expert.

The gasp and pain for Priestess Elba didn't last long. She collapsed onto the footpath. A passerby noticed her bleeding onto the concrete. Help came, but there was nothing the maverick medic could do for her. It was the work of a professional assassin, a priestess cutthroat that shouldn't exist but did. She had stabbed, withdrew her instrument of death, tucked it away under her garments, and walked calmly away. She did not run like a criminal so she could easily be caught by a patrolling maiden officer and her robots. That sort of clumsiness was for television.

One hour later, the High Priestess of Wollongong was given the details of Priestess Elba's demise, and for the first time in a while, found she had something to smile about. She would have the ridiculous priestess' remains sent to Egypt for burial. The person responsible for her death would never be caught.

CHAPTER TWENTY-FOUR

Toff was still in a quiet room away from everyone, hopefully getting better from seeing a good friend die. Elanora was glad he had only been in the arena the one time. If he had been forced to fight dragons a second time for the pleasure of priestesses, maidens, and mavericks, he would not have survived. *Toff should never have been made a knight,* she thought. *He's young, intelligent in his own way, and not made for fighting. Those damned priestesses that decided at his school what males should be knights and what should be mavericks got it wrong with Toff. Who knows how many others they also got wrong?*

As she gazed out the farmhouse's kitchen window, Elanora saw a rat scurry past a few feet away. It was big and grey, about the size of a small domestic cat. She wondered if the dead had been buried deep enough. It had been done in such a hurry.

The morning milking had been accomplished by Susan, Cybil, Ronald, Aayan, Gregory, and Eric. Aayan's blue heeler, Hector, who was eager to help get cows to do what his owners wanted them to do, was also there.

The cows had been taken out of the overcrowded cow shed and milked in groups. Susan had the knowledge required to get the machines back into the shed and hooked up, so the milking didn't have to be done by hand.

Elanora was glad there was plenty of good grass back of the shed and still on her land. For Ronald, Cybil, and Susan, she gathered that seeing to the cows was mentally an automatic process. It was what farmers and farmhands did; Cybil and Susan were farmers, and Ronald had been a farmhand. Elanora felt there was an absolute absurdity in doing the milking since life was not likely to go on at the farm the way it had much longer. Still, the children needed milk, and she did enjoy a few drops of it in her coffee, especially of a morning, so she made no objections to this activity.

The milkers returned to the farmhouse, having acquired a fresh supply. Ronald seemed incredibly happy. *If Ronald needs to be someplace, this is it*, thought Elanora, *either here or some other farm. Goddess knows he deserves to be content, as do we all.*

There was a chill in the air she didn't notice, but the priestess and the children commented on it as they gathered close to the kitchen fireplace, basking in its warmth. The children and the priestess sat on the floor. There weren't enough chairs to go around. A seat was left vacant for Elanora.

The furniture in this farmhouse was solid rather than attractive. It was worn but not worn out. She had such high hopes for the farm, but now, thanks to the dead and buried Knights of Saint George, it looked like she and the crew she had gathered around her would have to move somewhere else, but where?

"Two great battles we have fought and won. Now what?" Eric sighed, hissing at the end of what he had to say. He moved his black-spiked tail rhythmically back and forth. Elanora took her eyes away from the window, first looking at him and then the children. Some of the human young were watching that great tail of Eric's in motion.

"We knew those battles could not be the end of our troubles." Cybil's hands clasped together, her eyes looking this way and that, then focusing on Elanora. She didn't seem as frail as when she first came to the farm.

Then the phone rang. Cybil and Susan gasped. Elanora hissed at this interruption to her thoughts. She was in no mood for a strange phone call. She looked around at the dragons, knights, maidens, and children, knowing she had made some children jump with her energetic hissing.

"Answer it!" commanded Elanora to Gregory. He did so, said hello, listened for a moment, held out the receiver to her,

Dragon Queen

and said, "He wants to speak to you, Elanora. He's most insistent. He won't give me his name. He'll only talk business with you."

"You'd best find out what whoever is on the phone wants, Elanora," said Aayan calmly. "Maybe there's a way to prevent further bloodshed."

The adults present bowed their heads in agreement with Aayan, then looked to Elanora. The children also bowed.

"Hello?" answered Elanora when given the receiver. "Who is this?"

"My name is Nathaniel," said an imperious sounding voice on the other end.

"We will not sssurrender!" cried Elanora.

"Since one of your knights answered the phone rather than a member of the Order of Saint George, I take it you beat the odds against you," said Nathaniel.

"How do you know it was not a Knight of Saint George?" asked Elanora.

"He didn't sound formal enough to be a Knight of Saint George, plus he was able to pass the phone onto you. Why would the Knights of Saint George keep you alive? By your hiss, I gather you really are Elanora, an extraordinary dragon."

"Yes," said Elanora. "That is logical."

"You're trapped, and sooner or later, you will be overwhelmed by superior numbers. The Order of Saint George will not go unavenged. What's more, the High Priestess of Kiama will want to restore order in this area. That means eliminating you."

"We are aware of our situation," said Elanora, swishing her tail about in anger.

"Fine." Nathaniel sighed. "I would like to propose another option beside surrender."

"What would that be?" asked Elanora.

"I wish to alight in the valley below your farmhouse," said Nathaniel. "I am unarmed, and so are my companions. I wish to discuss your situation further with you face to face."

"And if I refuse?"

287

"Then I have had a wasted journey, and I will return to Wollongong, and, from there, I'll make my way back to Rome."

"And you want to take me back to Rome as your trophy?" asked Elanora, more swishing of her tail.

"No. I don't want that at all," assured Nathaniel. "Just meet me, and we will discuss what I can do for you."

There was silence on the phone that seemed to last a long time. When Elanora got back on the line, she said, "Very well, you may land, but no tricks. We are well armed."

Nathaniel hung up first. Elanora wondered if she had done the right thing or not in allowing him to land. *Who is this Nathaniel?* she wondered. *Why would he wish to help my followers and me?*

****

It took Nathaniel all of five minutes to leave the payphone in the Berry wine bar and return with Malcolm and Megan to the flyer. Twenty minutes later, Malcolm touched down in what he considered to be hostile territory. Nathaniel exited the flyer. An armed knight and an armed dragon came out of the farmhouse and trudged down the hill to greet him. Both knight and dragon had swords.

"You're Nathaniel?" asked a bold-looking knight, who carried his sword well.

"Yes, and you are?" Nathaniel already knew the answer from a mind probe but felt he should ask the question anyway.

"I am Gregory, and my companion is the dragon, Eric," said the knight. "We will escort you to Elanora."

"Can my friends come along, too?" asked Nathaniel.

"Yes," said Eric.

"Malcolm? Megan? Come on out. We're going to meet Elanora."

Malcolm and Megan left the flyer and joined Nathaniel in his walk up to the farmhouse. They huddled together. Neither could stop staring at the swords, which were bloody from battle. Gregory opened the door for them, and they went inside.

"Meet Elanora," said Gregory, pointing to a robust, black-scaled dragon that had the right curves to be a female.

"We've met before," said Malcolm. It didn't take much mind-reading talent on Nathaniel's part to realize this was true.

"Yes. Malcolm and Megan, right?" asked Elanora.

"That's right," answered Megan.

"What do you want of me, Nathaniel?" demanded Elanora.

"I want to save you," said Nathaniel.

"Why?" asked Elanora.

"You are unique," said Nathaniel.

"I would make a poor trophy."

Nathaniel could read in Elanora's thoughts she had visions of being sent to Rome in chains.

"I, too, am unique," said Nathaniel. "That is why I want to save you. That is why I want to take you to where you will be safe."

"Only me?" asked Elanora.

"Yes," said Nathaniel. "That is my intention."

"So you are to whisk me away to safety somewhere, and we are to leave everyone else you find here behind?" Elanora waved her arms, taking in those around her. Nathaniel then knew she wouldn't be separated from those she felt depended upon her leadership.

"It would be best," said Nathaniel, wondering if he could make her see sense.

"How do you feel about his offer?" asked Elanora of Gregory.

"If you were alone, you would be easily disposed of," Gregory offered. "I don't want you facing danger without backup."

"I say go with them," said Eric. "If they are genuine, you will be safer. You've done enough for us already. Besides, they have shown courage in coming here."

"My answer is no." Elanora told Nathaniel. "If my dragons and knights can't all go with me, I choose to stay and share their fate."

"But there are so many!" cried Nathaniel, looking around. "There are children, too!"

"And Berry's very own priestess," said Anna. "We would never abandon the children!"

"We could take three extra passengers in my flyer, maybe more," suggested Malcolm. He and Nathaniel noticed how the children were fascinated by his metal hand and leg. They followed the movement of his robot parts with their eyes.

"The answer is still no," said Elanora.

"This will take some organizing." Nathaniel sighed, realizing a simple mission had just gotten complicated. "There are so many of you!"

"You mean you're thinking of taking all of them?" asked Malcolm. "My flyer, as I have indicated, isn't big enough. It would take numerous trips to get them away to anywhere safe, and I don't believe that is wise."

"It can be done," said Nathaniel, after taking a few minutes to think about it, "and it must be done in a hurry."

"We haven't agreed on anything yet," observed Gregory.

"What do you propose?" asked Elanora.

"Four flyers to get you all out of here as quickly as possible," said Nathaniel.

"And where will we go?" asked Elanora.

"That's something I will organize," said Nathaniel. "Either go with me or die here. It's your choice."

"We should go," said Ronald.

"We could make our own way out of here," reasoned Susan. Nathaniel understood from touching her mind that she didn't like his smooth talk.

"I agree," said Cybil, taking Susan's side.

"Me, too," added Celine, the former maiden officer.

"Yes. That is a possibility. We have the transport. There are the Knights of Saint George trucks and our own pickup," said Elanora.

"But I will make you disappear!" Nathaniel fluttered his hands, wishing he had on a magician's cape for added emphasis. "It will be as if you, Elanora, and those with you never existed."

"How?" asked Elanora.

"With trucks, there is an easy trail to follow," said Nathaniel. "You must travel by road. You will need to stop for petrol and food, and those who provide you with these necessities can then be questioned by maiden officers with their robots. There are no doubt patrol cars with maiden officers and robots already en route to Berry. If you manage to get aboard a ship, you will be trapped on that ship until you reach port, and then, when you reach port, it is likely members of the Order will be waiting for you. Either that or officials will be there to greet you and send you back here to face what the High One of Kiama will no doubt call justice."

"True," agreed Gregory.

"Even now, they could be sending warriors from Constantinople to find out what has happened to the knights you've buried," said Nathaniel.

"So, what do you propose?" asked Elanora.

"If I can work it right," said Nathaniel, "travel by flyer will leave the Order with little if anything to go on. It may take the Order days, weeks, even months to discover their dead comrades. I take it they are buried deep. Eventually, they will use metal detectors. Even so, if they are not aided by either the High Priestess of Kiama or the High Priestess of Wollongong, they won't be able to connect flight plans with how you escaped. You will have simply disappeared."

"So, how exactly will you work your miracle?" Susan asked.

"Yes," said the former maiden officer. "I'd like to know."

"Slight-of-hand." Nathaniel really did wish he had on that magician's cape. "Let me get back to the flyer, and I'll let you know if I can work it or not."

"Nathaniel could radio the authorities now that he knows for sure we are here," said Gregory.

"I could have done that before we even touched down," replied Nathaniel.

"There is still a trust issue," said Elanora.

"Fine." Nathaniel sighed deeply. "Malcolm and Megan can stay with you, and Gregory can go back with me to the flyer."

"And they are important to you?" asked Elanora, pointing at Malcolm and Megan.

"Only if I want to get out of here," said Nathaniel. "I need a pilot, and Malcolm would not be in a good mood if anything happened to Megan."

"Agreed. I trust Gregory." *Once more, I am putting my life in the hands of a knight,* thought Elanora, and this thought was picked up by Nathaniel.

****

Gregory followed Nathaniel back to the flyer. There Nathaniel radioed the High Priestess of Hobart and arranged to buy an island off Tasmania. He then ordered three extra flyers and pilots to go from Wollongong airport to the valley below the farmhouse where Malcolm had landed his flyer.

"This will cost a fortune!" gasped Gregory.

"My money," said Nathaniel. "I suppose you could say I'm a millionaire, thanks to the Highest One. She pays me well because she likes to be seen paying her best advisers well, even if I am only a maverick and not a maiden or a priestess. I haven't had a great use for my wealth up till now, just food and accommodation wherever I am sent. I only need a small apartment in Rome, so the money has been accumulating."

"But why?" asked Gregory.

"Let's just say that getting you and your friends out of here will be the greatest magic trick of all time," replied Nathaniel, shrugging his shoulders and trying not to smile.

"I still don't understand," replied Gregory.

"There is no need for you to understand," said Nathaniel, frowning, his hand covering his chin and stroking it. "No need at all. Just please trust that I mean you and your companions no harm, no harm at all."

Next, Nathaniel radioed the Highest of High Priestesses confirming his buying of the island for friends he'd made. He also notified the High Priestess of Wollongong that if anyone from Wollongong caused trouble on the island he now owned, then a secret concerning a certain dragon would get out. What's more, if anything happened to him, an agent in Rome would forward the information about the dragon to the Highest of the High. She might then act against Wollongong's High Priestess in the best interests of the Great Goddess.

When Nathaniel and Gregory returned to the farmhouse, there was heated discussion on what should happen next. Gregory's view was that Nathaniel's solution, crazy though it happened to be, was the best way forward. The whereabouts of Elanora and her people would not be easily traced thanks to travelling by flyer. When they were discovered, they would be in the High Priestess of Hobart's territory and possibly under her protection.

"What plans have you for the Knights of Saint George that will be coming for us?" Eric asked Nathaniel.

"Secrecy is our best bet," said Nathaniel. "In this, I know the High Priestess of Hobart won't let us down. I've met her at several parties. Since the money exchanged for land she deems worthless to her is important to her financial wellbeing, and she doesn't want to mess with anyone close to the Highest of the High, she'll help us all she can."

"What about the High Priestess of Wollongong?" Elanora asked.

"I guarantee to you the High Priestess of Wollongong will do her best to cover up our trail," said Nathaniel. "Flight plans are, no doubt, already vanishing even as I speak. As for the High Priestess of Kiama, she won't make a move that will put her out of sorts with the Highest of the High, and going against me just might do that."

"So, the trail will go cold somewhere on the outskirts of Berry, and we'll be on this island," reasoned Eric.

"It's called Green Maiden's Folly, and it's five miles long by ten miles wide," said Nathaniel. "It has a herd of sheep and a dozen shacks left from whenever it was last inhabited. I have flown over the island numerous times on my way to Hobart. There's a little freshwater lake a pilot friend once told me about and a small forest. There's plenty of birds, and the fishing, I have been told, is good."

"What about supplies?" Susan asked.

"Once a month, I will arrange for a supply drop," said Nathaniel.

"We'll be in exile," said Priestess Anna.

"Yes," agreed Nathaniel, "but you'll be alive."

Before long, the other three flyers arrived and were quickly filled with children, maidens, knights, and dragons. They were also loaded with food and other essentials. Malcolm took Priestess Anna, Elanora, Eric, Ronald, and Gregory with him as well as Nathaniel and Megan. Room was also made for Hector, the blue heeler. The cattle were let loose in the hope they would be picked up by farmers.

The first stop of all four flyers was Hobart airport for topping up with fuel though the topping up probably wouldn't be needed, and for Nathaniel, the signing of the contract for the island. The next landing site after that would be Green Maiden's Folly.

The reception at Hobart airport was generally cordial, the staff friendly toward Nathaniel, the maidens, and especially the children. They ignored the dragons and the scruffy-looking knights.

Nathaniel bought sandwiches for every one of his charges, which made the maiden behind the lunch counter grin. He also gave money to Ronald to purchase enough food at a nearby grocery shop to last those he wished to save for a month. Nathaniel told him it had to be dry food packets that would not weigh the flyers down too much or take up too much room. Ronald thanked him, and Nathaniel watched Ronald, Cybil, and Priestess Anna race to the shop where they bought the packets and then speed back to the airport and the flyers with what they had acquired.

The added fuel and the deal, Nathaniel discovered, took no time at all. The official with the documents for Nathaniel to sign beamed at him. He was eager for Nathaniel to sign for fear that it wouldn't happen, and he would have to return to Hobart's High One without that precious signature. It didn't take much effort to garner from this official wearing a top black hat with red swirls that neither he nor the High One thought the island much of a bargain.

It was raining when they touched down at Green Maiden's Folly. Ronald helped Nathaniel, Celine, Priestess Anna, and Susan unload the dry food packets and what blankets there were in the flyer and put them in a dry place in a shack.

"It is green," offered Nathaniel after seeking shelter in a nearby shack that leaked. Elanora, Malcolm, Megan, and Ronald came in with him.

"It's probably green because it rains a lot!" grumbled Susan as she joined Nathaniel and the others, seeking out a dry spot.

"The shacks are in disrepair," said Nathaniel. "I knew that when I purchased the island, but I am sure, for now, it is possible to find dry corners in each of them."

"I want to go home!" cried the youngest of the children, bursting into tears as she entered with Priestess Anna and the other children. The other children also began to weep.

"There! There!" soothed Priestess Anna, arm over the little girl's shoulder but addressing the others as well. "It'll be better after we've been here a while."

"We're alive," reasoned Aayan, while dodging a drip, "and we can fix up the shacks, make them more liveable."

Only Hector seemed at all impressed with Green Maiden's Folly. Despite the rain, he sniffed around for a good twenty minutes, putting his nose in this bush or that, before joining Aayan in the shack.

The flyers left. The pilots in them undoubtedly were contemplating if this odd colony, whatever its purpose might be, had much of a chance of lasting in such a locale.

"I wish I could have stayed with them," confided Nathaniel to Malcolm and Megan as they flew away into the darkness, "but my destiny, as always, lies in Rome."

"I don't understand you," said Megan. "Why have you done this?"

"Why save them?" asked Malcolm. "You're a bastard, right? You work for the Highest of the High."

"I'm a complicated bastard," answered Nathaniel.

****

The following morning, when the clouds parted on what became a sunny day, the new inhabitants of Green Maiden's Folly got a better look at their new home.

"It really is green," said Susan after leaving the shack she and Cybil had claimed the previous night. "And smell the air! It's so fresh! It's even fresher than at Berry."

"I'm glad I have boots on," countered Cybil as she joined her. "It's still cold, and you have to watch out for that white frost on the ground. Step on it in bare feet, and it'll freeze your toes blue. But I do love that crunch, crunch sound when you walk on it."

"I bet you the trees are vibrant with wildlife," said Ronald as he walked to them from another shack.

"I saw wild sheep and a few goats this morning as I took an early jog," said Elanora, coming up to Ronald and smiling at him. "The sheep and the goats can be tamed. There are also wild ducks."

Later that day, Susan found a beehive and showed it to Ronald. "We could have fresh honey for the children," she told him. "That will brighten them up."

As it turned out, the children didn't need much brightening up. When they awoke and did their own exploring, they concluded that Green Maiden's Folly wasn't so bad after all.

When Hector went walking with Aayan, he located some rabbit warrens. He sniffed inside one, indicating it was occupied.

"I will bless our new start," said the former Berry priestess at breakfast who was now the priestess of Green Maiden's Folly.

****

On their return, Malcolm and Megan were warned by a representative of the High Priestess of Wollongong, as were the pilots of the other flyers, not to mention where they had been to anyone.

"What happened to Priestess Elba might happen to you if you speak out of turn," a priestess told Malcolm at the airport soon after his flyer had landed. "Priestess Elba's death has already made the news."

Jens later pressed Megan for details about where she and Malcolm had been and what they had done there. This was at their favourite coffee shop.

"All I can tell you," Megan said to Jens, "is that Malcolm has been working on a secret project for a representative of the Highest of the High."

"The Highest One?" wondered Jens, gasping.

"Yes," said Megan. "Nathaniel, after all, does represent the Highest One, and it would be my life and yours if I said any more about it."

"But why did it involve you?" asked Jens.

"It just did," said Megan, shrugging her shoulders. "All hush-hush. I can't go into it without risking your life and mine and, of course, Malcolm's. When you are called upon to do something for the Highest One's representative, it has to be like that."

"Yes, I see. The Highest One's representative," murmured Jens before taking a sip of coffee, "And it would mean your life to say any more about it. I'll pass this on to Dean Renate. I just wish it was safe for you to say more."

"So do I," agreed Megan. She finished her coffee then left Jens in a bewildered state.

*****

A week later, Nathaniel made the journey back to Rome. His buying of the island the Highest of High Priestesses fobbed off as a mere curiosity. However, she was amused at the High Priestess of Wollongong's insistence that the purchase was all above board and nothing to worry about. *There is now something Nathaniel will want to protect*, thought the Highest One. *He now has a reason not to betray me.*

"Was it a foolish buy?" asked the Highest of High Priestesses of Nathaniel over sherry in her office.

"I hope not," replied Nathaniel.

"Is it a social experiment?" asked the Highest One. "You wanted a small kingdom of your own?"

"Yes," answered Nathaniel. "I suppose you could say that."

"Then, if it doesn't interfere in any way with my governance," said the Highest of High Priestesses, "I will allow you to keep your island. What's more, I wish it every success. It has my blessing."

"Thank you," replied Nathaniel.

****

Two weeks after Elanora's people settled on Green Maiden's Folly, five Knights of Saint George arrived in Wollongong, via flyer, from Constantinople. Three days later, following the twenty's path of destruction, they arrived at the valley where the trucks they had hired were still parked.

The five knights looked around for signs of what had happened. There were scorch marks on the hill leading to the house. Some of the grass was brown and looked uneven, but no damage inside the house to suggest a violent confrontation.

A Berry farmer from a nearby farm was found rounding up some cows near the cattle shed. He thought it would be safe enough by now to gather them, via the use of his dog, and take them to what was left of his property. "Please don't hurt me," said the farmer to the Knights of Saint George. "If you want them, you can have the cows."

"Do you know what happened to the twenty brave Knights of Saint George that have gone missing?" asked one of the knights.

"I know five of them were killed in the centre of Berry," he told them. "I have no idea what happened to the others. Please don't beat me! I swear that's all I know."

"Go!" one of the knights snarled, pointing at the cattle. "Be off with you and take those Goddess damned breasts with you."

The five knights moved on to the next farm in line, and the next after that, until they arrived at the next town along from Berry, Jasper's Brush. Everything was peaceful there. Fearing they had missed something, the knights returned to the farm where the trucks were and had another look around. One of them found a broken chest plate in the valley not far from the trucks. They then went back to Kiama and obtained metal detectors to fully explore the uneven ground. The metal detectors worked. Berry knights were brought in to dig up the missing Saint George Knights.

Slowly, the bodies were retrieved and put into coffins to be sent, via commercial plane, to Constantinople for reburial. The wounds, in some instances, were peculiar. All of the Order expected to die in battle, but all dreamt of a clash of equals on a great battlefield. They did not care to die in the middle of nowhere like this. The bodies of the five knights found in Berry's constabulary building would also be included in the transportation of the dead to their final resting place.

"You shall be avenged," said the lead knight as he witnessed the last body being dug up.

The five investigating knights examined train records and questioned railway personnel. No runaway dragons had gotten onboard a train at Kiama headed for Wollongong, and there had been no new sightings of renegade dragons in Wollongong.

The airports also proved to be a dead end. There was nothing to indicate that dragons had, in the last two months, been transported by air from Kiama airport or, for that matter, Wollongong airport. The five investigating knights were baffled. Everyone was afraid of them, and still, no one had the answers they sought.

Examining the petrol stations and rest stops on the road from Kiama to Jasper's Brush proved fruitless. Beyond Jasper's Brush was wild country in which creatures, affected by radiation, had long ago drifted up from Melbourne and had made their home there in the dense forest. If the dragons had wandered past Jasper's Brush, they would most likely be dead. There was now nothing left for them to do but return to Constantinople.

CHAPTER TWENTY-FIVE

Green Maiden's Folly, Elanora understood, would only be a paradise in the making for some time. The roofs on the shacks needed better maintenance. There were stainless steel ladders left from an earlier time that would help in this.

There was plenty of wood in the forest, but it had to be cut and shaped into slats to marry up with those already there on the roofs. Gregory told Elanora that with the right tools, he and Eric could do it. This was on the first day after their arrival.

"The walls of the shacks have been made solid. It would take a hurricane to topple them," Gregory told Elanora after he had examined each and every wall. "The steps leading up to the porches are worn but not dangerous. The porches need plank replacements here and there, and we'll get onto that when we can. The front doors are sturdy, and the hinges on them in good shape. All they need is a paint job."

"Anything else?" asked Elanora.

"These shacks were not built with electricity in mind, so they had to have been constructed long ago," said Gregory. "They have chimneys and stoves that require firewood."

"What kind of condition are these chimneys in?" asked Elanora.

"The chimneys need unclogging because they haven't been used in a long while, but we can clean them out with sticks," said Gregory. "We can do that today. Some of them smoked badly last night, choking those inside. We need the fires inside these shacks for warmth and to cook, but Eric and I can get right on it now, so not a major problem. The bricks making up the chimneys look all right."

The shacks, numbering seven, were two-room affairs able to house three adults comfortably with proper bedding. They had wooden floorboards. Each shack had two windows. There were adjustable slats on each window that could be taken up or left down for privacy and security against the wind.

"It may be a while before we have proper bedding," Elanora told Gregory.

"We'll just have to make do with the blankets we have," reasoned Gregory.

The trees in the forest areas were solid and tough, or so Gregory informed Elanora. During a casual walk, she found plenty of logs and fallen branches to gather for kindling. Apart from creatures previous humans on the island had let loose, such as rabbits, Elanora noted there were possums, lizards, and snakes. Underbrush and puddles provided for small birds and frogs.

There were caves near the inland lake and waterway that needed exploring. *If anything were to happen to the shacks*, thought Elanora on one of her walks, *maybe we could shelter in these caves until new dwellings could be built.* For now, and for a long time, Elanora and her followers would leave the caves be. When they were explored, they were found to be long and damp. Sheltering in them in summer would be fine, but not in winter when inside it would really get cold.

The beaches encircling the island were cut off by large rocks going out to sea. These rocks made perfect platforms for fishing. There were also high cliffs near the sea Elanora thought might prove dangerous. Sea eagles and hawks nested there.

Back at the shacks, Elanora noticed how Gregory remained uncertain for some time about Nathaniel's good intentions. The same could be said for Eric. She understood that Nathaniel was too smooth for them, and even she suspected a trap of some sort would be sprung sometime in the future.

In the weeks that followed, Elanora observed how Gregory and Eric remained ready for a fight, practicing combat moves with their swords.

Meanwhile, Ronald, Susan, and Cybil became familiar with the island and what it had to offer. They reported back to Elanora with information that was relevant for an extended stay. She didn't have the heart to tell them she had already made these discoveries on her own.

"There is fresh water here," Ronald told her. "There's a stream and a lake."

"Whoever was here before us brought with them goats and sheep," added Susan. "So we have fresh meat if we need it, and if we don't, there's milk from the goats and wool from the sheep."

"Some of the boys have made fishing rods out of long branches trimmed of leaves and spare string and wire they took from the fliers before they left," said Cybil. "They found grubs in the bush. At least one bream was interested enough to bite and so became supper for one boy."

"That doesn't sound very encouraging," Susan mused after a moment's thought, "Only one fish."

"It is!" cried Elanora. "It means the fish are out there. When certain knights and dragons stop messing about with swords and looking out for trouble, they will make us better fishing rods. Aayan is looking into it, but we need Gregory and Eric too. Nets might even be possible if we had the right material to make them."

"Gregory, Eric, and Aayan did a marvellous job in patching up the holes in the roofs of our shacks. But we need them to do more along those domestic lines if we are to survive here," reasoned Ronald, moving his silvery tail for emphasis.

"I do understand the fears of Gregory and Eric," said Elanora, now motioning her spiked tail in rhythm with the movement of Ronald's tail. "You are right. We can't have Gregory and Eric continually on high alert for something that might not happen. Gregory will exhaust himself, especially with what he is also doing for Toff. Aayan seems more willing to just get on with what needs doing here."

"You have posted lookouts along the shoreline in case of trouble," added Ronald, tail still moving. "Each group takes turns. Gregory and Eric have been part of this posting. That is enough for now. Preparation for battle with swords has to stop. Aayan appears to be in agreement with this."

"I'll talk to them about this," said Elanora.

"Do that with the maidens and Priestess Anna for support," advised Ronald.

"Why the maidens and the priestess?" asked Elanora.

"I have seen Celine in tears over what she calls primitive conditions," said Ronald. "Priestess Anna was the one, with the help of the children, to use large leaves to sweep the dust out of the shacks. They will help you get those two to see sense."

"How is Toff?" asked Elanora. Her tail stopped moving, as did Ronald's.

"Toff is slowly getting better," Susan told her. "Gregory, Celine, and Priestess Anna look in on him every once in a while, talking to him and bringing him food and water. I get the impression Celine does most of the talking."

"It took almost a week, but Gregory, Celine, and Priestess Anna coaxed him out of the shack they had placed him in," added Ronald. "I believe the fresh smells of the island have helped as well as Celine's continued talk. Within another week, he was looking for things to do to help everyone. I think he is as handy with mending as any of the other knights, or he could be if properly taught by them. I have spoken to Aayan, and he is willing to teach him."

"I am pleased with hiss progress," said Elanora, hissing gently. "We need Toff to be more active. How is everyone coping without electricity?"

"We are barely doing so." Susan sighed. "Fires can keep us warm, and there is plenty of firewood in the forest areas. Our clothes, however, are turning to rags, and that's not good against winter winds."

****

A month after their arrival on the island, a flyer piloted by Malcolm landed. Elanora was delighted to see him and was almost overwhelmed by what he brought them. He had with him more food, including liquorice for the children, medicine against colds, metal buckets for gathering water, soap, and shampoo, plus warm clothes for those living there on Green Maiden's Folly.

The clothes were nothing fancy, but none of the knights cared to dress up like mavericks ever again. Priestess Anna was pleased to wear white robes once more rather than tattered robes that should have been white but were grubby instead. Elanora gratefully burned the coat she had worn to cover up her femininity. She would wear a shirt and a pair of pants made for dragons to wear from now on.

Nails, saws, and hammers were now provided to make future repairs easier. Before this, they had only one hammer from a flyer and no nails or saws.

There were also solar panels and the necessary wiring that goes with them for one shack to have electricity. Malcolm also brought a two-way only computer and printer to be installed with instruction manuals for both solar panels and the computer.

"For now," Malcolm told Elanora as he got everything out of his flyer with Gregory and Eric's help, "when it comes to the computer, you can use a tall tree and the aerial I have with me to help boost reception, plus a long-lasting battery for those days when you don't get much sun. There's a tall tree near your shack, so that's not a problem. Nathaniel tells me he is anxious for you to get the communication set up, so you'd better get started on that as soon as you can."

"Understood," replied Elanora.

Malcolm didn't stay long, just enough time for Elanora to notice the children staring at his artificial hand and leg.

"Is he a robot?" asked one of the children who was hiding behind Priestess Anna.

"No," replied the priestess. "He's a friend."

It took Elanora, Gregory, Eric, Aayan, Susan, and Ronald a couple of weeks to get the panels up and working and then the computer.

Elanora noticed the surprise and delight on Nathaniel's face when he first made visual computer contact with her. His eyebrows went up, followed by a great big grin.

"Elanora!" cried Nathaniel. "I take it you are in good health?"

"Yess!" hissed Elanora, showing more emotion than she either expected or wanted to show. "The maidens are having a rougher time adjusting to life here, especially Celine, the ex-maiden officer who got too used to having robot servants. But they're all managing."

"That's fine," said Nathaniel. "Are conditions there improving?"

"Susan, one of our farmers, knows about plumbing and how best to gather water from the stream and lake as well as what to do about both dragon and human waste," revealed Elanora. "I know from books, but Susan has a better understanding because she knows from experience on her farm, getting her farm hands to do the work properly. Ronald, with Gregory and Aayan's help, has started rigging up hot water showers, powered by fires, outside the huts. I was the first to try one, followed by Priestess Anna, who gave the enterprise her blessing."

"It seems you are doing remarkably well," observed Nathaniel.

"Thanks to ducks Eric has managed to corral," said Elanora, "We now have fresh eggs of a morning. Ronald is working on ways to get honey from a beehive. We catch the occasional rabbit with a snare and have a stewed rabbit with dumplings."

"That is promising," Nathaniel mused.

"What's happening in the outside world?" asked Elanora. "Are the Knights of Saint George still on the hunt for my followers and me?"

"They will always be on the hunt for you," Nathaniel replied. "I think you must know that. What I can say is the Knights of Saint George, who were looking for their dead, found them, but there's no sign of those dastardly dragons and whoever else might have been in league with them."

"That's good," said Elanora, shrugging her shoulders and then smiling. "I wish I could say eat with us, but I take it that isn't an option for you."

"For the safety of both of us, I shouldn't visit you," sighed Nathaniel. "Eyes are on me most of the time, and I don't want outsiders to find this place and have the information get to those knights hunting you."

"That is sensible of you," agreed Elanora, "but why have you done so much for us and say you will do more? I know I have brought this up before, but I still don't understand."

"No need to understand for now," Nathaniel said, frowning slightly before smiling again. "I am my own bastard, but I choose not to be so to you and your people. Make a list of your needs and contact me again when the list is complete."

Computer transmission ended with Elanora feeling bewildered. *What does he want from us?* She wondered. *How far can we trust him?*

The computer, Elanora knew, gave her access to Nathaniel's computer only. Elanora understood, without being told by Nathaniel, it was a safeguard. If she could contact too many people with it, and they could contact her, then before long, her cover would be blown. Vengeful knights from Constantinople would invade the island, killing everyone. Through the computer, though, she knew she could now request the supplies her colony needed, plus gain information on any advances in technology that might be useful to her.

Elanora understood, from what they told her, that both Gregory and Eric looked upon the computer at first with suspicion. "Why has this Nathaniel given you this communication device?" asked Gregory of Elanora after it had arrived. "Why has he given us anything at all?"

As the months rolled by, Elanora believed both Gregory and Eric had come to realize the computer was for the best. She had also reached this conclusion, though she still had no idea why Nathaniel was helping rather than hurting.

Elanora grew closer to the gentle Ronald, who found farming a joy. "It reminds me of my youth in Berry," he had told her on numerous occasions. "Now, however, there is no maverick overseer to tell me what to do, so I feel wonderful about what I can do."

The wheat Ronald planted from seeds provided by Nathaniel took to the soil very well, and the same could be said for the yellow corn seeds. After the first harvest, both children and adults delighted in the taste of boiled corn on the cob. Elanora had never had anything like it and hoped corn on the cob could be an annual event.

Thanks to the help of farmers Susan and Cybil, Ronald corralled female goats for milking. They were not as easily milked as cows. Still, to Elanora's delight, Ronald did persist and eventually succeeded in milking one of them. Both Susan and Ronald then did future milking together.

Sex between dragons was not something anyone understood, much less being comfortable with. Nathaniel had no information to offer Elanora when she inquired. Regardless, Elanora and Ronald experimented. Despite the tails getting in the way, especially her barbed tail, they found a method that satisfied both of them.

Somehow, Elanora understood, Priestess Anna held onto her faith despite the strange departures from some of it she not only had to experience but condone as well. Elanora heard the children talk about their priestess. They couldn't work out why she was sad about change one minute and joyous about it the next. It may also have baffled the priestess, but not Elanora, who had perhaps a better understanding of how the Great Goddess religion, from her earlier education, had come about in the first place.

****

A year after they had come to Green Maiden's Folly, Elanora came down with stomach problems. There was pain and movement no one initially could explain. No one else had been affected, so bad food was ruled out. She began to swell in places where she hadn't before. Thanks to her farming experience, Susan came up with the answer to Elanora's malady and the reason why no one else was coming down with it.

"You're pregnant," she told Elanora.

"Is that possible?" asked Elanora. "I thought I was dying. Nowhere in any of the books I have read or any of the computer talks I have had did the subject of pregnancy for a dragon ever come up. But since I am not supposed to exist as a female dragon, it wouldn't, would it?"

"I hope Susan is right," said Ronald, pacing. "I'm not sure about becoming a father at my age, but I don't want to lose Elanora."

Nathaniel was turned to, via computer link, for advice, but he had none to give. Ronald was there with Elanora anxiously listening in.

"As far as I know," said Nathaniel, "no dragon had ever given birth to young. For that matter, there are no records of a male dragon ever impregnating a female dragon. All the accounts I can find concern mavericks impregnating maidens, and then, instead of the maiden giving birth to a human child, a dragon claws its way out of the unfortunate maiden."

"If I can give birth without being harmed, that would be better," murmured Elanora.

"Yes," agreed Ronald wringing his claws, "that would be much better!"

"Apart from sending Elanora extra blankets, a couple of water bottles, and towels, there isn't much I can do," Nathaniel told Ronald. "Even sending her painkiller drugs that are okay for human pregnancies might be wrong in her case. I will, however, send bottles of multi-vitamins. I think they might help, and since dragons have the same dietary requirements as humans, they should be fine for her to take."

Everyone, including Nathaniel, waited anxiously for the event, hoping it would indeed be joyous. No one wanted Elanora, their leader, to die in childbirth.

Before long, Elanora produced a great, white egg.

"What do I do with it?" asked Elanora, perplexed.

"I think I know," said Ronald. "I hope I know. I've handled duck eggs that would hatch on the farm before, though this isn't a duck egg. It's much bigger."

Ronald carefully wrapped the egg in towels, blankets, and hot water bottles. "This is the best care I can give it," he said, fussing over the placement of the blankets and hot water bottles. "There! Warm and safe!"

By the end of the month since the egg popped out, Elanora noticed movement inside it. There was a tiny crack, and minutes later, a small, silvery creature broke through and wiggled its way out of the shell, towels, hot water bottles, and blankets. Like any newborn, it howled for attention.

"You have a daughter!" pronounced Susan.

"A daughter!" cried Elanora, tears rolling down her facial scales, making them gleam. "Whoever thought thisss would be possible? But why did she arrive in an egg? I have been asking myself that question, but I have no answer."

"It must be the way dragons naturally reproduce," replied Susan.

"But I'm black-scaled," said Elanora, picking up the infant and putting her to her breast, "and she is silvery. Why is she silvery?"

"Your mate, Ronald, is silvery," offered Susan.

"So he is," said Elanora. "That does make sense from a genetics standpoint. I should have thought of that myself."

"What will you name her?" asked Susan.

"I will talk it over with Ronald before I decide," Elanora said.

After much thought, Ronald suggested Elaine because it was similar to Elanora. This was rejected for Ronda because it was as close to Ronald in the feminine as Elanora could get. Ronald felt honoured.

Over the computer, Elanora told Nathaniel the good tidings. He was excited over the baby at first. He was all smiles, then he put on a grim face. "I am sorry to say this," he told her, "but new danger is looming."

"What new danger?" Elanora asked.

"The old girls' club of High Priestesses might tolerate the existence of one female dragon that shouldn't be in this world," he told her, hands on chin, "but quite possibly, not two such dragons. Yet, there is nothing to be done except to keep moving in the direction we are going in. I'll send baby clothes. They'll be designed for human infants, but I am sure you can adjust them to suit a very young dragon. It will be a matter of cutting a hole in each garment for her tail. "

There was a magnificent feast in honour of Ronda in which everyone on the island attended. Elanora wished Nathaniel could have been there but knew that would have endangered them all, including Nathaniel. He was nevertheless pleased to receive a report via computer on the festivities. "I will continue to support Green Maiden's Folly," he told her via computer after receiving the report. "It is all coming together. You have a lovely and loving community. I envy you."

The flyer drops of food and other essentials on both Nathaniel's understanding and Elanora's insistence became less frequent as Green Maiden's Folly's occupants became more and more self-sufficient.

Little Ronda grew up well with plenty of human playmates older than herself. She adored her stern mother, who smiled at her when she wasn't looking but had a special affection for her father, who was always introducing her to something new on the island. It was with her father she might spend an hour studying a butterfly or a praying mantis. He might show her a flight of terns or introduce her to the wonders of food preparation. Elanora sometimes watched them from a distance, amazed at how Ronda and Ronald got along.

****

Every Mary-mass, which was once a year like the old Christmas of legend, Nathaniel had presents dropped off to the children of Green Maiden's Folly. *If there is a temple on that island,* he thought in one year, *it's most probably Priestess Anna's shack. I can imagine singing, feasting, and asking of the Great Goddess's blessing for the coming year and games, lots of fun for the children.*

This dropping off of presents would, he knew, be the closest Nathaniel would ever get to having children of his own. He could not risk the possibility that if he did marry, his wife might give birth to a dragon because of the dragon DNA he carried. The Highest of High Priestesses, he knew, would not allow such a union for the exact same reason.

****

One year, Ronda got a skipping rope. She wondered what it would be like to be a pilot in a flyer bringing presents to all the good girls and boys, whether human or dragon.

Ronald, her father, not only entertained everyone with his stories of daring-do but helped to feed everyone. She loved his stories about the sneak thief Toff, the one-eared fighter called Phips, and Craft, the big eater. Toff, though long since reformed, said to Ronda that he didn't mind the stories about him, which tended to be exaggerated anyway.

"Why was Toff such a good thief?" asked Ronda one day as she was having lunch with Ronald down by the lake.

"He had to be clever to survive in a terrible city," Ronald had told her, "but don't you ever steal, my girl. Your friends are here, and you don't steal from friends. And Toff doesn't steal anymore because we all need to trust one another."

"Why did Phips have only one ear?" Ronda asked on another occasion.

"He lost one of his ears in a fight," said Ronald. "I hope you never get into that sort of fight."

"Me, too!" cried Ronda. She felt her ears, and Ronald smiled with amusement as she did so.

One evening, just before supper, Ronda asked her father why Craft had liked food so much.

"It wasn't a case of liking food so much," Ronald told her. "He remembered those times when he was starving, and there wasn't any food. So when there was plenty to eat, he ate plenty. But he was a good friend. I miss him, just like I do Phips. We were such an odd combination me, Toff, Craft, and Phips, but your mother had us all working together."

One thing that touched Ronda was that her father could discover something new in every season. Ronda understood that her mother was more the scientist and had facts at her disposal, but her father was the little dragon that never quite grew up. Even the harshest of winters wasn't as terrible to her father as it was for others, or at least that was the impression he gave her. "If it is possible to have shelter and to put food on the table every night," he once told her, "it isn't as awful as some of the times I have been through when I was younger."

Just before Ronda's birth, Nathaniel sent better bedding along with more blankets and pillows. Hence, Ronda was not acutely aware of the harshness of earlier conditions at Green Maiden's Folly. She couldn't really imagine how her parents had lived in Wollongong or the horror of being trapped in a cattle car where the stench was almost overpowering.

Ronda realized that Toff was too quiet and skittish to form any meaningful relationship with any of the children. However, he was a big help to her father, Ronald, with his farming. Hector, who was firmly Aayan's dog, always had a paw and a kind wag of the tail for Toff, so she and the rest of the children figured that Toff mustn't be so bad after all.

****

The high winds one year in winter on Green Maiden's Folly killed two sheep, but they were able to put the rest, plus goats and ducks, into a shack to keep them warm and safe. The dead sheep were butchered for their meat. This horrified Ronda, who was not used to the sight of blood spilled from creatures she had cared for.

"This is wrong!" Ronda cried. "I think I'm going to throw up."

"We cannot waste the meat," said Ronald, his claw on his daughter's shoulder. He walked her away from what Aayan and Eric were doing to the dead sheep.

"I remember the farmhouse and the fight for survival against those horrid knights," murmured one of the older children. She moved away from the butchering, shaking her head as she went.

"No!" cried Toff, running away from the blood. This put him in a bad mood for a week. It took Celine and the others that long to get him out of it.

****

The spring that followed that terrible winter was welcomed like spring had never been welcomed before. Every sign of new growth was a triumph, according to Ronald and accepted as such by Ronda who was sick of winter and was glad it was going away.

Unfortunately, Hector had come to the end of his life. He died peacefully under the branches of his favourite tree. Everyone mourned him, especially the children. He was buried not far from Aayan's shack, and Priestess Anna was called upon to say a few words on his behalf. She had never done a service for a deceased blue heeler but realized that everyone was counting on her for words of comfort.

"Our friend Hector was a good dog," she told them over his grave. "He was a friend to all and an enemy to none. He enjoyed playing with the children, chasing rabbits and butterflies, and rounding up sheep and goats. He was Aayan's blue heeler, but we will all miss him. I am certain there is a corner of heaven where he is right now chasing rabbits and butterflies and rounding up sheep and goats. We will miss him, but someday we will join him in the great beyond."

A month later, Nathaniel had a male and a female blue heeler flown in to make up, in some small way, for Hector's absence. The dogs took to the island very well, but it was a while before the children, including Ronda, warmed to them.

That spring, Gregory and Aayan worked on building a barn for the animals for next winter.

Meanwhile, Ronda told her mother about how silly some of the children were about her tail and how a bad boy wanted to cut it off. Elanora thought to interfere at first but then decided it would be better if Ronda told the bad boy off herself. Elanora would not always be around to fight Ronda's battles for her. The bad boy turned out to be just a child who didn't really mean to upset her. The next day, Elanora saw them happily playing a game of marbles together, all strife between them forgotten.

****

Eleven years after the farmhouse incident, the Knights of Saint George were still looking for those renegade dragons and their helpers but never in the right place. It seemed that Nathaniel's vanishing act for Elanora and her followers was as complete as it could ever be. Every once in a while, a few members of the Order would venture to Australia in the hope of picking up an already cold trail, but there was nothing for them to latch onto, provided Malcolm and Megan kept their mouths shut, and the others who had flown to Green Maiden's Folly also continued to do so.

In the meantime, Nathaniel happily realized, the Highest of High Priestesses had found no reason at all to spoil his Green Maiden's Folly social experiment. Still, she was continually amazed at how much of his funds had gone into it without any sign of profit to be acquired on his part.

"I don't understand your continuing interest in Green Maiden's Folly," the Highest One said to him one day as they gazed out at Rome from her balcony.

He was shocked by this, as he had not always been able to read her mind. He had hoped she had forgotten all about that island and his acquisition of it. Apparently, she was keeping tabs on his spending.

"It goes well," replied Nathaniel. "Have I not been performing skilfully as your emissary and confidante?"

"Yes, you have," replied the Highest One. "Now tell me what you think of the High Priestess of Wollongong."

"She's doing fine," Nathaniel told her.

"Yes," agreed the Highest of High Priestesses. "Wollongong has gone back to being a city to be reckoned with, and the games they now have twice a year there are exceptional."

"She has long since repaid the loan given to her by the High Priestess of Liverpool," said Nathaniel, "and I believe her city coffers are in excellent condition."

"Yes, those items are in her favour," agreed the Highest One.

"The Knights of Saint George are not the disruptive influence they were even five years ago. That also favours Wollongong."

"But their quarry still goes missing," the Highest One said in a teasing voice.

"Yes." Nathaniel had to agree since it was the truth.

"If it is not possible for them to find this quarry, we must give them something else to do," said the Highest One, giving away nothing and being difficult to mentally read.

"That does seem logical. What did you have in mind?" Nathaniel couldn't quite get what the Highest One was up to, and this frustrated him. He looked away from her for a moment, and the black patch in the distance where the Vatican once stood caught his eye. It was forever a warning not to be too sure of oneself or those around you. Over the years, the Highest of the High had gotten good at hiding her thoughts from him. She wasn't one hundred percent able to do this, and so he looked for leaks.

"I have been informed that the High Priestess of Kiama has once more breached our trust in her," said the Highest One.

Nathaniel looked again at the woman who ruled over a great empire.

"How so?" Nathaniel tried once more to peer into the Highest One's mind but without success.

"She has a new lover. At her age, she should know better." The Highest One was frosty in making this announcement. It was forbidden for those who had entered the priestess-hood to have sexual encounters, but that didn't mean it didn't happen.

"She has done this before, and you have let it go. What has changed?" Nathaniel sensed in the Highest One something dark.

"Her lover has become a distraction for her." The Highest One knew this not to be true but said it anyway. This much Nathaniel was able to gleam from the Highest One's mind.

"I have been monitoring the situation in Kiama and also the towns just south of Kiama that come under her jurisdiction," informed Nathaniel. "Nothing seems amiss. I can confirm that milk production at Gerringong and Berry has been **very good** for the last five years."

"Yet there has been unrest among the dragons of Kiama and the knights," said the Highest One, clasping her hands together.

"That's true. There is the feeling among Kiama dragons that if a group of renegades can escape from involvement in the games, then they can also refuse to participate. There have been executions." Nathaniel wondered if the Highest One had made the connection between missing knights and dragons and the island.

"But there have also been Kiama knights shying away from the games," the Highest One continued. "The executions can only go so far, and we do not want to thin out the ranks of participants in the games too much, do we?"

"I understand. What do you want me to do?" Nathaniel remembered he was a servant and not a partner.

"I want you to go to Constantinople and enlist the help of the Knights of Saint George. After all, they are pledged to my service. We need both her lover and herself arrested and taken here to Rome to stand trial for breaching our trust in her." Nathaniel noted that the dark spot in the Highest One's mind had grown.

"Very well. Do you have anyone in mind for the position of High Priestess of Kiama when it becomes available?" Nathaniel concentrated, but couldn't get through the mind barrier the Highest One had set up.

"Perhaps it is time to appoint a maverick to the role of overseer." The Highest One smiled.

"Has that ever been done?" Nathaniel suspected it of being a first.

"Yes, but not in my lifetime. I believe the last Maverick Overseer lived a hundred years ago." The Highest One, Nathaniel knew from what little he could pick up from her thoughts that she was making it clear this was not an illegal move on her part.

"Some maidens and mavericks will find such an appointment shocking, to say the least." Nathaniel knew it would upset quite a few priestesses, maidens, and mavericks.

"Regardless, it is my decision." The Highest One was firm in this.

"Who will be this overseer?" asked Nathaniel. From reading what little filtered out of her head for him to read, he had his suspicions on which maverick it was likely to be.

"Why, you, of course!" cried the Highest of High Priestesses.

"Me?" Nathaniel gasped.

"Yes, you." The Highest One smiled.

"Are you serious?" Nathaniel was giving her a chance to change her mind.

"Quite serious." The Highest One looked stern.

"It is a great honour, but I am not suited to the position." Nathaniel knew he wasn't a priestess, and priestesses were normally chosen.

"I am the best judge of that." The Highest One folded her arms.

"What if I refuse?" Nathaniel asked. His voice was calm, but there was fear in his eyes. His eyebrows had gone up, and his pupils seemed larger than they had been a moment before this announcement.

"You have no choice but to accept," claimed the Highest of High Priestesses, "unless you wish me to end your little social experiment. It has been going on now for quite a few years, hasn't it? Perhaps you are sick of that island by now and those who dwell there."

"Please let it continue." Nathaniel's voice was no longer calm. "I have put so much effort into it."

"It will do so if you become my Maverick Overseer," said the Highest of High Priestesses in an imperial tone, "but first off, you will go to Constantinople. I radioed the High Knight of the Order, and he is expecting you."

"I go in your name," said Nathaniel in a humble voice. He bowed as he left the balcony.

Nathaniel's mind was racing. He had a feeling the Highest One would pull something like this, but didn't realize it would happen so soon. Even with his ability to read minds, she could be unpredictable. Last time he spoke to her, he was sure the High Priestess of Kiama was safe. Now she was doomed.

A quick look through old documents put on computer revealed to Nathaniel that the last maverick overseer was assassinated during a popular uprising in support of a traditional High Priestess taking the role. He was stabbed through the heart while showering. *At least he died clean*, thought Nathaniel. He hoped he would be able to avoid that fate through the use of his mental powers. Knowing when attempts on his life were coming and being able to act in time to save his skin might help him live longer in that dreaded position.

Nathaniel decided on Malcolm as his pilot. He knew he'd just arrived in Rome after dropping a diplomat off and was planning on going back to Wollongong. It was to be a simple flight from Rome to Constantinople, but Nathaniel felt better having with him a reliable pilot.

"No," said Malcolm when Nathaniel asked him to fly him to Constantinople.

"You are in no position to refuse," replied Nathaniel. "This is a mission for the Highest One."

"I am afraid," said Malcolm, crossing his arms and frowning, "and I have every right to be."

"Do you wish me to tell the Highest One you refuse?" asked Nathaniel.

"No," said Malcolm in a timid voice. "I'll pilot for you. I just hope you know what you are getting us into."

"I hope so, too," replied Nathaniel.

****

It was a drizzly morning in which Nathaniel and Malcolm set out on their journey. At one stage, a giant creature with many rows of teeth, whose ancestors may have been whales, came out of the Mediterranean Sea to attack and devour. Unfortunately for the behemoth, it could only gain so much height out of the water before it had to let gravity take it back to where it belonged. Malcolm knew to keep a certain distance from the water below, and Nathaniel saw no reason to interfere with the creature's mind since they were never in any real danger from it.

Malcolm made a smooth landing at Constantinople airport. Despite the journey not being long, Malcolm was pleased to rest up overnight in a nearby hotel before Nathaniel was set to greet the High Knight of the Order the following morning. As a precaution for a quick exit, Malcolm made sure the flyer was fully refuelled before checking into the hotel.

****

The following day, Malcolm was pleased to go from his hotel room to his flyer and wait for Nathaniel. The city made him feel uneasy. Ordinarily, he liked spending time at seaports, and this was one of the oldest still in existence. It even smelled of fish. The notion, however, of meeting up with some Saint George knight who might, for any reason, take an instant dislike to him was not comforting. He didn't want his throat slit over a look or a stray comment. There might even be a knight who doesn't like the appearance of his robot hand and leg.

****

It was a short amble for Nathaniel from the hotel to a castle built along medieval lines. Within this castle, there was the hall of heroes, and at the end of this hall sat the High Knight of the Order of Saint George. On the way to meet up with the great knight, Nathaniel passed portraits of famous knights and battles. Various dragons were shown being slain in a multitude of ways. He was escorted by two large knights whose armour rattled as they walked.

Nathaniel approached the High Knight with trepidation. He was an aging man on a throne with fish and cross symbols carved onto his armrests. There were two guards with pikes on either side of him, looking as menacing as it was possible for them to be. One had a scar down the left side of his face. The other was missing a finger on his right hand. Nathaniel knew from a quick read of their minds that they were battle-hardened and not likely to give quarter.

"I have come from the Highest One," said Nathaniel.

"It must be a sensitive matter," reasoned the elderly knight, "otherwise she would have simply radioed her request."

"That is true, Noble One," said Nathaniel.

"Out with it then!" cried the High Knight.

Nathaniel gave him the message, and then left the hall of heroes. He met up with Malcolm in the flyer. He sensed Malcolm was anxious to get going.

"Did you do what you needed to do?" asked Malcolm.

"Yes," replied Nathaniel.

"Good," said Malcolm. "Let's get out of here."

****

Malcolm took the same route back, arriving in Rome in good time. From there, Malcolm said farewell and good luck to Nathaniel. He then had his flyer topped up with fuel for the first leg of his trip back to Wollongong.

When Malcolm got home, Megan was glad to see her husband again and in one piece. He had already told her, via radio, about his journey to Constantinople.

"I hoped you would have nothing more to do with Nathaniel and his mad schemes, "she told him after greeting him with a kiss, "but I know I can't hold you to that. Nathaniel has power and influence, and you and I are such little players."

"Yes," agreed Malcolm.

"One thing I am determined to prevent is you being stripped of your right to be a maverick," she said firmly. "Still, I don't want you to die a maverick from some crazy stunt Nathaniel has talked you into doing. The drops at Green Maiden's Folly are dangerous enough."

"Yes," agreed Malcolm, "that they are."

****

Over the period of a week, the High Priestess of Kiama was kidnapped by knights of the Order of Saint George and put on trial in Rome.

The following day, the maverick executioner, an expert at his trade, made the former High One's last moments on earth bearable. Her neck was thick and so presented a problem by its thickness for the executioner, but nothing he wasn't aware of or couldn't handle. Her arms and legs were tied so her corpse wouldn't walk about once the deed was done. Her head rested comfortably on the block. Her fingers twitched. Her head was then swiftly removed without any fuss and bother. Moments later, by the hand of another executioner, her lover was hanged.

All of this took place in the square of the Highest One's main temple in Rome. Priestesses, maids, and mavericks gathered in adjacent buildings to watch.

Very few priestesses, maidens, and mavericks mourned the passing of the High Priestess of Kiama. In an edict, the Highest of High Priestesses made it all too clear the deposed High One of Kiama had abused her position and so deserved her fate. "The purity of office, in one form or another, has to be restored," the Highest One told the public in a television interview. "How this will happen will no doubt come as a shock to the people of Kiama," added the Highest One without going into any detail.

A week after the High Priestess's untimely end, Nathaniel was installed as Maverick Overseer of Kiama. The High Priestess of Wollongong protested, but the Highest of High Priestesses upheld her decision. "I will have my Maverick Overseer," the Highest One told the High One of Wollongong over a two-way computer linkup. "Do you wish to share the former High One of Kiama's fate?"

"No," replied the High One of Wollongong. "You can have your Maverick Overseer."

Nathaniel went from Rome to Kiama and was seated on the throne of office usually reserved for High Priestesses. Serving priestesses were unsure how to address him. "We've never had a Maverick Overseer before," a young priestess told him.

"I know it will be a learning experience for everyone," said Nathaniel, smiling.

"We don't want a Maverick Overseer!" cried a high-ranking priestess.

"We don't need a Maverick Overseer!" shouted another.

"Jail them for insolence," said Nathaniel to a maiden officer. "See to it your robots are gentle with taking them away. I will decide later if I will pardon them."

The offending priestesses were taken away. Watching them go, Nathaniel wondered if he really would pardon them and decided it would for now be the better option. *I will keep them in lockup for a week*, he thought. *That should give them time to think things over. Killing priestesses outright is not a good idea. Besides, sometimes a show of mercy can do better for one's position than a show of force.*

A day later, a couple of mavericks who failed to obey him were demoted to knights. He didn't like doing this, but it was expected of him, and he understood just how tenuous his hold on Kiama really was. *I don't fancy their chances of survival come No-*

vember in the games, he thought. They pleaded for their lives, but an example had to be made of them. "I can't have a maverick rebellion," he told the press.

How will they try to remove me? Nathaniel wondered, knowing his appointment to Maverick Overseer was not popular. As he adjusted to his seat of office, he was approached by a priestess carrying a glass of wine on a tray. She offered him the glass, but he made her drink it instead. She fell frothing at the mouth and died. He had her corpse taken away. He said to his official scribe, "Please make a note. I will need a food taster."

That night, two assassin knights, armed with daggers, entered his new sleeping quarters. They stabbed away at a body in his bed which turned out to be the priestess who had hired them. Nathaniel had arranged for her to be tied up and placed in the bed after he had read in her mind what she had planned for him.

The assassins were arrested and hanged. One of the first things Nathaniel did to quell the discontent among knights and dragons was to create a minimum wage for them. It was now illegal to employ a knight or dragon for less than this wage. Of course, as tradition suggested, knights would get more than dragons.

He would have liked to have been fairer, but he knew that if he did, he'd have problems with the maidens and mavericks. He also raised the accepted price of milk by two cents a quart to give the farmers in Gerringong and Berry incentive to expand and employ more hands. He realized how important dairy was to the economy and wanted to make his city more prosperous.

Nathaniel looked into the finances of Kiama and discovered that its coffers were almost bare. He also found a fortune in the dead High Priestess' bank account, so he had that money transferred to the coffers. He was amazed at how much the High Priestess of Kiama had gotten away with and how many priestesses, maidens and mavericks had been part of the corruption.

The Highest of High Priestesses was pleased with Nathaniel's initiatives and said so over the phone. She also told him that she missed him being close by.

"Still," the Highest One added, "you are now in a position to more firmly keep me in power and also to safeguard your island in the event the High Priestess of Hobart ever has a change of heart over the financial deal you struck with her."

Any sign of impropriety might well mean not only his demise, but the end of those living on the island.

Nathaniel now made sure that any drops to be made to Green Maiden's Folly would be done by Malcolm alone. He also had a maiden computer expert make sure that the computer he was using to communicate with Elanora could not be accessed by anyone else. Then he had that computer expert sent to a dairy farm in Berry where she was to be an overseer and have no further contact with computers. He didn't want to do this to her, but it seemed to him the best way to protect not only himself but also those on Green Maiden's Folly. As it turned out, she liked her new role in life.

CHAPTER TWENTY-SIX

On Green Maiden's Folly, special occasions arose to give life on the island added meaning. When Ronald turned fifty, Elanora arranged for a birthday party for him. Susan baked a cake with cream on top. Sweets were fashioned out of honey, flour, and water. The presents were simple. His daughter, Ronda, made a drawing for him of a butterfly.

Toff fashioned a kite out of strips of wood, paper hardened by flour and water, plus string from one of the packages sent by Nathaniel. Ronda got more fun out of that particular present than Ronald, who delighted in flying it with her. The blue heelers were happy to chase the kite and bark at it.

"I wish I was a bird," Ronda told Ronald, holding the kite. She smiled, but Ronald could tell by her eyes she meant it.

"Me, too!" Ronald replied, looking at the kite. "There are times when I think my old mate Toff also wishes he could fly."

"I don't understand Toff," said Ronda shaking her head.

"He doesn't always understand himself. But he's one of us. We care for him, and that's enough." Ronald sighed. Toff was hard to explain to anyone who had never been in combat.

"Sometimes I think he's afraid, but there's nothing here to be afraid of, is there?" Ronda smiled. She had gotten to the heart of what made Toff what he was.

"He doesn't want the past to catch up with him," said Ronald. "He was once in a bad way and not wanting to go back there sometimes plays on his mind."

"But he won't be going back there, will he?" asked Ronda.

"I hope he won't," Ronald reasoned, "because if he does, the rest of us will be going with him, including your mother, but that's not likely to happen. Our refuge here hasn't been invaded. We're not in chains being taken off to one of those horrid cities. We're safe on Green Maiden's Folly and have been so for a long time."

"What can we do for him?" asked Ronda.

Ronald took her claw for a moment, gently squeezing, then said, "Do what I do. Be patient, and any sign of him joining in, you let him but don't make too big a fuss. I love this kite he made, don't you?"

"You like him, don't you?" asked Ronda.

"I suppose I do," replied Ronald.

For Ronald's birthday, Gregory had carved a likeness of a tern, one of Ronald's favourite birds, out of wood. Eric fashioned three bowls out of clay and a drinking cup. He then had them made solid by fire.

Aayan created fishhooks out of bone for Ronald, and the human children sang songs they knew Ronald liked. Priestess Anna blessed them all and added a sponge cake she had baked to the occasion.

After the festivities, came the question on everyone's mind. Just how long could Ronald live? Usually, dragons went into the life-or-death games at sixteen and were lucky to live to be twenty-five. Ronald was more than double that and still going strong. When asked by Ronda about his age and how he kept on living, he put his longevity down to the love of a good dragon queen and the scampering about of young ones always at his feet. No one seemed fit to argue about those conclusions, not even Elanora.

That night over supper, Elanora looked at Ronda and at her husband, Ronald, as if seeing them for the first time, and smiled. She wondered how she got to be so fortunate. She could have stayed all alone for the rest of her life on that remote island off the coast of New Zealand. It was a choice she could have made.

The High Priestess of Wollongong was in favour of her doing so. She could have lived out her life in relative comfort with very few people anywhere having any idea of her true existence as a female dragon. Instead, she embarked on a great adventure that landed her on another island, this time off the coast of Hobart.

She was, however, not alone and gathered she was never likely to be so again. Sometimes she missed her solitude but realized that was a very small price to pay for the life she was living with people, human and dragon, she could care about and, at the same time, be herself caring for them.

Every once in a while, she went out to the forest with treats for the magpies to make friends with them. She knew she should take Ronda with her on these outings to form a closer bond with her but felt inadequate to explain what such outings meant to her. As a scientist, she could talk about magpies, giving details about every aspect of their existence, but not concerning the feelings she still had for them. Perhaps someday she would try to tell Ronda of her past loneliness and how those birds on the island off the coast of New Zealand helped her. Then she would take Ronda into the forest in search of those wonderful black and white magpies. Meanwhile, she had an island to run and people to look after.

ABOUT THE CONTRIBUTORS

Author Rod Marsden was born in Sydney, Australia. He has three degrees, all related to writing and history. He spent nine and a half years as a civilian clerk with the Royal Australian Navy. His proudest moments there were in the publications area.

He enjoys wildlife photography and in recent years, joined Illawarra Birders. He went on a birding expedition to the main north island of New Zealand, where he came upon wildlife unique to that country. There he also met up for the first time with correspondent, friend, and novelist Lyn McConchie. He shares his fascination with nature with his entire family, including his niece Jasmine Perala. Her pet, Kiki, is a young, female eclectus parrot and, soggy from a recent shower, is featured on Rod Marsden's shoulder on the back cover of this book.

His stories have been published in Australia, England, Russia, the USA, and Canada. He has work in the Australian anthology *Small Suburban Crimes*, the American anthology *Cats Do it Better,* the American steampunk anthology *Break Time,* the Canadian anthology *Morbid Metamorphosis,* and in the Canadian anthology *Grey Matter Monsters – Takers of Souls*.

Many of his short stories, including "The Antarctic Pineapple," have been published in *Night to Dawn* magazine. *Undead Reb Down Under and Other Vampire Stories* is a collection of his early short fiction on vampirism. *Disco Evil* is his first venture into the vampire novel. *Ghost Dance* is his first undertaking into dark fantasy involving a quest plus secret agents out to prevent demonic takeover. It has been reprinted with a new cover. *Desk Job* is his salute to Lewis Carroll.

His short plays, *Zombie Vision, Hyde and Seek,* and *Smarty* were well received at Cronulla Arts Theatre, south coast, New South Wales, Australia. Both his plays *Smarty* and *Hyde and Seek* made it into Sydney's Short and Sweet contest.

He has a short story in *The Twofer Compendium* edited by Ruth Littner and Ann Stolinsky (2020) in which he mentions the Berry Celtic Festival, which took place every May in a farming community on the south coast of New South Wales, Australia. It is a festival that, unfortunately, had to be cancelled in 2020 because of the coronavirus but will hopefully resume in May 2021. http://rod-marsden.id.au/

SCAR: As the creative team SCAR, Steve Carter and Antoinette Rydyr have been pushing the boundaries in art and comics in Australia for over 25 years. They create in the genres of science fiction, fantasy, horror, and satire, all injected with a liberal dose of surrealism and weirdness. Together they have produced graphic novels, award-winning screenplays, and esoteric electronic music with their band TeknoSadisT, which can be sampled on Bandcamp.

They have recently published a series of graphic novels including a collection of fantastic beasts and strange monsters titled *Bestiary of Monstruum*, a science-fiction fantasy anthology called *Fantastique,* the dystopian *New World Disorder,* the out-of-this-world anthology *Weird Worlds – Subversive Science Fiction Stories,* and Australia's most controversial comic book resurrected in the graphic novel *Phantastique – Tales of Taboo Terror,* among others.

In 2018, their debut steampunk western novel, *Weird Wild West* Parts 1 & 2 was published by Bizarro Pulp Press, USA. And *Weird Wild West* Part 3 was published in 2019. View more of their books on their Amazon Author page: Carter Rydyr.

In 2010, their original unproduced screenplay *Curse of the Swampies,* a horror sci-fi film, won Best Feature Film Screenplay at the A Night of Horror International Film Festival.

Although SCAR's work polarises viewers, their art cannot be ignored and introduces readers to other worlds of possibilities.

View more of their work at http://www.weirdwildart.com/

www.ingramcontent.com/pod-product-compliance
Lightning Source LLC
Chambersburg PA
CBHW020216260626
47156CB00002B/410